GODDESS KINDLED

RAVENS NIGHT SAGA
BOOK ONE

HOLLY MACGREGOR

Triquetra
BOOKS

Hardcover ISBN: 978-1-7381864-4-0

Paperback ISBN: 978-1-7381864-0-2

EBook ISBN: 978-1-7381864-1-9

Audio Book ISBN: 9781738186419

978-1-7381864-6-4

PROLOGUE

For the one to see the futures past,
Is thrice blessed to conquer lightfast.
Fire be true,
With leadership firm.
Changing destiny right.

CHAPTER 1

*H*arlow looked on in a daze as the director spoke, not hearing a word he uttered. It was all she could do to keep herself upright. With the exhaustion of the past few days, and the full body numbness from the arctic wind blasting them. Turning to glance up at her son and then her twin brother. She noticed they weren't faring much better than her. Their eyes stared unfocused ahead, with hands shoved deep into their jacket pockets. Her only advantage was that they both were taller. With them standing behind her, they offered much-needed shelter. Not just from the weather, but the rest of those gathered. It was nice they came with her today. She needed the support.

They were burying her one and only friend today. Cora Lewis was the sister she had never had. The one person other than family, of course, that accepted her. The stubborn girl never wavered in her persistence to become friends. She always defended and protected Harlow when they were young. Teaching her how to stand up for herself. Just because she wasn't like 'them', it didn't matter.

Shivering from a chill running up her spine, she could feel the eyes of everyone else gathered staring at her. Looking around their small graveyard. She took note that no one was paying any attention to the director of the service. They were staring at her with either curiosity, suspicion, or disdain. Sucking in a shocking breath, Caden bent to whisper in her ear.

"Pay them no mind, sister dear."

Squeezing her shoulder in reassurance.

Cora had died only a few days ago. All she could remember was, she had been looking for something, and couldn't find it. It must have been important. Her friend was in a state of panic and fear. Asking only that Harlow trust her while keeping this secret. She agreed reluctantly, only to ease the pain she saw in Cora in her distress. Wishing her friend trusted her enough to confide in her. Maybe they weren't as close as she thought.

Now she wondered if she should have shared with Caden about Cora's behavior. Could they have helped Cora? Or even have saved her? They would never know, sadly. Shivering again from the cold, this time she wrapped her arms around herself. What was she going to do now?

With an inward smile, she thought back. Cora and she had been friends forever. Even if she was Caden's friend first from school, and the only other one outside of Caden who didn't laugh at her. She believed she was just like everyone else. Having hair, check, even if hers was just a wild mass of crazy curly ginger ringlets. Everyone prided themselves on pointing out and teasing her. 'Crazy ginger' they called her for her lack of straight light or dark hair. It was always said that she lacked any intelligent thought because of it. Cora always teased that Harlow's hair just had a life all its own, and everyone else was just jealous.

To prove everyone wrong, she had become the archivist within the compound's library vault. She was now fluent in many of the dead languages. A personal joy of hers. She loved the multitude of sounds each word made, not to mention all the different ways of expressing yourself. Often wondering why the ancestors had given up on them. Her ability to consume knowledge allowed her to hope that someday she might be normal. Maybe it could help them find a solution to saving their dying planet.

Her only other standout quality was she walked with a limp on her left leg. Being born into a world where doctors could fix and heal anything. It was unusual that they didn't help her by repairing the damage. Instead, they chose to believe the focus of those involved was so fixated on the fact of a twin birth, an event only written about in history books. Or the fact their mother had died giving birth to them. They forgot to go about the repair.

Since they had no family other than each other, the Overseer took them to live within the main compound building under his supervision. The Overseer singled out Caden, either because he was a boy or because he was the oldest, and favored him more. Even though he too shared many of the same traits as she. From the color of their ginger hair, green eyes, and fair skin dotted with freckles. He received celebration and favoritism, while she, sadly, did not. Learning the hard way, no one valued her. Only her twin, and then Cora had.

Shaking her head to rid herself of her wayward negative thoughts. To berate herself, she should focus on today's events, not her misgivings. They were attending Cora's burial, followed by the celebration of her life. An event so rare, she was being honored with a proper burial on the grounds. A task that required the setting up of protection from the elements or lack thereof outside the compound.

Regardless of the fact that they cremated her, Cora was being granted the privilege of resting with the ancestors for eternal sleep. She had her suspicions about why that was. It costs too many precious resources for cremation. Someone was hiding something. But who?

Soon they would all leave this sacred place, to the dust it had become, to safety, such as it was anyway. Focusing back on the director. Letting out a long breath, she swiped at her falling tears. God, she was going to miss her. Bending to grab a handful of dirt, she straightened, tossing it onto the small box of cremated remains in the equally small hole. As was tradition, the last goodbye of a loved one.

Turning away, she took her time walking through the throng of gathered guests. Giving Caden and Rowan room to repeat her movements. Making her way to the cemetery gate, she stood with her back to them, waiting. Refusing to look behind her.

Sighing in relief when Rowan threaded his fingers through hers, and the comfort it brought.

"Come on Mom. Let's go celebrate Cora's life. She'd want you too."

Tugging on their joined hands. She allowed her son to lead the way. Like always, they all walked at her pace, with one on either side of her. It was a blessing to have a twin, and a son as caring and demonstrative as they were. She loved them so much and would do anything for them.

With the party in full swing, Harlow wasn't in the mood to celebrate. It felt wrong somehow to her. Why would we want to celebrate life when Cora's life was cut so short? Fidgeting in her seat, and trying to straighten out her one, and only, pretty dress, she began looking around the grand room at everyone in attendance. Noticing other than herself and her family, only the True Guard was present. All dressed in the finest clothes of their position or rank. Strange how no one else was from the community was present. She tilted her head to the side to study those gathered. She saw just how truly fake it all was. Appearing a caring and protective leader.

They held the gathering of the celebration of life within the grand ballroom. Housed in the Overseer's estate. A room with huge ornate mirrors installed on all the walls. Adorned with gilded stucco moldings and large crystal chandeliers. A room of sparkle, and shimmering light. It took your breath away every time you entered. It also allowed her to see around the room. To know that it was total crap. A show. Put on to simulate caring.

Not one person truly cared about Cora, only what they could get out of showing up here. Making their presence known in flamboyant displays of caring. Connecting with the uppers was more important. Constantly striving to get ahead. Well, except for her and her family.

Slumping in her seat, she pondered. What did it matter, anyway? Their ancestors had destroyed the planet. It was fading away, with humanity in tow. All attempts to reverse the damage, and save it, have failed thus far. Why bother going through all this facade, only for it to end soon?

Maybe this was what Cora had been working towards. Saving the planet or humanity. That would explain her odd and protective behavior. Why else would she have died so young? They labeled her death as suspicious and planned to interview everyone close to her. Would point in that direction. However, these techniques have not been in use for centuries. Now you were innocent or guilty on the spot. With The True Guard handing out a ruling on The Overseer's behalf.

They thought Cora had some important information or something. Possibly sharing that relevant knowledge with those who knew her. Why else go to all this trouble? Her friend was caring, giving, and supportive. However, she was also private and secretive. She did not open up and share.

Thinking about this over and over for the past few days. Harlow believed that rather than a suspicious death. Cora's death resulted from someone seeking information. Information she either didn't know or wouldn't share. Possibly even tortured for it. Why else would they have cremated her? It was a practice they only allowed if the death resulted from a sickness. It just took up too many precious resources.

Harlow just knew when her interview time came up, she would hold her tongue. Even being interrogated, she would never reveal what she knew or give up something they wanted. She was confident, however, that she didn't have the information wanted. Her sister needed protecting, even in death.

The question of who bore the responsibility twisted her gut. There was someone in this room who had a connection to or knowledge of who had killed Cora, and for what purpose? There was just a minor matter. She had zero proof. Only her feelings and suspicions. Which hurt her heart. Cora needed justice, dammit. Every time she thought about it, it just made her more angry.

Just like every other time her thought process went down this road, she found herself with her hand resting over her heart. Trying in vain to rub away the hurt of sadness, anger, and disbelief. It just wasn't fair. The only person who valued her outside of blood was now gone forever.

Deciding if she was going to get any answers, any at all, she would have to socialize with this crowd. The idea made her feel a little queasy. These were the people who teased and mocked still. Not on the daily, but whenever they seemed to feel the need. Knowing they did it to bust themselves up was one thing. It just hurt. Over time, it had gotten a little easier to take.

Straightening her spine, and squaring her shoulders, she glanced around again. Someone here had to know something. Even if they didn't realize it. For her friend, she decided she would do this. She would find her killer, or at the very least, whoever ordered her interrogation. Tossing her hair to the side, she stood, straightening her dress again. With determination, she would get some answers for Cora.

Grabbing a drink from a nearby table, she glanced around. Wondering where should she start? With as much grace as she could muster, she drifted. Trying her damnedest to blend in with the crowd. The less attention she garnered, the better. Gathering as much information was the name of the game. What a game they all seemed to play, too.

Using this room only reaffirmed her suspicions. The only grand room left from the old days. Too beautiful, she guessed, not to possess. Moving along the edge of the room. She didn't feel like weaving her way through people. Her subtle limp made it difficult to maneuver that way. She stopped when she could see how almost everyone had gathered.

Gathered into many groups, scattered apart. They were laughing and talking, with drinks in their hands. Arms wrapped around each other or arms flailing about in a storytelling. It seemed they were all enjoying themselves. She squinted to look closer, trying to see if she could recognize individuals. An enormous challenge for her. Not being allowed to be educated among them like her twin had been. It was hard to remember who was who. Just then, she saw him.

Caden was talking with his current love interest, Sally, and her

8

team. They were laughing at something one of them was saying. Most were bent over, holding their stomachs. Everyone looked like they were having a grand old time. Sally, however, looked as if she had other ideas. She couldn't keep her hands off Caden, like a cat in heat as she nibbled on his ear. Her brother didn't seem to mind; he looked as though he rather enjoyed it. Scrunching her nose in disgust, she shook her head. Yuck, Sally annoyed her. She behaved like a teenager most time. How she was a team leader for The True Guard she didn't understand.

Caden's team, however, was standing amongst Jasper and his team. They all seemed to have broken off into a few here or a few there. All looked to be discussing something deep. Their brows were all furrowed, with tense body postures. As if each were ready to pounce on the other. Strange, the contrasting groups. Tilting her head in closer study while wondering.

Noticing then that the three other True Guard groups and their leaders weren't present today. Oddly, they were likely off on a mission somewhere. One very secret, and confidential. At least, that's what was always said. So who knew the truth? They could be the very ones she was looking for, for information. Would make sense then that they were not here. If that was the case then, what hope did she have? Her mission ended before it could begin.

Deciding instead, she made her way towards Caden. Even though she wanted to find some answers, she needed her twins' support. She knew he didn't believe the reasons announced by the Overseer either. Being a member of The True Guard meant he had to hold his tongue. Maybe they could help each other find answers. Like she thought before, perhaps someone had knowledge of something and didn't realize it. If she could just muster up the courage to talk with people, she might get some information.

Frustration filled her as she rubbed her eyes while making coffee. Last night, the celebration of life had revealed no information. Well, not anything she didn't already know or suspect. People were only there because they had to be. That the better food and drink were being served was the side benefit. The likely factor in swaying the dictated attendance presence of the True Guard at the party. This being the only information learned last night was as they left.

Also odd was the absence of the Overseer. He only appeared at the service held before burial, and the departure to the graveyard. Sharing his condolences while also announcing interviews would begin the following week. As they looked into the suspicious death of a valued compound member.

Yawning, she grabbed the ties of her robe, tying them around her waist. She couldn't shake the chill from the graveyard yesterday. Her bones still felt like ice from that arctic wind. Shivering, she rubbed her arms to get more blood flowing. Anything to warm up a bit before her coffee. Her one vice. The only ones she shared were with her twin and her son. It seemed like a family trait to her. Smiling to herself, she allowed a small giggle to escape at the thought of a family trait.

But who knew? She shrugged her shoulders, thinking about how a nanny had raised her and Caden. Never being told anything about their parents or extended family. If they even had any alive, no one would say. Their only knowledge was that their mother had died during childbirth. Given the health care techniques they had, it was a bafflement to them, just like her limp while walking was.

Reaching into the cupboard, she grabbed three mugs, placing them beside the coffee machine. She decided long ago to stop asking questions regarding either issue. It never garnered answers, only trouble, and negative attention towards Harlow. So what was the point?

Yawning again, she pulled a hair tie from her robe pocket, attempting to secure her mass of wayward curls. With some success, she again thought back to last night. So much for finding anything out. Frustrating too. Especially with almost everyone drinking. Some tongues should have been telling some tales. But all she could hear were tales of old missions or childhood rememberings.

Maybe her thoughts last night were right, and those responsible hadn't been in attendance. Somehow, though, she knew that to be false. If only partly. She just wasn't sure how she knew. It was just a gut feeling again. Rubbing her eyes and yawning once more. She needed to be a mom this morning. Regardless of how tired she was. Shaking her disappointment off in order to focus on her son.

Rowan was on his way to master training today. He was to become a member of the True Guard. The program began at fifteen and continued for five years. After this, a member of high standing takes students under their wing as an apprentice.

She didn't like that he would have to move into the dormitories on the far edge of the compound. Only to come home on the odd weekend. Despite suppressing her own emotions, she felt pure joy for him. He wanted this calling. Ever since, he had understood Caden's position and role. He looked up to his uncle and always wanted to be just like him growing up.

Proud that he was pursuing his dreams on his terms. What mother wouldn't burst with happiness upon witnessing his accomplishments? She would help him in any way he needed. Always, and with love.

When the coffee pot beeped to announce that it had finished percolating, she grabbed her mug. Smiling, she poured the sweet-smelling brew. Closing her eyes and inhaling, loving the wonderful smell. Wrapping her hands around the heated mug and making her way to the table. Sitting at the table, she sipped, waiting for the others to wake. Closing her eyes again, she sighed with pleasure. Hoping the wonderful brew will warm her chilled bones.

After hearing a door open, she looked up and was surprised to see

Sally leaving Caden's bedroom. Well, maybe she shouldn't be after how she was crawling all over him last night.

Whispering as she snuck across the room.

"Oops, sorry. I thought I could duck out before anyone got up."

Pretending indifference with a shoulder shrug.

"I didn't know you were here Sally"

Reaching the door, and for the hand scanner, Sally turned. Still whispering. This time with a smirk on her lips and a twinkle in her eyes.

"Oh, well, I stopped by after the two of you left the party. You know how one thing can lead to another."

Looking into her steaming cup and mumbling.

"Sure,"

Just before taking another sip. She wished this woman would just leave already. How her brother didn't notice she did this every time, or why did he put up with it? Was anyone's guess. Although she knew her view of sex was different from everyone else. For her, it hurt a lot. She felt hurt and betrayed by the person she had trusted, who turned out to be selfish and cruel. Bragging later on about how he had had the limp girl. Like she was some kind of trophy. She had thought he cared until he showed his true colors.

Those became even more apparent when Rowan became the result of their coupling. He had become violent towards her. Making Caden and Cora angry. They were all fifteen. With Caden off at the master training program. Therefore, only Cora could be there for her in the beginning.

After the attack on her, she needed to be in the hospital ward. When her twin found out, he was furious. To say the least, he did not want to come back. Only Cora, who was also furious, had kept Caden where he was by moving in with Harlow. Helping any way she could with Rowan until he came home years later.

Pulling herself out of her memories, she looked up at Sally. Mustering up as much kindness, she smiled while whispering over the brim of her cup.

"Bye, Sally."

Tilting her head, Sally studied her a moment before whispering, "Bye" and letting herself out.

Hearing the quiet click of the door auto-locking, Harlow shivered as the tingle zipped up her spine. There was something about Sally that rubbed her the wrong way. She couldn't put her finger on what it was. Frustrating her to no end, trying to figure it out every time. At least the knowledge of her twin's tweaking of the locking mechanism allowed her some comfort. Relaxing back in her chair, there was no point now in thinking further about Sally. Not when she had her steaming brew to finish. Moaning with pleasure, she continued to drink.

Just as she finished filling her second cup, both Caden and Rowan emerged from their rooms. Each scratching their heads, making more of a mess of their crazy hair. A family trait, it seemed, one they had better luck at taming. In unison, they yawned with garbled.

"Morin,"

Smiling with a chuckle.

"Morning. Sleep well?"

As she made her way back to her chair, she took a sip of her cup.

Rowan just grunted his reply, heading right for the food she had made earlier. Piling food onto his plate in a giant heap. At her raised brow, he shrugged as he sat across from her.

"What Mom? I don't know when they'll feed me next. Plus, I'm really hungry."

He dug into his food with gusto. Barely coming up for air. Caused her to chuckle once again. Caden, however, headed for the coffee. Filling the largest cup they had. Guzzling it. He didn't come up for air till the cup was half empty. Sighing in pleasure.

Raising his mug to her.

"Thanks, sis. I needed this this morning."

Shaking her head with laughter. As she copied his gesture.

"You're welcome."

Caden then piled food onto his plate, placing the remaining onto a plate for her. He handed her the plate before topping up his coffee and sitting down to eat.

They ate in silence. Enjoying their food and each other's company. It would be a long time before they could share this again.

CHAPTER 2

*S*eeing Rowan off had been hard. Rowan's education, unlike the others attending the master training, primarily involved being raised at home with a tutor. Their upbringing was similar to the way she and Caden were brought up. Well, Caden could attend some classes with other students. As orphans, the Overseer appointed a governess to raise them. Still, their education had been odd. Everyone else moved into an educational boarding house at four years old. At fifteen, you either continued training in a specialty or began working within the compound.

No one understood the close connection they all shared as a result, making them different. Their visual distinctiveness made them a target for teasing and ridicule more than others. Sadly, she in the end received the most negative attention. By now, however, it just became a way of life. Though sometimes it still hurts.

No one knew the reason behind their unconventional upbringing compared to the norm. Being the only ones along with the Overseer to live in the main building was odd. An estate large enough to house many. This too also caused rumors and stories. Someone constructed it for a large household eons ago. Now it was more of an empty shell of a home. Thinking of it as a home made her laugh. The place was a palace for the elite, big enough to house a small city of its own.

At one time in history, that had likely been its purpose. Now, however, it had strict restrictions imposed on it. During the day, it allowed the True Guard a home base of offices on the main floor. However, at night they all headed to the barracks, except for her brother, of course. Only a very select few had access to the lower levels. Her brother's team was among the few. Furthering rumors of a paranoid Overseer.

Caden and she were the only ones to see Rowan off. An emotional send off. Many hugs and tears were exchanged by them. The plan had originally included Cora to be involved in the grand goodbye. Unfortunately, that was not to be, and that seemed to tip all of their emotions overboard. A broad smile spread across her face as she witnessed her son being included with the others on an equal footing.

They offered their condolences and extended their support, showing great compassion. He was quite happy about it, even if he had some trepidation about being included. Caden had seemed to fare well when it had been his time. Her heart swelled with hope for him.

After their last see you later, she shared a quick goodbye with her brother. Each of them had to return to their own responsibilities. Life had returned to normal. Regardless of how she felt inside.

With a sigh of exhaustion, her trek back towards the principal estate was slow. Hanging her head, she wallowed in her sadness. She traveled at a slower pace than usual. Not caring who saw her, she didn't even bother to hide. She didn't care if anyone shouted remarks at her or not. The murder of her best friend and her son leaving home left her feeling devastated. They should expect her to be melancholy.

Arriving at the grand entrance of the building, she slowed her movements even further. Glancing up, she looked at the always gloomy sky above the dome. It seemed to fit her feelings. Dark with an ever changing wind. Taking a deep breath, she took care going up the steps. Entering the main building, she made her way to the stairwell that would take her to the archive library. She knew this place like the back of her hand. So it didn't matter that it was poorly lit to conserve power. Every bit they could do helped, or so they were told.

These halls and levels had been hers, and Caden's playground when they were small. It was a beautiful labyrinth. Containing many rooms and levels designed for a multitude of functions. Most of which people have forgotten over time. They spent many hours over the years exploring and playing. Discovering many hidden secrets within their grand home. As they grew, it became more about sneaking away to find more treasures. Until at some point they had just stopped. She couldn't remember why.

Gripping the handrail, she cursed herself for forgetting to bring her walking stick today. She felt the fatigue more than usual after the trek from Rowan's send off. Too bad the lifts within the building no longer operated. Would be nice to have access to one right about now. Just one of the many joys of trying to conserve power whenever and wherever they could within the compound. Even the library in which she worked every day only had one working security camera, and a single row of working lights by the main door. She always used a small portable light when looking for books and reading. Most times, however, she just used it for reading though. Shaking off her internal complaining, she continued.

With steady care, she made it to the archive library door. Sighing in exhaustion, she moved to place her hand on the scanner. Chuckling at the icy surface that was worth locking this way. They could have just relied on the old key mechanism instead of a power sucking scanner. Waiting for the telltale chick sound of the door lock opening before moving forward again through the automatic door.

With shuffling feet, she made her way to her favorite chair. Pulling the books from her bag, she slipped the strap over her head. Tossing the bag, hoping it would land by the chair's front feet. When it did so, she pumped her clenched fist in the air, shouting.

"Score"

Laughing at the little game she always played with herself, she smiled for the first time in days, it seemed. Her morning brew didn't count. Making her way over to the shelving. Yesterday's borrowed books needed to be put back. After which, taking a few minutes to scan the section of books she had yet to read. Quickly making a few choices for today's reads, Harlow took them back to her chair. Placing them on the side table today, she moved the footstool into position. She needed it today. Grateful her former instructor had insisted it be here for her.

Sitting and lifting her leg onto the stool, she sighed with pleasure.

Leaning back into the comfort of the chair. Loving how this chair felt like it was always giving her a warm hug. This felt so good and comforting. Something she needed at the moment. Needing to shake off this melancholy, she shook her head at herself and focused on work. Such as it was.

Picking up the first book in the pile, she first looked it over, before going through the pages to see if anything stood out to her. Sometimes there were notes written in the margins or passages highlighted. Those books she wanted to read first. It seemed their contents were of some importance. Other times, however, the contents were no longer of relevance. It was amazing all the things she had learned.

Language was a favorite of hers. Having gone through all the digital references years ago, the physical books were fascinating to her. She had taught herself many of the dead languages. Even ones that were dead within these books. Odd, how later humanity could resurrect a language only to forget it again.

A perk she enjoyed was being able to tell people what she thought of them in another tongue. Their expressions were always that of confusion at first, followed by anger. Sadly, it wasn't a practice she did much anymore. Most thought she was doing something to them, or that she was off. She grew tired of always having to explain herself to the True Guard personnel. For her brother's sake, and now her son's, she kept quiet. If only she had the guts to speak up in a language, they understood defending herself.

Alas, that would never happen. She would much rather just hide away in her familiar surroundings. Among those whom she trusted and loved. The daily routine became a great comfort, along with her favorite things.

One of which was her favorite kind of book to read. Aside from the multitude of language ones, were the old romance novels. At one time, they were very popular. She could understand why. She often would put herself in the heroine's position. Disappearing into the fantasy world where anything was possible. If only someone could love her so deeply.

That love life amazed her and started a deep seed of wondering. Since discovering that section of the library, she had been taking a new book almost every night. Her nightly routine was to read a few chapters before dozing off, replaying stories while she slept.

Her dreams were always so wonderful, bright, colorful, and full of beautiful sights, smells, and sounds. With people so real she felt like she could reach out and touch them. Filled with mystery, intrigue, and suspense. How she could see the past, however, was strange to her. The world now was full of browns and shades of gray.

Only within the greenhouse dome structure that surrounded them did she know a little about how colorful plants could be. They could only survive thanks to the dome that enclosed the once grand city. It had created a mini world within. Allowing people to live, well, survive was more like it. Leaving the dome without sufficient outfitting would cause death.

Like they had been for Cora's burial. Only instead of outfitting them, they created a small channel of temporary domes. Allowing those permitted access to the ancestor's cemetery for the event. After which, it collapsed, and the tech team removed and took it back to the safety of the compound. Devices, and technology their ancestors had crafted and created. Giving them a false sense of hope.

Humanity had created this high tech little world for survivors hoping to find a cure or a solution to save the planet. They were still looking, however, with no success. Harlow had only helped by forwarding information about greenhouses and agriculture to the appropriate departments. They put the forgotten methods into use. They had improved the food supply.

The compound expressed immense gratitude for the one thing she had contributed. Many had lessened their heckling of her since the discovery. Believing she was of some value, after all. She couldn't contain her happiness as she lent a hand, finding comfort in remaining unseen. Finally becoming somewhat invisible.

Time had treated the compound unkindly, causing its technology to fade and energy to dwindle. We needed to resort to the old ways again. Being less reliant on devices, and more on the real. Thus the very reason for her position. Even though people considered it useless at the time of its creation. She was proud to be part of a generational responsibility, going back to the beginning of the compound.

At first, she liked it because she could hide and get away from all the taunts. Greta, the elderly woman she replaced, radiated warmth and compassion. Learning from her teachings in those first few years was eye opening. For the first time, Harlow held a position of responsibility within the compound. This caused her to feel like she belonged somewhere. Just like everyone else with the ability to pull their weight and contribute. Even if others thought it a waste of time. A position created just for her. Never mind the fact that responsibility has always existed.

It was once a public library for everyone. Now, however, it was a dark, and dusty, forgotten space. Along with every other room beneath the estate. At one time housing many. Full of life and hope. Now housing only the ever growing paranoid Overseer, his personal bodyguard, Caden, and herself. With The True Guard, the only others allowed access during the day. The structure ultimately became a ghost. A sad foreshadowing for humanity.

Taking pride in her work, she came here every day. Taking books from different topics each day. She read them to see if she could find any useful information. They thought there might be an answer to all the problems with the library. Rumors of the like have circulated for generations. Even she had heard them through the years.

So she continued to read and read every day. How she never got bored baffled her brother. He never understood how much you could learn from the old teachings. Of course, some topics were boring and didn't interest her. But you never know when it could be helpful. Just like the advanced gardening had been. The scale may be different, but the principles still apply. Maybe she would even one day find what humanity had been looking for.

She had just rounded the corner from the stairwell that would lead her back to her rooms when she walked right into someone. Flailing her arms at her instant backward descent. Gasping then in shock as the person grabbed her upper arms to steady her, and keep her from falling. Harlow stiffened at the contact that caused an icy shiver raced down her spine. Knowing instantly who her savior was.

Dreading it, she still whispered a "thank you" looking up into Sally's smug but laughing eyes.

The enormous grin that displayed on her face never reached her eyes. Chuckling.

"You gotta watch where you're going, Harlow."

Trying not to sound annoyed.

"I know Sally. I'm sorry. It's just been a long day, and I'm tired."

She shrugged off Sally's gripping hands.

"I'm alright now."

Turning to go around her, only to be stopped again when. Sally reached out, touching her shoulder, and chuckling.

"Slow down. I'll walk with you. Make sure you don't fall."

Rolling her eyes at Sally's attempt at caring while grinding out through clenched teeth.

"Fine".

To once again shake off Sally's touch, and the shiver it always caused. She paused, taking a deep breath while counting to five. Squaring her shoulders, she started again towards the safety of her rooms. Walking at a slower pace than normal for her pace, Sally seemed to think it was appropriate.

"Perfect."

She sang, skipping alongside her.

"I'm glad I was here. Imagine what could have happened if I wasn't."

Shaking her head as if sad, but with a huge grin on her face. One that this time reached her eyes.

Shaking her head, what a strange woman. If she hadn't been here, Harlow wouldn't have walked into her. Someone clearly dropped this woman on her head as a child. That was the only explanation she could come up with. How she became a member of the True Guard was baffling. Groaning, she rubbed her forehead to gain the release of her thoughts, and the growing headache.

Sally reached out again as if to touch her. Pulling her hand back at the glaring look she got when Harlow turned towards her.

In a hesitant sing song voice.

"Are you sure you're ok, Har? You know, we could head on over to the medical wing at headquarters. I'm sure they could fix you."

Odd choice of words, fix her. As if she were broken. She just had a headache. These last two weeks had been tough and emotional. Her best friend's odd behavior was followed by her death. Knowing it was murder and not being able to say anything. Her son is going off to master training, and Caden is gone scouting for work. Leaving just this morning after the send off. Leaving her alone, alone for the first time.

Just trying to focus and read today had been more work than usual. Turing off her thoughts has been harder than ever. Shaking her head. She increased her pace, ignoring the pain in her leg. She was almost there, home.

With a wave of her hand, she stated.

"It's just a headache, Sally. I'll be alright after dinner, and a good night's sleep."

Raising her arm again for a goodbye wave, she hastily rounded the corner. Quickly placing her hand over the scanner. Rushing in at the first opportunity without looking back. There was just something about that woman that gave her a distrustful vibe. Far above the airheaded routine. She wore too many faces.

After today's emotion filled day, Harlow was ready for some much needed sleep. On autopilot, she went through her evening routine of getting ready for bed. Forgoing the evening meal and not bothering to take any medicine for her headache. Hoping a good night's sleep would heal instead. She would just eat a big morning meal tomorrow. Sighing in comfort as she snuggled down into her bed. She agreed with herself, it was a good plan. Trusting tomorrow would bring about some normalcy.

Someone was laughing, well giggling. It sounded like a little boy to her. At least Rowan had sounded very similar when he was young. Curious, she opened her eyes to investigate. Knowing she was no longer in her bed, blackness surrounded her. Inhaling deeply to calm her fear, she gripped her fingers into fists. Taking slow, and even breaths while focusing still on the far away giggles. With an inward thought of courage, she reached out to feel around her. Surely she could figure out where she was through touch.

With her hands out in front of her, she took a hesitant step forward, hearing the snapping of twigs beneath her foot. After a few more steps, her fingers felt the leaves of the tree. Blinking, she realized if she squinted she could make out the shape of trees around her. She must be in a dense forest. She had read about them and saw pictures of them.

This thought towered over the others, proving its unrivaled superiority, even with her limited sight. Scary, yes. However, a fresh, earthy fragrance stirred up as she walked across the ground. She was quick to bend forward, holding a branch close to take a deep inhale. It smelled sharp, sweet, and refreshing. Closing her eyes with a smile, she inhaled again. Truly wonderful.

This began calming her fear until hearing a sharp cry of pain. Forcing her maternal instincts to kick into high gear. Turning her head in the sound's direction, beginning to make her way towards it. Pushing branches aside, she weaved her way through the dense woods. Seeing a light in the distance, she quickened her pace. The closer she got, the faster her heart beat. When the crying stopped. Fear took hold. No longer caring about the branches, she hurtled her way towards the light. Scratches and all.

At the edge of the dense trees, Harlow came to a stop, frozen in place. Blinking rapidly, only to allow her eyes to adjust. There was so much bright light. Squinting again, she realized she was standing at the edge of a large clearing. Filled with lush, vibrant grass, and colorful flowers. Birds and insects flying all around. Bringing her hand up to shield her eyes, she looked towards the sky. A big beautiful blue sky with white fluffy clouds, and the brightest yellow sun she had ever seen. It was amazing.

"Wow"

"Come now, children. Focus, and concentrate."

Whipping her head toward someone talking. A man from the deep sound of his timber voice.

Remembering the giggles, and the crying, she turned. She moved closer towards the voices, where a small group had gathered. Tilting her head, she wondered what they were doing. There were three children. Two boys, a girl with an older gentleman. Their teacher? Must be a lesson or class of some kind, she guessed. Based on how the older man was giving instructions, it seemed likely. Still not knowing what the children were supposed to do, she moved closer, wanting to find out.

In front of each child, there was a small pile of wood within a dirt circle. One little boy seemed relaxed looking at his pile, which smoked in the middle. Quickly turning to an orange fire flame. With a huge smile, he looked towards his teacher, receiving a nod. The second boy. The one who had been crying, she guessed, was still wiping his tear stained cheeks. Looked from his friends' burning piles of wood to his own with determination. Slowly it too smoked, then turned to a tiny orange burning flame. Grinning at the teacher, he too received a nod.

A curly redheaded girl. Much like herself stared at her pile of little logs. Her cheeks turned a bright red the longer she focused. No matter her intention, her pile did not react the same as the boys. Whipping her head in the boy's direction as they giggled at her. She stood ready to march towards them, halting only at their teacher's gentle voice.

"Enough"

In unison the boys, looking contrite, muttered.

"I'm sorry, sir."

The little girl, however, stomped her foot while shouting.

"Well I'm not, they were laughing at me."

The instructor crossed his arms, shaking his head as he scolded.

"Children, I believe we've had enough lessons for today."

Raising his head, he looked into Harlow's eyes. With the wave of his hand, the flames went out, and the wood vanished. Pivoting on his heel, he glided from the clearing. His long robes floated behind him.

Gasping, Harlow raised her hand to her chest in shock, whispering.

"Did he just look at me? ….. How did the flames and wood disappear?"

Focusing again on tiny voices, she watched as the children bickered with one another. She glued her gaze to the moving figures.

"What the?"

As all of them vanished in a poof. Before she could investigate, she was being pulled upward into the sky, with blackness surrounding her once again.

Bolting upright, she tried to catch her breath. Looking around, realizing she was now home in her bed. Slouching back into her pillows in relief. Letting out a large exhale, she had been dreaming again. What an odd thing to dream about, too. Maybe it was all the books she read. She had splendid dreams when she read the romance books she enjoyed so much. Scenes in some of those inspired some very racy nights. Though never had she dreamed of children other than her own son.

Odd. Shaking her thoughts away, she looked at the smart screen for the time. At 5:45 am she might as well get up and get her day started. Her alarm went off at 6:00 am, anyway.

CHAPTER 3

*N*ervous didn't even describe how Harlow was feeling this morning. After her early wake up from a crazy dream, she noticed she had a summons to appear in a meeting at the Overseer's office. Which scared and freaked her out to the point of a near panic attack. A scalding shower followed only half a pot of hot coffee. Was she able to calm herself enough to think more clearly? Were they trying to throw her off by holding her interview without her family around for support? Hoping she would then crack with some information. As if she thought. That is what they used to say right in the past. Her mind still kept coming up with all kinds of wacky ideas. Right until she came to the office door.

With a polite acknowledgment to the guard standing outside the door. She had taken a deep breath. Attempting to clear her mind, while squaring her shoulders, he scanned his hand, allowing her entrance. Her jaw dropped and her heart raced as she learned the purpose of the meeting. Curiously, she asked why her family wasn't performing the task. Only to be told they weren't available to do so. That was strange. Why wouldn't they be available? Has something happened to them too?

The more she pondered it, it was odd she remembered they hadn't appeared at the celebration of life either or any of the services. Where had they gone? Or more likely disappeared too? Deciding to keep further questions to herself, she murmured an acceptance and left as fast as she was able.

Harlow shivered as a zing ran down her spine, thinking of this morning. It gave her a bad feeling in her gut that grew every time it popped up. Which seemed to happen at an increasing rate. Maybe this was something or someone trying to tell or warn her of something. Deciding to be extra cautious, she would use all the teachings Caden could give her on his breaks from classes. Now, however, she was glad he had insisted on teaching her everything he could. As those lessons might now be useful.

Making her way towards Cora's building that housed her suite of rooms, she could rid herself of the tingling on the back of her neck. Having a strong sense that someone was watching her with more than curiosity. It was a great struggle to not glance around. Wrapping her arms around herself instead for some sense of security, she trudged along. Again, her thoughts were getting the best of her. That couldn't happen. It was too dangerous. Especially considering Cora's fate.

Was this some kind of test for her? To see her reactions to going through all her friend's belongings. It wouldn't surprise her. Someone had previously conducted this as a test. Like she was some kind of lab rat. She found their treatment of her disgusting. Didn't they understand she was a human with feelings just like everyone else? Being physically different didn't warrant the treatment she received. Mumbling to herself.

"Enough"

Going down the road of the past served her no good. She also couldn't let on that she suspected anything suspicious. This would be done with honor and respect. Cora deserved that above all else. Holding her head up high, relaxing her arms, and marching her way as best she could, she continued forward. Anyone would see only what she wanted them to see. Making her way into the building and up the flight of stairs.

Arriving at the familiar door, she stood staring at it for a moment. Taking a deep breath before stretching her arm to place her hand on the scanner. At the telltale chick, and the swoosh of the door opening, she allowed herself one last deep breath. She could do this. Squaring her shoulders, she entered Cora's suite of rooms.

A shocked gasp escaped as she took in the state of the first room. Covering her mouth with her hand.

"Oh my god. What the hell happened?"

As she turned, she saw that someone had tossed and shredded the room. Rushing into the rest of the rooms, which each looked the same, with nothing left untouched. Surveying the destruction, her heart hurt. Who would do this, and why? Was this before or after her friend's death? Did whoever tossed the place did they find what they were looking for? Or get the reaction out of Cora they needed? Too many questions, and not enough answers. If Caden were here, his skills would be loads of help. He could never teach her everything he had learned. She slumped her shoulders while trying her hardest to hold back the tears.

Tiptoeing her way through the debris and pondering where to begin. Her gaze surveyed her friend's belongings, very much disrespected as her life had been. Allowing the tears to fall in full. Covering her face with her hands, she sobbed. Wouldn't do to have the neighbors hear and come with questions or accusations. Everything always seemed to be her fault in the compound. Slouching to the floor, and bringing her knees up to hug herself tight. Allowing herself this moment of sadness and grief. Resting her head on her raised knees, she continued to cry.

After a while, her tears had dried out. Raising her head to once again survey the damage and destruction. The disrespect disgusted her and fueled her anger. Brushing back her wild curls and gathering it into a tighter ponytail, she stood. With confidence she didn't feel, she announced to the empty room.

"The bedroom. That's where I'll start,"

Nodding her head at the great idea.

With her affirmation, she maneuvered her way through the maze of destruction. Stepping over the threshold of the bedroom and placing her hands on her hips. Harlow continued her pep talk. While deciding what to start with. With a decision made, she got to work.

She had been making great headway in the bedroom, wondering what it was they had been looking for, when the click of the front door echoed. Sucking in her breath, she froze, listening. No one else should have admittance. They had stated it as such in the meeting this morning. Unless …….

"Hello. Harlow, are you in there? Hello?"

Rolling her eyes and dropping her head whispering.

"Great just, great. Will my luck ever change?"

Lifting her head, she shouted her reply while mentally cursing her luck.

"Hello, Sally. I'm here, in Cora's bedroom."

Hearing movement, and an eager reply.

Hearing her rush into the suite, stopping in the doorway with a look of relief at seeing her.

"Oh good. I'm glad you made it here, OK? I was worried I'd have to go get you."

Not bothering to hold back her irritation, she snapped.

"Why would you get me?"

Only then remembering her plan to act normal. Well, as normal as anyone could in this situation. It wouldn't do well to have more suspicion on her. For what, she wasn't sure. Just because she was close to Cora wasn't reason enough for her. There was more to it. Of that, she was positive. Looking up at Sally's smiling face as she laughed at her.

"Well, you know."

Shaking her head and frowning.

"No Sally, I don't know."

With a tick on one side of her face, and a shrug, she declared.

"Well, never mind. We're both here now. Let's get this done, and over with."

She nodded her head as if all was agreed, then turned and fanned her arm as she left the bedroom. Headed for the kitchen. As if she were in charge.

"I'll work in here. You can continue in there."

Fearing the answer, she asked before holding her breath.

"Sally, why are you here? I was asked to perform this task."

Laughing as if her statement was some kind of joke.

"Oh well, I was asked too. You, of course, couldn't do this all by yourself."

Knowing that was how most people saw her as a joke. Most people always treated her as a joke. Like she had no feelings. It still hurts. No matter how hard she tried to not let it get under her skin. Her head knew she had her brother and son in her corner. She used to have Cora too. Her heart, however, was always harder to convince. With an internal head shake, she mumbled.

"Enough of wallowing."

There was a job to do. She noticed a stack of bins placed by every door and grabbed one from it. She piled the trash in. So far, I have found nothing worth keeping. She wondered then why the person who had taken the time to stack all the bins hadn't filled them first. So far, nothing had been worth saving. It was heartbreaking. There were people within the compound that could have benefited from the contents. Those who held lower responsible positions were most in need. It was one reason she had such a sparse wardrobe and furnishings. As did Caden and Rowan, they needed very little.

Bending, she grabbed the last bit of shredded clothing. This room then would be done. Frowning at the destructiveness, again, Harlow mumbled.

"Enough already. Let's just get this done with."

She felt something hard in what she had just picked up in a soft garment. She gingerly turned the remnants of the pants, sticking her hand in the pocket. Her fingers met the cool hardness of an unfamiliar object. She wrapped her fingers around it, careful to pull it out. However, once it was within her grasp, it caused a humming of her blood. Along with a feeling of great importance. Pulling her hand back and slowly opening her fingers to reveal the object. Just as icy hands grabbed her shoulders.

"What have you found, Harlow? Let me see."

Letting out a scream of fright and wrenching herself free of the ice fingers. She dropped it. Placing her hand over her heart and gasping.

"God Sally. What the hell? Why sneak up on me?"

In a dramatic gesture, Sally placed her hands on her hips while jutting one to the side. With a lot of attitude.

"I did not sneak. If you didn't hear me enter, that's your problem, not mine. Now give me what you found."

Shrugging her shoulders

"It's nothing, Sally. Just more trash."

Not sure why she felt compelled to lie. Tilting her head up, she studied Sally. This behavior of hers seemed more true, as different as it was. Just when this thought came to mind, Sally's entire body shifted. Like she was putting something on physically. Once she firmly settled the mask, she looked into Harlow's eyes. Causing a full body shiver. It was like she could see right through her. Causing her to suck in a breath, and hold it.

"If you're sure."

She bent and picked it up. She looked into her hand, rubbing her thumb over it.

"I suppose you're right. Just a stupid old stone. Why Cora would have this crap is beyond me,"

Tossing it to Harlow as she spoke her last words. As she left the room, turning over her shoulder, she announced.

"You can take the main room. I'll do the bathroom. Then we're done here."

Releasing the breath, she sagged in relief. Holding the stone in her palm and whispering to herself.

"Why indeed?"

She wondered. She opened her fingers to reveal the stone. It wasn't anything impressive. Rolling it around in her hand. She observed it was smooth, but she also noticed a covering on it. Coated in something to keep it hidden. Strange, why would someone disguise a rock as a rock?

She looked back at the doorway, making sure she was alone. She bent down, tucking the stone into her sock, while also picking up the pants remnant. Just in case she was being watched, no one could know she took the stone. Pretending to adjust her shoe after tossing remnants into the bin. The shoe in question was on her limp foot, anyway. So it wouldn't be out of character for her to fix it. An action she did often.

A feeling of excitement, curiosity, with a hint of dread filled her. Having found something that might help Cora. She hoped. Now, there was just finishing this trash gathering. Then she could go about investigating the stone. A heavy cloud of sadness engulfed her as she observed how one person's life could be reduced to this. Shredded clothes, smashed items, empty scattering of products, and broken furniture. She shook her head at her growing melancholy. This needed to be cleaned up. At least she could take care of the cleanup. Rising, she made her way to the main room.

Looking around at the distraction, it seemed like whoever did this hated Cora. Furniture was destroyed beyond repair. However, whoever did this shredded and tore all personal possessions into pieces. Sending an obvious message. Making her way around to the stack bins, pulling them all out this time. She lined them up for easy access. As quickly as possible, she filled each one up. Until only a small pile lay on the floor. Just as she looked up to scan for any more empty bins, Sally sauntered in. The thought that she behaved as if was some kind of royalty popped into her head. This woman always had to have a grand entrance with all eyes on her. It was all she could do to stop rolling her eyes when her fake sing song voice rang out.

"My rooms are done."

Stopping, she looked around.

"Ah, good, you're almost done."

Nodding her head to herself, she repeated.

"Good."

Pointing her thumb behind her with a quick jerking motion.

"There's an empty in the bathroom if you want it. I'm out of here. See you later."

With a huff and a salute, she left.

Snarling at the closed door, she mimicked her salute while replying.

"Well thank you, Sally. How very kind of you."

Bending to massage her sore leg again, she made her way to the bathroom, once again pondering. That woman is strange. What did her brother see in her, anyway? Her behavior today was more peculiar than usual. Perhaps because it was just the two of them without Caden. Though the day she had walked right into her the usual Sally appeared, more concerned perhaps. This was all so strange. Shaking off the thought while bending to pick up the empty bin, she settled it on her hip, making her way back. In no time at all, the last pile filled the bin. This was it. They placed all of Cora's destroyed things into bins, along with the bigger broken pieces of furniture, to discard them. So sad.

Taking one last look around, Harlow let the silent tears fall. She turned, leaving her best friend's suite for the last time. Allowing her feelings to come to the surface.

CHAPTER 4

*O*nce she entered her suite, she sunk into her usual spot in their main room. A wingback chair of pillowy softness that would engulf you in its embrace every time. With a sigh of pleasure, she leaned back, closing her eyes in comfort. She would rest here for just a little while before she made herself some food. She experienced a range of feelings throughout the day - physical, mental, and emotional. Like so much of the last few weeks. It was exhausting.

A surge of happiness filled her heart at the idea of getting a little extra shut eye. Not bothering to open her eyes, she felt around for the blanket. Grabbing it, and shaking it out as best she could, she covered herself while also tucking her feet up and under. Yawning, and burrowing deeper into the chair, she gave into sleep.

Once again; she found herself amid darkness. With a fresh, earthy fragrance in the air. This time there was a small breeze wafting smells of earth, trees, and flowers. Inhaling, she smiled, enjoying the lovely smells, fragrant and sweet. The familiarity of the aromas helped her settle into a calmness. With the knowledge, she has been here before. A dense forest. Confident she was beginning in the same place, and with arms stretched out in front, she set off towards the clearing.

Allowing her eyes to adjust. It was easy to enjoy her lazy wander through the trees. With each additional step, the sunlight began streaming through the trees. This was the only place she had ever imagined the sun so bright. Knowing this, she raised her hand to protect from the glare to come. Just as she did, she could hear the muffled sound of people shouting. Whipping her head in that direction. It sounded like a woman and a man were arguing. Harlow moved quickly and quietly to get a better look.

Well, as best she could, anyway. When she rushed, the clumsier she became. Something she preferred to steer clear of. So the fact she only fell twice wasn't so bad, she guessed. Since no one saw. With only one knee scraped, it could count as a win. Still, the voices grew louder, making her realize she had reached the clearing.

Stopping at the edge, Harlow stood gazing at the scene before. Perhaps it wasn't an argument like she thought. A man was sitting on a large stone with his head bowed while rubbing the back of his neck. Worry crossed his face as he looked up at the woman shouting at him. Pleading with the woman. He begged her.

"You can't do this. It's forbidden."

Attempted to grab her hands in his.

The woman was oblivious to him, still shouting while throwing her arms about.

"You don't understand. You never did."

Stomping her foot in a tantrum, and spinning, turning her back on him.

Harlow felt her pulse increase and gasped in shock. Blinking, she was looking at herself. Covering her heart in disbelief, she kept blinking. Maybe her eyes were playing tricks on her. Taking a few steps back, she needed a tree for support. The woman was her. How was this possible? Also, why were there two of her? Shouldn't she remember arguing with the man before? Plus, this place only existed in her dreams. Curious, she moved closer. No longer concerned with the argument they still had, she got close enough to realize this woman was quite taller than her. She also didn't walk with a limp. She moved with a fluid grace as if she were floating on air.

Squinting, she studied them both. They seemed familiar to her. Recognition hit, these two had been in her last dream. Now, though, they had grown up. Why was she dreaming of people she didn't know? Still, she felt a pull towards these people. Moving until she was standing between them, she had the desperate urge to touch and comfort the young man. Strange. It felt like an internal pull, growing ever stronger.

Before she could make contact, an intense feeling of worry and fear overcame her. She got ripped away just as quickly. Being pulled upwards into the sky. Screaming, she braced herself for some kind of impact. Fear filled her.

Harlow woke to the peeling sound of someone at the door. Disoriented, and confused, and gasping for breath, she looked around. The room was now dark, meaning she slept longer than she intended. The auto shutoff for nighttime had kicked in. Sighing and taking a moment to calm her racing heart. Sitting up, she rubbed her eyes, hoping she could focus enough to see in the dark. Rising slowly, allowing the blanket to fall, stepping over it, she carefully crept to the door. Who would be banging at this hour?

Not bothering to look at the smart pad by the door to check, she opened it. Revealing a True Guard member. He questioned.

"Harlow? Harlow Faxon?"

Fear gripped her. Had something happened to Rowan or Caden? Trying to swallow, she looked up into the man's deadpan face.

In a barely audible whisper.

"That's me."

As his body posture slightly relaxed, he shoved a box she hadn't noticed toward her. Announcing

"Here, this is yours."

Confused, she looked at the box.

"I don't recognize it."

Glancing up again at his face, before questioning.

"Are you sure this is mine?"

His eyes connected with hers.

"The box belongs to you. It is to be given to you at Cora Lewis's request upon her death."

Shoving the box into her hands, he turned and left. She stood staring unseeing at the direction he went. Cora what? Why would a

True Guard member she never met make a delivery in the middle of the night? Odd, very odd.

Numbly, she closed the door to her suite. Woodenly, she moved towards the coffee table. In a shaky voice, that took multiple attempts.

"Lights on at fifty percent."

Blinking to adjust to the light change while placing the package onto the table. Harlow paced, fixing, and adjusting her wild curls to no avail. With her worry and anxiety growing, she thought aloud, while also ignoring the pain in her leg.

"Why now in the middle of the night?... Why wait so long after Cora's death?... Was this to reveal some clues?... For her or them?.... What is going on?"

With an unintelligible sound of frustration. A stomping of her foot, throwing her arms up in a tantrum, she collapsed in the seat. Expelling a large huff. With her elbows resting on her knees, she rested her head on her hands. This was crazy. She needed to focus. Something bigger than the death of her friend was going on within and around the compound.

Sitting up and resting back, she focused on the ceiling. If only Caden were here. At this moment, his help would be wonderful. Not to mention his expertise. He may even have knowledge she didn't. His presence alone would be a dream come true. He seemed to help her think through things when she was flustered. This was definitely one of those times. Sadly, she'd have to muddle through on her own. Maybe that was for the best. It was safer for Caden and Rowan to not be involved.

Turning her focus over to the box sitting on the table. Finally able to see it. It was a very plain box. Put together from mismatched metal pieces, held together with pins and rivets. Reaching out, she touched the icy surface. Rather odd looking the more she studied it and ran her fingers along it. Maybe someone fashioned it in a hurry.

Willing herself to pick it up. With shaking limbs, she grabbed it. Placing it on her lap. With a closer look, she noticed there was a carving on the lid. Tracing a finger along the beautiful work. It was an emblem of a raven, its wings spread standing atop intricate interlacing line work. A present moon entwined within a triquetra surrounded by a circle. After tracing the emblem, she felt a warm energy fill her. Odd.

Squinting, she tilted her head for a closer look. This was old, old. She sensed it held something more valuable in the past. Something of a great power. Someone made this box for a coveted object.

How she knew the intended item was no longer housed in the box, hadn't been for a while too. Was definitely strange. Good thing too, as it seems someone opened the box before giving it to her. Tilting the box, see realized the latch was no longer secured with its lock. Half of which was missing. Who else had wanted what was in this box? Was this the reason for Cora's murder?

Just as she opened the lid, and look inside, the smart screen peeled with an incoming written message. Slumping in annoyance, she mumbled.

"Now, who could it be?"

With a frustrated sigh, she put the box down. Rising and making her way to the panel by the front door to check the message. At this time, it could only be Caden or Rowan, she hoped. Through with Rowan in training, he wouldn't have access to a public com at night. That could only leave Caden.

After a few taps, she found the most recent message. It was from Caden. Soon, he would return. There were some technical issues with equipment that he and his team were encountering. In the morning, he requested Harlow's presence for a meeting. They could use her help with a language issue. Seems all the tech was now displaying in a language they didn't recognize. Laughing, she shook her head. Well, if her brother needed her help for sure, she could be late to the library.

Replying, she would stop by on her way tomorrow. The archives weren't going anywhere. Remembering all the times she had tried to teach him the languages she had learned. Laughing again to herself, she smiled. He was hopeless.

Turning, she went over to the coffee table, picking up the box, continuing towards her room. Might as well open this tomorrow now. She was tired, needing more sleep than a simple nap could grant. Once in her room, she placed the box on her bed. Going into her ensuite bath, she slid the mirror to the side. Going back to the box, she placed it in the cavity behind. Reaching into her sock, she pulled out the stone, placing it beside the box. Pulling down the top cover of the cavity this time, before sliding the mirror into place.

With a sense of security, she wasted no time in putting on her snug sleeping attire. Climbing into bed, telling the smart screen lights out. As soon as Harlow's head hit the pillow, she fell into a deep, dreamless sleep.

CHAPTER 5

*H*arlow had almost made it to the bunker room door when she heard shouts of swearing. Followed by clunking and banging. Laughing followed as she scanned her hand at the door. As the door opened with a swift click, she had to bite her lip to hold back her laughter. Caden seemed to have a physical altercation with his equipment. Her twin had a very long fuse. So seeing him in a ballet with his equipment like this was a rare sight.

Clearing her throat rather to alert her arrival, she couldn't contain one last chuckle before asking.

"What did your equipment do that you needed to attack it? Or are you trying to beat it into submission?"

Moving into the room, she wondered what could have happened. Stopping beside her brother, she looked at the offending item in his hand.

"What is the problem with it?"

With a loud grunt of frustration, Caden dropped the device onto the tabletop before him. Running his hands through his hair as he turned towards her.

"I'm not entirely sure what is wrong with it. One issue is the native languages."

"Ok. How am I to help you? You speak and read almost as many languages as I do. However badly."

Hinting at his butchered attempt when she tried to teach him. Elbowing him in the side, she smirked at his sour expression, before back peddling.

"More if you count the tech languages."

As she gestured towards the room of tech. His later learnings happened while away at master training.

They had taken it upon themselves to continue to speak many languages at home. First for fun, and later, however, hoping Rowan would pick them up as well. Whenever they were obliged to attend community gatherings, they swiftly transformed it into their game. Which always garnered several glaring stares from others.

Turning back to look at his equipment, speaking in a defeated tone,

"I know that's true. All of our tech just started going haywire, and when we tried to fix it, this strange language was all that appeared."

Picking up the device as he spoke. Turning to the display screen. In a defeated tone.

"No one understands it or has ever seen it before. We can't repair the other issues until it's displaying a language we know."

Looking into her eyes, he pleaded.

"Any chance you could read this or at least attempt to figure it out?"

Speaking, she placed her hand on his arm before taking the device from her brother's hands.

"I'll give it a look."

This strange looking hunk of cold metal didn't seem worth all the fuss to her. Glancing back at her brother, she asked.

"Is there somewhere I can sit? I'm assuming you don't want me to leave with this?"

Instantly on alert at her question, he shook his head as he spoke.

"No, it mustn't leave here. The fewer people that know, the better."

He took her elbow, leading her over to a working desk with a few chairs.

"Over here. No one is using this desk at the moment. Maybe with the two of us, we can figure this out."

Easing herself into the chair, she asked.

"Where were you when this happened?"

Curious, she now looked the device over. Turning it around in her hands. It was cold and warm at the same time. She continued to flip it until the home screen was facing the correct way. She zeroed in her focus, tapping on the touch screen. It came to life with a cheery beep while lighting up the entire display.

This felt foreign while also familiar to her. She had finished searching the digital archives years ago. Now she only read through all the very delicate books. She felt immense gratitude as she saw the delicate books being carefully stored in a controlled room on the lower levels. The fact they still felt the power required to uphold the environment spoke volumes. She just wasn't sure which direction required the most attention.

Caden answered in a forlorn voice. He seemed mystified by the event.

"My team and I were on a scouting mission. That's odd."

Looking up at her brother. Confused, she asked.

"What is odd?"

When he spoke again while taking the device back, he glared at the screen. It seemed to have a life of its own. Peeling a sound along with a light display across the screen.

"This has never made that sound before. Or lit up like this."

Confusion and curiosity filled his expression as he turned it this way and that. Before shaking his head and handing it back to her with a shrug of his shoulder.

Looking again at the screen, she studied it. These caricatures seemed familiar to her somehow. This wasn't a language she had taught herself, though. Nor had ever seen it in any of the archive books she came across. Something was tugging at her in the back of her mind, though. Like an instinctual understanding. Taking a deep breath, she decided to just trust her instincts. With her finger, she started tapping on the screen, scrolling through the many options. Until a large hand appeared in front of her, covering the display and halting the movement of her tapping finger. Glaring up at Caden, she asked with her brows furrowed.

"Why stop me?"

Staring her down, he then asked. He emphasized his questions by tilting his head, and his stern look.

"Do you know what you are doing? Have you figured out the language already?"

Pulling back from his covering hand, she sharply started.

"No, and no Caden."

Glancing again at the screen.

"Just be careful. Ok."

Then he slumped back in his seat, running a hand down his face. Attempting to deal with his nerves.

Nodding her head for a reply, she heard him huff in frustration. This was interesting the more she looked through. It was as if on some level she knew exactly what to do, and how. Was this the excitement Caden felt when on a mission? If so, she could understand the thrill. Giddy, she tapped a few more times before revealing the standard normal home screen. With a very large grin, she looked at Caden. Who was leaning back in the chair staring up at the ceiling now with unseeing eyes!

As she stretched out her arm with the device in hand towards him.

"Here Caden."

As he looked questioningly at her, he asked while raising a brow.

"You finished already?"

Smiling ear to ear, she shoved the device into Caden's hands. She giddily stated.

"Yep, here, have a look,"

Stunned, he kept looking from the screen to her.

"How'd you do this so fast? I thought it would take a while. I mean, neither me nor any of the team could figure this out."

Finally, he studied her work for himself.

Shrugging her shoulders. Turning, she looked at all the equipment laying out on all the other tables.

"I just followed my gut and kept tapping. It worked well, it seems."

Jutting her chin in their general direction.

"So, those are all affected in the same manner?"

Looking up from the device, he followed her line of sight.

"Yes. I'll need your help with all of them. Only this time, walk me through it so we can both tackle the reprogramming. Will be much faster that way."

Looking back at her, his features softened, he said. Frowning.

"I don't think you'll be making it to the archives today, anyway. There is just too much to work through."

Placing her hand on his arm, she squeezed.

"It's ok Caden. I'll help as long as you need me to. Come on, let's get started."

Rising slowly from her chair, grabbing one of his hands and forcing him to follow along.

Together they made their way around the room, working on each device one by one. Teaching Caden what she did, and how, was quick. Once he could focus, he grasped the technique in no time. Commenting, the task was much easier than he suspected. He was used to using his gut within a mission, just not with the tech used while on a mission. They continued in silence. They were halfway through before he spoke up again.

"Harlow?"

She looked over at her brother.

"What is it, Caden?"

She could feel he was about to reveal something important.

"Please don't mention this to anyone, ok. I'm not sure why or how this happened yet. I do know it was only my team this happened to. We used you and our family relationship for my team to come back. Sighting, I just needed to make sure you were okay after everything this past month."

"I'm doing ok Caden. Really."

Placing her hand on his arm. The need to touch him and reassure him was strong. She knew he needed the comfort. Smiling, she continued.

"I'll go along with anything you need, you know that."

Pausing, she pulled her hand back as she hesitated to ask.

"What is going on Caden?"

Slumping his shoulders, he said.

"I'm not sure yet. But there is something amiss."

Wringing her hands together, she took her time to say, "Caden," in a whisper. Before looking down at the floor. Feeling the need to hide was so strong.

At the worry in her voice, his focus zeroed in on her.

"What is it, Harlow?"

Moving closer to her, he took her hands in his with a light squeeze before letting go.

She looks up to her brother.

"There have been things happening here too, you should know. I just can't tell you here, though."

To nervously glance around the room while breaking eye contact. The speed at which she went from happy to scared only amped up her worry.

"It might not be safe. Plus, I need to show you something. Come on."

With a nod of her head for him to follow her through the door. The rest of the devices would need to be dealt with later. Preferably by Caden and his team.

Feeling anxious, she walked as fast as she dared back towards their suite. Her twin followed in quick pursuit. Catching up to her in no time at all. With him walking beside her, she could slow her pace, feeling safer. Though she wasn't sure for how long.

Once they were back in their suite, Harlow offered to make some coffee. They might as well have something to enjoy while she filled him in. While she was in the kitchen, Caden swept through the rooms one by one checking for additional devices for sound, and video that did not belong. Why she never thought of thought, had her mentally kicking herself. Of course, he would think of such things though it was part of his job.

Sad he had to do so, though she was glad he was here to check. It just went to prove something was going on. She just didn't know what, or who, all the players were yet. They needed to be careful. Grateful also for the fact her son was away from it all while he was attending master classes.

When her brother reentered the kitchen, he held up three fingers before bending them to raise them again. Showing three in one room, and three in another. Followed by pointing towards their main room and her bedroom. Shocked, she stopped what she was doing. Only her room, and the main room. Covering her mouth to muffle her shocked gasp.

Caden was quick to embrace her in a comforting hug.

"It'll be ok sister dear."

As he rubbed his hand up and down her back before he released her. Holding her steady by her upper arms.

"We'll get through this like we always do. Together, as a family."

Nodding his head with a raised brow, he waited for her silent reply. He was speaking in code. Something they did when they were little. Whatever they said always held a double meaning.

Taking in a deep breath, she nodded in understanding.

"You're right Caden. It just hits me sometimes."

Turning she poured each of them a coffee, leaving them for Caden to take to the table, she grabbed the light sandwiches she had made before leaving today. Making their way to the table, sitting, they dug into the food.

Caden had about cleared the plate before mumbling loudly with a mouth full,

"Mmm, these are good. Are there any more?"

Laughing

"Yes."

Nodding her head.

"They're in the cold cupboard. Help yourself,"

She finished just as he sat with the rest of the sandwiches.

"Wow Caden, you are hungry."

She smiled happily at her brother as he nodded vigorously. He finished eating while she cleaned up, pouring one more cup of coffee

47

for herself. She would need the jolt to fill in her brother on everything since he left. Stopping beside her brother, she stated,

"I'm going to take this cup into the main room."

At his nod, she headed to her favorite spot.

Just as she sat, and got cozy, she was taking her second sip when Caden entered. Holding up a small black rectangular device. At her nodding in understanding, he turned on the scrambler. This one was one to have likely made himself. Verifying it was, therefore, tamper free.

Unlike their suite. This was just crazy, like one of the many stories she read about in the books she brought home to read. She then explained everything that had happened in the last few days. Despite his unhappiness, he was not happy about her plan to find Cora's killer. Understanding the need for justice, he wanted it not only for their friend, but also for their sister. With all the goings on, he seemed pleased that she could not continue in her search.

She agreed it seemed a little strange, that anyone to be asked to go through Cora's things. Disguised as a clean up, that was what she was doing, while under watch too. Practice was for a team to go through or family, and redistribute the belongings to people in need.

Caden confirmed her suspicion. It should not have been her. They were betting on the fact that she would find or stumble onto something of importance. Before she could finish filling him in, the smart screen peeled with an incoming call.

Frustrated, Caden rose, holding his hand out to halt her movement.

"I got it, Harlow. It's likely for me, anyway."

Picking up the scrambler, he handed it to her, saying.

"Keep this on you and turn it off in a few hours or so. Unless someone comes calling, turn it off then. Ok?"

Staring her down waiting for a reply.

Taking the device from his outstretched hand, and put it into her pocket. Nodding in understanding.

"OK, Caden. I'll do that."

As he turned and made his way to the smart screen, she asked.

"What do you think they want?"

Looking over his shoulder, he replied.

"First, the interruption to whatever we are doing. They're no longer getting information from here."

Gesturing around the room.

"Second, I'll likely be called in and allowed some leave. Second, they will probably summon me and grant me some leave, ensuring that we can be watched together."

Raising his brow for effect before turning back towards the door, he continued.

"Oh"

This was not what she wanted to hear him say. Even if he was one hundred percent right. Sitting back, she let out a long exhale. Well, now what? She had only gotten to the point about being left a strange looking box from Cora upon her death. Still, she hadn't mentioned finding the stone in her suite of rooms, either.

Why she felt the need to protect that information, she wasn't sure. The box, however, he would learn about from all the here says. Everything was always talked about here. Unless you were the Overseer or those working for him. The deeper she dug, the deeper she was becoming in this mess. If only she knew all the what. Well, all she had to do for now was wait.

She just finished tidying up the after meal mess when the peel of someone at the door sounded. Thinking that was rather fast, she switched off the scrambler in her pocket. It had only been about two hours since Caden was called away.

Walking towards the door, she attempted to tame her wild mass of curls. A nervous habit, after years of teasing. Opening the door before said person could ring again. Wanting the recording devices to pick up her visitor's voice first. Notting it was Sally at the door. Did this woman have some kind of radar for her brother? It was all she could do not to fool her eyes.

With a voice far too chipper. Sang from Sally.

"Hello Harlow"

Gripping the door frame for support. Hopefully, she came across as sincere.

"Hello, Sally. What do I owe the pleasure?"

With a flip of her perfect blond hair, she once again sang.

"Oh nothing dear, I just swung by to see how you are doing. I mean, after yesterday."

She seemed to fidget for a moment like she was trying to remember something.

"Plus, with your brother and son gone. You're all alone."

Wow, state the obvious, she thought before she said. She lied.

"Actually Caden is back. We just ate before he left for a meeting. You just missed him."

Pretending curiosity and sincerity in her reply. Before taking off as if a bee stung her.

"Oh really? Well, how nice I guess. I'll just let you be, then."

That woman was odd. You never knew which face you were going to get. She allowed the door to close as she stepped back. At least it was a quick check in. She knew Sally already knew her brother had returned. Why had she not played the calling love story? Why the fake concern for her? Glad, though, it was a brief conversation.

Probably because she turned the scrambler off. What did they hope to gain from her? Someone had already opened the box willed to her and knew the contents, if there were any. They were very well listening to her at Cora's during the clean up as well. Clearly, Sally was watching her. That was at least some comfort knowing she was only dealing with listening devices. It was the library that had a lone active camera for surveillance.

Questions only kept increasing every time an answer would come. What did they know that she didn't? Did she perhaps know something she didn't know she knew? Who was involved? What were they looking for, and why? Who killed her friend?

Ack, rubbing her temples in frustration, she leaned against the closed door. Her head was hurting with all the questions, secrecy, and duplicity. Maybe if she took a nap, the thumping in her head would stop. After she could hash out all the questions with Caden. Maybe between the two of them, they could make a plan of attack of their own. Or at least answer some questions.

Making her way to the chair, she picked up the blanket. Sitting on her favorite chair and covering herself. Harlow drifted off to sleep.

Blackness once again surrounded her. An uneasy feeling forced her to shiver in dread. Wrapping her arms around herself for warmth and a false sense of security. Harlow listened intently for anything. Not hearing any voices this time, or anything else either. She took a deep breath, and gambled in a direction, she began her trek forward. Cautiously moving through the dense trees.

Quickly stumbling, this time upon the clearing. Looking skyward, she noticed a hint of sunlight streaming through thick layers of clouds. It reminded her of the sky from home. Only this sky was still a fraction brighter.

Returning her attention to the clearing itself, she scanned the glistening area. A young man was sitting hunched over with his head resting on his hands. He sat perched on one of the large rocks forming a circle within a circle. As he shook his head, she could see he had been crying. Tilting hers, she studied him a little more closely. This was the same man from all her other dreams. What could have caused him so much sadness?

Overwhelmed by the need to comfort and soothe, she made her way to him. She was a few steps away when another man appeared as if from the air. Freezing in shock, she covered her gasp of shock with her hand. It was the same elderly man from her first dream. She recognized him. Similar to how she would know Caden and Rowan. So strange.

Again, as if gliding across the ground, he moved closer to the younger man. Placing his hand on his shoulder. He soothed.

"I am sorry, my boy."

Looking up at the elderly man with hope.

"Why? Why would she choose this path? Knowing where it will lead......I don't understand why?"

Sighing with a gentle squeeze of the shoulder. The elderly man guided them to stand in front of the younger one. He spoke in a soft and stern voice this time.

"You already know why and don't want to believe it."

In a heated rush, the young man jumped up shouting. Angry, he stormed out of the clearing.

"NO. It can't be true. Not her."

Shaking his head with a smirk. The elderly man turned and looked right at Harlow. Speaking to her.

"It will turn out right."

Then, just like that, he was gone. Rapidly blinking, she shook her head in disbelief. How did that man do that? An overwhelming feeling of nauseousness hit her. Covering her hand over her mouth with an arm wrapped around her middle. She closed her eyes, breathing in air through her nose and out through her mouth, hoping for relief.

Abruptly she felt a grounding, followed by the sounds of shouting, grunts, and metal clanging. Her eyes widened in disbelief as she found herself amid a brutal battlefield. Righting herself in defense, she took in her surroundings. There was so much going on she whipped her head from side to side. "How the hell did this happen?"

Movement to her left caught her eye. Turning in that direction, she watched in shock and awe. People of all sizes and strengths fought each other. She was now standing in the middle of a battlefield. Her jaw dropped in shock as she watched, transfixed. Some had weapons, others wielded makeshift ones. While others appeared to not need weapons at all. Relying on some kind of force to overpower their opponent with an imaginary force, an element, or a bewitched item.

Realizing this must be what they had called magic eons ago. Positive in thinking, that only happened in fairy tales. Something created for entertainment. She had been wrong. Here she was seeing the proof it was not so.

With an overwhelming sense of familiarity, Harlow zeroed in on a woman with hair very much like her own. Sucking in a breath of unease, the realization came that this must be the girl from her earlier dreams. She was fighting in this battle, too. However, she seems to be on the side of the people using weaponry. Not the side of beings relying solely on their gifts. That seemed odd. She was one of the gifted, wasn't she?

With time, Harlow noticed this woman seemed to garner some discontent for those like her. People looked at them with hatred and shouted grueling remarks in their direction, while others shouted orders.

Whatever had angered this woman, he was using those lesser than her to achieve her goal. Whatever that was? Perhaps it had something to do with the fact she wielded both a weapon and used her gifts. Or she was righting some injustice. Maybe it was just plain old jealousy and greed. Wasn't that what war was about in the end?

Now, though, it didn't seem to matter to her who was on what side. She was casting down anyone in front of her. Using the pile of dead bodies she had created, she used it like a stepping stone to launch herself towards the man leading the charge of the gifted. Raising her weapon mid leap, and a few whispered words, she gripped it with both hands in a spin maneuver. With significant force, she slashed her blade through the man's neck. Severing his head cleanly.

However, not before he raised his hand, sending a powerful bead of energy that grew brighter as it traveled directly through her heart. Both bodies hit the ground, dead. All the other fighters immediately stopped fighting when it happened, as if someone had broken a magickal spell. All heads turned toward the fallen leaders.

With everyone frozen in place, Harlow rushed towards the fallen couple. Filled with a compulsion, she needed to be right there. Weaving her way through the sea of bodies, she noticed the young man she had seen before was doing the same as her. She believed he was going towards the young woman, but she was shocked when he disregarded her corpse and instead opted to kneel at the body of the leader.

Howling in anger and pain, he grabbed the hands with his. Holding them over his heart. In a gravelly voice, he spoke in another language, an ancient one.

"Thar ceann a oinigh.
A lá gaile.
Tá sé de bheith orm.
í gcónaí."

At his completion, sparks of light surrounded both men, causing the younger to gasp and shudder in a wave of pain. His face, though, spoke of a different story. One of pure shock and awe.

Once again, the elderly man appeared from thin air standing behind him. Placing a supportive hand on his shoulder.

"His ultimate gift to you."

Again, this man raised his head, looking at Harlow. With a sad smile, he gently spoke.

"Your time to help will come, my dear. Have faith and patience. You have more power than you believe."

Before she could open her mouth to reply, something pulled her upwards towards the sky. Tossing her arms out for balance as she screamed in fear. Feeling hands on her upper arms shaking her brought her to fight back. Balling her fist, and with a shout "NO" she lodged it into someone's nose. At the sound of a familiar voice cursing, she opened her eyes. Caden was holding his nose with one hand. The other held out to stop a further attack. At the sight of blood dripping between his fingers, she was instantly regretful.

"Oh, Caden. I'm so sorry."

Rushing up, she ran to the kitchenette for a towel. Grabbing it, and some ice from the cold box. Returning to Caden. Offering him aid, she said.

"Here. Why did you wake me?"

Using the towel to sop up the blood he mumbled,

"You were dreaming Har."

Rolling her eyes she voiced. Placing her hands on her hips with her demand.

"Well ya. But why wake me?"

At her pointed look, he mumbled again. Sitting on the edge of the sofa, he readjusted the ice.

"You were screaming."

Taken aback, she sat as well, on the edge of her chair. Looking unseeing into her memory she questioned,

"I was screaming?"

Pulling the towel back, he checked to make sure the bleeding had stopped.

"Ya. Your voice was audible down the hall. I thought something had happened to you. When I entered, I discovered you sleeping.

Coughing, he removed the ice towel.

"I know now to be careful when waking you. At least I now know you really were listening when I taught you how to punch. Your instincts are spot on."

Touching his nose gently as he spoke.

"I think I might even turn a lovely black and blue. Thanks to you."

Remorseful. Reaching out towards him for a hug, only for him to back away. Laughing as he did.

"Oh Caden, I'm sorry,"

Smiling, he muttered as he got more comfortable on the sofa.

"No worries, I'm just glad I know you can protect yourself. Want to tell me what you were dreaming about?"

She hesitated before whispering,

"I don't remember."

Why she just lied to her twin, she didn't know. She just felt this was to be private. She couldn't take any more analyzing. Like dreams were the mind's way of sorting out your problems. This thought felt somewhat different, almost real. At Caden's raised brow, she knew he knew she had lied to him. They could never hide the truth from each other.

Rising from the sofa. He spoke before he quickly disappeared into his room.

"Well, when you're ready to tell me, let me know. You can always count on me to listen, Har. I'm going to go to bed. I'll talk to you in the morning. Night."

Defeated, she stood staring at his closed door for a moment. Before heading to her room. Shrugging her shoulders with a sigh, she might as well go to bed, too. Once her night routine was done, and all the lights were out, she lay in bed staring at the ceiling, unseeing. Her mind was a flurry of activity. From Cora, life, and her dreams. Everything was jumbling together. She wasn't used to this much activity.

She found solace in the shadows, satisfied with her hidden existence. Now she was front and center, involved in something she was clueless about. It had nothing to do with her defects or differences, either. Only someone she knew, and the potential knowledge. Maybe that's why her dreams have been so odd. Perhaps she just needed something to focus on. One thing, just one. Then she might not feel so scattered. Deciding tomorrow she would look in the box, Cora left her. That was her last thought before drifting off.

CHAPTER 6

She felt grateful that Caden had received another summons for a meeting this morning. When he left, he said he'd fill her in later. They had just enough time to eat a quick boring meal with a coffee before his call came through. Luckily, it was a member of his team calling, giving him a heads up in the code they had developed. Therefore, the extra eyes and ears would only know what Caden wanted them to. He even apologized for having to put off opening the willed box with her. Followed by a wink. Letting her know she could open it without him.

That was what she had done. In her bathroom. She started the water in the shower, creating a good steam. Carefully, and quietly, removed the box from its hiding place. Opening the box on the floor only to find a letter within it, written on paper. A scarcity in their time, for sure. As soon as she unfolded the letter, tears fell down her cheeks upon seeing its beautiful handwriting.

Dear Harlow,

If you are reading this letter, then you have received my last will, and testament to you. Sister of my heart, I'm truly sorry to have left you so soon. Hopefully, *my demise was from natural causes, and not nefarious. But never mind that, someone has already done the deed, regardless of the circumstances.*

Just know I love you with all my heart, the sister I never had. Tell Caden the same. I love him as if he were my brother. To Rowan, I love that boy as if he were my own. My heart overflowed with gratitude as I proudly embraced the title of his aunt. That nephew of mine is something special.

Please keep on reading my crazy red headed girl. I know you love to learn and discover new things. For you never know what wonders the library holds. Just promise me not too many romances. Ok. The pages of the books within hold many wonderful and incredible things to behold. I know you will find many answers but also so many more questions too.

So farewell sister of my heart. Take care of our beautiful family.

Yours forever,
Cora Lewis

Thank goodness for the running water muffing her crying and sniffles. After reading and rereading Cora's letter, she had to put it and the box away. I was all becoming too much. She was grateful for having discovered that secret hideaway hole years ago. She could keep her special things hidden.

Hoping into her now cold shower preceding a quick cleaning rinse down. Harlow then scurried around, getting ready all she needed to go to the archives. She would ponder the many meanings of the letter later.

Obviously, whoever opened the box before her thought there was a secret meaning within the letter. They just couldn't decode it. If she was positive, why else give it to her? Then there were all the listening devices installed around her. They hoped she would understand its true meaning. But could she decode it? Or was it what it looked to be, a simple and loving goodbye letter?

When they were teenagers, it was a game they had always played as children. Cora loved creating phrases with a double meaning. Harlow felt a deep sense of gratitude towards them. It was like having their very own secret language. Especially the times when they had to all gather. Harlow had always been the topic of conversation. Why wasn't she in all their other classes, like her brother was? Or why was her hair so crazy, and not like everyone else, smooth and straight? Or her freckles that lightly dotted her face. Kids could be so mean.

The dual meaning she and Cora shared lightened the mood in those stressful times. Over time, as they grew, Harlow understood she was different. They just made fun of her because they were either afraid or not sure how to approach her. Now, as adults, they mostly ignored her. She preferred it that way. She felt safer. Oh, they still stared, usually with curiosity. There were still a few people who disliked her, as well as her twin and son, by extension. They wouldn't dare stare at Caden or Rowan. Their responsibilities helped with that. So that left her.

Perhaps some of the animosity was because they lived within the Overseer's estate. No one was sure why, not even them. They learned at a very early age not to question it. Having it drilled into you by your nanny every morning helped with that. If anyone ever asked about it, the True Guard would immediately take them in. It had instilled a level of fear and jealousy. Sadly, it was mostly always directed at her. She didn't like it. Who would? If it meant however Caden and Rowan could live easier, then she would take it.

Now to the matter of Cora's letter. It had some double meaning in it. Of that, she was sure. Since she was being watched. Either by recording devices or True Guard members. For Caden's sake, she hoped she could figure this out. With him being a member, and Rowan soon to be, it would be best if she did this alone. The less they knew, the better and safer for them.

For Cora, she would figure this out. Her challenge would be doing so in secret while being watched. All the while keeping this from Caden and Rowan. Now thinking of that, she should create her testament should something happen to her. Though she would hide hers in a place only Caden and Rowan would know of. They could provide more information to them in that case. Harlow took a deep breath, and an exhale of relief at the decision she just made.

It was like lifting an enormous weight off her shoulders. Even though she was still about to do something risky and take a step into the unknown. She would solve the clues Cora had left for her, hoping to finish her work. Whatever that may have been. While also making sure her family could find all the information should something happen to her.

With a new sense of confidence, Harlow left her suite and made her way to the library archives. Today would be the start of her new mission. She was pretty sure some of the double meanings had to do with the library books. Especially the ancient ones. She planned as she walked how she could avoid the active cameras in the archive. That was the simple part. How she could change her habitual routine was another matter altogether.

Whoever monitored the recordings of the library log would know any changes made by her, and likely the reason behind them. There was also the possibility the recordings were now live, considering the situation. The need to appear as normal as possible was paramount. Guessing she could allow for moments of grief here and there. Could be useful to her in seeking what she needed.

Luckily, today she made it to the archive with no interruptions. She would consider everyone except Caden, and Rowan a suspicious person from here on. The information Cora had but not revealed was of great importance. Perhaps the undisclosed information that Cora had was even connected to the current situation the planet was in.

Why else would all this secrecy and deception be going on? As it was dying, and then along with it, that was very like the case. If that were true, then she needed to hustle. Finding out and solving the clues. Then putting everything into action and completing the task. She would do this for her family, Cora included.

Placing her hand on the door scanner she waited to enter the library, shifting her weight from foot to foot. Today was going to be an interesting and fun day. It was all she could do to appear normal and not rush in. she was to be overwhelmed by sorrow, crumbling under the weight of the willed box from Cora.

As she walked to her usual comfy chair, she began pulling out the books from her side bag. The book into which she tucked Cora's letter, she placed it on the side table. This way she could have it close for reference should she need it. A thought she had while getting ready this morning. Going back to the hidden place to remove the letter. It was like bringing a piece of Cora with her today. In hopes, she could help her in revealing the clues and discovering the answers.

Allowing her bag strap to fall off hers shoulder, her bag landed with a soft thud beside the table. She had to go through all the same motions. She was a person who kept to a routine. Hesitating for only a moment, she turned and went about putting the books away in her arms. As she did, she figured it would be best to pick from her latest usual section. Best not to alert anyone to her change in plans. At least not yet, she hoped.

Once getting settled in her chair, she arranged the books into a reading order, tucking the book she had borrowed into the middle of the pile. When she would get to that book, she took a bathroom break. It seemed like the perfect timing to her. Putting her plan into action.

A restroom was in the back of the library. To scan the other shelves in the back would be easier for her. Her hunch was that was where she had to look. Even though there was very little lighting back there, she was glad to have thought, and worn dark clothing today. It wouldn't do for her to be caught on the loan camera searching the library.

Picking up the first book, she scanned through like she always did, continuing like so for each book. Thankfully, this pile she had gathered seemed to not contain anything of note. They had no need for financial economics within the world now. It was a trade or barter type of life now currency was a thing of the past. She still fulfilled her job when all she wanted to do was go through the motions. It meant too much to her.

This would work well for her plans, though. The bland topics with no relevance would allow her to alter timing her routine. Rising from the chair, she collected the stack of books, returning them. When it came time where her back was to the camera, she quickly slid the letter from the book, sliding it into her front cardigan pocket. When she pulled her hand out, she made a display of the handkerchief. She pulled out. Using it to dab her eyes and wipe her nose before putting it back into her pocket.

She asked the smart screen the time before nodding and heading towards the restroom. Saying she might as well take a minute before once again rubbing her nose. May as well make it look real. With a heart full of gratitude, she navigated her way through the maze of bookshelves, finding solace in the thought that the restroom was just around the corner. It meant that the camera wouldn't pick up her opening the door. It was the only room back there with an automatic light still worked. This way, she could grab a few books on her way to check them in the light.

After reading and rereading Cora's letter, she was to get a few extra romances to take home each night. She also had an inkling that the very letter itself was a clue. Like maybe someone wrote it on a page from one book. If Harlow was right, she was in for a challenging task. With so many books housed here, how would she find the right book? Hoping she could rely on her gut intuition to find it or not zero in on its general location. Lately, her gut feelings have been very helpful.

Once she knew she would be out of the camera's sight, she paused only long enough to place her hand on her stomach. With a deep inhale, and a quick exhale, she mentally asked, where? Heading in that direction, she felt the strongest pull she weaved in and out. It took her around the corner, past the restroom corridor to the back wall. Where there were several doors along the wall leading to forgotten rooms. Only she knew one door held a secret. Cora must have learned of that secret, too. However, she wasn't sure. She had told no one, not even Caden when she had discovered it many years ago. It was something she had kept for herself. Feeling the need just in case.

Refocusing on her mission led her to a shelf lined with many ancient books. The spines of which looked to be made of leather. They were lovely. In the distant past, they had discovered a way to preserve and restore these ancient masterpieces. How Cora could have torn a page from one of these was horrifying to her. Looking closer, she reached out her hand, feeling the same vibrations she felt when she had touched the stone in Cora's suite. So weird. Maybe there was a connection between them. With that thought in mind, she hovered her hand over the books until she felt the strongest tremor. Carefully wrapping her fingers around the spine, a very pleasant warmth filled her.

This was all strange. Why, when touching a book, could she feel like she was coming home? It made little sense. Shaking her head to dislodge the thought, she needed to stay focused. She pulled the book from the shelf. Without even looking at it, she made her way into the restroom. Once the light was on, and the door closed, she turned the old turn lock securing the door. It was a relief to have taken precautions, just in case. It would give her a notification should anyone try to enter. Leaning against the wall, she took some quick breaths. This was exciting, but scary at the same time.

How and why could she feel these things? It made little sense. Had Cora been the same? Was that why she had been acting so weird before her disappearance? More and more questions kept coming to mind, and no answers yet. This was getting frustrating. Her emotions were all over the place, too. Making it difficult to know what she was feeling. Not trusting there not to be planted devices in here, she went and sat. Turning on the faucet as she passed it. Just in case, she had to be careful.

Looking at the book in her lap. It didn't look like something special. Running her fingers along the spine, she could feel that there was expert knowledge held within. The cover of the book, though different from the spine, is also composed of leather. A very plain looking but thick book. Almost seemed as if it was wearing a disguise to fit in. Shaking her head, she wondered where that thought had come from. When she turned it, she realized the book had a lock. Two metal arms were stretching across, one near the top, and the other near the bottom. A lock mechanism in the middle connecting each.

Leaning back with a frustrated sigh. Well, isn't this just great? How am I supposed to look at it now? She didn't have time to try and figure this out in here. She had to get back to her chair and look at the other books. Fritters! Was she to hide the book in here? Put it back on the shelf? Or take it with her somehow? As she was panicking, she remembered. Romance novels. That's what she would do.

Jumping up, and turning off the tap, goodness she had been wasting valuable water lately. Never mind that she had a job to do. She moved swiftly, unlocking the door, and then making her way to the romance section. Grateful that this section was well out of sight for the camera as well. So it wouldn't seem odd or out of behavior for her to be seen with an armful of romance books. The letter did reference them, after all.

First, she looked for a jacketed book the same thickness as the leather-bound book. Once she found one, she removed the dust jacket, placing it onto the leather-bound book. Well, as best she could, anyway. After shelving the jacket free book she randomly grabbed some books she could add to the pile. Before she left the section, she grabbed one more book cover, just in case. Tucking it, the letter in the stack of books.

Moving quickly until just before camera range, Harlow slowed. She could take her time now. Once back in her chair, she sat placing the stack of books onto the side table. Bending to pick up her bag, she put each of the books into it. Being careful not to reveal the locks on the special book to the camera. It had to be kept a secret. For the camera's sake, she continued as usual.

Returning to the section of study, and selecting more books. For the first time, she was bored. She wanted to be in her room trying to open this special book. Not here reading over boring books filled with numbers and financial advice.

CHAPTER 7

As luck would have it, she once again bumped into Sally. Though this time she suspected it was not her fault. Having seen her, and trying to walk around her. She wasn't in the mood to talk or deal with the multiple sides of her personality right now. However, she wasn't so lucky, as per usual.

Sally barked as she grabbed her upper arms.

"Harlow, you really need to watch where you are going. Are you really so absent minded not to be aware?"

Trying to free herself from the firm grip.

"I was trying to walk around you, Sally."

Her struggle was in vain. The harder she tried to shake free, her grip only tightened. Through clenched teeth, she begged.

"Please let go, Sally. You're hurting me."

As if burned, Sally released her with a little push. Causing Harlow to stumble back a few steps. To which she gladly sneered.

"See my point, you need to watch where you're going."

With a frustrated sigh, and trying with all, she had to be polite. While remembering this was a member of the True Guard she was dealing with.

"I'm sorry Sally."

She took a moment, pretending to fix herself, before she asked.

"Is there something you wanted? I'm headed back to my suite."

Patiently waiting, she studied Sally's face. The woman looked like she was sucking on a lemon with the expression she displayed. It seemed like her true colors were shining through. Sadly, though, only with her. If only her twin could see this person standing before her.

With time, it seemed like she made some internal decision, and her face relaxed as she turned on her heel, heading back in the direction she had come from. Turning over her shoulder to grumble.

"Never mind."

Then stomped off like a petulant little child.

Rubbing her hands on her upper arms to relieve the pain and the sudden chill. She mumbled.

"The many faces of Sally were exposed. That woman is nuts. Why doesn't anyone else see it?"

Shaking her head to clear her mind, she continued home to her suite. Once she entered, Caden's presence in their kitchenette, busy cooking, surprised her. Also, making one heck of a mess.

Maneuvering her way through the room, she dropped her bag into her favorite chair. Asking.

"What's with all this?"

She waved her arm, showing the set table, and him cooking.

With a huge smile in her direction.

"I felt I should cook for you for a change. You are the one to always take care of me and Rowan. Don't worry about cleaning up either. That's all mine."

He turned back, working his magic.

Wow, this was nice, even if it felt wrong to her. She enjoyed taking care of her family. It made her happy. Making her way to the table.

"Thank you, Caden. Is there anything I can do to help?"

While waving his kitchen utensil in the air he murmured,

"No, no, I'm good. I have everything under control. Even if it looks like a tornado hit. Have a seat. It's almost ready."

Shrugging her shoulders, she pulled out the chair in front of her, taking a seat. Sitting back in the chair, Caden brought over plates of food. Taking a deep inhale, her tummy grumbled. With her appetite growing, she pulled her seat closer to the table.

"Caden, this smells amazing. So how did all your meetings go?"

Sitting across from her, he displayed the biggest grin she'd seen on him in a long time.

"Well thank you sister dear. Digg in, I'm starving too."

After shoveling in a mouthful, he moaned before stating.

"Skipped the midday meal again, did you?"

Nodding her head in agreement, she too ate. At the first bite, she moaned, looking up to Caden. After swallowing, she commented,

"This is great. Thanks for cooking."

After that, they continued to eat in silence. Caden even helped himself to the rest of the food. He completed his meal before she finished hers. Laughing, she asked him.

"Do you breathe at all or just inhale?"

He replied as he cleared the table.

"Ha ha, very funny Harlow. Why don't you go do whatever girls do to freshen up? That should give me enough time to clean up. Then I can fill you in on the meetings I had."

With that, he turned and got straight to clean up.

Accepting his offer was easy. She wasn't sure how she could tell him she opened the box. Found the letter, and read it. Then figured out some of it. Let alone the book she found in the archive today. Maybe she could come up with something while cleaning up. Getting up from the table, she thanked her brother again, picking up her bag from the chair as she passed by. Once in her room, she leaned against the closed door. Today was turning into a strange day. That was saying something, considering the past month. Pulling herself up, she tossed her bag onto her bed. Opening it, she carefully took out the special book. She had the urge to pet it. Like it was a living thing or something. It deserved to be appreciated. Her reaction to it was so strange. It was just a book, right?

Reaching in the bag, she pulled out the extra book jacket she grabbed along with the letter. Taking them with her. Once in her bathroom, she opened the secret hiding place, placing them in along with the other things. Quickly closing it, she moved about the room, doing all she needed and wanted to do. Back in her room, she pulled out her favorite comfy clothes.

Putting them on, she thought about what to discuss with Caden.

Perhaps she could bring up the many interactions lately with Sally. As well as all her many personality changes. Believing only she got to see the real Sally. While everyone else got the fake sunshiny girl. Even though she didn't like the woman, she was glad she got the real one most of the time. However annoying or horrible she could be.

Just being in her presence made her gut sing with ill ease. It was the fact she didn't trust her that bothered her the most. Or that no one else seemed to see what she saw or feel the way she felt. Like her feelings or experiences held no value. Arg, anytime she thought of Sally, she became super frustrated.

Try as she might to braid her wayward hair into pleats for the night. She gave up with a sigh.

"Good enough guess."

With curls sticking out at every angle. Opening her door and shuffling into the main living space. Another wave of shock crashed over her, leaving her speechless. Caden had lowered the lights and had two steaming cups of hot cocoa on the center table. Scanning the room and she did not see him.

Shrugging, she sat in her favorite chair. Wrapping herself in a blanket and grabbing a mug. Harlow nestled deep into her chair. Taking a careful sip. Mmmm, this was divine. Closing her eyes, enjoying the warmth and the smooth flavor.

There was a big scream in her mind, though. Her brother never did stuff like this. Did he want something? He could have just asked. Or did he have bad news to share? That seemed more likely, and he was trying to soften the blow. He prepared dinner for her, followed by cleanup and hot cocoa. She liked it. Yes, it was different. In the middle of her thinking, Caden emerged from his room all freshened up, too. Raising her mug, she smiled.

"Thanks, Caden."

He nodded a welcome, so she asked.

"What's with all the buttering up? Got some bad news or something?"

Watching as he sat took his mug, taking sip after sip before replying.

"Well, kinda ya, but not really."

He leaned back into the sofa for more comfort. At her scrunched brows, he said,

"I was given some time to spend with you. Bereavement leave, they said. But they temporarily assigned my team to someone else.

Holding his mug now with both hands, he drank it sip by sip until it was empty.

"I think that you take more care of us than we do around here."

As he waved his arm around, indicating their suite. He said, shrugging his shoulders.

"It's not fair. You have outside responsibility too. I figured this was something I could do to give back to you."

Smiling at her twin as she continued to sip.

"Awe, that's sweet of you Caden. I feel thankful for it. I don't mind taking care of you or Rowan. You're my family. I'm happy too. So is that all your news?"

Holding his finger to his lips, he then said.

"Yes, that's all. We can just relax tonight. It's been a very stressful month. Finish your cocoa, I'm going to turn in. I'm beat. Night sis."

He rose from the sofa. As he passed her, he squeezed her shoulder, mouthing. 'In time.' After he cleaned his mug, she said her good night. Watching him disappear into his room.

Well, that went easier than she thought. Remembering now about the listening devices. That would explain some of their choice of conversation topics. How could she have forgotten those? Caden must suspect what they are hoping to hear. So sad that they were being treated like this. How they thought they didn't know or wouldn't find out was another confusion. She just wondered who was listening to them. After pondering, she was willing to bet it was Sally. It would explain her erratic behavior. She just wondered how her brother didn't see it. She had long ago stopped bringing the subject up. Maybe he just didn't want to see it. Or she only allowed him to see what she wanted him to. Though he too was a True Guard member so it baffled her how he couldn't.

Enough of this train of thought. Rising from the chair, she went to the kitchenette and cleaned her mug. Told the smart screen lights out and felt her way to her room. After closing the door, and getting into bed, she snuggled into its comfort, hoping for a good night's sleep. She felt drained and had no energy left. The past month had been the most eventful of her life for sure. Perhaps even the entire compound, too. Living with the fact that time was running out was driving people to craziness.

Why couldn't she just turn her brain off so she could get some sleep? With all these thoughts and questions running through her mind. An endless loop of all the same things. She started to toss and turn. Trying in vain to get comfy enough to relax and sleep. It wasn't happening, though. Cora had been right. There were more questions than answers. It didn't seem to have an ending in sight.

With a frustrated growl, she tossed back her covers. Sitting up, she swung her legs over the edge. Rubbing her hands over her face. She asked the empty room.

"What am I supposed to do?"

Waiting for an answer she knew wouldn't come, she stood. Stretching her arms up, she realized her leg had not pained her today. Odd, for the stress and life happenings it would flare up.

"Huh, guess I'll count one blessing."

Making her way to the bathroom, and closing the door quietly. Turning on the faucet, she splashed some water on her face before opening the hidden hole in the wall. Retrieving the book, she closed the opening.

Returning to her bed, she sat asking for lights at twenty-five percent. Why was she compelled to pet this book? It was so strange. Looking it over in closer detail, she turned it this way and that. Studying it from every angle. Maybe she could learn something by just looking at it tonight. She knew she couldn't open it. She needed a key for that. Maybe she could look up in the archive, how to open it without a key? After making that, her plan for tomorrow along with recovering one of her books with this cover. She would return some books as well.

As she felt the book, she noticed that the leather covering was a jacket itself. The leather covering laid over an embossed cover beneath caught her attention. Why would someone do that? She wondered. This book must be important to disguise it in such a way. Now she wanted to see what was inside. Plus beneath the leather cover jacket. Turning the book to the back, she figured if she was going to remove it, she would then start there. The leather wrapped its way around the metal straps. She would have to cut it.

Not happy with that, she still reached into her nightstand drawer, grabbing the knife Caden had given her. Removing it from its protective covering, she held her breath as she carefully sliced at the book's edge. She sheathed the knife after completing the deed and filled her lungs with air. That was painful, kinda. Tossing the knife back in the drawer, her curiosity won out. Gently, she lifted the corner of the leather. With a sigh of relief that it was not stuck down with some kind of adhesive. As she pulled back, she revealed a stunning cover. A brilliant white with scrolls of picture art and ancient lettering. It was colorful, bright, and luminous.

Wow, this was stunning. A beautiful work of art. Every inch displayed a swirling pattern combined with both art and text. She just wasn't sure what the text said. It was unlike any she had ever seen before. The more she revealed, the more it sparkled and shined. This must have taken a significant amount of time to create. Gently turning the book, she revealed the spine. It contained similar markings, however much darker and demure. Interesting.

She hesitated about revealing the front. This felt almost wrong to her somehow. Like she was stripping the protection of the book. The leather had afforded the decoration to survive this long. Safe from dirt, oils, and germs. Someone covered it prior to creating the restorative technique. Perhaps someone concealed it because of its contents. It would seem that was the case, based on all the events happening. Needing to know, while setting the book on her bed. With careful hands, she lifted the leather to reveal the front cover.

Gasping at its beauty. It had a similar appearance, with scrolls of picture art and ancient lettering forming a circle around a large embossed emblem in the center. It looked very much like a protective circle around something very important. As she studied it further, she recognized the design. It was identical to the one etched on the metal box. The raven with its wings splayed, clutching an entwined design with its feet. Triangular figure composed of three interlaced arcs, with a crescent moon threaded through it.

The imagery was like a thunderstorm, striking with immense

force. It felt as though it was vibrating through her. Like a connecting thread from the book to her. Strange the only other time she felt like this was when she held the stone in Cora's suite. Like this book, it too seemed to have a covering. More for disguise, she was guessing than for literal protection. She intended to research the covering of it first before revealing it. Now though, that could be a luxury she didn't have.

At least for tonight, however, the book was her focus and not the stone. That would come in time. Running her fingers over the book cover, she was in awe of the talent it took to create. Wishing she possessed the skill to produce something similar. What did the symbol mean on the front? she wondered. The symbol on the front had a connection to the box and held importance. Was it only on the box to identify the book? Or were there more out there? Caden had seemed to look at it weirdly now that she came to think of it. Something she would have to think more about later.

She was getting sleepy. It was late, after all. With all the activity in her life, she felt like she was on the go all the time. She experienced busy dreams during her sleep. Her brain seemed to never truly rest. No matter how many naps she tried to sneak in. Maybe tonight would be better, as she was having trouble keeping her eyes open. Studying the book, and finding an opening, it would have to wait for another day.

With great care, she placed the leather covering back over the book. To keep the leather in place, she also covered it in the book jacket. Sliding off her bed, she took the book to her bathroom, sliding the mirror over and she put the book next to the box. Funny how something so skillfully created could have commonality with something fashioned out of scavenged metal. Smiling, she slid the mirror back into place.

Yawning as she shuffled back to bed. She struggled to tell the smart screen lights out as she crawled under the covers. Borrowing in, she sighed in comfort. Her next plan of action was searching the library for information on picking locks, creating real looking rocks, and ancient languages with symbols. For now, sleep was the goal. Smiling as she closed her eyes. Her plan was a good one. One that no one would suspect she was doing anything other than her responsibility.

Her plan was a great one. It seemed no one had guessed she was up to something different. As far as she could tell, anyway. She went to the archive every day. Picked out books on various topics to read through. Took some books home to study further. Her run ins with Sally had stopped for now at least. Letting her know her plan had been working. At home, however, that was a different story.

Caden seemed frustrated and moody. He knew she wasn't telling him the whole truth. Keeping secrets from him. He also couldn't confront her about it, either. The recording devices were still in place, and very active. They were walking on eggshells with each other, not wanting to use the scrambler device again. It was only a matter of time before the dam broke. That so was this morning. Two weeks to the day since Caden was granted bereavement leave. The gates snapped.

Sitting in her chair in the library, she thought back on the last two weeks. Everything appeared to be just fine, and they were content with their lives. When the suite doors closed, however, the tension just grew. The adage 'ignore it, and it'll go away,' seemed to be the game they both were playing. Those listening in likely had figured that out as well. Hence, no physical interference. They just kept listening and waited. Likely enjoying the growing tension.

It was like any other morning routine. Get up and get ready for the day. She started the coffee like always. She made the best brew, but in reality, was just the first one up. As they had each finished a cup, washed it, and put it away, she turned to grab her bag when Caden had asked.

"Why have you been lying to me, Harlow?"

She had spun around and her head was dizzy. Taking her time to focus on him standing, their arms crossed, a scowl on his face, and a rigid stance. Lifting her chin in defiance.

"I have not."

The hurt showing across his face also followed throughout his body.

"That hurts, sis."

Pivoting on his heel, he went to his room and grabbed a bag that had been sitting on the floor. Tossing it over one shoulder. Without looking at her, he said.

"I'll be at Sally's if you need me."

She had just stood there, frozen in place, as he walked out the door without a backward glance. However, her internal monologue had sprang to life. Was he the reason there had been no more run-ins with Sally in the hall? Or maybe he was on the side of those who wanted what Cora had? Other than showing him the box that one time, it never came up again. Was that why he was mad? They never had that 'in time conversation.' His behavior confused her. Yes, they had fought as children, what brother and sister didn't. Never like this, though. It wasn't even a fight. Until she could figure this out, she'd give him his space.

Going to Sally was an obvious message to her. He had chosen her over his twin. It hurt, yes. Maybe it was time, though. She just wished it was anyone other than her. She couldn't stand the woman, neither could Rowan. No matter how many times in the beginning they had together, and separately broached the topic. Shaking her head to physically try to dislodge the thoughts and hurts. She turned and grabbed her bag, leaving the suite.

Her journey to the archive had been uneventful as always. Therefore, her thoughts were up front and center. No matter how hard she tried, she couldn't get rid of them or even change them. An ache was forming in her belly. The worry, and the unknown, were festering. Instead, she pushed herself to move faster to exert energy, removing the worry and guilt. That realization had stung.

Telling Caden only partial truths and withholding information was necessary. It was for his protection along with Rowan's. Was it in itself a lie, whether or not by omission? Guilt consumed her as she acknowledged the truth of her lie. Even if she still believed she was right in doing so. Being called out for it hurts. This was her twin. Someone she shared a close bond with. Yet she should be able to tell him anything, and vice versa.

He was keeping things from her, too. She was positive. Talk about double standards. Their close connection they shared allowed her to know and feel the truth of her knowledge. It was okay for him, but not her. Throwing her hands up in the air with frustration, she had continued her fast pace to the archives.

Now she had to move things along. If she didn't have Caden on her side at the moment. Time was crucial. There had been no luck on the lock pick front. None of the books referenced the lock type. Now the picture language was, but the definitions were all over the place. It differed depending on the geographical location. So the meanings seemed endless. Causing her endless nights of frustration. She was looking crazed. For when she became that frustrated, she always attempted to tame her curls. The continuous handling only ended up causing them to frizz and grow ever larger. Thus, she'd taken to doing plats while it was wet before bed. Now she looked like a greasy bedhead girl. Why she even cared after all these years was anyone's guess.

The stone, however, was an easier find in this difficult situation. She wavered, unable to decide. There was a possibility she could apply mix soap and water or an agent to break down a bonding glue. The result would be to just smash the outer stone, hoping to not damage the one within. Talk about stress. She had tried the soap and water technique with no success. The breaking down agent was an absolute no for her. So that left the smashing technique. Which she hadn't had the gumption to do yet.

It seemed, however, she was running out of time. If today's events were anything to go by. She would just have to hope that the stone residing within was the key to opening the book. Hopefully, she could read and understand the contents once she opened the book. She felt like crossing her fingers and praying. Many of the books she read referred to this. Perhaps that would help and bring her some much needed luck.

The desire to run back to the suite was so strong. Only she knew it wasn't a smart option. Everything there would have to wait until later. For now, all she could do was study more of the picture language. With hope, it may be helpful. This morning she had found some ancient books depicting similar styles of art and shapes from the cover of the book. She no longer cared about being seen going to the back of the library.

She had sensed when she entered this morning it could be her last time to visit. Whether that meant the back area or the library itself, she wasn't sure. These feelings of knowing were growing stronger and happening more frequently. She often wondered if it was something more than intuition. Her reason for questioning was Sally herself. When she first met her, it was more like an inkling of dislike. Since all this craziness began, it was full of knowing she was untrustworthy.

She had also kept this quiet because it was another thing that would make her different from everyone else. She stood out enough as it was. With her crazy curly mass of red hair, her tiny stature, and the fact she was a freckled face twin. Oh, and she can't forget her green eyes. Why people chose those things to make fun of her baffled her. Her nerve damage in her leg caused her to limp. That made sense. The technology to repair it exists, and it wasn't. Why will forever be a mystery? All the persons present for Caden's and her delivery were deceased.

When they were younger, they had asked their nanny. She, however, didn't know either. Always assured them it is a trivial thing to worry about. Just appreciate the opportunity to live deeply. Twins were very unusual and rarely survived past birth. We shouldn't complain or ask too many questions. We also got to live in the principal estate, and were extremely lucky, counting ourselves as blessed. The world we were born into was dying at a rapid rate. It was all humankind could do to save it. Never once mentioned it was humankind who killed it, to begin with.

Rubbing her temples in gentle circles. A headache was forming. This trip down memory lane, finding answers was taking a toll.

Caden's anger seems to be the icing on the cake. Cora had been right in her letter. For every answer, many more questions arose. When would this ever end she wondered? She could use a break. Leaning back in the chair, she closed her eyes, taking several slow breaths to calm herself. Maybe she should just head back to her suite. At least then she could take a brief nap and rid herself of this headache.

CHAPTER 8

*A*s she ate her meal alone that night, she pondered the best way to well smash the stone. Not to mention where would the best place be. With the listening devices all within the main living space, that left them out. Even if she were to use the other rooms, the possibility of the sound caring was high. It would be even more suspicious to leave the suite to try elsewhere. Didn't leave very many options open.

With Cora now gone, she did not need to leave the suite. Other than seeking Caden and Sally, that was a big definite no. No way was she ever giving that snake of a woman any information. Sadly, that left her private rooms then. Should she use her bedroom or bathroom? Either would work. Her bedroom had a carpeted floor. Ancient yes, but it could still muffle some of the sound. It was, however, the room closest to the device in the sitting area. So, not such a brilliant choice. Plus, it might be harder to clean up after.

Now her bathroom had a thick tile floor. It would be great. However, the sound would bounce around that room. Alerting anyone listening, she was up to something. Cleaning up would also be much easier. The room's construction, like that of a very large wet room, made it great. However, the sound would bounce around the room, alerting anyone listening that she was up to something.

Cleaning up would also be much easier. Why it was so big, she wasn't sure. She also didn't even want to consider Caden or Rowan's rooms. That was their private space. It needed to be protected. Even from her. If this went bad, evidence would point all her way.

Well, the only option was to pick the lesser of the two evils. Her bathroom, it was then. Maybe she could use some towels and rags to cushion some and muffle the sound a little. Plus, then she could just wrap up the debris in them, tucking them into the back of the small vanity cupboard. Provided no one searched the rooms, she could keep the evidence hidden. At least until she could dispose of it.

With her decision made, she went about cleaning up after her meal. Grateful that when she cooked, she had, out of habit, cooked for two. So now tomorrow was all set for her. One less thing to worry about, taking time out of her crazy life. Grabbing a few rags and towels from the kitchenette, and making her way to her bedroom. Picking up her bag on the way. Just before closing her door, she told the smart screen lights out. Closing her door, not bothering with her lights here, she tossed her bag onto her bed. Making her way to the bathroom.

Whispering close to the smart screen, lights on. Standing straight, she looked at herself in the mirror. A person familiar, and yet foreign, stared back. As much as she held herself straighter with her head held high. Her skin was just a little washed out, gray bags lined her under eyes. Even her many freckles seemed to blend away. Life was taking a physical toll. More like sucking the life from her. Whispering to her reflection.

"We will figure this out."

Squaring her shoulders.

"Let's do this."

Turning, she lay out some towels and rags she had collected on the floor. Hoping to cushion the sound on the tiles a little, plus collect the mess. Standing again, she slid the mirror to the side, revealing her hiding hole. She had to take everything out, opting to do so one by one. She had placed the stone at the very back, just in case it slid out, and she didn't notice. Figured it would be safer this way. She couldn't resist pulling back the leather to reveal the book. It was stunning to look at. Sighing, she finished pulling the box, letter out, then the stone.

Holding it in her palm, she wondered why she kept calling it a stone. Turning it in her hand, it was more like a rock. It was almost the size of her palm, a little oval like. Some thickness to it. To her, it had never felt right when holding it. She had noticed that when Sally had held it, to her it was just a plain old rock. How she didn't feel the energy within it, or the fact this wasn't its true face. Made her question why or how she could.

Taking a thick rag, she damped it a little before placing the stone in it. Kneeling on the floor with one hand, bracing her weight. The other held the gathered ends of the rag. Starting back over her shoulder, swinging forward, allowing it to hit the ground with a thud. Arg, she was hoping this would work on the first swing. Just wasn't her luck. She repeated this process, and again till she could hear the telltale signs of cracking and crumbling. Finally! Her arm and shoulder were getting sore.

Releasing the rag, she interlocked her fingers, turning her hands, and stretching out her arms. She prepared herself to see what might be revealed. She had built this up so much in her mind the fear of disappointment was strong. Releasing her fingers, she gently pulled back the rag. It looked like just a pile of broken rocks. Had she been wrong and broken this for nothing? Or was this pile of debris something special? Reaching in to the debris of scattered pieces, she moved a few before seeing something white. Just as she touched the next piece, she felt a sharp sting.

"Fritters."

Pulling her hand back to see a decent slice along her finger. Cupping her hand while keeping pressure on her finger, she meandered to the sink.

Frustrated, she wasn't doing a good job of containing the blood. Creating a trail as she went. This cut was deeper than she thought. Taking a clean rag, and wrapping it around her hand, she rummaged around in the cabinet beneath for supplies. After finding them, she went to turn on the faucet, dripping blood onto the exposed book cover. Cursing herself, she just stuck her injured hand under the water stream. With her other hand, she was about to try tripping the blood away with the now dirty rag. A loud click followed by a pop that echoed through the room.

"What the?"

Pulling her hand back revealed the clasps holding the book sealed were now laying open. How was this possible? Looking at her injured finger under the running water, a thought occurred. Could it be? Looking at the cover again, she noticed a drop of her blood had landed in a small crevice on the right hand side of the book, in the middle of where the straps were located. Was that the key? Blood. It would seem so.

In an excited rush, she took care of her finger. Cleaning and dressing it. Putting all the supplies away. Turning, she almost forgot about the rubble on the floor, and the stone she had been trying to reveal. Having an idea, she rummaged around in a drawer for a pair of tweezers. No sense in cutting herself again. As much as it revealed blood was the key, there was no desire for a repeat injury. Delicately, she pulled back pieces to see a beautiful white stone carved and inlaid with gold. Wow.

Dropping the tweezers, she took the stone. There weren't words to describe how this made her feel. Wow, didn't cover it. Looking closer at the stone, she realized two things. First, the carvings and inlay were identical to the book. This meant that they either went together or someone made them together. Second, she had seen this stone before. Around Cora's neck, set in a yellow gold setting on a simple cord. She remembered growing up always asking about it. Only to get the same reply, "Oh, this old thing. Just an old family trinket." As she shrugged her shoulders. Come to think of it, Cora had stopped wearing it the week she disappeared.

This must have been the only way she could think of protecting it in such a short time. With a prayer, the right person found it. Or not found at all. No one will ever know the truth. Was she killed for this thing? It was unlikely it was the book. That had hidden in the library for eons without being disturbed. Did Cora even know about it?

Wrapping her fingers around the stone, she held it to her chest. Now she had to protect it. How could she do that? Her hidden hole in the wall wouldn't likely stay hidden for long. Now that she had, every-one's eyes centered on her. For now, though, it would have to do.

Moving, she tucked it and box back into hiding. Finishing up the floor clean up, she took the book into her bedroom. Checking the time on the smart screen. At least she had most of the night to read this book, and hopefully come up with a plan. The sooner the better.

Getting comfy to read hours on end with the lights dim. She opened the magical book. It was the only way to describe it. Why else would it sparkle and shine? Or require blood as a key. Opening the cover to see it was just as stunning on the inside as well. She observed this book had no torn pages. So where Cora got the paper for her letter was still a mystery. Just one that wasn't a priority now.

Burrowing deeper into comfort, she took a deep breath before beginning. Turning the first page, she read about a great battle fought between good and evil. Where evil coveted the power and position, good had. They would do anything to get it. Even enslave those weaker than themselves. Whereas the good battled to free the enslaved and defend what they had. In the end, both sides lost, and the enslaved found themselves without protection or masters to fend for them. Thus decent began.

This story sounded very familiar to her. It was so much like the one told in the education program they had here at the compound. Weird, theirs wasn't about good or evil, though just people. A planet wide battle amongst each other, only to realize what they were doing had a cost to the plant. Resulting in a unity of a common issue to come together as one to try and solve it. They were still trying to fix all their ancestors had done. With no success to be seen. The messages from other compounds had long ago ceased that all feared the worst. Still, they would not give up.

This also reminded her very much of the dreams she's had. Especially the one in which she is standing amongst those in battle. That battle seemed to be an evil vs. good scenario. On the good side, being blessed with special gifts along with the use of weapons. The evil side only has one gifted individual with a weapon. To which Harlow shared an uncanny resemblance. It scared her. Others from that side only had makeshift weaponry and no gifts she could see. It was a scary, and sad dream, one in which she always woke up screaming and crying.

Looking up from the book in shock. About to shout, oh my god, when she remembered the devices on the other side of the door. She was reading the book. Actually reading the book. When and how? This was weird. She had a knack for language printed or verbal, but this was just outright strange. She had never figured out a language this fast before. Not having any time to ponder further, she forced herself to read on and on. The more she read, the more she understood why Cora protected all this information. She must have been aware of the book, just not its location.

Now the responsibility was hers to handle. One she would do, to the best of her ability. Only she had something Cora didn't. This book, and all the secrets it contained.

Glancing over her shoulder, she noted the time. She would have just an hour to plan. Then immediately put that plan into action. The thought scared her. What if she failed or something went wrong? She'd be leaving the mess to Rowen and Caden. She would just have to work them into the plan somehow, just in case. Crossing her fingers, she hoped for the best. Closing her eyes, she whispered in her mind. 'Cora, I'm doing this for you, and my boys. I will protect my family.'

With that, she sprang into action. Whether her boast of energy came after a no sleep night or the weeks of lack of sleep was anyone's guess.

Harlow waited around the corner, holding her breath. Knowing she was just out of sight of a working camera. Two True Guard members were taking their time walking and talking in the hall. She just didn't want any personal interactions, so she could avoid it. So far, everything had been working the way she planned. Hiding away what needs to be hidden for each desired person. Where they could easily find the clues, they needed to decipher the hidden objects.

Pretending to have an issue with her leg, she rounded the corner. Needing to account for the delay in her camera appearance. It wouldn't do to have more suspicion placed on her. She had garnered enough already. Today was not the day to add to it, either. She felt an overwhelming sense of gratitude as her limp leg saved the day.

As usual, she went to her responsibility in the archive. Only today she wouldn't be staying there. She would use a door in the back of the library that opened to another hallway. A long ago forgotten one. There were some definite advantages to growing up within the principal estate in the compound. Especially one that was built like a full city of concrete that spanned many, many levels below ground. A maze of rooms, corridors, and their contents were all forgotten. Today she would make use of them.

She would need what was in them if she was to go forward with her plan. The hope was everything would still be in working order. The only challenge was getting the information she needed. That would be her make it or break it moment. Again, she was crossing her fingers and hoping for luck. So far, so good.

She made it to the library with no big issues. She only had to stop to avoid being seen by the men. As planned, she tossed her bag like always. Instead of the usual happiness, she displayed greater pain in her leg.

Moving closer to the chair, she set the books she had pulled out for the camera show. Rummaging around in her bag, she grabbed her pain meds. Making a big deal when she found them. Ever so slowly, she made her way limping to the restroom. Internally laughing all the way, trying to keep a pained face on display.

Rounding the corner, she took a few more slow and steady steps just in case. Moving to the door she needed, and reaching for the last book on the last self. Long ago discovering held all the keys to the doors. Grabbing the key, she unlocked the door. Reaching into the carrier bag she had disguised beneath her cardigan, she removed a large utensil. Wedging open with it, she returned the key and the book. Swiftly moving through the door, she tucked the utensil by the doorframe in the hall. It may be necessary to use it again.

Now she had to move fast, even if she was in pain. Her fake out would only give her so much time. Less she suspected than usual, given the suspicion towards her. In the first room she entered, she changed from her everyday clothes to that of an original True Guard member. Lucky for her, she found an outfit that fit her perfectly. Using the inner connecting door, she moved to the next room. This one was a gamble. It housed all the old tech. Hoping it all still worked, she held her breath. Where she was going, she would need it.

With meticulous attention, she examined each item, evaluating its quality and worth. She filled every pocket and compartment in her uniform. This stuff surpassed what is being used. Only they couldn't repair this equipment if it broke down. The technology didn't exist anymore. Hence, it's being left to collect dust. On her way out of the room, she saw a zippered sweat with an extra large hood hanging on a hook by the door. She smiled to herself and thought, 'This would be perfect.' With its signature color and its kinky curls, she was instantly recognizable. This jacket would go a long way in aiding that issue.

With a skip in her step, she retrieved the sweater, putting her arms in the sleeves. Zipping it up, she sighed in delight. It was a perfect fit. Pulling the hood up over her head, it landed to just cover her brows. Smiling to herself again, 'This was perfect.' She had braided her hair in the shower that morning, so when she put the gear on, she could tuck it down the back of the top. This hood graciously covered the rest. Giddy with excitement, and another skip in her step, she left this room, moving on to the next.

Her third room was an easy in - and out affair to get what she needed. This one, however, was the other big gamble. This was the room she had visited Caden to help with his equipment. She needed the location coordinates of the device's malfunctions. None of this would work without them. There was also an exit from this room to the led out to the wasted. The land outside their domed compound. It's where she needed to go for this all to work out.

She cautiously peered around the corner one more time, seeking reassurance. Confirming she was alone, and with a bundle of gear tucked under her arm, she scurried across the hall to the door. Hoping and praying her hand scan would work. The other flaw in the plan. Now that she thought about it, there were too many flaws, but that's what she got in the hour she had. No way to get around it, though, without Caden here. He was much safer in the less he knew the better category, at least for now.

The telltale click sounded, and the door opened. Slipping inside, she breathed a sigh of relief. Looking around, she found what she needed. Moving quickly, placing her stuff down on the table. To then pick up the device she needed and clicked away at the screen to find what she was looking for. She was so engrossed she didn't notice the person coming up behind her.

"You won't find what you're looking for there."

Startled, dropping the device, she whirled around with a hand over her heart.

"I wh.. what?"

She asked. She was staring at one of Caden's men. At least that was something. Still not good though. Asking louder this time.

"I won't find what?"

Calm and resolute, the man said.

"You won't find what you are looking for there."

Hands on her hips, she asked a little rudely. His gentle calm demeanor, juxtaposed to his large stature, put her off a little.

"And what is it I won't find? Huh?"

Crossing his enormous arms, he simply stated.

"Well, the coordinates, of course. Your brother had us scrub them."

Defeated, she dropped her shoulders.

"Oh. Well, crap."

On the last, she stomped her foot with meaning. She opened her mouth to complain more when tall, and enormous arms said.

"Here. I wrote them down for you, though."

As he held out a folded piece of paper. Looking up at him in disbelief, her shaking hand took the paper. Before she opened it, he spoke again.

"There's no need to study it. I have already programmed it into some equipment over there."

He showed, pointing directly to a table next to the exit to the wasted land. This time, with no hesitation, she asked,

"Why are you helping me? Also, how did you know?"

Before she could get an answer, he was moving. She had to run to follow him.

"Come, we talk as you get ready."

Turning his head to make eye contact

"OK?"

At her agreed nod, he nodded with a smile.

"Good."

As they reached the table, he gestured to check her equipment. At her nod, he worked efficiently, and quietly. Nodding at each approved item. He even loaded her up with more and some duplicates.

"You did good. Your Brother will be proud."

Gasping aloud.

"What Caden."

She took a step back, shaking her head.

"No, no, no, he can't know yet that I'm here. It's not safe."

His arms reached out, taking her arms in his gentle hands.

"Shhh, little one. Your brother knows nothing of this. This is because of Cora, and well, I guess me too."

Confused, she tilted her head, relaxing her tense posture.

"Cora, set this up with you? But how did she know?"

Closing her eyes for a moment to shake her head to put the pieces together. Unable to, she opened her eyes to look up at him again.

Sadness covered the gentle giant's face.

"She didn't know for sure, little one. She could only hope and strategically place the pieces, hoping they would fall where they were needed."

Studying his sad face, she realized, sucking in a breath as she covered her mouth with her hands. At her realization, she spurted out.

"You loved her. Didn't you?"

Nodding his head, he dropped his arms, whispering. As he looked down at the floor.

"Ya."

Wanting to comfort him, and unsure how or what the protocol was, she touched his arm. Whispering.

"I'm so sorry."

Nodding once again in acknowledgment, they got back to work, gearing her up to face the environment of the wasted. He then explained the device with the coordinates she needed, and what to expect for a visual if it was available to her to see. The wasted was forever a guessing game, and very dangerous. She also carried extra nose pieces of air and an additional set of coordinates in case she needed them or failed. He gave her a loaded up back sack he strapped to her. Before they finished, though, she had to say.

"Thank you."

"You're welcome. Now you better get going. Rest assured, I've erased the evidence of your hand scan in here. Also played with the recordings for the archives. Who knows how long it will take them to realize you're suddenly wearing yesterday's clothes again."

He chuckled to himself. Again, before she could open her mouth to ask, he answered the question.

"Your brother will only know what he needs to know when he needs to know it. Ok? Now you get going. I'll need to erase the log of this door opening."

He ushered her out with his hands. As she moved, she put in her nose piece and pulled up her face guard just above her nose. Securing it in place with her goggles and its strap. Pulling her hood up, she nodded and gave a thank you wave to her big rescuer. Without waiting for a gesture, she walked out the door into the Wasted, pulling at gloves again for reassurance.

Her heart brimmed with thankfulness for her colossal friend. She needed to learn his name. Calling him giant wasn't fair, especially since he was one of her family's offshoots. Loving Cora and being her partner meant he was instantly one of them. Why she never met him before was anyone's guess. However, she could come up with many reasons for keeping him hidden. Mostly, his protection was top of the list, given recent circumstances. She wondered if Caden knew of their relationship.

She appreciated the gear he had set her up with. It was helpful, for the Wasted was like a gray desert storm out here. Even though the GPS wrist smart screen was most definitely needed. Her favorite was the velcro headband holding her hood in place. Who knew something so simple would be so great? By walking this way, she could balance herself on the terrain and also found it easier to use the GPS. God only knew what her hair would look like later without that layer of protection.

From what she had been told, she needed to look for the remains of a brick building at the coordinates. What she was after was likely in the basement of the remaining structure. Since ground levels have changed drastically, there was a significant possibility it would be down there. Its importance would have guaranteed its protection and preservation.

Sad that her friend knew this was an outcome. Having to plan events for after your death to protect a secret. One that even Harlow still did not know yet what it was. It was a scavenger hunt so far. Solve the clue to reveal the next, and so on. It was sparking her curiosity for sure. The sneakiness at which she had to go about, though, kinda sucked. Having your privacy removed also sucked. While that spurred her on to hurry. It was not the exact way she would have preferred. Also, she would have liked to include her twin in this. He was an excellent sleuth.

Ah well, no sense in worrying about the past. It was over and done with. They lived on a planet showing the whole truth of that statement. It was dying because of humanity. Now humanity was still trying to save it. Chances weren't looking favorable right now. At least from where she stood. Quite literally. Gail force winds filled with lifeless earth moving constantly. No structures or vegetation left to slow the winds or maintain the ground.

Plus, it was cold, so very cold. Her body convulsed, her teeth clattering together behind her mask. Rubbing her arms to get warm, she continued. Hoping she wasn't far from her destination.

It was hard to track the time having nothing to reference. The speed at which she walked depended on the winds and her footing. She was also getting tired, so she knew she was moving slower. Not a good thing with timing an issue. She couldn't confirm if someone had followed her or if someone had also figured her out. Even with her big gentle giant helping her out.

It was even possible Caden could be close behind her. They had a weird twin bond. Knowing things about the other without communicating. Not seeing the connection between other siblings they knew, they assumed then it was the twin thing. It could just be that someone raised them differently than everyone else too. So they weren't sure.

Ignoring the pain growing in her leg, she tried to keep up her pace. From what she could see of the GPS tracking dots, she was close. The challenge was the unit also showed topography. Since its creation, things have changed so much that the accuracy of the unit is no longer reliable. It changed daily out here. To her, it seemed to change hourly with these winds. They were getting stronger, too. It was all she could do not to topple over. Grateful that the blinking dots on the screen were almost on top of each other now.

Using her hands, she cupped them to frame around the protective eyewear. From the look of the dots, she should see the structure remains a little to her right. That is, if there was anything left of them. Or could this crazy mess of dirt and debris have covered them up? On her next step, she failed to lift her limp leg, her foot then connected with something sending her sailing forward. She let out a sigh of relief, grateful that she had extended her arms just in time. This was a common occurrence when she was tired and pushed herself too hard. She had lots of practice. Still, she'd carry some bruises for sure.

Rolling to her side, she rolled her wrists and ankles, and moved her limbs. Just checking to be sure. Sitting up, she placed her hands beside her to stand when the ground beneath her gave way. Screaming as she plummeted down, hitting her arm and knocking her head on her descent. This time, she didn't expect the landing on the stone-clad floor. Moaning in pain, it took a minute or two to catch her breath.

"Well, that sucked."

Grumbling. She ached now from head to toe. Moving ever so slowly, she took stock. Raising the arm, she felt hit something. It was sore, but her clothing was still intact. Assessing if anything was broken, she opened and closed her fingers and rotated her arm. Sitting up, nausea hit her. Freezing in place, she tried to breathe with slow, even breaths. Once it passed, she remembered she hit her head too. Raising her banged up arm, she felt her head. There was a minor bump growing. Great, just what she needed. Pulling her hand back, she noticed blood. Sucking in a breath to try to calm her nerves. She was about to rummage through her pack when she thought she heard something.

Fritters she had better move; she didn't have time to tend to her wound just yet. Maybe once she found what she was looking for. Whatever that was. All she knew was what the book had told her. I guess this was the location based on her brother's experience when he was here. She had brought the stone with her. Since the book didn't require it, she speculated she might require it here. The book itself, she had left in a different hiding place for either Caden or Rowan with instructions. In case she failed, someone needed to pick up where she left off. Crazy, and sad about how Cora had done the same.

Grunting as she pushed herself up. It took a moment for the world to stop spinning. Reaching up, she held her head as if to stop the spinning. Feeling the pain at the contact.

"Ouch,"

That goose egg was a good size now. Gingerly, she took in her surroundings. It seems she had found the basement of the structure Giant had talked about. Noticing a set of stone steps, she headed towards them, keeping one hand on the wall for support. She couldn't afford another tumble. Slow and steady, keeping her hand on the wall, she followed the stairs downward. This structure reminded her of the pictures she'd seen of turrets and their winding stairs. Stopping at the bottom to steady herself, and glance around, there was only a doorway that at one time held a door.

She was growing sleepy. That was a bad sign. Hitting her head caused a concussion? It would be her guess, based on how she was feeling now. She had to stay awake now, though. That was becoming a challenge with every minute that ticked by. Gliding her hand along the wall as she made her way through the doorway, Harlow was stunned at the beauty before her on the other side. She was still in a stone built room with an archway at the other end. Bright and colorful light illuminating from the archway shone around the room. Surrounding it were carvings thick with picture art, and multiple texts. Just like it was in the book. The desire to rush over to it was so strong that she was holding herself back, but only just. With her head still spinning, she moved, again keeping her hand along the wall. Reaching out with her other hand to run her gloved fingertips along the stone.

It was beautiful. This must have taken great skill and time to complete. The weathered stone showed its age with grace and integrity. Whoever constructed this should be proud. A stunning masterpiece of craftsmanship. Its survival to this day is a testament to someone's love and care.

Side stepping she moved along taking in its wonder. Wishing she could take her glove off to touch it. Sadly that was not an option. This was what the clues had led her to. Now what was she to do? Looking closer she noticed a notch carved on the inner side of the archway, which was a good foot, and a half wide. When she got closer, tracing her finger around the edge, it was the same shape as the stone. Could that be it?

Bending to reach the stone from one of the many pockets, she cried out in pain at the pressure in her head. Uprooting herself again she held her head as the pounding persisted. Awkwardly she maneuvered to the pocket to retrieve the stone. As she did so she heard her name being shouted.

"Harlow? Harlow, where are you? I heard your scream of pain, Har."

That sounded like Caden.

"Caden, is that you?"

She tried to shout, but her head just hurt too much. Moving, she put the stone into the opening. Well, she tried too. It was getting harder to see straight. Using both hands, one at the cutout and the other on the stone. She manured till she felt the stone was in place. The blood on her gloved fingers wasn't helping either. The stone kept slipping. Once it was in place, she noticed she could push it in. Like a secret button. Before she could, however, Caden stepped through the opposite doorway. He shouted.

"Harlow, what are you doing?"

His voice rang in her head. Grabbing her head again with one hand leaving the other on the stone arch for support. She squinted and looked questioningly at her brother.

"What?"

She tried to ask. However, she could only manage a whisper.

As Caden shouted

"You're hurt"

He lunged towards her only to be pulled back. Jerking roughly out of the grip caused him to stumble a few steps into the tiny room. Turning, and moving himself between her, and whoever was at the bottom of the stairs. He stood firm radiating anger instantly.

"I see you followed me, Jasper. Where would your other half be then?"

At least Caden was talking loud enough for her to hear. Why would Jasper follow Caden? The other half, who was that? She got her answer as Sally walked into the tiny room. Waltzing over to Caden, she tried to touch him. He shrugged her off with disgust. Finally, she thought. Blinking rapidly, she tried to focus, it was getting harder, and harder with each moment. Trying to zero in on the conversation hurt. Everyone still talked as if she wasn't there, typical.

Caden loudly snapped.

"What do you want Sally?"

Trying again to snuggle up to him only to be rebuffed again. She sneered.

"Oh come on it wasn't all bad, you liked it."

Crossing her arms trying in vain to push up her cleavage.

"Enjoyed, ha"

Caden laughed. He actually, laughed.

"You really can't tell when it's fake, eh? I was using you like you were using me."

Shaking a pointed finger at her, he said in an angrier tone.

"But you should have left Harlow out of it."

Turning to look at her. Again concern grew in his eyes as he lunged for her only to be stopped by Sally this time. They grumbled, and argued, all while struggling to free themselves from the other.

Her vision was tunneling. Leaning on the wall for more support her hand slipped pushing the stone into place with a click. Bright colors of lights seemed to come from everywhere now. In pain and shock, she screamed.

"Caden."

The light was too bright causing more pain. She saw both Caden, and Sally turn in her direction, frozen with confused looks on their faces. As Caden's face changed to worry she saw Jasper move in behind him on the other side. Just as she was about to shout, to warn him, she was forcefully pulled her backward, causing her to be knocked off her feet. With her arms, and legs flailing about she screamed at the pressure building in her head.

Closing her eyes to block out the kaleidoscope of colors surrounding her. She tried to raise her arms to hold her pounding head. No such luck, however, just as she moved her limbs, instead of the intense backward pulling force she dropped from it to free fall. Before she could even blink, she landed with another thud. Forcing all the air from her lungs. Trying to move hurt as did the little bits of air she got. Cracking open her eyes she saw a black sea with twitching, twinkling dots.

"Oh, that's nice."

Before the blackness surrounded her, she thought he heard someone chuckle.

CHAPTER 9

*O*nce again, she found herself amongst the dense trees of a forest. Inhaling deep, the sweet earthy smell, it filled her with a sense of familiarity. This place was growing on her, like a sense of coming home. With excitement, and a little bounce in her step, she began the trek towards the clearing. An enormous smile spread across her face as she did so. This time there are beams of sunlight poking through the treetops, creating a mystical feel to the forest. It also made it much easier to see through the dense foliage.

Why hadn't her other visits here looked like this? She wondered. Filled with so much life, singing birds, scattering animals, and the warmth of the sun's rays. Taking her time, she'd stop to feel the rough bark of tree trunks and the silky texture of their leaves. Feeling the needles of some trees were smooth and sharp to the touch. Whereas others had a soft ruff like texture. The variety was stunning to her.

So lost in her experience, she jumped, startled when she heard voices shouting. With her hand on her chest, she took a few breaths to calm her racing heart. Would she ever not react every time something scared her? Once she calmed and started her way towards the clearing, again she focused in on the voices. They weren't clear enough to understand yet. They also didn't sound like an argument either. More like tons of people are just all talking at once. She questioned the reason behind so many people being gathered in the clearing.

At the edge, she hesitated, the group of people mingling there was enormous. She'd never seen so many people gathered together at one time. Her heart was beating a little faster. Seeing this many people frightened her a bit. Wrapping her arms around herself, attempting comfort in a hug.

As she calmed and was remembering all the times she had been here before. No one had ever hurt her or had seen her. Well, except the old man, that is. She still couldn't figure that one out. Why she would create this dream world was beyond her so far.

Inching forward, she relaxed her arms. As she reached the edge of the gathering, she began weaving her way through the throng of people. Wanting to see who was running this shouting match, and why. Her curiosity grew stronger with every step. As she passed people, she could hear requests for something to be done, that it needed to be done. Plus, what were they going to do about it? Noticing in fascination too, this group was adults of all ages, men and women speaking their minds. Wanting a way to work together and solve the issue. Whatever that issue was, she wasn't sure yet.

She was not used to such commonality and community spirit on an issue. It was the Overseer who just dictated a result on any issue he saw fit. Even when no issue existed. The True Guard was there to enforce the desired outcome. She was kinda liking this way better. Even if it was too confusing for her at the moment. The desire to learn more propelled her further.

Making it to the front of the group, a line of people standing like statues taking in each, and every voice greeted her. Amazing, she thought. Their eyes shot around the mass connecting to each individual. Wow, what must that be like to process information at a rapid speed like that? Inching a little closer, she froze in her tracks. The elderly man she had been dreaming about stepped out from somewhere behind the line of people, raising his arm in the air. It was then she noticed the staff he was holding as he stretched it above his head. There was something held within the top of the wooden staff. When he twisted his wrist slightly, it sparkled for all to see. Silencing the crowd. With a booming voice.

"I thank you all for coming, and voicing your concerns. The elders have heard you. Trust your will to be done through them."

Lowering his staff, he then pounded it on a flat rock at his feet three times.

As if by magic, the scene in front of her changed, in a poof the once shouting mass vanished. Once gone the elders, she guessed, now standing in a semicircle speaking with a small group of men and women. Among the small group was the older man she saw die in the battle dream she had. She also recognized two other men from her dreams as well. They were all animated about their discussion, nodding in agreement with each other. As they decided, the older man thumped his fist over his heart three times. Announcing them loud, and proudly.

"I will prepare all for battle."

Bowing his head to the ancient ones, he gave his thanks to them, leading most of the group away.

The elders stopped three of the group. Worry and curiosity shone on their faces. The two men were the ones she recognized earlier. The woman, however, was new to her, and still hidden by the others. When the elders spoke, they had an eerie voice. A unified high pitch sounded like a slurring whistle. Causing shivers to race down her spine.

"The destiny you three share will differ from the others."

She thought the elders acted like a hive mind. For each spoke a sentence in the same high pitch whistle, one after the other.

"Long, and hard is the road ahead.
For together you create that, what will be the saving grace.
To heal for all is holding your hand.
The Raven shall light your way."

Pulling her eyes away from staring at the elders to look at the three. Who all stood proud, firm with shock and awe across their faces. Turning, they looked at each other. The man she had seen most often stepped forward, bowing his head in respect and thanks. Rising his head, he opened his mouth. However, the elders interrupted him before he had the chance to speak. They all spoke as one this time. Causing Harlow to cover her ears in vain.

"Never fear Kieran. Your destiny holds even greater gifts."

Moving as one, the five elders shifted on the breeze back a few paces before continuing.

> "For the one to see the futures past,
> Is thrice blessed to conquer lightfast.
> Fire be true,
> With leadership firm,
> Changing destiny to right."

With that statement, in the blink of an eye, the five elders vanished from sight. As too did her dream. She became aware of herself again. She hurt all over and was vaguely aware of voices in the distance. Trying to move, she groaned in pain when she did. Opening her eyes to see what had happened to her, she screamed, this time in pain caused by the intense light. Shutting her eyes tight and locking down her jaw. She started breathing through her nose to stave off the rising nausea. She felt a nice cool cloth moving around her forehead, sighing at the comfort as she relaxed into the bed. Hearing a whispered, "Shhh little one. You are safe. Rest, just rest." With a comforting whisper, she drifted off into a blessed dreamless sleep.

Finding the woman who had fallen from the sky fascinated him but also aroused his curiosity. He hadn't known why he had been so drawn to that location today. He hadn't been there since he was a tiny child, and that was eons ago. It was a sacred place. One from the ancient acceptors. Today, he felt a powerful compulsion to be there.

He could not even make it to the sacred site when he saw the woman falling through the air. Instant worry filled him and had him rushing to her aid.

A good thing too, when he found she was lying there unconscious, and bleeding from the temple. A surge of knowledge filled him, confirming that he was sent to help her. She looked as though she had been in a battle, bruises covering every inch of showing skin. Which wasn't much at all. Her clothing and armor looked strange to him. Where had she come from? he wondered. Bending to kneel at her side, he tore a piece of his clothing to place on her temple, hoping to stop the bleeding. As he touched her, however, a spark of familiarity and energy zinged through his veins. She hissed in unconsciousness at the pain of the pressure. At her sound of pain, his entire being screamed MINE. With the need to protect and care. As if zapped, he pulled back.

"No. It can not be?"

That wasn't possible, it was just a fairy tale they were told.

Putting his thoughts aside, he lifted the woman into his arms. As she cried out in pain once more, he shhhhh'd, and she calmed. Still, he questioned, shaking his head, 'it can not be.' Rising, he began the long road back home. Every so often shhhhing as she cried out. Amazed that at the sound of his voice, she would relax. Could this be true? He wondered. It was too much to hope for.

She fascinated him regardless if it was true or not. She was tiny compared to him, but he sensed a strong, vibrant inner strength. He wanted to learn more about her. Like the color of her eyes or her hair. Did she blush, as her fair skin suggested it would? He'd have to wait till all her bruising held to see. Just looking at her soft skin marred with a kaleidoscope of greens and yellows forming filled him with anger. Who would treat a woman so? It wasn't right.

His heart eased as he opted for the safer, albeit longer, route. Instead of his home, like he planned, he headed toward Cormac's cabin. She would be safer there, especially in her condition. She needed healing. Since Cormac was a shaman and healer, it was just the place to go. The fact he was also an ancient one was an added bonus. His powers and knowledge would be a significant asset. His gut was screaming to protect this woman at all costs. As gingerly as he could, he quickened his pace without disturbing her. Needing to reach his destination a little quicker.

He had just rounded the corner in the woods surrounding the shaman cottage when he saw Cormac rushing toward him. Shaking his head at himself, he should have known they would have a greeting. As Cormac skidded to a stop, Kieran continued to walk right past him. He'd never seen their wise man as frazzled before. He was usually so calm, collected, and resolute in his surroundings. At this moment, this man showed another side.

With a whisper heavy in concern, he asked.

"What happened to her, Kieran?"

Looking over his shoulder, he said with more venom than he intended.

"I know not. But whoever did this to her will pay."

Turning back, he marched up the steps of the cottage, through the open door. Finding a cot already prepared in the middle of the room, he laid her on it. Turning again to find Cormac right behind him, whispering this time.

"She has quite the bump on her head combined with a gash. It was bleeding when I found her."

Posture shifting before his eyes, the ancient one seemed to call on all his years, and knowledge to treat the woman. Kieran suspected no one had ever seen him in a vulnerable state like the one he just witnessed. He also suspected he never would again, either. Suspecting also, it was the woman who had brought out that side of him. Expressing his worry and concern. She had not arrived in the condition he had expected. Based on his soft mumblings to himself while he worked. Her injuries must be worse than they look too, by Cormac's continued reactions. Which also caused his worry to grow. Quietly, he asked.

"Will she be ok? What can I do to help?"

Not bothering to look away as he worked, he too spoke.

"She will be fine. Could you warm up some more water, then bring some clean clothes over with it."

Without hesitation, he jumped into action and continued to fulfill all requests. Anything to help her was never too much. Once the shaman felt satisfied with everything being done, at least for now, they both sat by her bedside. He couldn't help but take her hand when she started mumbling and moaning in her sleep. Rubbing his thumb along the back of her delicate hand. Once again calmed her from his touch. Scrunching his brow in curiosity, her reaction to him fascinated him. They had never met, but she seemed to have a great trust in him. Very strange. He did like it, though, which made him feel superior.

"You feel it, don't you, my boy?"

Looking up at Cormac, confused. He asked,

"Feel what?"

With an air, and a relaxed tone.

"Why the pull, of course! She is yours. Is she not?"

Raising his brow this time, but as a challenge.

"You know, the instant knowledge of recognition. That internal screaming."

Understanding now, he asked.

"You mean the mystical pairing? The kind the ancient ancestors had. The kind we were taught in lessons so long ago."

Nodding his head in agreement.

"Yes, my boy."

Still, he questioned.

"We always thought it was just a myth told by elders. To support the reason for arranging magical bonds. No longer was the luxury of waiting for their True Mate. With magical beings killed off, and fewer descendants being born."

Giving him a stern look.

"Now you know differently."

Looking at the woman with worry

"Yes. Yes, I do."

Reaching with his other hand, he used a finger to brush aside a wayward curl.

"I never really noticed until now how eerily similar she is."

Nodding in agreement,

"Yes, she is. However, it is very different at the same time."

Rising from his seat, he looked Kieran in the eyes. He said, moving his head towards the outside.

"You know that won't matter to them."

Frowning, Kieran agreed,

"I know. I just don't know what to do about it."

With confidence, Cormac said.

"Go and gather Ravens Night. Together, make a plan after you tell them what she means to you."

Nodding, he too rose from his seat. Before he could turn to leave.

"She will be safe here with me, rest assured. Might I also suggest planting the seed of growth for preparations to be made to celebrate at the festival?"

Opening his eyes large in shock at the suggestion he was about to ask when the old man turned and stated.

"Why wait."

With a shrug, he disappeared into another room.

As he was making his way to the clearing, he summoned the members of Ravens Night. He agreed they should meet and discuss options of protection for the woman. Why would Cormac suggest planting the seed, though? He didn't even know her name or her his name yet. Running his hands through his hair in frustration. His instincts were screaming now. They seemed in full agreement with the suggestion, only they wanted it now, and not what till the festival. So he understood somewhat. His head, however, was the holdup, being all logical and questioning. With one last tug on his hair, he left his muddled thoughts to focus on more important ones.

Picking up the pace, he made it to the clearing first. Which didn't help his thought process. The more he debated, the more he agreed with Cormac. Pacing and mumbling to himself over the pros and cons of each decision. Anxiety built, till he couldn't take anymore. Sitting on a nearby stone, he dropped his head into his hands. Fisting his fingers into his hair. He was about to pull when Aidan sauntered up laughing at him.

"You make a decision yet?"

As he sat down on the stone beside him.

"What's got you all tied up, anyway?"

Lifting his head, he peered at Aiden. Might as well tell him the truth. Whether he would believe him, he was unsure. But if you couldn't share with your best friend, then who could you share with? He blurted out.

"I've met my True Mate."

Aidan's eyes grew large, and his jaw dropped opening, and closing a few times before sputtering.

"Really?"

Relaxing again, only to tense moments later. He then really looked at Kieran. With concern, he asked.

"What's going on Kieran?"

Exhaling, Kieran told him how all the stories were true about knowing the instant you touch your True Mate. You feel it everywhere, both physically and mentally. He hadn't figured out yet why they taught them otherwise. It was on the list of things to find out. He also shared their shaman's recommendation and planned to follow through with planting the seed for the addition to the celebration in two weeks. They would perform the official ceremony here before the festival.

Aidan's jaw dropped in disbelief, and he couldn't hide his astonishment. Only saying that one day he would understand the growing pull that only ever seemed to expand. Then, he informed him about how he also found her after someone had assaulted her and she had lost consciousness. Then there was her uncanny resemblance to Neera. Her followers would come for her eventually. So secrecy regarding her was paramount.

Stern, and on alert, Aidan asked.

"Do you know who attacked her?"

Shaking his head. He sharply stated.

"No, I don't. When I do, though, they're dead."

Aidan shrunk back at the venom in his voice. He'd never seen his friend so serious and focused before. He rather liked it. After they all had assumed Neera was the one to fulfill the prophecy given by the ancients, only for her to betray her people and start a war. Resulting in her death, and the death of Kieran's father. He still had a hard time adjusting to the fact that his friend was now their chieftain. Also, how do you deal with the betrayal of someone you thought was close? The other members arrived at Kieran's last statement. With varying amounts of concern, asking in unison.

"Who's dead?"

Turning to the mass, he growled.

"Whoever laid a finger on my True Mate."

Snarling, he stood and paced. Leaving Aidan to explain to the others. Who had no issue believing after observing Kieran's increasingly odd behavior? As if overnight he had changed. Physically, he seemed taller to them, and more accepting of his position of power. Many had commented 'finally' to each other. Liking the changes they saw in him. They wasted no time in making plans for extra protection spells around the village and his dwelling.

Only the leaders of the group would know of her correct hiding place, in unanimous agreement. Hoping to protect the location, and each other, deciding that it was best to send out travelers as well. They would get feelers on any gossip about Neera's followers. Then, they would provide updates on any news, so that they could set plans in place to further prepare.

All agreed they were likely aware of her and would make attempts for her. As for his other plans, Aidan would see to the arrangements needed for the ceremony.

All the other members were too giddy about that part of the meeting to focus on anything else. Most agreed it was about time Kieran took his role seriously. It was his position by birthright. There had always been a leader among them. Feeling still that he hadn't earned it, that became his the moment his father had died. It wasn't right. Still coming to terms with all of it, he also struggled with the added gift his father had bestowed on him.

Another thing they all thought was folklore and fairy stories. The apparent transmutation of power and knowledge. He now possessed his own, and his father's, knowledge. Everyone on the battlefield witnessed it. Saying it was a show of power, lights, and energy flowing around the two of them as he held his father's body. What they didn't know, and he couldn't share with anyone, was he also processed the power and knowledge, leading back to the beginning of their kind. How did you share that kind of information? He was still trying to sort through all of it in his head. He waited and decipher the knowledge until after settling the issues with his mate. Her safety is the top priority.

A burning question for him still was, why? Why had his father not shared the knowledge with him? Did he not plan to share this gift at all? Or did he share only because he died in battle? Or was it because he never got the chance too, diving far too soon? He would never know the answer to these questions. He needed to leave this type of questioning behind. It was pointless. Reaching up, he started pulling at his hair again. His poor head was hurting in more ways than one. Stopping in his tracks, he looked up, looking around, realizing it was just him, and Aidan left, and it was the abundance of knowledge that allowed him the simple acceptance that the mystery woman was his True Mate. Smiling from ear to ear. He heard Aidan chuckle.

Aidan asked. Slapping his friend on the back.

"What evil plan have you cooked up now?"

Shrugging his shoulders, he replied.

"Nothing, just looking forward to the ceremony is all."

Laughing again, Aidan stated.

"I bet that's not all you're looking forward to!"

With one more pat on the back, Aidan strolled back toward the village, whistling as he went. Leaving him staring at his retreating figure. He seemed as happy as Kieran felt.

Now, if only his mystery woman would wake up. Whistling his tune, he turned and headed towards Cormac's cottage. Just in time, when he was making his way up the steps to hear her moaning in agonizing pain again. Rushing through the door, and asking how long she had been like this. Rushing to her side. Whispering

"Shhh little one. You are safe. Rest, just rest."

Shocked again, her body relaxed at his words. When he picked up her small hand to hold in his, she smiled. Forever imprinting herself inside him.

CHAPTER 10

The next time Harlow woke, she tried to remember what was so important and came up with nothing. Why couldn't she remember? She opened her slow eyes. Blinking to gain some focus. She couldn't see anything. Alert she took an inventory, her body felt stiff, and a little sore. Her tummy didn't hurt, but she was hungry and thirsty. Very thirsty. At that thought, she reached up to rub her throat, trying to swallow. Moaning at the difficulty. When she heard someone next to her say.

"Here, try this. It should help."

Followed by a rustle of movement.

Looking towards the very blurry image of a person, her need for a drink outweighed her fear for the time being. Using her elbow to prop herself up and accept the help of a drink. Taking one tiny sip after another. The sheer joy of feeling the cool water glide down her throat was delightful. Closing her eyes again as she savored it. Once finished, she murmured her thanks, laying back down. Realizing then she was not in her bed. Tensing, she panicked when a large hand rested on her shoulder.

With a soft caring voice, she heard.

"Shh, it's ok. You are safe here. No one will harm you."

Scared, she tried again to focus on the blurry person and asked.

"Where am I? Who are you?" Do I know you?"

The voice was familiar. Frowning, she asked.

"Do I know you?"

Hearing some more rustling, he then said.

"You are at my cottage, my dear. I know of you. However, we have never formally met."

Not sure how to take his answer, she asked instead.

"Why is my vision blurry?"

At the sound of movement, she could tell he leaned back into his chair.

"You took quite a knock to the head. It'll take some time to heal. Don't try too hard, the strain will only make it worse. Ok?"

Before she could agree to his sound, reasoning her tummy took that moment to grumble. Alerting anyone around she needed sustenance. Embarrassed, she wrapped both arms around her middle. With a murmured sorry. She couldn't remember the last time she ate, much less anything else, for that matter. More rustling and laughter.

"No need to be sorry, dear. I have something here that should quiet that tummy grumbling."

While she heard him stand, and moving about the room, she took the time to pat herself down. She seemed to be in her clothes. Only her boots were missing. Why could she remember her clothes but not what happened to her? Her memory was so foggy. Every time she tried remembering, the more her head hurt. Scrunching her face in pain, she raised a hand to rub her head. Only to come in contact with a rather large goose egg.

"Ouch."

Pulling her hand away. From across the room, she heard.

"Careful dear. Healing takes time. I was able to help you some. The rest you must do on your own."

Hearing him shuffle close to her, and sit again next to her. He continued.

"Here, let me help you sit up. Then I can pass you some food. Ok."

"Alright."

Accepting his help, she sat, and he supported her back with blankets, she guessed. To which she mumbled,

"Thank you."

Sighing when she relaxed back into comfort.

Smiling, he answered.

"You are welcome, my dear. Here, now eat."

Placing a piece of food into her palm. She enjoyed a quiet meal of bread and cheese pieces. When she was full, she murmured a thanks once again. She felt exhausted again after removing the extra blankets with his help and laying down once more. Sleep would be a blissful escape, with a full belly, a quenched throat, and healing to do. In a whisper to her caregiver.

"I'm just going to close my eyes for a little bit."

Kieran returned to the cottage every morning. He wished he could just keep her with him at his dwelling. She was safer here with someone to watch over her all the time. He couldn't guarantee to be available all the time. Issues always came up in the village or someone needed and wanted something from him. Thankfully though, yesterday he began setting up a system to allow him some more free time. The time that he could spend with his mystery woman. Rubbing his hand through his hair. He needed to find out her real name. Calling her his mystery woman was wrong.

When he arrived this morning Cormac said she had woken up, but that her vision was blurry. Knowing he could heal that for her, he had frowned at him, only to receive a stern look. A Shaman had his reasons, he guessed. Choosing not to confront him about it, he asked if she could eat. Not only did she eat and drink, but she kept it all down. Which was an excellent thing. Making him happy, if not a little more reassured, she was on the mend.

Cormac had been called out to see a village member, leaving him alone with his mate. With instructions to wake her every so often, and also feed her something light, followed by plenty of fluids. That he should talk to her often, since she only seemed calm with the sound of his voice or the touch of his hand. Above all, she needed the rest to heal.

Remembering the edict, he prepared a light meal and some tea. He placed everything on a tray before making his way back to her cot. Set it on the small table beside the chair. Turning, he sat in the chair, and with a deep breath, he prepared to wake her. Only when he looked over at her, her eyes were open. He watched as the color drained from her face. Unsure what to do, he reached out to touch her. Only for her to abruptly retract.

With a shaky voice, she asked.

"Whoooo.....who are you?"

Trying to calm his inner beast for her. His mate should never fear him, never. Instead, he calmingly said.

"I am Kieran."

Suddenly her face changed. Furrowed brows and a scrunched up little nose pointed toward him.

"Kieran? I know that name from somewhere."

Dropping her head in confusion.

"I think, anyway. Arg, why can't I remember?" She raised her arms only to clench her fists, pounding them onto the cot with frustration.

Curious, he asked her.

"What do you mean, you can't remember?"

She started rambling on as if he weren't there.

"Well, my mind is foggy. I mean, I know who I am. I know my name is Harlow. I was to do something important. But I can't remember what. I remember my best friend's funeral. But not how she died. I remember my son going off to training........."

She continued to ramble on but his focus zeroed in on the word son. She had a son? How old was she? How old was her son? Did she already have a mate? Realizing she had stopped talking, he asked.

"You have a son? How old is he?"

Holding the edges of the seat, he sure hoped it wouldn't break. Wouldn't do to break the shaman's chair, when he was tending to his True Mate.

She answered in a strange voice.

"Oh Rowan, he's fifteen now, just saw him off to training for his responsibilities."

Nervously he asked.

"And his father?"

Rage coursed through her veins, boiling her blood. Her cheeks darkened in a heated blush. Gritting her teeth, she spoke.

"That bastard is dead, I hope. He disappeared before Rowan's birth."

Oh, maybe he should stop with the questions for now. She seemed to be emotional all over the place. Perhaps food and drink were a better idea.

"I have something for you to eat, and drink if you'd like Harlow."

He liked her name. Liked how it sounded as he said it. She seemed to think the same saying, her posture relaxing, and a small smile touching her lips.

"I like the way you say my name. Yes, I'd like some food, please."

Cautiously, she eased herself up into a better sitting position.

"What would you like first?"

Hesitating a moment, she said.

"Drink please."

Handing her the drink, he picked up a small piece of meat. After she finished, he took the cup and held the meat to her lips. His heart sang when she opened her mouth and took the meat. Moaning as she slowly chewed. Licking her lips when she was done.

"Can I have some more? That was wonderful. I've never tasted something so full of flavor."

"Of course."

Holding another piece to her lips, the cycle continued til she had eaten and drank everything he had prepared for her. With her eyes drooping, he helped her to lie back down.

"Rest Harlow. I'll be here when you wake up."

"Mmmm" was her weak response before producing a light little snore.

He discovered, to his surprise, how much he enjoyed feeding her by hand while sitting back. He suspected it was not something she was familiar with, but she still found enjoyment in it. Was it because it was him? He sure hoped so. His mind wandered to the mention. She had a son off at training. Where was he training, and with whom? What responsibilities? At least no mate or father in the picture. He would have to get the full story on that, though. Perhaps he should wait till she was ready to share it with him. She likely wouldn't remember any of her ramblings later if she was having trouble with her memories.

What troubled him when she expressed anger was fear, panic, and shame beneath the surface. Every emotion she had showed across her face. He saw them there clear as day, even if they were just a flicker. She should never have those feelings, let alone they linger for fifteen years or more. Mates are to be protected and loved. Determination filled him as he promised her he would be there for her. That never again would she feel fear, panic, or shame.

This was how the rest of the week continued. He cared for her daily while she rested and continued to heal. Each sharing a little touch here or a caress there. Each day better than the one before. They each learned a little about the other in their daily conversations. The more they shared, and the closer they got, it was as if the magick string tying them together was getting ever shorter. While he was not shy about staring and checking her out. She would study him when she thought he wasn't looking. He liked the idea she found him attractive, even with her limited vision. That seemed to improve day by day.

He loved the way she always blushed under his touch. The way she touched hesitant, but curious would always send a zinging thrill through him. What would they be like together? He always wondered. Her reaction to her son's father gave him pause every time he wanted to take things further. It is likely that someone did not treat her well. You should always cherish your partner. He wanted to kill any man who dared hurt her. He would just have to bide his time and wait.

Curiosity was growing daily, though, he suspected. However, she had no memory of her first ramblings. Revealing she had a son or the death of her dearest friend. She repeated things, however never that first conversation. Not sure how to broach the topic again, he let it be for now. This time spent together, just the two of them were perfect. Tomorrow, he planned on showing her his favorite places around Cormac's little cottage. She could make out enough things if they were close. Plus, she had hinted many times about being stir crazy.

Whatever that was, he wasn't sure. If he had to guess from the repetitiveness of the statement, she wanted out of bed.

Perhaps if she was up to it, they could go further and introduce her to the village. He didn't like the idea of sharing her with anyone, though. Seeing as they hadn't heard a word about her, and no attacks had come against her. He figured it was time. He wanted her to see his home. Still, they needed to exercise caution. They always needed to be prepared.

Especially since he still didn't know what had happened to her or how to leave her in the condition he found her in. Plus, her memory was still out of reach for her. Then there was the fact she so resembled Neera. In looks only, Harlow differed by being a sweet, caring person, whereas Neera was a tall, slender harpy. Who only thought of herself, and what she could gain from others? No matter what, her followers would turn a blind eye to the differences. Placing Harlow, who was shorter but by far sexier, in his opinion, in danger. Grateful that he and the fellow members of Ravens Night had agreed to secretly guarding his Mate. While monitoring the known followers of Neera. Thus easing some of his worries so he could focus on her.

CHAPTER 11

*H*arlow woke feeling well rested, and happier than she had been in a long time. Her time spent with Kieran while she healed was lovely. Other than her twin brother and her son, no man had ever treated her with any kindness. Well, Giant could be considered belonging in that category. Even then, though, no man had cared for her this way. Feeding her, caring for her, and touching her. Those accidental grazes, and the soft touches every so often, always set her blood on fire.

Bolting upright, she realized she just remembered. She had a twin brother. How could someone forget that? Rubbing her head for a nonexistent hurt. Her insides were screaming at her to protect them at all costs, as she remembered. They were her only family left. She would use the skills her sibling had taught her as best she could. Until she had all her memories back, however, she couldn't be sure of anything. Was she looking for them or them her? Or could it be both? For now, though, they would have to keep her little secret, at least till her memory returned.

Now, who was this other person? Trying to remember why she could remember Giant. Not a name, but a description of the man who had helped her. With what, she wasn't sure. Only she had decided he was now family, and to be treated as such. Thumping her fist down on the cot in frustration. This was becoming a routine for her as of late. This trying was getting her nowhere, instead she took in her surroundings.

It was then she realized she could see too. Having almost given up hope that her vision would return to normal. Taking her time, she looked around the room. Taking in where she had been living. It differed from anything she had ever seen before. The furniture, walls, ceiling, and floors were all made of wood. Although lacking in extravagance, the kitchen still had an efficient design and served its purpose. She could attest to that, having eaten throughout the week. The food was delightful and flavorful. Never had she eaten meals so full of flavor.

Looking closer, all the pieces of furniture seemed to be crafted by hand. The tool marks, seen here and there, added character to the piece. The skill and knowledge that went into creating such things were clear in each and everyone. This person was very talented. She also noticed fabrics like she had never seen before scattered around the place. Some were bright and colorful, while others were plain.

Excitement grew while her heart beat a little faster the more she saw. She noticed at the far end opposite her that there must be windows. The fabric covering them was moving in the wind. Without thinking, she jumped up only to get tangled in her blankets from the cot, and face planting onto the floor. Unraveling herself, and center her breathing, she then stood and rushed to the door.

Grabbing a hold of the large handle, pulling with all her might, she swung the door open. Stumbling a little at the ease with which it opened. She wasn't used to opening a door this way, nor the surprise that greeted her on the other side. The large yellow sun blazing its light stung her eyes. Gasping at the surprise and discomfort, she cupped her hands around her eyes. Stepping over the threshold, her jaw dropped in utter shock. Trees, lots, and lots of fresh green trees. Ignoring the burn from the brightness, she rushed down the cottage steps, tilting her head up. There was a clear blue sky up there with a glaring sun, with a scattering of white fluffy clouds.

"Wow"

With excitement, she turned to look at the cottage where she had spent her last week. Another work of art. Crafted of logs, and what she guessed was called a thatched roof. Books were a source of pure joy and enlightenment. But seeing with your own eyes was a wonder to behold. Seeing was believing.

It was rather large in its setting, though perfectly settled. They would add rooms to the building when there was a need. Somewhere in the back of her mind, she knew that this building seemed out of its time somehow. Like her, it didn't belong. Shaking off the thought, the trees surrounding the cottage seemed to embrace it in a protective hug. Except for the small clearing in the front where she stood by the front steps. Remembering the curiosity of trees, she whipped around, only to collide with a solid wall of muscle. Big, powerful arms wrapped around her. Instead, instant panic and desire filled her.

"Kieran."

Laughing as he spoke.

"Careful there, little one. Where are you off to in such a hurry?"

Inhaling deep. She loved his scent. It did crazy things to her. Trying to free herself but enjoying his hold just the same. Opening her mouth to answer him, a moan came out instead. Which had him responding by tightening his hold, and what she thought was him smelling her hair. Looking up with her brow furrowed, she asked.

"Did you just sniff my hair?"

Relaxing once she got a good look at him.

She could see him. He was beautiful, but rough. A large man with a kind heart. Sensing he carried many burdens. Tilting her head, she studied his face. A few scares here and there decorated his face. Reaching up with her hand, she felt his jaw, and the little bit of stubble there. She rather liked it, smiling at the thought. She noticed he had arched his brow. Shy, she ducked her head. Never been this bold before, she wasn't sure about protocol.

As he lifted her chin with his hooked finger. He asked, looking softly into the eyes.

"See something you like?"

Unable to speak, she nodded her head yes enthusiastically, before blushing a deep scarlet. Not liking his response. She pushed against him, freeing herself with a huff. Remembering the trees, she marched towards them. Taking in their beauty, she took a deep inhale. Clean, earthy, and sweet, just like in her dreams. Running her fingers along the bark of the tree trunks, needles, and leaves. She felt amazed, even though these were the same too. If that were so, was she dreaming? Whirling around to face Kieran with her hand on her chest. She loudly asked, fearing his answer.

"Am I dreaming?"

Confusion covered his face.

"Dreaming? No, you're not dreaming."

As he shook his head. Stretching his arm to her,

"Come. I want to show you my favorite place. It's very close to here."

Taking his outstretched hand feeling his warmth as he closed it within his own. Together, they made their way around the cottage along a footpath. Full of worry and fear, she tried her best to hide it. Where was she, and what had happened to her? The more she tried to bottle it up and push it down, the worse it got. She was shaking.

When Kieran announced proudly.

"Here it is."

He pulled her forward to stand in front of him, resting his large hands on her shoulders.

Having been stuck in her head on the way here, she had seen little. So it took a few moments for her eyes to focus on where he had taken her. Gasping in shock, she covered her mouth with her hand. It wasn't possible. However, Kieran took her gasp differently.

As he moved around her speaking

"I know right? It truly is a wonder, and so peaceful and free."

As he slowly spun around, he shared a side of himself again that no one else had the privilege to see.

Putting one foot in front of the other, she moved her way into the clearing. The same clearing with two centric circles of stones. A place she only thought she made up in her dreams after reading way too many romance books, combined with her other literature. This was an actual place, and she was here in it. But how? Her head was hurting again. Frowning, she rubbed her temple. Looking at Kieran, she asked.

"What is this place?"

With his arms out wide, and a grin from ear to ear.

"Why, this is our sacred grove. A place for ceremonies, gatherings, and handling of affairs."

This time, he looked at her. Concern marring his face.

"What is it, little one? What's wrong?"

Rushing to her side, and picking her up into his arms. Before strolling to the stone circle to sit on one.

Pushing one of her curls aside. He continued to twirl it, saying "Tell me."

Taking a deep breath, she wasn't sure what to say, and she felt shocked when she blurted it out.

"I've been here before."

At his confused look, she continued. Telling him about her many dreams over the years. Most were the same over and over again. Lately, though, they had been changing. Still the same people, but older, aging. Then there was the battle, as she went into more and more detail. Kieran became bigger and harder somehow. It was strange. Stopping to ask.

"Kieran, are you alright?"

Tilting her head, realization struck her like being hit over the head. Jumping from his lap, she cried.

"You. It was you. I've been dreaming of you."

Taking a few deep breaths, she asked him.

"Why?"

Kieran just shook his head slowly before he answered.

"I know not, little one."

She knew he was lying, or at least not telling the whole truth. Her memory was foggy, but this rang a bell for her. Now knowing what it was like to be on the other side. She didn't like it. What had she lied about, and to whom, and was Kieran doing it now? Instead of asking, hoping someday he would tell her the truth. She just accepted his answer and asked.

"Can we go back? I'm getting a little tired, and hungry."

Slowly he stood, taking her hand.

"Of course, little one. Don't worry, we'll figure this out."

Nodding in agreement, she let him lead her once again. Having not paid attention to getting here, she did not know where here was. Or let alone where the cottage was. How did she get herself into this pickle of a mess? What was she to do now? With a thumping in her head growing, she let the worry be tomorrow's problem. She should just enjoy her time with Kieran.

When Harlow had drifted off after their meal, he snuck outside to the porch. Cormac sat there on the steps, keeping his hands busy. The man could never just sit still; he had to be doing something. He would always say 'a man who does nothing is useless.' So he created wonderful things out of wood with whatever tool he could. The only exception to the rule was talking. A pleasant conversation had to have undecided attention. Rolling his eyes, he laughed internally. He sat down beside his Shaman. Looking ahead, he stared at the trees that had fascinated her so.

"So has she told you then?"

Confused, he turned and watched the hands at work creating three interlocking open triangles encasing a crescent moon. When he asked.

"Has she told me what?"

Shaking his head in confusion. The old man seemed to always be one step ahead. Likely his gift of sight. Though he suspected that was not always the case. He had a way that allowed people to open up to him. Though he suspected this time, it was not the case.

"When she's from?"

Before he realized what he had been asked, he quickly replied, "N..."

"What do you mean? Isn't it where?"

His mind buzzed with curiosity, eager to delve into the man's knowledge. There was a great deal of magick at work here. Which put him on edge a little.

Putting down his carving, he turned to look at Kieran.

"No, I do mean when. You need to get her to open up to you, and fast. She may not like it, but you don't have a lot of time. I'm telling you this only once. She is the KEY and needs to be protected and treasured. Your road will not be easy. You will also have to take some leeway with the ceremony and rearrange the order a bit."

With that he rose, snapping fingers, making the tools, and the carving disappeared. Turning to look down at Kieran.

"Oh, I almost forgot. Have Aidan with you to train her. Their gifts will align well. Gotta go, later."

With a two finger salute, he vanished in lightning with a pop. That man had the oddest way of speaking sometimes. It was like he was from a different time. Time, that word kept rolling around in his head. Standing, he turned, entering the cottage again. Looking at Harlow, he wondered. Could it be? He had been heading towards the ancients sacred arch. Could the stories be true? Moving across the room, he sat in the chair beside her cot. It had become his favorite as of late. Anything close to her didn't matter where.

Reaching out to push back the curl to look at her. She was stunning. Ivory skin with a dotting of freckles. Her mass of red ginger ringlets, which seemed to possess a life of their own, reached down her back. He loved to touch and twirl his fingers in it. She seemed to enjoy it too. An audible hmmm always followed. He spent the past week contemplating whether his attraction to her was because of her or because of the magick of the True Mate. It was giving him pause in the ceremony. With what Cormac had just said, it added to the building pressure. In the end, he knew he would do what needed to be done. He just didn't want to hurt her. He had to plan things just right.

Then there was the thing about Aidan and his training with her? What was that all about? He could only guess. That man sometimes spoke in more riddles than the elders did. They were the creepy ones you never crossed. Shivering at the thought, he shook his head to dislodge it. He would attempt to understand what it was all about based on the suggestion. His task was to decipher the meaning behind taking leeway with the ceremony and rearranging it. In order to get any ideas, he would have to ask Aidan.

Focusing back on her sleeping form, he wondered. Could the

when be right? Her clothing was different. Then there was her reaction to the cottage and its surroundings. Also what she had said in the
clearing. He had forgotten to ask Cormac about that. It had to either
do with the mate tether or the archway. His gut was now screaming at
him; it was a bit of both. If that were so. Then his world, and hers,
were about to change.

CHAPTER 12

*K*ieran had enlisted help from Aidan to carry out many plans and duties as chieftain. Therefore, they were both able to be available to Ravens Night, and Kieran could spend more time with Harlow. Time he enjoyed, she got any, and every free moment he could give her. He wasn't looking forward to sharing her with anyone. The connection they shared was growing stronger every day. So was the tension between them. He couldn't seem to keep his hands off her. She also always seemed in contact with him. Either sitting on his lap or snuggled up beside him. Over the last few nights, he dreamed of hot and sweaty action filling his dreams. Never had he wanted to devour a woman in kisses. With Harlow, however, that's what he wanted to do. He wanted to taste every inch of her ivory skin, play connect the dots with her freckles. Rousing her desire till he was devouring her mouth as he sank deep inside her. Their first time together couldn't come soon enough.

Her safety, however, came first. His desire to take things further would have to wait. It was best he took all the cues from her. Just knowing those he trusted with his life, and their fellow tribe's people, would look out for her. Put his mind at ease. He felt things were about to get rocky for them before it got worse. Hoping, though, they were prepared for whatever was coming their way, was what was getting him through each day. Well, that, and his time spent with his Mate.

After talking with Aidan last night about his conversation with Cormac, he now understood what he meant about rearranging the ceremony. The more he thought about it, the more he liked the idea. The issue was how to go about it if time wasn't on their side. So far, his only decision had been that Harlow would now live with him in his dwelling. Plus, if what he suspected about her history on the subject was true. Treading carefully was at the top of his list. She deserved to be treated like the wonderful woman she is. Even though he wanted to do things to make them sweat.

She would not be meeting all the village members, however, only those who were members of Ravens Night. He and Aidan would walk her back to his dwelling this morning. Tomorrow night was the planned meeting. Members had agreed it might be a little easier for her to first see how they operate, and what their plans were. Since she was a part of the topic of discussion, it would help for her to be included and get her opinion. Then introductions could flow from there. Liking the idea, he agreed. Between him and his other two cofounders, the meeting should be a success in both ways.

Placing his hand over his midsection, he tried to silence his intuitive gut. Feeling he should have listened to his instincts this morning. Something had felt off, the sensation growing stronger as time passed. As planned, he and Aidan walked to the Shaman's cottage. Maybe they should have brought along more members for protection. They didn't want to alert anyone watching to secrecy. In hindsight, they should have thought of that while he had been coming here daily to see his Mate. Well, he guessed that what he had done was done, and he had to hold on to his trust of the others.

While they strolled along, Kieran had been answering all of Aidan's questions regarding the Mate connection. How it felt physically and mentally. It is an energy of sorts engulfing within and around you. A knowledge that you don't know how you ever survived without it. Words were hard to describe the truth of it. Experiencing it outweighed any kinds of words, period. Though for his friend's sake, he had tried.

However, there was still more to discover about their connection.

He hadn't even broached the initial subject with Harlow yet. Not even sure how to, or when. Then there was the other discussion he needed to have with her. How to bring up that one baffled him. She was one of them, and not aware of it or couldn't remember yet. Whatever the case may be, it had to be broached soon, though. It was driving him crazy, being so close to her and not doing something about it. He suspected she felt the same. At every opportunity, they were in constant contact. Him touching her; her touching him. Most times, he would just pick her up and place her on his lap as they talked. Any distance between them seemed to hurt.

Also, the joy of feeding her from his hand was a very intimate connection they shared. Even the chaste kisses they had shared were hot. Always sharing a little kiss with her to say good morning or goodbye. They grew at length each day. He wanted that always, and so much more. The limits of his restraint were being tested to their limits.

When they arrived at the cottage, they found Harlow sitting on the steps, talking adamantly with Cormac. Hands in the air as she explained whatever they were talking about. The enormous smile that spread across her lips, and reached her eyes as she saw them coming. Was like a bolt of lightning right to his heart. Sending a lovely warmth that filled him. Smiling in return, he asked.

"Ready to go, little one?"

Nodding her head, before declaring.

"Yes, I'm ready."

Turning, she hugged Cormac, whispering something in his ear. Standing, she said her thanks as she made her way to him. Launching herself into his arms. Thank goodness for his fast reflexes or he wouldn't have caught her in time. Holding her close as she wrapped her legs around him. With one hand, he fed his fingers into her mass of curls at her nape, positioning her head just so. Lowering his head, he touched her lips with his in a hungry kiss. Before he could take it further and devour her mouth. Aidan coughed into his hand, interrupting them by saying how cute they were. Pulling back, he smiled as Harlow moaned at the sudden loss. Turned then to give his friend a stern look for being called cute. He was about to tell him to get lost when they heard someone running down the path behind them.

On alert, he turned, letting Harlow to the ground. Turning to stand shoulder to shoulder with Aidan in front of her, with Cormac coming to stand behind her. With her guarded, they waited. Only for one of the usual messengers from the village to appear rounding the bend. Seeming to come with a message. Only a select few could come to the cottage because of their worry for Harlow's safety. This man had not been one of those select few. This was sending up some serious red flags for him. They waited as the scrawny came as close as he dared towards them.

In his whiny voice, this little man demanded,

"My Lord, you must come quick to the village."

With his arms showing as such, to follow him. He continued to repeat his display.

Who was in charge here? Surely this messenger didn't think it was him. Staring down at the man, Kieran straightened his shoulders at the same time as Aidan. This messenger was hitting a nerve for both of them. Everyone knew he and Aidan would see to an important matter today. They were not to be disturbed. If there was an issue, they were to go to the elders. Not him. So why this, and why now? Curious, he asked, interrupting his whiny tirade.

"What is so important for you to have bothered us, and not the elders, as instructed? Hmm?"

With both he and Aidan staring him down, it seemed he would soon pee his pants. The matter wasn't of that great importance then. They waited what seemed like a while to receive any response.

When the men had created a protective, physical circle around her, Cormac had whispered into her ear.

"Whatever you're going to do, do it quickly."

She knew what he had meant. Bending to her side, she reached into one of the leg pockets of her pants. Grabbing the device inside, slid it over her wrist, pulling her hood over her head for added measure. Tilting her wrist, she started tapping a sequence into the device to activate it. In the blink of an eye, she became the unseen woman. Hearing the praise.

"Very good."

Coming from the Shaman filled her with happiness. Smiling to herself, it felt good to have approval. However, she felt a surge of malice.

With Kieran still speaking to the creepy man on the path, she lifted to her toes to whisper in Aidan's ear.

"We are surrounded by more of them. Their intent is not truthful."

At the same time, she slipped her hand into Kieran's, squeezing it. Which he held onto tight. He seemed to need her touch more than she had needed his. As she lowered from her toes, all three men growled. Sensing what she had moments before, watching as the man shifted from whining at Kieran to displaying a face of pure hatred and snarling.

"You'll pay for what you have done."

Before lunging in their direction. Harlow felt scared for Kieran. Her fear evaporated, then turned to anger at the wee little man. Gazing at him, she was stunned when he burst into flames, screaming and howling in pain. At that moment, the others revealed themselves, coming from all around them. Cursing, and spitting at them.

"Look what you have done."

She was about to speak when Kieran squeezed her hand. Snapping her jaw shut. These people were creepy and strange. Desire to defend her man, and his friends, is only natural. If Kieran thought it best to keep quiet, then so be it. Then she remembered she had cloaked herself. If she spoke, she would endure revealing herself. Grateful to him for knowing her so well, in such a short amount of time, too. The thought of being without him was inconceivable to her. Despite not understanding, she appreciated the level of connection they had. She experienced a greater sense of being grounded.

Focusing on the now, had her wondering how had the man caught fire. Why weren't his supposed friends doing anything about it to help him? They all seemed to focus on the group of them. Saying more hateful words, promising to return before taking off the way the scrawny man came. This place was turning out to be so strange. Who was she to say, though? She had devices for many things. Like the one she had just used to hide herself. Or one that allowed the user to breathe fresh clean air, for hours at a time, when none existed. There were many more hidden within her many pockets, and compartments of clothing. She knew without doubt she was no longer in her time. That much was very obvious. It was how it came to be, was her lingering question.

This was the place she had been dreaming about. Having confided in Cormac this morning when her worries had become overwhelming. She trusted him. He felt like an old family member to her. That was how she saw him, anyway. He listened to her uncertainty regarding her situation. Confirming her suspicions but assuring her all her answers to her questions will reveal themselves in time. She had to be ready and open to them. Only then could she hear them. The man always seemed to speak in riddles. When you spoke with him, it was only after you realized you now had more questions than answers. That thought sounded so familiar to her. From where, though, she couldn't say.

When she noticed her surroundings again. Cormac was circling them, chanting. His movements were fluid and steady, falling in a perfect rhythm as he moved around. She could see physically the energy flowing around him as he did. "Beautiful," she whispered. The colors flowing from his hands in motion looked like expanding ribbons. Combining to create a dome like circle surrounding them. She had seen something similar before. Just couldn't remember where. Whipping her head in Kieran's direction as he asked her.

"What's beautiful little one?"

"Cormac, and his movements. I can see the energy he is creating with his dance."

Once again being pulled into watching his movements. Serenity settled in, creating a soothing ambiance akin to a lullaby. She swayed with the music she heard in her head.

Kieran and Aidan shared a look between them. It took a few times for him to call her name before she heard him. Turning to face them, she asked.

"What is it, Kieran?"

With a quiet laugh he asked.

"Will you reveal yourself now? We would like to see you."

How could she have forgotten? Tapping the command into the wrist device, she appeared to them in a blink.

"There is that better now?"

Tilting her head for effect. Before smirking a smile at Kieran. She did like looking at him. He had the most stunning eyes. Eyes filled with lust, desire, and compassion. Then there were his kisses. Gliding her fingers along her lips, she remembered their kisses. She liked his kisses. They always sent a zing through her body. Shivering at the memory, she smiled to herself.

Shaking his head, Kieran rolled his eyes and snapped his fingers in front of her a few times.

"Harlow, we need you to focus. Ok."

Once her eyes refocused on him, and she nodded, he continued.

"We have some questions for you, ok?"

Shrugging her shoulders, and a nonchalant

"Sure. Whatever you'd like to know."

She was finding it hard not to be drawn towards Cormac. She wanted to join in. Shaking her head to clear it, and focus on her man. She enjoyed thinking of him that way. Smiling.

"Harlow, I need you to focus ok."

Again waiting for her to nod, and they shared eye contact.

"We'd like to know how you were able to become unseen, but that will have to wait till later. First, though, you can see the physical magic?"

As he hugged his head in Cormac's direction. Again, she nodded.

"Second, you saw the messenger catch fire?"

Nodding for the third time.

"Ok. We're still going to head to my dwelling. However, this time you will do your own becoming unseen, and walk in between myself and Aidan. Should we encounter another issue, whoever grabs for your hand, you take it. You stick to them."

Looking sternly at her.

"Yes,"

All but shouting as she nodded enthusiastically this time. Not wanting another encounter like what they just had.

With a hooked finger placed under her chin, he tilted her head up just a little. Speaking in concern, he asked.

"Lastly, are you ok little one?"

She blurted out.

"I didn't like those so called friends of his. They tasted funny."

As she spoke, her entire body shimmered in distaste.

"I didn't like it, Kieran. They were going to hurt you."

Moving closer to him, and into his open arms. Sighing in comfort, he wrapped his arms around her. What she did not see was the look shared by all three men. Shock at the younger, and the firm I told you so from the elder.

With a final tight squeeze, he said.

"Alright, little one, let's go. Cormac will stay here."

Answering her unasked question. Taking a step back, she lifted her wrist, tapping away, looking up before they lost sight of her. Aidan whispered, "Fascinating." Made her chuckle.

"You'll need to remember not to talk while unseen. It will seem strange to others that a woman's voice is amongst us. Should we run into others, that is! Which we shouldn't."

He rushed to assure her.

"That's what you said before. Look what happened. I'm not even sure what that was."

Placing her hands on her hips, not that they could see. Frustrated, she stomped her foot.

With both of them laughing at her, they said together.

"Come on."

Forcing her to leave the safety she felt at the cottage. Stepping out into this new world. One she thought only existed in her dreams. How wrong she had been. Yes, it was colorful, filled with magick and mystery. She couldn't wait to discover and explore. Did everyone have gifts? According to her dream, they didn't. Could this mean some of the other books she had read that claimed to be fairy stories were true, too? If so, which ones? There were too many questions.

Then there was Kieran, and oh those possibilities. They made her toes curl. It would do no good to disappear into her head full of questions. Every fiber of his being honed in on the present, leaving no room for anything else. Abandoning her wonderings and fear, she focused instead on keeping up pace with the men. She was running as they just displayed a simple stride. Staying in the present was more important now. If the last hour had taught her anything. It was to be prepared for any scenario. It was with this agility they made their way to Kieran's hut with no more interruptions.

CHAPTER 13

*H*aving made it to his dwelling, all three breathed a sigh of relief once inside. Their journey had been free of any more interruptions. Though it seemed they had exhausted Harlow. After preparing a quick snack. They all sat in silence to eat. They hadn't even finished when his Mate began struggling to keep her eyes open. Before she could keel over, he picked her up and settled her on his bed. Wishing her a pleasant sleep, he kissed her forehead before returning to Aidan in the main room. Sitting beside his long time friend. He, for once, didn't know where or how to start.

"Did you? Can you believe it?"

Shaking his head at his indecision, he opened his mouth only to have Aidan answer.

"That wasn't me, you know. It had to be her….. How did she do it?"

Shaking his head in question, leaning back in his seat. He seemed to struggle with what they all had witnessed. Rubbing his chin

"She started it didn't she?"

Turning to look at him, pleading.

Kieran nodded, still struggling himself

"I believe so, yes. Cormac had said she should train with you. Now I understand why."

Running his fingers through his hair.

"I don't see why, though. You saw. What could we ever teach her?"

Nudging his chin in her direction.

With a half laugh.

"I feel the same. But she did not know it was her. Did you hear her whisper to me?"

Displaying a pleading look on his face.

Shaking his head. Further surprised by this woman.

"No. I only felt her squeeze my hand before I was about to lunge at that guy. What did she say?"

Eyes wide and impatient for an answer. His seat couldn't contain him. With all the energy pulsing within him, he needed an outlet. Folding his fingers around the seat's edge. To contain himself.

Aidan seemed to have the same issue. His leg, however, was bouncing ever faster. Answering in awe as he spoke.

"She told me more of them surrounded us. Their intent is not truthful."

Thinking, he then blurted out,

"I didn't like those so called friends of his. They tasted funny."

Twisting his head to face Kieran

"What does she mean by that? I've never heard of a gift like that."

Shrugging his shoulders, not having a clue himself.

"She saw the physical manifestation of Cormac's protective circle, too. She was called to it. I've never seen anything like it either."

An idea formed. He asked his good friend.

"You think the prophecy is about her? He said she is the KEY. I just thought he was talking about the mating connection."

Standing abruptly, he paced.

Aidan sat stone still and upright. So deep in thought. Before asking.

"You think so?"

Rubbing his chin, returning to his pondering. Lowering his head, he leaned back again, frowning as he did so.

Quickening his pacing.

"It must be."

Before stopping in his tracks. Looking seriously at Aidan.

"That means the elders got it all wrong."

Returning to tuning his fingers through his hair and blurting again.

"Or was that their intention, to lead us astray?"

Sitting up straight with hyper focus. Shaking his head.

"No, they wouldn't. Couldn't."

Pausing in thought.

"Would they?"

Falling back again in defeat into his seat. His body displayed the physical signs of hurt. These were their elders. The ancient ones. Their connection to the ancestors is so full of knowledge and power.

They were both on the same path of thought. Were they intentionally misled? Or could there be a reason behind it? They believed the link between Neera and the prophecy because they received teachings about it throughout their entire lives. Or were both women linked? Could it be? They both seemed to come to the same question. Looking at each other in wonder and hope.

If they were right, then the possibilities were still open. They could all still have a fighting chance. With grins growing from ear to ear. They worked out a plan. How to help Harlow harness her gifts, and learn about their people. Well, hers too, it would seem. Hopefully, all will go according to plan at the meeting. Executing dealing with Neera's followers would be swift and final. That woman had caused enough damage. Even dead, she was still wreaking havoc on all their lives.

That plan of attack was for after the festival, in a week. During this, Harlow could learn about their history and the ancient ones. Taking her to the clearing to learn and practice her gifts, they agreed, seemed the best option. It was far enough away from the village she could work without being seen or heard. Also close enough to Cormac should an emergency arise. Their evenings would be theirs alone. He liked that idea. Hoping she did too.

Thankfully, the festival was on track. Even with the extra add ons. The villagers had been more than thrilled with announcing the ceremony being added to the celebration. Each day, there was a flurry of activity with preparations. Excitement hung everywhere in the air. with a smile on their face, and a skip in their step. It looked like each was trying to outdo the other, as well as work as a team. It seemed crazy and confusing to him. They had taken over everything, tossing him aside. He just wanted Harlow. How it happened it didn't matter.

Conceding that yes, it needed to be proper. He held a seat of power, and with that came responsibilities. This just seemed over the top to him. If it resulted in people's happiness, then so be it. On the plus side, having extra guards posted hadn't seemed odd with all the activity. Everyone assumed he wanted the preparation protected. The only challenge would be how to tell Harlow or perhaps when to her. He planned on waiting, kinda. He needs only to tell her about the festival. Aidan said that was a bad idea and he should tell her the truth. To which he just shrugged. He'll deal with issues as they arise.

However, after today's events, they couldn't be sure someone wasn't after Harlow. There was also the possibility they were after him. They would just have to prepare for both if they had the manpower. With everyone already performing multiple duties, it would be a stretch. Hopefully not too far.

He watched as they entered the dwelling. Once inside, he crossed to the other side of the village. It was easier to get away from there. He had been there this morning and seen all that had transpired. Following the so called leader, and his right hand, the Shaman's cottage. The three had been holding their leader prisoner there. Today was the day they planned to move her. Well, they had planned to free her. They just all needed to be in their right positions. Once the plan was in motion, they sat back and waited. Watching as the three men held their dear Neera captive. Covering her with their magicks in an effort to deceive them. As her followers tried to save her.

Could these men not see she wanted free? Who would want to be trapped between them like that? Even when trying and displaying her magic, they did not free her. They kept her hidden until they could demean her.

As their comrade lay dying, turning to ashes, all the others fled in fear amid shouts of hatred. All he could do had been to look away until, once again, they covered her with magic and took her away. Only he had been smart.

He had stayed in his spot in the trees. Waiting, watching, and learning. He had followed them back to the village. Watching and waiting again. When enough time had passed. He used his skills taught to him to disappear. Well, he really couldn't disappear like Neera had. But he could become that which no one noticed. For most of his life, no one had seen him. That was until Neera, she saw him. She had had a need for him, and his skills. She said she liked the way he worked and would be rewarded. He believed her.

Making his way through to the edge of the village, he slipped away. Slinking along the path in hopes he could make it in time to tell him he had found her. She would need rescuing, for why else would she stay with those people? He hated them. Gifted powers they refused to share with others. Why should they have all the power? They thought themselves better, living with their own, always celebrating. Never with those lesser than them either. They deserved what was coming for them.

It will be funny to see how they like being at the bottom of the pecking order when the Master, and then take what's owed to them. First to go are the ancient ones. She had said so, promised even. Then the rest would go one by one. I mean, it was their fault for killing Neera the first time. They would see to it she finally got her revenge. All other magical creatures would die until only they were left with the powers. The world would be theirs to remake as they saw fit.

Yes, he liked the plan. He was very sure he would be rewarded for finding their leader. She had a great many talents. It would seem in her first death she received more powers. That would be good, because she would need the extra boost this time round. He couldn't imagine the magics being too happy about dying. They would just have to deal with what they deserved.

Happy he was far enough away, he straightened to walk. He would hold his head high. He was the one who found her and would be the one to tell him just where she was being kept. He knew where, when, and how. Proving he was smart and capable. The Master would definitely be getting his powers soon. He whistled as he walked. Thrilled with his plan and himself.

Harlow woke feeling a little stiff. Blinking a few times to allow her eyes to adjust to the dim light. Sitting, she stretched her arms while rotating her neck. Tossing back the cover, she swung her legs over the edge of the bed. Looking around, this must be Kieran's bedroom. The last thing she remembered was the three of them eating by the fire. With every bite she had taken, her eyes grew heavier until she could no longer keep them open. Someone must have carried her in here. Turning to look behind her, the other side of the bed was empty.

Kieran wouldn't sleep elsewhere because of her. Would he? She hoped not. They have been getting closer and closer to each other every day. They couldn't keep from touching one another longer than a second. It was like they were magnets drawn together. Very much how she felt right now. Her heart beat faster at just the thought of him. The distance between them is too much to bear. Hopping down off the bed, she looked for which way to go. There were two doorways, but which one to choose? Deciding on the one that had a brighter light coming from it was the direction she went.

This home was stunning in a different way to Cormac's. Sections divide the large rectangular structure inside. Rooms in the like with walls that were more dividers, stopping at the base of the roof line. Looking up in the dim light, you could almost see the detail in the thatched roof. Turning her focus back to where she was going, she ran her hand along the wall. The texture felt nice under her fingers. Woven panels of reed or willow, maybe. If she was remembering correctly, not sure where she had read that. But she could picture the book pages in front of her. This was odd how she would have a flash of memory.

She admired the intricate design that the artist had incorporated into each panel. Beautiful pieces of art each of them. Kieran must be of some importance to live in a place beautifully crafted. She pondered how the detail would appear if someone had incorporated color. Making her way to another door opening. This one reveals a large central area, with a roaring fire in the middle. Along the wall, there were some cupboards and tables. A kitchenette, maybe. Around the fire there were chairs, and benches circled and draped with blankets and fur. Opposite that was the entrance they came in. This space was far larger inside than the outside dimensions. Magick could do some amazing things.

Turning back to the fire, sitting on the opposite side, was Kieran. His body position said he was looking at the flames. As she moved closer, she realized he was looking off into his memory. With eyes glazed over, unseeing of the flames or her getting nearer. Trying not to startle him, whispering.

"Kieran."

Not getting a response, she moved in closer, touching his arm and saying his name again. Blinking a few times before he turned his head towards her. It took a few more moments for his lovely blue eyes to zero in on her.

Concern flashed across his face as he opened his mouth to speak. She squeezed his arm.

"Shh, it's ok. I only just woke up. You weren't with me, so I came looking for you."

As she spoke, he lifted her onto his lap. Bending his head to hers, taking a deep inhale. Smiling to herself, she gave up asking why he did that or even why he liked it. His only answer was a nonverbal one, a shrug of one shoulder. Curious, though, she turned to look at him and asked.

"Do I smell good?"

The response she received while teasing surprised her.

He growled. Really growled before vigorously nodding. Grabbing her head with both hands, tilting her head up, bowing his to devour her mouth. Moaning at the spark it ignited within her, twisting so she could wrap her arms around his neck. When he pulled back, "Nooo" she whined. Moving his hands to her waist, he lifted her, so she was now straddling his lap. Liking his train of thought, she moved in and began devouring his mouth, wrapping her arms around his neck.

She felt him run his tongue along the seam of her lips, demanding entrance. Opening for him, she wasn't so sure what to do. Hesitantly, she moved her tongue along his, causing him to growl again. Scared, she pulled back. When his hands massaged up her neck into her mass of curls. Cupping the back of her head to tilt her to the perfect angle, he ran his tongue around her lips. Before he deepened the kiss. He tasted so good. So this is what it felt like. Now she understood the appeal. Relaxing into him, she moaned a no when he pulled back again. She could feel his smile as he left little kisses along her jaw. At her ear, feeling the tiniest pinch, and trying to turn, she gasped.

"Did you just bite me?"

His only response was a "MMMM" as he continued to make his way down her neck. At her shoulder line, he moaned like he was eating a decadent treat. The feelings he inspired within were new and exhilarating. Tingles ran from her head to her toes. Heat began in her belly, and grew, expanding throughout. Not sure what was happening to her, but she liked it. A lot.

She felt a pinch, followed by the soothing movement of his tongue along her skin. Try as she might, she couldn't seem to find her voice. All she wanted was more, more of him, and his magick touch. In a barely there whisper, she begged, "Please, Kieran." Not sure what she was asking for. She felt his wandering lips moving again, back the way they came. She was so impatient. Grabbing his head, she pulled him to her. It was her turn to taste him.

She heard him chuckle at her enthusiasm, which only spired her on to drive him as crazy as she felt. As her lips touched him again, she had to rise to reach. Her core contacted his rock hard abs. Moaning at the contact of both, and closing her eyes in bliss, liking her body's reaction to him. Kieran growled, his hands swiftly grabbing her ass. With a firm squeeze, he began a gentle rhythm of motion. The friction of his abs started a wonderfully tingling sensation in her core. Groaning into their kiss, she grabbed fistfuls of his hair as she quickened his pace. She wasn't sure what she was racing towards, but she wanted it. Wanted it with Kieran.

Kieran moved his large hands as he pulled back for their kiss. All her attempts to pull him back only resulted in him slapping her ass. Eyes flying open, she glared at his amused face, only for him to tighten his arm around her lower back. Adding to the pressure she felt in her core. Letting her head fall back on a deep growling moan, only for Kieran to lock his fingers in her curls at her nape. In a firm panty melting voice.

"Eyes Harlow. I want your eyes on mine when you come. You will come for me, and only me."

Growling as she placed her hands on his shoulder for support and digging her nails in as her body tightened.

"That's it, little one. Let go and fly. I will always be there to catch you."

She looked at him, confused. In an attempt to shake her head, his grip there tightened along with his demand.

"Come."

As if an elastic snapped, she came falling apart in his arms, tipping her head back in a howling scream.

"Kieran."

She wasn't aware he had moved his supporting arm until she felt his fingers apply pressure over her core. Blinking to regain her focus on his eyes.

"Again little one."

Opening her mouth, she was about to ask how. However, he increased the pressure of his fingers and pinched hard, sending her flying over again. All she could manage was a whisper.

"Wow"

The ability to keep her eyes open was becoming more difficult as the moments passed. Her body felt like jello, heavy, relaxed, and satisfied. Grateful for Kieran's strength, he easily lifted her. Cradling her in his arms. With her head resting on his shoulder, she smiled. Looking up to see he was staring at her with awe. Trying to blink away the fatigue, she whispered.

"That was amazing, Kieran. I always wondered..." her eyes falling closed, losing the battle as sleep embraced her.

CHAPTER 14

*K*ieran came awake with a start. Something was wrong. Opening his eyes, he scanned the room, seeing nothing amiss. It was then he heard a groan followed by moaning. Turning his head, Kieran saw Harlow tangled in the bed coverings, fighting an unforeseen foe. Murmuring words he couldn't make out, she cried in a continual fight. Not liking the tears streaming down her cheeks, he reached for her. He intended to hold her close and calm her. However, as soon as his fingers made contact, her body reacted on instinct. Turning with a flip in the air, her arm came forward, thrusting the heel of her hand up and into his nose from beneath.

Surprise took him by her swift movements. As she moved for her next assault, he grabbed both her wrists. Using his momentum, he pushed her onto her back, raising her arms above her head. He held them in place, using one hand to pin them while stroking her cheek with the other. While repeatedly saying her name. His voice gained volume as he spoke. Till demanding.

"Harlow wake up"

Feeling her body tense beneath him, he watched as her eyes fluttered open.

As she scanned his face, she asked.

"Kieran, why is your nose bleeding, and why are you on top of me?"

Tilting her head at the last question.

He could tell she liked their body positions. Her body gave her away, as a lovely blush rose from the collar of her shirt and continue up to her cheeks. The slight unevenness of breath as her eyes fluttered closed. She lifted her hips in an attempt to make contact. She was enjoying being pinned beneath him, and he liked her there. Oh, the things they could do together, and will do together. He couldn't wait to get started. Tucking this information away for later. He stated.

"You clocked me in the nose, little one."

Her eyes sprang open, filled with remorse. Shaking his head as she opened her mouth to speak, he said.

"It's ok Harlow. I am glad the instinct for you to protect yourself is so deep within you that your body just reacts. Skills like that are a life-saver. I'm grateful to whoever taught you. They did amazingly well."

Gently, he released his grip on her wrists.

"Am I safe now, little one? No more flying body parts coming my way?"

Laughing at her scrunched angry face, he shifted, in a move so fast she missed him with the pillow she tossed. He was up and standing by the bed as she flopped forward from the momentum and weight of the pillow. At her face plant into the tangled mess of a bedcover, he let out a roar of laughter. She further mumbled into the fabric, slamming a fist down beside her head. With the back of his hand, he cleaned away any remnants of blood.

When she raised her head, he expected tears, but her laughter once again took him aback, matching his own in intensity. Gone was the anger from a few moments ago. Instead, his woman was laughing at her misfortune. Could his Mate be any more perfect? This is what love was all about. With the thought of love crossing his mind, he froze. He loved her? But they were still getting to know each other. Yet he suspected he had more knowledge of the real her than anyone else in her life so far. The same was true of her knowledge of him.

Then there were the events last night. Making his woman come had been the highlight of the evening. Watching and hearing her scream, his name filled him with joy and pride. He suspected he was the first man ever to bring her to orgasm, and to bring her to such a powerful climax that she slept like a baby next to him all night. He had never slept so well. Just seeing to her pleasure had been a thrill he wanted to repeat over and over again. He suspected he was the first man to have ever brought her to orgasm, and to have brought her to such a powerful climax that she slept like a baby next to him all night.im to taste her even further. Feeling his body stir at the thought, he licked his lips in anticipation.

Feeling the delicate touch of her fingers on his arm, he focused his vision. Looking down to see she was now kneeling up at the edge of the bed. Concern spread across her face. He must have been away with the fairies for a while. Raising his hand, he cupped her cheek, running his thumb over the soft skin there. Searching her eyes, he asked.

"What is it, little one? I was remembering last night, and thinking I would very much like to repeat it."

Again, she flushed with a lovely blush. Glancing further down, he noticed her nipples were peeking out as if to say hello. So lovely, he circled each puckered nib with his other hand.

A deep moan followed quickly by her sharp intake of breath. Filled him full of male pride, that he could cause her to want. He moved, sliding a hand around her nape, and holding firm. Locking his eyes with hers, he lowered his mouth to hers. Both were moaning at the contact. She tasted so good, even in the early morning. Deepening the kiss, he growled in delight as she tilted her hips closer to his. Wanting better access, he gripped his fingers into her hair, tilting her head back. When she opened her mouth in surprise, he took full advantage, surging his tongue in. This time she responded with gumption of her own, dueling her tongue with his.

Liking she could hold her own, he upped the ante. Increasing the pressure of his circling finger, he took charge of the kiss. She melted into him, trying to gain contact with her hips to gain that much wanted friction. Instead, he pinched her lovely little nipple and tugged. His woman came, breaking their kiss to scream his name. She was stunning when she came. Smiling, he could do this all day, every day, and never tire of seeing her like this. Holding her in his arms as she collapsed into him. He chuckled when she said.

"Thank you, Kieran. That was wonderful."

As she moved to sit at the edge of the bed, she asked.

"What about you Kieran? You didn't get any satisfaction?"

On alert, he sat beside her, taking her hand in his. With his other, he placed a finger beneath her chin, lifting till they were making eye contact. Worried about what she said, he informed her.

"Listen little one. I have never enjoyed myself as much as I have with you. Anything and everything we do together brings me so much happiness. You understand."

Staring, he waited till she nodded before continuing.

"Now when you say satisfaction are you referring to finishing or … Cumming?"

Smiling again as she attempted to lower her head, to which he shook his. Only for her lovely blush to flush bright again. Her reactions were always so telling. He hoped that would never change as her experiences grew. When her eyes fluttered back to him, she whispered.

"Yes, Kieran."

Biting her lower lip, she looked at him with pleading eyes.

"OK. Just so you know, Harlow, I am very satisfied with everything we have ever done and will do. I don't have to come for that to happen. I wanted very much to make you come last night, and again this morning. I'm pleased I was able to do so for you. Did you enjoy yourself?"

Feeling her nod her head with a sheepish smile, he continued.

"Good, I'm glad. We will have plenty of time to explore. We have the freedom to enjoy ourselves and have fun. It's not just about procreation."

Squeezing her hand for reassurance, he said.

"Come on, let's get our morning meal. Then we can head to the clearing for some practice and training, ok."

"Ok, Kieran."

Twisting to face him, she swung her arms wide, engulfing him in a firm hug. Taking a cue from him, she nibbled on his ear, moving with traveling kisses. Making her way to his mouth where she kissed with enough passion to have him stirring once more. If she kept this up, they wouldn't make it through the day. As he was about to take it further, Harlow pulled back, smiling, unaware of her effect on him. Jumping down with an excited giggle.

"Thank you, Kieran. You are amazing. You are the first to treat me in such a way. Well, except family, they have always had my back. I'm excited for today."

Bouncing on her toes, she continued.

"Can we hurry? I don't want to wait."

Without waiting for an answer, she quickly left the room.

He doubted she was aware of what she had revealed to him. More pieces of her memory were returning each day. At the random sprinkling of them, she hadn't quite realized she was remembering. Perhaps because they were small tidbits of information. He suspected, though, when the day came that she remembered everything, it would be a crushing blow. The condition he found her in, and the time it took her to recover, something big had happened. Hoping with all his might he was with her when the dam broke.

Having to contain his feelings of anger, curiosity, and suspicion wasn't something he was used to. Today's training couldn't come soon enough. Every time she revealed her past mistreatment, he felt the urge to break something. Women were to be treasured and respected. They held great power of their own, the ability to create life among many others. She was already a mother, and her son was now grown in the eyes of her clan. To now continue in the defense of them. Was not only hard to believe he was in awe. How could anyone turn their backs on her and treat her in the manner they did? A deep sense of appreciation washed over him for her family. She deserved everything. Hearing her shout, then giggle.

"Are you coming, Kieran?"

He smiled to himself, rising with a shout.

"Yes, little one."

The first day of training went well. After their quick morning meal, and take a few minutes to change for the day's events. They had both met up with Aidan and made their way to the clearing. This morning had been a history lesson with training in the afternoon, and as would every lesson thereafter. The ancients decided she had full knowledge of who she was and where she came from. In case her memory never fully returned, assuming she ever knew this information. The more she learned and remembered about herself, it became clear that was not the case. It seemed everyone assumed she had come from somewhere close by. Only her internal self screamed that wasn't quite true. Every time she tried to remember, she only ended up with a headache instead. Then there was Cormac saying things like when she came from, and not where. Could she have come from a different time? But how could that be?

Still, she couldn't contain her excitement upon discovering that she and her family had a history, and a fascinating one as well. Sitting on the circle of stones, Harlow listened intently as they each took turns explaining the world in which they lived. About their people who were hers as well. She was a descendant of a God race. Who knew? The more she thought about it, the more she still had trouble wrapping her mind around it. It would seem she had learned that gods were a myth. A fairytale taught to children to entertain their minds. They no longer regarded it as truth, only a fantasy.

In the beginning, the Gods had flourished within this land. Many of them live in harmony together. As they grew in numbers, they formed tribes or clans of their own, spreading out amounts of the land. Again, their numbers grew, as did their need for vanity. Many tribes created life in the likeness of themselves, with the need to be worshiped and tended to. Only these creations lacked the magick gifts. While others saw this creation of life as a degradation of their kind and way of being. They sought to destroy the created life and bring about a return to purity. With these groups at war with each other, some never sided with either side. Instead, they turned to protect the created life and their kind.

The god wars caused the loss of many, many lives. Most suffering were the gods, whose numbers were now lesser than the created. As a result, it said the ability to find one True Mate became impossible. She noticed Aidan giving Kieran a strange look while he was telling this story. Wondering why she asked him about it later when Kieran continued. However, they now knew that True Mates were indeed a real thing, which rendered the fairy tale they had been told incorrect. When you found your one, you were forever connected. With so few ancients from that time left, no one dared question them or their teaching. For fear of earning their wrath. No one had ever suspected that they would have lied for any purpose.

How nice would that be to have a partner dedicated forever? Shifting around in her seat, she remembered thinking it would be nice if she could have that with Kieran. As a man, no God, he was a work of art. With his tall, large body, his strength is like no other. Those eyes, eyes that could see right into her. Knowing what she needed at any time. Not to mention the way he made her feel. The connection she felt with him was like none other than she had ever felt before. How she knew that to be true, she did not know. It was just a gut feeling so strong.

After her small mind wandered, she zeroed in on their stories. Knowing she needed to learn everything. This was very important. Not only for her, but for others as well. Who they all were, she wasn't sure, yet. One day she would know, soon. Closing her fingers together in her lap, she looked between the two men as they each told the stories they had learned in their teachings. Along with all the pieces added to it. Lies told to protect their kind to continue life. Only having just discovered the lies told it was unsure if there were more waiting to be revealed.

It was recently discovered. The True Mate way of life was gone in favor of any person of fancy hoping to procreate, and quietly. The ancients abandoned waiting, hopeful of replenishing what was lost.

That was their best guess at the moment, regarding the lies told. Only the plan never worked as they thought. Yes, the gods were still here in much fewer numbers, decreasing as time moved on. Soon they would be gone. With them gone, all other magic would also die from the world. When that happens, it would only be a matter of time before everything else would die, too. Sad that even though they had sworn to protect their kind, and those created. They would fail in the end, it seemed.

They made attempts in the past to increase the number of magicks, hoping it would be beneficial. They encouraged many gods of the past to enter the world of the created ones and find partners. Some did so and were happy and successful. The result of which are many kinds of magickal creatures. Others went out with intending malice. Blaming those lesser than them for the fate they now lived in, causing chaos and destruction. While some individuals took advantage of those we swore to protect, they actively created harmful beings that preyed upon others. The numbers are dwindling ever faster now.

The most shocking news was hearing Kieran, and Aidan along with one other were the last of the God's offspring born. They were in the created one's terms, ancient themselves, being hundreds of years old. A created one's life span only being about one hundred years. Now, however, knowing that one's True Mate is legitimate, there is hope for the future. Plus, her appearance, even not knowing where she is from, points to a hopeful future. For there were more gods out there than they believed. What other explanation can there be for her presence?

Her brain felt weighed down by all the information, so she expressed gratitude for the noon meal. A simple one filled with finger type foods of delicious taste. The men seemed to know she had needed time to ponder. Allowing her time alone. She was a God like them. How was that even possible? She had thought this afternoon's training was just going to be more self defense. They were to discover her gifts bestowed upon her at birth. Then teach her how to harness and use them.

This just didn't seem real to her. This was her dream world, but how she became stuck within it was a mystery. Of that, she was positive. It made her uneasy to open up about that to anyone. Believing they would think her crazy. Maybe they wouldn't after hearing their history. She was feeling like she was coming apart at the seams. It was only a matter of time before she snapped. As they all finished eating, she decided to just go with it. Let them teach her all they could. What would it hurt, anyway? As if she had any gifts, ha.

Turns out the joke was on her. She had many talents. Discovering first like Aidan, she had an affinity with fire. Not only could she start one at will, which scared her the first time she had tried. She could also touch it, hold it, and move it to her will. Her skill level was almost that of Aidan, and he'd been using his ability for centuries. The question was how powerful could she become. The thought made her a little queasy to think about. All she could remember is she wanted to hide as she grew up. The desire to blend into the background was strong. Still not sure why yet. Arg, would her brain ever give the answers?

The afternoon continued. She learned how she was much faster, stronger, and more agile than other magickals, and the created. Repeatedly, she had to rely on her gifts to complete a range of scenarios set up for her. With each triumph, a swelling of pride washed over her, mingled with a touch of trepidation. She felt as though she was becoming herself. There was also the possibility, however, she would possess greater gifts than most gods. Why that would be or how was a mystery.

Then there was this growing little inkling they were holding back some information. Important information. Maybe she would find out later in the week. They planned to continue training every day in the clearing. They didn't want to overload her all in one day. Considering she still hadn't regained all her memories yet. She might never.

That scared her the most. Not being able to remember her life with her son or her twin. What must it have been like? She wondered. She knew she loved them and would do anything for them. Missing them was getting harder every day. She wished she would have confided in Kieran about them earlier. Now it just felt like it was too late. In her sullen mood, the men called it quits. They would head back to Kieran's dwelling to eat a meal, and so she could clean up before the meeting tonight.

CHAPTER 15

*S*itting cross legged on the bed, Harlow attempted to braid her hair. Like always, it was winning the war, with springing curls popping out here and there. Wondering why she cared so much. No one here seemed to mind. Well, those she had met anyway. It was important to her to make a good impression. She would meet the members of Ravens Night tonight at their impromptu meeting.

Bringing the braid around her shoulder, finishing the end, and tying it off. She let it drop. After eating a meal together, Kieran and Aidan had left to go prepare for meeting their other founding member. Which gave her some time to rest and freshen up. Thankful for the time, because she needed it. After this afternoon, she was feeling kinda dingy. Blessedly, someone had made her an outfit for her to train in. A lovely garment that allowed her to move with ease. It also felt amazing against her skin. She planned to ask about it while they ate but wasn't able to.

The men had chattered about everything. Discussing the meeting again with her and explaining its history. She felt fascinated to learn and hung onto every word as they discussed. She felt thrilled to attend. They explained their surprise at how well she also took the information and history of their people. Their chests had stuck out with pride during that topic. She tried so hard not to laugh, failing when Aidan had stuck his tongue out at her. Once she started, she couldn't stop, even though they joined in.

When it was time to clean up the food mess, they continued with their praise. It was strange for her to hear so many positive things. Like how impressed they were with how she had controlled her gifts so soon. Rambling on further about the possibility of discovering more seemed to excite them. With the cleanup finished, she could now have some me time. They would come back and collect her, so they could all walk together to the meeting.

Feeling lucky, and nervous at the same time. This was a secret society, formed in the wake of a call to war. They kept order while remaining unseen. Performing dangerous feats to protect all living creatures. Sometimes even nefarious tasks, which they were considering for her situation. Not to mention the guard duty some members have already been performing for her safety. Never had she felt this treasured or valued.

Jumping down off the bed, she grabbed her footwear from beneath and pulled them on. Feeling more secure in her clothing, physically and mentally. The confidence it gave her was what she wanted to show at this meeting. Standing, she rotated her shoulders with a mental pep talk. 'You can do this. It's only a few people. Plus, Kieran will be there.' Looking up and taking a few deep breaths to center herself, tilting her head from side to side. 'Let's do this.'

Making her way from the room, and down the hall. Stopping when she heard whispers coming from the main living space. Odd, why would the men be whispering when they were getting her for the meeting? Knowing she promised to be ready to go when they got here. She moved closer, stopping again when she heard a nasally whisper.

"She has to be here, the Master said so."

A female whisper demanded.

"How would he know? He wasn't here when she apparently came here."

They continued to shuffle around in the main area. At some point, they decided it was no longer necessary to stay super quiet, and began turning things over. Their whispers became murmurs. Deciding these two were nuts. Harlow's heart swelled with gratitude as she recognized the value of her decision to wear her clothes. With a grateful smile, she reached into one of her leg pockets and pulled out her device. Praying there was enough charge left within it. Slipping it on her wrist, tapping the familiar sequence. She became the unseen woman just in time.

Nasally and cranky were coming around the corner. Harlow sucked in a breath, plastering herself against the wall. Hoping they would walk right by her. How did these two get in here, anyway? There was to be a protection spell around the dwelling. The protection spell only allowed Kieran, Aidan, and her to enter. They were supposed to physically stop all others from entering.

"You know, thissss place issss kinda nice."

Nasally hissed as he looked all around while walking past.

A scrawny, greasy female smacked the male upside the head.

"Don't be stupid. We're here to confirm that redhead is here or not. Either we take her now or tell the Master. So focus."

Grabbing his upper arm in a crushing grip, she tugged.

"Come on, let's check the bedroom and get otta here. This place gives me the creeps."

She pulled him along as he hissed in pain, making their way down the hall.

Gingerly, Harlow crept around the corner. She froze, taking in the destruction the two intruders made. The two intruders had upended everything, broken furniture, and shredded the once beautiful fabric. Shaking her head to keep the tears at bay, she made her way around the room. Trying not to step on anything or make a noise took great concentration.

She planned to hide where they had already looked for her. She couldn't be sure there wasn't someone outside keeping watch. Even though she was the unseen, a moving door on its own would be a dead giveaway. So hiding inside it was. She had just got herself tucked into one of the table shelves in the little kitchenette when they came rounding the corner in a rush.

The female was dragging the nasally man by the front of his shirt. Chattering on as they hurried along. Her strength was surprising, considering the image she presented. The man was running on his toes, trying in vain to keep up. What an odd duo, she thought.

Without a care, they stomped their way through the debris and out the door. Only for a mass of shouting to occur. Harlow curled herself as tight as she could. It was sinking in. Someone wanted to know where she was and wanted to take her.

Trembling, the fear was taking over. This dream world that wasn't a dream had wonderful people and scary people. She wanted to go home. She missed her son and her twin. Finally, she allowed the tears to fall silently and wished to regain her memory. Then maybe she could figure out how to get back home. Plus, why she left in the first place? It just felt odd for her to do something like that. The shouting grew louder, like a booming of thunder. She could feel the rage, and the fear, so thick in the air she could taste it.

Suddenly, the front door swung open with a bang. A tall, dark shadow stood in the doorway, surveying the mess and destruction. Sending her fear into overdrive, Harlow covered her head, retreating into herself. Hoping to remain hidden.

Kieran's heart swelled with gratitude towards his friends who had made the preparation for the meeting a breeze. They were taking all the extra steps for this one. With Harlow in attendance, they would take every precaution to ensure her protection. They had added a complexity to the protection spell that required the three of them to perform. As the founders, and leaders of Ravens Night, only they could cast the spell. His only qualm had been leaving Harlow alone at his dwelling. Yes, there was also a protection spell enveloping it, though it wouldn't hold to darker magicks. It was not as sophisticated as this one. Could that be why his guts were screaming again?

They had guards placed all around. Inside and outside the village. They didn't allow anyone inside the circle area where his dwelling was located. Only those whose dwellings were also within, who were some Ravens Night members along with trusted tribe persons. Still, something was wrong. He could feel it.

Scanning the clearing, he looked for Aiden. He was on the other side, and closest to the village. In a thunderous shout.

"Aiden"

His friend spun concern stretched across his face.

"Harlow"

That was all he could say before his good friend bolted. He finished his and Aiden's portion of the spell before making his way in the village's direction. He could hear the shout.

"Keep calm for your Mate, for fear does funny things."

Did she mean his fear or Harlow's or both? Filled with a comforting feeling of safety, he opted to choose both.

Arriving at the village, it was in utter chaos. People were everywhere. Shouting, and scurrying about in anger, and fear. What the hell had happened? Having to weave his way through the maze of people, his fear was quickly turning to anger. He was their chieftain, after all. They should move aside to allow him to pass. Instead, it was like he was invisible to them, even pushing through they never acknowledged his touch. If they were this upset, shouldn't they shout at him too? At least his friend seemed to be faster than him.

It took far too long to make it to his dwelling. When he did, he found two of his guards unconscious a few feet from his door. Another two were busy wrangling with a greasy, scrawny woman, who seemed to believe she was above all else. Making demands left, right, and center! While her companion tried to slink away unnoticed. As the pair of guards focused on dealing with the obnoxious female. He didn't recognize these two. They weren't a part of their village. They must be from the next one over. Though how they got this close to his dwelling was a mystery worth looking into. But first, his mate was the priority.

Turning, and trusting the guards with those two, he made his way to his door. Or what had happened here, what the hell had caused damage to his door? Fearing for his Mate he made quick work of getting into his home. It looked like a tornado had ripped through. Destruction had ravaged everything, leaving nothing untouched.

Whoever had done this was mad or sending him a message. He was betting on both. He could hear Aidan shouting for Harlow. Hadn't he found her yet? Panic was creeping its way in.

Following the sound of Aiden's shouts, He found him in their bedroom. He was attempting to move pieces of the remaining bed. Rushing to help, he took the other side, and they tossed it aside.

"You think she's here?" Showing beneath the pile of bed debris.

Focused on his task, Aiden never looked his way, only growled.

"I don't think so, no. Have to check just to be sure."

The sweat dripping off his friend's brow showed how bothered he was about this, and how hard he had looked thus far.

With the last of the debris pile gone only to reveal nothing, Kieran asked,

"Where all have you looked? Do you think she left?"

Standing straight with a stretch and a twist of the neck.

"This was my last room."

Scrunching his brow in thought. Tilting his head to the side, he asked.

"You don't think she used her... what did she call it? …. oh yes, her device. Do you?"

Why hadn't he thought of that?

"It's possible. Could be why we can't find her. If she's here, why not answer?"

Did she use the device to escape or could she have injured herself again? Before his panic could grow, he felt Aiden's hand on his shoulder. Turning to his friend.

"I know you're worried. I am too. But calm yourself. If she really is your Mate, you're each a half of a whole. Try to feel her. I know you can. It was her fear you felt when you sent me."

Realizing he might be right. It wasn't his screaming gut, just an instant knowing. He felt overwhelmed by fear, her fear. Eyes growing large at the amount of Aiden's insight. He took a deep breath, closed his eyes, and thought of Harlow. How he needed to find her. Searching, it felt as if he were floating. Reaching out along a cord, pulling himself forward. He felt overwhelming trembling with fear. Snapping his eyes open, he moved. Allowing the pull he felt tugging at him to move in her direction.

She was here in the hut. Trembling in fear, he could feel the vibrations as if they were his own. Whispering with confidence.

"She's here Aidan."

They made it into the main living area, stopping in the middle of the great room. He took a moment to focus. He wasn't sure where in this room, just knew she was here. Taking another deep breath as he scanned for places she could hide. He zeroed in on the kitchenette area. He glanced over his shoulder, confident that his concern didn't need to be verbalized because it was already understood. Making his way around, the debris called to her softly.

"Harlow. It's me, Kieran, little one. I'm here now."

Not sure where she was hiding in this area, he crouched low, speaking softly again.

"I can't see you, sweetheart. Will you turn your device off and come to me."

Waiting silently, his heart hurt with her pain and fear.

"Please, little one. I need to hold you."

With his last words, he felt something inside him click. He could hear her heavy breathing. In the blink of an eye, she appeared on the bottom shelf of the kitchen prep table. Moving to her, he pulled her out before she could even attempt to. Holding her close as she wrapped her limbs around him tight. Cradling her head with one hand, he inhaled her scent before kissing the top of her head. There were no words, only feeling her in his arms. Turning, he followed a concerned Aidan out.

No longer caring who saw her. Everyone knew where she was now, and with whom. Going forward, she would be with him always. Never again would she be in a position of fear. Especially in their home. As his anger brewed, so did her trembling. Rubbing a hand up her back, he reassured her.

"Never again, little one. I'll keep you safe. I hear by promise you."

Kissing the top of the head again, he felt her relax and gave a small nod. He allowed Aidan to lead their way. Grateful his friend was heading towards the clearing. The safest place for them at the moment. They would still need the meeting. Harlow's introduction to everyone would have to wait till another time. Her safety, and dealing with Neera's followers, were the top priority. Plans would have to be revised and adapted. They were now dealing with persons dabbling in the darker magicks.

People such as those were unpredictable and unstable. Planning had to be for multiple scenarios at any time. That took more strength, powers, and persons. They sadly had to postpone in-depth planning until they learned how the act was accomplished. They would have to make do with what they had put in place for the time being. Inadequate as it appeared to be. He had to hope keeping her with him could suffice. How quickly they could gain information from today's events would determine everything.

Reaching the clearing, he breathed a sigh of relief crossing over the threshold of the protection spell. Seeing as they were the only three here thus far, he headed for the stone circle. Sitting on one of the lower stones. Closing his eyes, and wrapping his arms tighter around his woman. He just enjoyed having her in his arms. Warm, soft, and all his. Instinct told him she would not be loosening her hold anytime soon. Which was fine with him. He enjoyed having her so close. The fact she trusted him filled him with pride.

Hearing the murmurings of others arriving. With Aidan standing just a few feet away, allowed them their moment together, such as it was. His frightened mate clinging to him. He'd like her clinging to him in the throes of passion. Another time, perhaps.

Instead of moving again and disturbing his precious bundle, he looked to Aidan and showed to send people this way. They might as well meet over here. That way, he could hold her, keeping her close. If she could, she could then hear all the discussions and plans. He felt she was still blocking things out. Since now, tweaks had to be made. Hopefully, they would receive news of this attack against her and the village before the meeting's close. Since two members were missing from the gathering, he assumed that was their goal. Just as everyone sat, however, he felt Harlow relax. It seemed being surrounded by the members she could succumb to sleep. Smiling at her increasing trust filled him with pride.

CHAPTER 16

$\mathcal{H}$arlow realized many voices whispering. She was also not in a bed. Well, it would be weird to hear so many voices in a bedroom now, wouldn't it? Becoming more alert, she realized she was clinging to someone. Breathing deep she recognized the scent, Kieran. She was in his arms. She smiled, her safe place. Opening her eyes, she had to blink several times to adjust to the light difference. Looking up into the most gorgeous crystal blue eyes. Light always seemed as if it was dancing around within them. It was magical. Smiling at him, she reached up and cupped his cheek. With a whisper.

"Thank you, Kieran."

Using her other arm to pull herself up and him down, she sealed her mouth over his. Moved at the zing that rippled through her at the contact. She enjoyed kissing this man. She was becoming addicted, never getting enough. What would it be like if they shared more? I mean, he had already made cum multiple times. The intensity was so overwhelming that it took her by surprise. It's no wonder everyone repeated, and again.

Her one and only time had been nothing like this. Everything she had shared with Kieran was thrilling, exciting, and real. Most of all, it felt amazing. Before, it had hurt and stung. A saving grace was it was over quickly. What followed, however, was betrayal, denial, and accusations. They blamed her for tempting a star recruit who showed no interest in her. The resulting pregnancy was trickery or someone else's. They believed he was justified in his actions, which resulted in her needing to visit the hospital wing.

Her son was a blessing, however, one that she would go through all that again to have him. An amazing young man, too. Caring, and smart with the ability to learn at a rapid pace. It was no wonder that they recruited him for a higher responsibility. She was proud of the man he was becoming. She only wished she could see more of him.

Pulling back from their kiss, she scrunched her brows, rubbing her temple. One moment she was full of desire, the next she began comparing. Why would that memory surface now? Realizing the murmuring of voices had stopped, she turned to look behind her. First seeing Aidan, who smiled from ear to ear, commenting.

"Nice kiss" winking at her.

Blushing, she ducked her head back towards Kieran. Hearing him chuckle as she did so. It was then she heard a woman's voice. It was so familiar to her, she just couldn't place where she had heard it before. The more she spoke, the faster Harlow's heart beat. With a tremble, she untangled her limbs, removing herself from Kieran's lap. Standing, she turned to face the woman. Taking a cleansing breath, she looked up to see who had been talking. Everyone was now looking at her in curiosity.

This woman was only a little taller than her. With long flowing hair and a pair of bright blue eyes staring in question. There was a familiarity about her, but differences as well. Taking a step towards her while reaching out, the woman asked.

"Is everything alright, Harlow?"

As she spoke, her hand contacted her arm.

Harlow sucked in a sharp breath while placing her other hand on her chest. It couldn't be, could it? Recognition had hit. Followed by a barrage of all her other memories. Shock spread across her face as she exclaimed, "Cora? Cora, is that you?" Gasping for breath, she doubled over at the waist. Placing her hands on her knees while breathing far too quick. Ears ringing, it was hard to hear any of the commotion that erupted around her.

Before she knew what had happened, she was again sitting on

Kieran's lap. Only this time, they were with his front to her back. She was now staring at a concerned Aidan and Cora. But how could that be? The time she came from the planet was so close to death that they were too. But here she was in a lush, thriving world filled with magickal beings of every kind. Tilting her head in question, she told Cora, and said.

"But you died. We went to your funeral, and celebration of life."

Taking another deep breath, she said in a shaky voice.

"You left me."

Watching as if in slow motion, Cora placed her hand on her knee, squeezing. Speaking softly.

"My name is Corrina. I am the third founder of the Ravens Night. I'm not sure how it is you know me?"

Upon making contact, Harlow immediately recognized this woman as the same one she knew from home. The how of it would be a later problem. Steading her breath, she answered.

"I know you as Cora in my time. The sister I never had, but a sister of the heart. You were there for me when no one else would be. My friend, protector, and defender."

Taking a glance at Aidan, he shared the same surprised look as Cora. Turning back, she looked her square in the eyes.

"Someone murdered you. I took it upon myself to investigate how, who, and why. In my search, I only found the why. Well, sort of."

Squinting, she tried to sort through the jumble of memories. It was so chaotic it hurt. Rubbing her now thumping head, she continued.

"I'm having trouble sorting through all my memories. But what I'm trying to say is I KNOW YOU. Maybe not the you now, but the future you."

Expelling a breath, she slumped back against Kieran. Relaxing into his folding arms. Smiling, she looked up at him.

"I remember now."

Frowning.

"Though it's all jumbled up in my head. It takes me a while to sort through."

Turning forward to face the crowd. It was then she realized she had told everyone there. Oops. With a shy smile, she covered her mouth.

Aidan laughed.

"It's ok Harlow. Honestly, most of us,"

Turning, and showing everyone.

"Suspected something of the like."

Turning to look at Corrina as she spoke.

"He's right, Harlow. There's no need to be shy with us. Though I am curious about the hows of you and me. Plus the why's. I suspect your time is of great distance?"

The fear spread across her face. Made her heartache.

"I believe so, yes. For in my time, the planet is dying. We possessed no clues how or when it started. They attempted to save it, but in the end, they only made it worse. Some populations were able to survive by building massive domed compounds. As far as I am aware, ours was the last one left."

Looking at her crowd. Many who had been standing were now sitting again. Some of their faces displayed shock, fear, or sadness. Curiosity still filled most of them. Even Kieran remained motionless. So she continued.

"I was the compound archivist. My responsibility was to comb through the archive library for any and all information that could be helpful. I started this when I was very young. Being an outcast within the compound, I liked I could hide away. In my own way, I could help."

As she spoke, she could see their expression changing. From impressed to curiosity, shock, and anger. The last had her confused. So she explained.

"I was born different, in a time where any ailment or dysfunction could be fixed. For some unknown reason, mine was not. Nerve damage in my left leg resulted in impeding my ability to walk 'like a normal person.' Then there was the fact about my crazy curly mass of red hair. No one else had anything like it, and people constantly mocked me for it. For all my faults Cora,"

Looking at her friend with affection,

"Was there turning any negative into a positive?"

It was then she realized her leg or rather her limp was gone. Surprise and curiosity spread across her face. Turning to look again at Kieran, she asked.

"My leg. How? Since I woke up here, I have never once had a problem with it."

With pleading eyes, she waited.

He took such a deep breath his chest moved her forward a little before he said.

"Cormac."

As if that was enough of an explanation.

Well, ok, guess she'd have to ask him to explain later. Turning back around to face the others, she was still questioning. Why she wasn't sharing everything, and why she was editing her story to keep all mention of Caden out? It was just a gut feeling she had. He had always been the one to protect her. Now it seemed it was her turn to protect him. Or maybe she was protecting them both. Not understanding any of the reasons, only knowledge and time would reveal all. Time, laughing aloud at her internal joke.

Kieran finally spoke, asking with a timber voice.

"What's so funny little one?

The more she tried to answer, the harder she laughed. Until she stuttered with a wave of her arm, "Thhhhhhis." Pointing at herself in the end.

"I mean, you're all here listening to me tell you I'm from the future. Not one of you is questioning me."

She stopped abruptly with tears leaking from her eyes.

"Why?"

Feeling Kieran take a breath, and open his to reply, Corrina blurted out.

"We believe you. That's why."

Simple, and factual. Her face displayed the truth of her statement.

Touched, she cried silent tears. Her emotions were all over the place. The last time she felt like this, she had been pregnant with Rowan. Realization hit, if she was in the past, and Rowan was in the future. She'd never again see her son. Shoulders slumping, she allowed her sadness to take over. Not feeling like talking anymore, she twisted and snuggled deeper into Kieran's arm. His warmth and strength comforted her. Feeling him move, followed by his whispered question.

"Are we finished for tonight little one?"

Not wanting to open her mouth for fear of blubbering, a simple nod was her reply. Tuning everything out, she focused on the warmth of Kieran. Not wanting to dwell on anything, she instead focused on her feelings for Kieran. This man brought feelings of desire to the forefront. Made her wish for things she wasn't sure were possible. Like the things she had read about in all those romance books, she loved so much. Long ago, she gave up on the possibility of ever discovering these sensations for herself. Maybe this was her chance.

Glancing up at Kieran, she tried to display all her wants and needs in one look. As if sensing her need, he looked at her, studying her face. How he understood she didn't care. Rising with her in his arms, and without saying a word to the others, they left. Making their way to Cormac's cottage. They couldn't seem to take their eyes off each other. Locked in a battle of discovery and wanting. It was a different way of communicating and she liked it.

Smiling, she reached up cupping his cheek. With gentle pressure, she guided him towards her lips. The instant they touched, it was like bolts of lightning zinging throughout her. But before they could go any further, Kieran pulled back with a wicked smile.

"Amazing little one, let's go somewhere more private."

Without waiting for a reply, he increased the pace towards the cottage. She just hoped they would be there alone. It seemed wrong if Cormac was there. Just thinking about it sent shivers down her spine. Just another thing to add to the list for analysis later. Tonight was going to be her night with her man. Smiling with anticipation of tonight's events, she closed her eyes, laying her head on his shoulder.

Kieran knew Harlow believed they were heading towards the cottage. Instead, he took her to the secret bunker room Ravens Night had created. They needed a place of security in case one of them was in desperate need. Sometimes they used it simply to hide, while other times they used it for healing. It wouldn't look good in the village showing up, and not being able to explain injuries. Yes, it took a lot to sustain an injury as a God race. Overall, we were adept at self healing. Still, it happened, especially when dealing with other magickals. Or like now when he and his Mate need a safe bed for the night.

He was feeling no guilt over letting the other members clean up his dwelling, and provide stronger protections around it. Seemed Like a great idea. The chance to have more with Harlow tonight was not something he would ever pass up. Even if it meant spending the night in a single room built within the side of a rock mountain deep in the forest. The entrance was both hidden and easy to reach for those who knew where to go. Additionally, they added every comfort they could squeeze in on top of all the magical protection spells.

So the more he thought about it, the more this place would be perfect for their first time together. Away from all the chaos and worries, they could focus on each other. He wanted to discover every inch of her. Even though she had made it clear what she wanted in the clearing, this was a first for her. Wanting to make it special for them both had him pushing back his urge to just take charge, and take her like a man possessed. He wanted to show her she was valued, treasured, and, above all, desired.

After making it through the entrance, he lowered Harlow to her feet. The fronts of their bodies enjoy close contact with increasing desire. He could hear the effect it was having on her with the quickening of her breathing. Placing a finger under her chin, he tilted her head back to just the right angle. Lowering his head, he kissed her with all the pent up energy he felt. Her subsequent moan, along with her leaning further into him, fueled him on. When she wrapped her arms around his neck, he moved his hands to grab her ass. Lifting her with ease, she wrapped her legs around him, grinding herself against him.

Growling at her instincts, he made quick work towards the bed. Again placing her on her feet, he sat on the bed this time. Looking into her sparkling eyes, he noticed they were a much brighter green at the moment. Smiling, he challenged himself to see if he could make them glow. Leaning back a little, he glanced up and down at his Mate. Liking what he saw, he said.

"Harlow, will you disrobe for me? I'd very much like to see you, little one."

As he expected, her blush started low, rising to her cheeks. Soon he could discover where it started.

She smiled shyly at him.

"Ok"

It was all he could do not to pounce on her then and there. Cautiously, she removed layers of clothing. Starting at the top and working her way down. He never realized she wore so much. At night she had only worn one shirt, and what she was standing in now. Only she never knew he had peeked once and saw her changing. This garb only had one piece holding her lovely breats, while the other covered her wonderful core. Seeing her hesitating when she was down to these two pieces, he took the option out of her hands.

Wrapping his arm around her middle, he drew her closer, sealing their lips together. She tastes so good. When she relaxed into the kiss and was sparring back with his tongue, he spun them. Switching placeless, he continued to kiss her. From her luscious lips down her jaw and collarbone. Taking his time, he latched onto one of her nipples, laving it with his tongue before sucking it deep. Causing Harlow to make a grunting, moaning noise deep in her throat while arching her back for more. Pulling back with a smile, he repeated the treatment to the other nipple. Her hands grabbed the back of his head to hold him in place.

His Mate enjoyed having her nipples sucked. Good to know. He would file that information away. Imagine her reaction without the clothing between them. This time it was his turn to growl, liking his train of thought. While looking forward to a repeat performance. Stunning him more was the fact that just as he started nibbling on her nipple, and escalating the pressure. She came arching off the bed and screaming his name.

Gently taking her wrists, he pulled her hands free of the back of his head. Placing them above her head, looking her sternly in the eyes.

"Leave them there."

Waiting for her acceptance, he grinned when she gave a slight nod.

Diving in for a kiss that ramped up her desire once more. When she started gyrating against him, he moved lower with his kisses.

Settling above her core, he noticed the lovely wet spot forming. Burying his nose, he took a deep inhale, growling deep within his chest at the center of her. Impatiently, he reached up and tore the dampening fabric away. As pretty as they were, she wouldn't be needing them again. The fewer layers covering her, the better access he would have. With a long, slow lick from the bottom of her lower lips to the top, he savored her taste. Sweat with a hint of tanginess. Perhaps a foreshadowing of their sex life to come. He used his fingers to open her, then swiped his tongue through each side before stroking deep inside for a better taste, causing her to arch her back once again.

Reaching up, he placed a splayed hand on her stomach, anchoring her to the bed. Looking up from where he was enjoying himself. A warm feeling of contentment filled his heart as he saw she had kept her arms exactly where he had placed them. Her lust filled eyes watched every move he made. With his eyes trained on her, he moved his other hand, he took a finger, and gently rimmed her entrance. Finding her little nub, he circled it before he slowly inserted his finger. With eyes growing huge, she sucked in a breath. Meanwhile, her internal muscles were flexing around his digit, making him wish it was another part of him. But he wanted her to come in his mouth first, he needed to taste it.

Twirling his tongue around before clamping down and sucking harder on her lovely little nub. When her eyes glazed over, he added a second finger. Harlow began shaking her head from side to side, moaning and groaning. When he added a third finger and bit down, she flew apart, screaming. Hands flying to the back of his head, holding him tight. Deciding to reward her for her passion, he switched places with his fingers. Pulling apart her pussy lips, he dove in deep with his tongue, mimicking the act of lovemaking. Taking his fingers, he circled her now protruding nub with her inner juices before pinching it tight, and pulling, instantly sending her over again.

Rising above her, he positioned himself at her entrance.

"Harlow."

Her eyes snapped open to look into his.

"That's it, little one. Look at me as I enter you. This is our moment."

Rubbing his tip in her flowing juices, he eased slowly forward. Groaning at how tight she was, he had to pause every so often to allow her to adjust. When he fully penetrated her, he lowered himself to wrap his fingers around the back of her neck, tilting to the perfect angle devouring her mouth. He sealed his lips to hers.

When she started raising her hips for more, he pulled back.

"That's it, little one."

Rising above her again, he moved. Slowly at first, then gradually picking up the pace till she was moaning in pleasure. When she had whispered for more, that's when he snapped. Placing his hands just under her armpits on the bed for support, he fucked his woman hard. Her arms came flying towards him, her hands gripping his forearms for support. Wrapping her legs around him, she joined in on the rapid movement.

Her moans and sighs of pleasure drove him higher. He also lost count of the many times she had come. Each orgasm seemed to spur her on for more. Until on this last one, her inner muscles clamped down on him so tight he could no longer move. She held onto him in a vice like grip as he emptied himself into her, filling her up with every last drop he had. Collapsing atop her, he rolled them to the side, not wanting to crush her. While both of them breathed heavily, he cradled her close. Both fell asleep entwined together, with him still happy inside her.

CHAPTER 17

*H*arlow woke the next morning in a tangle of limbs and bedding. The intense warmth made her forehead glisten with perspiration. After a few failed attempts to free herself without waking Kieran, she called his name with an increasing volume each time. Until finally he stirred, groaning before blinking his eyes open, and stretching his limbs. Now that both arms were free, she placed both hands on his chest, pushing him onto his back. Watching as his eyes rounded in shock at her force, she too rolled to her back, fanning herself to cool down.

Rolling again to his side with an elbow on the bed, he propped his head in his hand.

"What is it, little one?"

Before she could answer him, he began running his finger over her stomach. Drawing some imaginary pattern, but igniting her arousal. Enjoying the fiery trail left by his finger, Harlow arched her hips. In the hopes he would travel there. She felt the burning need for him inside her. His responding chuckle had her groaning in despair before she took matters into her own hands. With her hand closest to him, she grabbed his wrist, moving it above his head.

In one fast motion, she swung her leg around his hip, using the momentum to straddle him and forcing him to his back. With her other hand, she grabbed his wrist, lifting it to rest beside his other above his head. She rather liked this. His gaze filled with surprise, wonderment, and most of all, desire. Searching his face, she waited. Having a sense that her man liked to be in charge in the bedroom. Somehow, though, she knew he would grant her this.

She wanted to give him the joy he had given to her. Then there was the realization she wanted to explore. To discover what she liked or didn't. Even if Kieran seemed to have figured that out already, she wanted the chance to learn for herself. Her grin spread from ear to ear at his brief nod.

Reaching behind her, she undid the bra she was still wearing, tossing it to the side. Watching Kieran fist his hands above his head and lick his lips at the sight of her breast. Did tremendous things for her, and she felt desired. Transferring all her weight into her legs gave her the freedom to explore with her fingers and hands. The sensation she felt when she glided her fingers down his outstretched arms was like millions of thrilling pulses of energy. His skin was soft and warm under her touch.

His chest bore the signs of some battles with scars scattered around. Tracing each one, she followed with a kiss, to heal old hurts. This was a brave man who cared about his family and his people. With each kiss, he would groan and harden a little more beneath her. Gaining confidence, she circled each nipple one at a time before bending down to kiss. Only these she wanted to taste. After each kiss, she rimmed each nipple until it was nice and puckered. Only when his breathing increased did she suck, laving it with her tongue. With each turn, he growled and bucked beneath her.

Rising with a devilish smile, she asked.

"You enjoying yourself?"

Tilting her head at his vigorous nodding, she winked before traveling downward.

Grabbing him firmly, her hand wrapping her fingers around him. Hearing him hiss at the contact had her smiling. He was feeling the same sensations of electrifying pleasure as she was. With a desire so strong to please him, she took one last leading look into his eyes.

As if understanding her internal fear, he grunted out.

"Anything you do, little one, will be heaven."

Nodding in understanding, she bent, taking a lick of him from base to tip. Liking his flavor, she repeated the action, to which Kieran groaned, raising his hips towards her mouth. She struggled to remember what she had read in her books. Instead, she decided to just go with what felt right, and what he seemed to like. It looked like anything she did, he would enjoy. Smiling to herself, she stuck her tongue out to lave at the tip that began seeping the minute she had touched him.

His sweet, salty taste had her moaning in pleasure. Not sure what to do, she pumped him lightly with her fist while swirling her tongue.

When Kieran groaned.

"More….Harder."

Looking up at him, confused. She was relieved he again understood. With one hand, he wrapped it around hers, showing her the increased pressure he desired. The other around the back of her neck guiding her movements. Once she figured out the motion, pressure, and speed he liked, he released her. He moved his hands back into the position she had placed them in. Smiling around him in her mouth, she varied the pressure and the speed. Enjoying every groan, moan, and hiss he made. Wanting to explore him more. She used her other hand to massage below.

He grew larger in her mouth. On instinct, she took him in as far as she could, squeezing with both hands. She swallowed. The result was Kieran shouting her name as he arched off the bed. He was cumming down her throat, and she liked it. Moaning once more at his taste, she felt him jerk again in her mouth. Spurting a little bit more. As he groaned again, she felt him place his hands under her arms, pulling her up to him. He looked into her eyes as he kissed her. Man, could this man kiss.

He made her head spin, each and every time. As he wrapped her into his arms, she melted, moaning with her pleasure. Pulling back, she chuckled at his enthusiasm as he tried to pull her back in.

Trying to give him a fake pout.

"I wasn't finished, Kieran."

Very serious, Kieran looked straight at her.

"Oh, I know, little one. We are far from done. Since you have had your morning meal, it's only fair that I have mine."

Confused, she scrunched her brows, shaking her head in question. With a devilish smile, and a lift of a single brow.

"I want you to turn over onto all fours."

Still displaying the confused look, she hesitated till Kieran moved her into position. With him moving in behind her, in between her splayed legs. Blushing, she ducked her head. When she felt him smoothing his hands over her rear end. Causing her breath to hitch when he increased the pressure, not to mention the feelings his touch stirred within her.

Chuckling.

"Ah, so my little one likes it, eh!"

Before she could reply, she heard the slap before she felt the lovely sting. Not able to question him before he repeated the movement on her other cheek. She moaned while he groaned, peppering down slaps on her now tender ass. As soon as she started leaning into each slap he stopped, only to kneed, and rub her tender cheeks. It felt so good. She was so lost in the sensations that she didn't notice his hands were moving again. This time from the base of her spine up her back to her shoulders. Pushing downward, she understood his request. Dropping her shoulders to the bed, she rested her cheek on the bed. She licked her lips in anticipation, humming when she tasted him there.

Sighing with pleasure, Kieran roamed over her back with his powerful hands. With skill, he had her flushing with arousal, squirming for more. Working his way down, he squeezed and molded the globes of her ass. It hurt and felt wonderful at the same time. Hearing movement behind her, she was about to move when he pulled her lower lips apart with his thumbs. Gasping at the cool air when he blew across her.

With a delighted chuckle, Kieran spoke.

"My little one likes it! Doesn't she?"

When she didn't answer, she felt two stinging slaps, one on each side. Jumping at the surprise, she replied.

"Yes, Kieran."

It came out more of a breathy moan. At least she had answered.

"Good. I can tell. You are dripping for me."

Embarrassed by his comment, she tried to move, like it was something she should be ashamed of. When she felt firm hands on her lips, and a soothing voice.

"Shh little one. It is an excellent thing and makes me a proud and happy man."

As he got back into position, he continued.

"Now you stay nice, and still as I enjoy my morning meal. Make as much noise as you want, little one."

With that, she felt his thick tongue swipe from her nub to her entrance with vigor. It took all her concentration to stay still. Before long, she was moaning, groaning, and swaying with his movements. He had a very talented tongue. Just as she opened her mouth to beg for what she wasn't sure. She just knew she wanted, needed more. He pulled back. Voicing her displeasure, she felt his finger at her entrance. Slowly, he pushed forward, then pulled back, repeating the movement until her hips followed. Only then stopping and repeating the process, this time with two fingers. This continued in the like, till he was at four fingers. This time when her hips followed he stopped only to grab himself and thrust into her hard.

Screaming out at the pleasure of forceful thrust, she dug her fingers into the bedding. Needing something to hold on to. Once he was seated, she didn't move, but she tried to adjust herself to get the much-needed friction. Only for Kieran to grab a hold of her hips and hold her in place. Growling in displeasure, she heard him strain to chuckle. At least he was as affected as she was.

"Hold still Harlow. It'll be over too quickly if you move now. I would like to enjoy this a little longer, wouldn't you?"

Nodding, she sucked in a breath as he moved his hands to rub deeply into the globs of her ass. As he did so, she felt herself being pulled apart.

"Have you ever played here? Has anyone ever had you here, Harlow?"

As he spoke, his thumbs brushed over her rosette hole. Letting out the breath she had been holding, all she could manage was a whisper.

"No, and no."

She could practically feel his joy radiating from him, even in silence. Why she wasn't sure, but who could think right now? He shocked her when he moved around to the front of her and ran his finger alongside himself until it also entered her. Moaning at the fullness. Was this what he wanted to back there? Wanting him to move, she tried pushing back only for another slap of the check. This time it backfired on him because she flexed her internal muscles, squeezing him. This had him moaning her name.

He quickly removed his finger, rimming her rosette again with his now wet thumb. Slowly, he applied pressure until she felt a stinging pop. Gasping, she attempted to even breathe.

"Whatever it is you're going to do, Kieran do it quick, I can't wait any longer."

As she finished, she felt what she assumed was his other thumb enter her.

"Oh my god Kieran."

"That's right, little one. Now you can move. I want you to have yourself cum on me just like this."

Slowly, she moved. Groaning at the increased pressure, and how great it felt. Gradually increasing till she was fucking herself on him. Her skin was super sensitized, so her nipples rubbing against the bedding were growing harder by the second. Something was missing, and she didn't care what it was. Almost in tears, she cried out. Kieran seemed to understand. He bent at the waist, giving her just enough of his weight. Whispering in her ear as he nibbled on it.

"Come. Come for me, little one."

That was all she needed to fly. With a scream, she let loose. Cumming all over him. In her throes of orgasm, he pulled his thumbs free and wrapped his arms around her, pulling them up till they were both on their knees. One arm around her middle, the other with his hand holding her neck. As he licked and nibbled her ear.

"Now my little one, now we'll fuck."

With eyes wide, she dropped her mouth open and realized she had been talking aloud earlier.

"Yes, little one. Mate of mine."

Biting down on her earlobe at the point of pain.

Instead of crying out, she released a tortured moan. Kieran moved at a rapid pace. It felt so good. His hand around her middle started a downward trajectory, landing on her sensitive tiny nub. He explored her lips with his fingers, collecting her juices, and then rubbed her nub. It became so intense that she tried to buck away, shaking her head.

"No Kieran I can't."

The firm command in her ear.

"Yes Harlow, you can, and you will."

In a movement so fast he pinched hard on her nub, and a nipple sending her over in a display of colored lights. He held her tight as she continued to come fucking her hard till she felt him come hard deep inside her. Her last conscious thought was, wouldn't it be nice if she could have Kieran's baby?

Kieran collapsed with Harlow in his arms, trying to catch his breath while trying not to crush her. Being with her was ...... wow, mind blowing. A wave of gratitude washed over him at the thought of their future. Her final murmurings had him turning back to reality a little quicker than he would have liked. He liked the fact he could wear her out so. His concern was how sad and lost she sounded about wanting a child of his. Why would that make her sad? He wondered.

They needed to discuss her son and her past. Rather soon too, it seemed. Something he couldn't help was the timing. With the festival coming up, and their ceremony being added to it. Maybe though he could just ask her after, they had all the time in the world. He still hadn't broached some minor topics regarding their peoples or about his past. Thinking further, maybe the discovery of her past could wait till after the celebrations, and they had dealt with the threat of Neera's followers.

Followers who were now dabbling in dark magicks or with those who did. He wasn't sure which one scared him the most. Planning for both was the best scenario for an outcome that benefitted them. If only they knew why they needed Harlow. Protecting her would be that much better and easier. Turning to look down on his Mate he smiled at how she was curled right into him. Her trust in him astounded him. It was something to be treasured. Kissing her temple, she smiled in her sleep, mumbling some reply. Still smiling, he untangled their limbs from covering her as he rose.

He knew Aidan was just outside, waiting for him. He had arrived in the middle of their morning activities. Not wanting to end their fun too soon, he had ignored the summons. His woman was more important. Dressing quickly, and quietly in yesterday's clothes. He moved about, preparing something for Harlow to eat if she woke before he came back. Grabbing the extra blanket, he covered Harlow with it. Brushing a wayward curl, he kissed her temple and stepped out.

Aidan was leaning against the rock wall two feet from the door. A huge grin spread across his face. Shaking his head at his friend, Kieran nudged him on the shoulder.

"Don't even bother. So what's with the change in plans?"

Referring to his friends' presence here, and not just an internal message sent. This must mean someone has achieved some progress.

"I'm here to bring you both back. We have taken over the great hall."

Raising his hand when Kieran tried to interrupt. He continued.

"We've pooled our magicks, along with Cormac, to protect it. We need you both back to put the plan into action."

Cautiously glancing at his friend.

"Plan? What plan? After we left, they must have found answers and quickly come up with a plan."

Rubbing the back of his neck, he felt a little guilt over not having anything to do in the plan to protect his Mate.

Aidan rested his hand on his friend's shoulder, with a squeeze.

"Not to worry. She is your Mate. We will protect her as our own."

Straightening his posture, a sincere look crossed his face.

"I would do anything to protect her too. She has become like a little sister to me."

Looking down at his hands as he twisted his fingers together.

"After all the classes, training, and spending time together, she got to me."

With a quick pat on the shoulder, he again crossed his arms leaning to wait for the couple to be ready to leave.

Shocked, that his True Mate could instill a steadfast resolution for her protection from his friend that was like a brother to him. What was it about her that drew people in? To process such loyalty was impressive. He was very proud of his woman. Kieran came back and discovered Harlow awake, taking him by surprise. She was preparing herself and eating the food he had set aside for her.

"I'll be ready to go in a sec."

As she sat in a chair, to put on her footwear.

"Just let me put these on."

Sliding the dish of food his way.

"Here, finish this, you need to eat something too."

He was still just standing there watching her when she jumped up and reached into one of her many pockets. Pulling out a tie for her hair. He liked her hair, a thick full mass of fiery red curls. A fore-shadow he suspected for the genuine women hidden within. Only showing her real self to those she trusted. He would help her gain the confidence to show the world. His little one needed to shine.

He was so lost in thought he didn't notice she was now standing right in front of him. Her hand on his cheek was gentle and soft. Every time she touched him, he could feel it in his bones with a fiery, arousing flare. He couldn't believe his eyes as her caring gaze trans-formed into a blazing desire, mirroring his own. Tracking her move-ment as she picked up a piece of food, and brought it to his mouth.

Gratefully opening his mouth and chewing the morsel. All while gazing into each other's eyes. Who knows? He would enjoy this so much. He liked it when he fed Harlow by hand. She continued to feed till he had eaten it all. With the spell broken, it only took them a matter of minutes to clean and tidy the space. Leaving the one room den where they shared their first time together was a little bittersweet.

Stepping out into the world, he noticed Aidan was holding a hooded black cloak for Harlow. As he dropped it over her shoulders, he explained she was about to wear it on the direction of Cormac. He had blessed it for her. Pulling the hood up and over her head, it fit and covered her identifying fiery hair. The hood fell forward, enough to cover her eyes. It seemed as if the cloak grew, engulfing its wearer.

Overwhelmed with appreciation, he held back a laugh and thanked the Shaman for their foresight. Gifting his M's foresight. Gifting his Mate with a magical garment. It would now forever be hers, adjusting itself to her given needs. Only at the moment, it looked to be showing off a little. He aided Harlow in wrapping some of the fabric in her arms to prevent it from dragging on the ground. However, maybe it was a good thing to cover her eyes as well, considering their very distinctive appearance. She was the only one he knew of to have such vivid green eyes. Even with her resemblance to Neera, this was one thing they did not share. Neera had blue eyes. The only other person he could think of with green eyes was Cormac, his had green mixed with a little gold ringing the center.

Taking her hand in his.

"Harlow, let's leave the hood like this. Feed your arm through mine, and I will guide you. Aidan will walk on your other side."

This was how they made their way back to the village and into the great hall. On the way, Aidan explained a spell had ignited the rioting villagers. It had been one of their very people. It had also been her daughter, who was one of those who broke into his dwelling. They apprehended and dealt with both of them.

They firmly believed in Neera's teachings and embraced the notion that our people were far more advanced than others. As Gods, they viewed it as our divine right to rule, and dominate those that are lesser. In all the chaos, the other offender escaped. Both women are tight lipped on his identity and affiliation. They sang like canaries about their beliefs and plan of attack. They had hoped in kidnapping Harlow, who they believe is a reincarnation of Neera, that Kieran would see the light in their plans. Becoming a willing participant.

Their story has some gaps that are too easily explained to believe. It is certain, however, they created and cast the spell. While the daughter broke in with her accomplice, her mother stood guard. Inflicting more chaos. All that is needed regarding them is your decision on the sentence. The clan has spoken, and their wishes are final. As he spoke Aidan had glanced his way with an uptick in his brow, before turning and carrying on. Kieran understood his meaning.

His decision could put him in a difficult position. Harlow not knowing how their clan functioned being from the future. Who had knowledge of the handling process? He was thankful for his friend's double meaning. His ruling would either be life ending or life threatening. However, the moment his Mate was targeted, he decided. Anyone who harmed her in any way would suffer death. And one guaranteeing no afterlife. Only pure suffering.

In the hall, Kieran led Harlow to the platformed end. Wrapping his hands around her middle, he lifted her before stepping up to join her. Even though she was one of them, she was a lot smaller. Her size resembled that of those they had sworn to protect. He liked her just as she was. Her internal light was bright and pure. With his back to the rest of the room, he pulled her close. Tipping back the hood, he smiled at her sparkling, unsure eyes. Running the back of his finger down her cheek.

"It'll be alright little one. You will stand beside me. Hold my hand if you need to ok."

Nodding his head to her.

She too nodded with a whispered "ok" before raising her chin, and squaring her shoulders.

As he turned, he felt her delicate touch as she slipped her soft hand into his. Turning again to look at her, he raised their joined hands, kissing the back of hers. With a slight tug, he maneuvered them to the center of the platform. Glancing around, he made sure all were present. Only a select few remained out and on watch. With a slow, dramatic nod of his head, the official meeting began. The official paraded the accused forward, from the back of the room, through the center of the crowded room. They had stripped them of their formal garb and dressed them in rags, binding their hands in front with spelled ties to prevent the flow of magicks. A simple gemstone tied close around their necks prevented them from speak casting. To protect the accused from harm and restrict fast movement until a verdict was announced, they tied a heavily weighted gem around one ankle, resembling a stone in appearance.

As the women with their heads hung low stopped to stand in front of them, many in the crowd started shouting and cursing them. It was very clear whose side they were on. Once again, Harlow had endeared more people to her, and her well being. People she hadn't even met yet. However, when the accused looked up, squaring their shoulders in a superior prideful way, they sneered at those before them.

He was expecting shock from Harlow at their appearance, not for her to move in closer to him in a tremble of fear. Squeezing her hand in his was all the reassurance he could give her at the moment. Her reaction, however, just affirmed to him his final decision was justified. Raising his other hand, he called for the proceedings to continue. First to present were the investigation findings, followed by the clan's verdict. After which he would announce this for all to hear. These two individuals had their fates sealed, and no appeal would be heard.

He noticed Harlow placing her other hand on her middle as each of the findings were presented, most of which Aidan had already informed them about. The more time that passed, she rubbed in circles as if to calm down. Was this upsetting her, or was she unwell? Turning back to the gathering, he needed to at least appear to be paying attention. His concern for his Mate was growing. Just as the clan finished their verdict, Harlow bent forward, clutching her head, releasing an ear piercing scream.

With lightning speed, he caught her as she collapsed, just as Aidan, Corrina, and Cormac rushed to her side. Other members of Ravens Night took up possessions at all entrances. One of the clan's elders came to stand in his place until he could get Harlow to safety.

With a gentle hand on his arm, Corrina instructed.

"Bring her this way, Kieran. It's not safe to leave this place. Let Cormac and myself look after her."

Nudging her head in Aidan's direction.

"Aidan will stand watch as we focus on her care. You mustn't let this sway you from your verdict. Give it, and return."

Regrettably, he agreed with her. If this was an attempt to distract them or weaken his rule. It would not work. Even if all his instincts were screaming at him to stay by her side. The fact comforted him she would be here in the hall, still surrounded by friends, family, and Ravens Night members. Placing her gently on the cot laid out, Harlow was still moaning in pain and mumbling. Without taking his eyes from her, he swept aside some curls.

"She has a tendency to mumble revealing information when unawares."

Before bending, and placing a gentle kiss on her forehead. Standing, he looked at each one of his friends before turning and going back to his formal position.

Rage consumed him as he questioned if someone had deliberately harmed his Mate to manipulate the outcome of the verdict. If so, it wouldn't work. Without waiting for formalities, he announced his verdict. He was in full agreement and supported the clan's decision. They would do the deed in the wee hours of the day of the festival. The horrified look on the faces of the guilty had him smiling with a wicked grin. No one would cross him and get away with it. The resulting gasp, followed by a rising cheer within the crowd, added to the women's shock. Had they thought he would side with them?

Overwhelmed with gratitude, he embraced the peaceful silence that lingered after the uproar of the departing clan. Checking to reassure himself that members still stood guard at the doors, he returned to where he left his woman. Shocked to first only see Corrina, and Aidan still with her.

"Where is Cormac?"

Looking between the two.

Both shook their heads unawares. Aidan spoke first.

"Harlow was mumbling like you said. Even with our advanced hearing, we couldn't understand her."

Corrina continued.

"Something she said, though, sent a wave of shock through Cormac. Then, like a bolt of lightning, he shot out of here. He clearly understood everything she was saying."

They shared a look, and Aidan continued.

"After he left, she stopped. She's been calm ever since."

CHAPTER 18

*O*nce again, she was in a vortex of swirling rainbows. To move and balance herself, she tried to splay her limbs out. Fear consumed her when she couldn't. Something or someone was holding her in a vice grip. As her panic grew, so too did the pressure within her head. Shutting her eyes, squeezing them tight to relieve some of the tension. As nauseousness enveloped her, the bonds restraining her lifted, just as an ear piercing pitch vibrated through her. She reached up to cover her ears in vain, only to be abruptly tossed from the whirlwind in a whoosh.

Shocked by the instant change, she chanced opening her eyes. Revealing a crisp sunny blue sky with the song of birds singing their tune. The clean, crisp, and fresh smelling air wafts around her as she was free falling. Realizing she was dropping downward, her fear spiked once again. With her limbs flailing, about to do who knows what, she landed with a thud. One that forced all the air from her lungs in a single whoosh. Laying there limp in the tall grass, it took her some time and energy to refill her lungs. Blinking, she attempted to look around, but the blackness was calling to her. Just before she embraced it with open arms, she recognized this place. It was Kieran's world.

She could hear the soft murmuring of voices. Where was she? Her entire body aches just like it had just over a week ago. Fighting the call to sleep, she cracked her eyes open just a little. Things were a little blurry, thankfully, with no bright lights. Still, it took blinking a few more times for her eyes to adjust. Standing beside her huddled together were Kieran, Aidan, and Cora whispering away. They hadn't seemed to notice she was staring at them. Sitting up, there was still a rush to her head. Groaning, she rubbed her head as Kieran rushed to her side, concerned.

Speaking softly, as he tried to nudge her back.

"Little one, you should lay back down."

Shaking her head.

"No Kieran, I'm fine."

Swinging her legs over the edge, she sat there. Not willing to test standing up yet. Sighing, she looked up to the others as Kieran wedged his way in to sit beside her.

Aidan's smirk on his face showed he wasn't convinced, as he commented.

"Sure you are Red."

Confused, she asked.

"Red?"

Taking advantage of her man's warmth, she snuggled into his side. Closing her eyes in comfort as he wrapped his big, powerful arms around her. Sighing in the pleasure and security she felt. Opening her eyes watched as Aiden got some more chairs. Offering one to Cora, and taking the other for himself.

"Ya Red. It's a nickname, as good as any."

Shrugging his shoulders. Before tapping his finger on his chin as if pondering an idea.

"Plus, I think it suits."

Nodding his head as if making a decision made, he crossed an ankle over his knee, resting both hands atop it. Tilting his head with a thoughtful expression.

"Yes, Red will do. How you really doing, Red?"

Feeling Kieran relax behind her. She rested her head on his shoulder and started talking.

"I really am doing ok, just a little tired. It was weird, is all. Suddenly I had a strange feeling in my belly."

At their concerned looks, she sat up, raising her hands and shaking them. Attempting to reassure them.

"No, no, nothing ill, just like something was going to happen. It kept getting bigger and stronger. Until, well, it was gone. How did I end up here? And where is here? Are we still in the hall"

Looking around, she answered some of her questions. Yes, they were still in the hall.

Cora answered her, still whispering.

"As you can tell, yes, we're in the hall still. You blacked out Harlow only just coming to a few moments ago."

Ok well, that would explain a few things. Licking her lips before asking.

"How long was I out?"

She could tell the men were both unsure of the answer to her question. Smiling her eyes at Cora's nonchalant answer.

"Only about ten minutes. Kieran caught you when you collapsed. So no need to worry. You're perfectly safe."

Aidan then became serious.

"So this wasn't something done to you. It was you reacting to something else."

Rubbing his chin, she could see his brows furrowed, and eyes glazed over, deep in thought.

Harlow blurted out.

"Who is Neera? Her name has been mentioned before, but I don't know who Neera is. I assume she is of some importance."

When she said her name, all three of them hissed. Confused, she looked between them.

"Well, who is she then?"

Each displayed an odd look on their faces. It was like hurt, anger, disbelief, and shock all rolled into one. What had this one woman done to them? This time Cora chastised as Aidan seemed to sink into the floor.

"Kieran, you didn't tell her. She has a right to know, you know."

With a humf, she crossed her arms, turning to look anywhere else but at them. Kieran stiffened behind her, only to relax a moment later in defeat. In a hushed voice, he agreed she was right. He should have told her. It was just other things that had gotten in the way, and well stuff kept happening. So he had held off. Something pinged in the back of her mind, causing a shiver from head to toe. Just then, warm, powerful arms surrounded her, holding her close.

Resting his chin on her head, he complained in a grumpy tone. As if to reassure her, he started drawing circles on the backs of her hands with his fingers. Before threading his fingers through hers. Then using their joined hands to hug her close.

"See, now she's all worried, Corrina. Look what you did."

Snapping her head in his direction, her face displayed hurt and a touch of anger.

"Nice try Kieran."

Harlow, shaking her head, had Cora relaxing into her once again. Still, she was quick to assure otherwise.

"No, nothing like that. I was just cold."

Why had she just lied to them? She couldn't be sure. Looking between Aidan and Cora, she all but begged.

"Will one of you please tell me? I feel as if I'm missing something major."

Aidan spoke first, a little hesitantly. Relaxing his posture, his eyes looked as if he was seeing something in the past. Why he seemed so sad as he spoke she didn't quite understand.

"For the one to see the future's past,
Is trice blessed to conquer light fast.
Fire be true,
With leadership firm,
Changing destiny right."

After finishing, he rubbed a hand over his face. A habit she had seen him do when either frustrated or deep in thought. Kieran's tell was running his hands through his hair. It was interesting what you could learn while watching someone. After releasing a long held breath, he continued.

"This is the prophecy handed down through the generations of our people and taught to us all. At one point in time, we all believed this to be about Neera. Eons ago Cormac had a vision regarding the prophecy."

Pausing, he stood and paced before continuing.

"Neera, Kieran, and myself were all born around the same time. As we grew, she resembled the woman from the vision. Since everyone knew the description of her, they assumed she was the one. From an early age, she had that burden thrust upon her. Maybe it was from the pressure, or she was just all about herself. Neera never had powerful gifts from birth and always struggled in lessons with the two of us. She looked elsewhere for ways to gain more. Feeling it was her right to do so in order to fulfill the prophecy."

Sitting in his chair again, he bent, holding his head in his hands.

She watched as Cora, no Corrina, she needed to remember the difference in names. Even if she was positive, this was the same woman. How that could be was still a mystery. She extended her arm to rub her hand up and down Aidan's back in reassurance and support. As she did so, she continued.

"This is difficult for these two....... I have a little distance being a little bit older. But in the end, the three of them were great friends, or so they thought. Neera was deceitful and selfish. If it didn't gain her favor or benefit her in any way, she didn't do it. We were unknowing, as she gathered her own followers in a plea to gain more power. She made unmakable promises to anyone she thought would be of use to her."

Making a face of distaste before continuing.

"The same time, some of us suspected the actions she displayed were not entirely true. Her true colors also started to emerge."

Pointing with her head in Kieran's, and Aidan's, direction as she spoke.

"It was these two who first suspected and confronted her. Only once you sting the cat does she scratch. Oh boy, did she ever."

Rolling her eyes and shaking her head, a small laugh escaped.

"That woman put on a show that the gullible among us took it hook, line, and sinker. These two didn't stand a chance at convincing them of her true intentions. They faced years of shunning and were blamed for her leaving. Thus jeopardizing the result desired in the prophecy."

Before she could continue, Kieran spoke up.

"It wasn't as bad as she makes it sound, but it is true. However, I wish we could go back and change how we were proven right. For the result was an all out war. The cost of which was too many lives shed."

She could feel him shaking his head. As slowly as she could, turned to look up at him. She asked.

"Is that how your father died? With her beheading him, and she from his power bolt of light?"

Before she could blink, he maneuvered her to sit on his lap, facing him. With a finger under her chin, he demanded.

"How do you know that, little one?"

Opening his eyes larger, staring her down, waiting for an answer.

Behind her, she heard the question repeated in unison. Opening her mouth a few times, she wasn't sure how to answer.

"Well, I have dreams. One of them was of a battle. Most thoughts were of you two, and her."

Glancing over her shoulder at Aidan, then back at Kieran.

"We're in it. I saw a leader taken down in the like by the woman who looks like me."

Shrugging her shoulders, before looking down at her fingers, trying desperately not to fidget. All three of them made a noise of understanding in unison. Feeling his finger once again under her chin, she glanced up into his eyes, fearing judgment or ridicule. Instead, there was understanding with a sense of pride displayed on his face. Smiling, she wrapped her arms around his neck, kissing his cheek before pulling back and asking.

"You believe me? Really?"

From behind her Aidan spoke.

"Of course, we believe you, Red. It's just a bit of a surprise."

She could hear him shrug his shoulders. As he laughed.

"Every time we think we have your gifts figured out, you go, and surprise us with one more. It's starting to get hard keeping track of them all."

Relaxing, she began biting her lip.

"So the woman that looks like me, her name is Neera? Is that right?"

Kieran closed his eyes and nodded. Putting the pieces together, it felt like something was clicking.

"And it's her posse that is after me. Possibly for all her said promises? Or just because I look like her? Have I got that right?"

Glancing between the three, who suddenly seemed more interested in the floor. Using Kieran's shoulders for support, she stretched her leg around to turn and sat beside him. Rolling her eyes at them and putting a hand on her hip for effect.

"Oh come on guys, just answer."

With his brows scrunched and a head tilt, Aidan looked at her, asking.

"What does posse mean?"

Trying very hard not to laugh at the way he said posse.

"It means a group of people or followers."

As she answered, another question popped into her head. This time it was her turn to scrunch her brows.

"How is it I can talk to you all, and understand you? I mean, I have always had a knack for languages and could figure out most of the forgotten ones. Like the one picture language on the arch, and such. But I don't remember learning this one."

Rubbing her head, trying to answer her question. After a moment, she felt Kieran's hand on her back as he rubbed up and down.

"No idea, little one. We had always assumed you were just from a place distant from here. Then when we learned you were from here, but in a different time, we just assumed the same thing was said. You've never questioned till now. Plus, we wouldn't have suspected otherwise."

He was right. Her situation just kept getting stranger, and stranger. She liked it here and hoped beyond hope her family found her clues and would come through like her. Caden had been there when she passed through. Maybe he was here. That thought made her perk up. Just the thought of Rowan left behind filled her with sadness. Maybe she could get him? Perking up a bit, she asked.

"How does the arch work? I mean, it's a portal, right?"

Giddy with the possibilities, she anxiously waited.

Corrina's expression turned to sadness.

"We're not sure. Many have guessed. Those who came before us created it. Before our elder's time, even. Though they may know something about it. To us it is sacred, and to be protected. Twice a year, we give offerings and build upon the spells of protection. Sadly, its creators are long since gone."

Leaning forward, and very serious.

"Is that how you came here?"

Not able to form words, she nodded her head. She felt like her son was slipping away. She had only herself to blame. Taking up Cora's clues left behind to complete her mission for her. Still refusing to give up, if Cora knew her as well as she apparently did. Then not only were clues left for her, then likely for Rowan and Caden as well. For she knew how much family meant to the three of them, and that included her. Her only reassurance was knowing she had left clues and the book for Rowan to find. Here's hoping he finds them all, and puts it all together.

Their discussion ended after that. Her stomach chose then to make itself known. By growling, Aidan kept teasing her the rest of the night about a lion or a bear living inside her. He reminded her so much of Caden, and how their relationship was. She was missing the banter shared between siblings. A gift treasured in her time. As darkness fell, they all prepared for sleep. Home for now was within the great hall for all of them. Each had a section created for themselves, only she and Kieran would be sharing.

For as freeing as she felt in this world with the ability to just be herself, the weight on her shoulders seemed heavy. Missing her family, her resemblance to Neera, and the threat of her followers.

Furthermore, she had to consider the prophecy in the mix, which she guessed was about her, not Neera, as assumed. She would have plenty of time to decipher it if she dealt with the dreaded groupies.

Sitting on the makeshift double cot, she let silent tears fall as she twisted her hands in her lap. It was like moving so far forward only to travel further backward. How was she going to deal with all of this as well as learn all she needed to about magicks and this world? At least there were many willing to help. Like tomorrow, Corrina was going to be her instructor in applying and channeling her gifts. Gratefulness washed over her, realizing that the underlying connection they shared remained strong, both in the present and future.

There was also the matter of why come back here. How would that help in the future? Was Cora just trying to go home to a better time? Or was it something else? The more she thought about it, the more her insides were telling her this was where she needed to be. It made her miss her family all the more.

That was how Kieran found her when he entered their makeshift bedroom space. Wallowing in worry, and self doubt. She didn't hear him, so his gentle cupping of her head, tilting it, and kissing her surprised her. It was a kiss filled with longing and caring. Her desire rose to the surface. She tried to take charge of the kiss. Moaning when he backed off, taking a step back, with his hand outstretched.

"Up little one. Let me turn down, and we can get in, and get some much needed sleep."

Taking his offered hand, she stood where he had moved her to. Watching as he prepared the cot for them. Once finished, he made his way back to her. As his finger rested under her chin, he tipped her head back and gently placed a kiss on the tip of her nose. With her help, he helped remove the rest of her clothes before placing one of his shirts on her. With a soft tug, he guided her into bed, and she settled in comfortably. She felt like purring in contentment, snuggled in beside him wrapped in his arms, in a nice warm bed.

Maybe he was right, there were many faces of a relationship. It wasn't all the sex, though she enjoyed it with Kieran. Finally understanding the appeal, all the books had been talking about. This gentleness of just holding each other was just as intimate, if not more so. She looked up from snuggling into his chest. She smiled at his tired face. Maybe this could be why. He was tired. Thankfully, she raised sweetly, kissing him.

"Thank you, Kieran."

Kissing once more before snuggling in again.

"Good night."

"Goodnight little one,"

Was the last thing she heard before drifting off to sleep.

CHAPTER 19

Time seemed to pass by. Yesterday was her first training day with Corrina. To say she was talented would not be doing her justice. The woman had knowledge of all elemental gifts, and then some. She reminded Harlow of an encyclopedia, filled with every conceivable piece of information. She knew just how to apply it, too. Her way of instruction helped Harlow advance, and rapidly. It was like this woman could pull the very best from deep within the student. Who knew she processed many gifts, as they called them? For her, it was just a matter of feeling connected to something. Whether it be fire, earth, wind, or water. She had an infinity with them all.

A rarity within the world, but not unheard of. Yesterday morning, she dedicated half of her time to learning abridged versions of history, magicks, and rules or guidelines that they all lived by. Over time, there have been those who have broken the rules or to live on their own. That number had increased thanks to Neera, and her views. The still scarier part was not knowing her practices. Many have come to believe them to be dark magicks.

They never received teachings because the draw towards them was too great. Once on that side, the pull became ever stronger. Much like an addiction. No one has yet to come back to the light and stay. Also, the magick was so very unpredictable it bordered on scary. So many feared it, so for such a long time it became dormant for a time. Now it was on the rise at a rapid pace. If only they could slow its progression.

Learning the art of elemental magicks was both thrilling and exhausting. The physical training lessons she did with Caden have paid off, at least. It made combining the two that much easier. It also seemed to impress Corrina. Which was something new for her. Impressing anyone with her abilities made her feel, well, she wasn't sure how to describe it. Other than her twin and her son, it had never happened before.

She knew they were training her for a fight or an outright battle of some kind. Hence the condensed versions of stories, and verbal lessons. With the focus being on how to apply her gifts. She felt frustrated because she instinctively did what came naturally instead of following instructions to work with a specific element. Not thinking beyond that to a certain pathway or spell, so to speak. Therefore, each result of the same task had a similar but different approach to the outcome.

Her head was feeling like it was a maze. Each new lesson and skill added a new link to her head. Without a thread or a crumb trail to lead her back, she felt the maze-like feeling in her head would trap her. Maybe this afternoon's lesson on the once again abridged version of spell formation, and casting would help. It was like she was missing something. Just couldn't quite put her finger on what that something was.

Today was her last training day for this week. After her spells and casting lessons, she would get some one on one time with Kieran. She was looking forward to that. Last night she was so tired afterwards that she ate her evening meal and then fell asleep as soon as her head hit the pillow. Tonight she wanted a little more than sleep, though. Tomorrow was preparation day for the festival. Everyone in the village took part. It seemed it was just as big and as important as the festival itself. She was shadowing Corrina most of the day. As woman and men had different tasks that they performed to get ready. She was excited about learning their ways but also nervous about not being near Kieran.

Within the great hall; they set up a mini course of battlements for her. She was to go through using one elemental magick at a time first, to then, in subsequent rounds, combine them. It felt kind of mundane at first, and she questioned why. Until she had to run through the course facing opponents. Some contained gifts, while others did not. Having the familiarity helped her to think on the fly for defense and offense.

After only learning she had these gifts a little over a week ago, she was proud of herself for what she had accomplished thus far. She was nowhere near as skilled as most of the God race to which she belonged. She could at least defend herself and be of some help when the time arose. At least she had a vague idea of what she was facing with Neera's followers. With the prophecy, however, that was anyone's guess. Important but the when, what, and where, were unknown still.

Her body ached from the last two days. At least today would end with a less physical lesson. Though she suspected it would still be just as taxing. Having to learn yet another new skill set. One she was having trouble wrapping her mind around. Even her gifts gave her a headache trying to fathom the how's and the why's. For the first time, however, she felt like she belonged, and was a valuable member of the clan. Every person she encountered had radiated warmth and open arms. Taking great interest in her as she did them.

The current situation resulted in limited contact with clan members. Only those approved of by Ravens Night members could interact with her. For their safety, and hers. Her first meeting was with a woman who had an amazing talent for cooking. Having prepared all their meals for the last few days. The food was so delectable that Harlow couldn't resist inviting her to join them, eager to learn and ask questions while they savored each bite. This had shocked her and was an honor, why she didn't know but didn't care. Even with the odd looks coming from the others.

Then there were the men and women she had been training with in the last two days. They were all skilled, gifts or not. Corrina kept getting frustrated with her because she would stop to talk and ask questions after each round. They had great insight and suggestions on how she could improve, and seemed grateful for her interest. Taking all their advice and putting it into action improved her confidence, and for the first time, she didn't care what anyone thought of her. She was just happy being herself.

After freshening up, she went in search of Corrina. She found it amazing how they could transform the great hall. It was like a massive indoor arena and could house any type of event needed. Of course, when they used magicks to construct it, she could only guess at the number of functions it housed. Still, this place had allowed for security, housing, meeting place, and training all at once. Absolutely amazing to her. The architecture alone was ornate and beautiful for something so utilitarian. People mostly used it for everyday affairs, she heard, rather than for grand occasions.

So the detailed carving work, and massive decorations spanning the rafters, and the walls were stunning. She would like some time just to look at and study each one. Only she suspected it would take years to do so. It had become a haven for her. One she could relax in and blossom. It felt strange sometimes, to feel so content while not having her family with her. Somehow in the back of her mind, there was the tiniest inkling it was going to be ok.

Finding Corrina sitting at the far end of the current training area, she made her way there. With a simple.

"Hello,"

She sat in the only other chair. Sitting back in the chair, she crossed her hands in her lap. Giving all her focus to her teacher. She felt this was going to be the most challenging for her. Her instincts proved to right. Struggling with basic spells, they worked right through the evening meal, with Kieran and Aidan coming to investigate afterward.

It took the three of them working with her late into the night before her aha moment occurred. It was then a domino effect, and everything seemed to connect. Like one big spider web within her head. No longer the chaotic ever growing and changing maze. She could do this, maybe not as well as others, but in her way.

That had her smiling, as they all agreed to call it quits for the night. She and Kieran didn't get their night alone like they had planned. But when had any of their or her plans ever worked out? So far, her record kinda sucked on that one. She felt a sense of pride and satisfaction for all that she had achieved so far. Both Kieran and Aidan wore expressions of genuine delight. Corrina had been the only one to comment on how impressed she was with how much they could cover, and in such a short amount of time, too.

Everyone saying their goodnights, she couldn't wait to crawl into bed. Every muscle in her body ached from the exhaustion. She needed some sleep. Cuddling up next to Kieran, she murmured her pleasure as he wrapped her in his arms. Her last thought was maybe they could have their one on one time after the festival. Tomorrow was the preparation, and the next day was festival day. Sleep welcomed her with open arms.

Each day of Harlow's training, he and Aidan had snuck in to watch her progress on multiple occasions. Every time, she found herself impressed with what she could do. The fact she will learn not just from Corrina but those she was mock batting with spoke about her integrity. After every round, she'd go over and talk to her opponent, asking questions, and genuinely listening to their advice. Her actions not only impressed him but the others as well. The word was spreading throughout the clan.

Further cementing his growing belief in one's True Mate. The desire for a partner who encompassed all things good consumed him - someone who could effortlessly charm others, possessed remarkable strength, and had an unyielding resolve. Harlow was displaying everything required within such a position. Although he suspected most of this was new to her and out of her comfort zone. At least it was in the past, or was it the future? Well, her past anyway. This situation was troubling to think about in too many ways. Some of it was best left alone.

When they weren't sneaking into the great hall to see lessons, they were attending meetings. Finalizing the ceremony was his top prior-ity. Well, that, and getting his dwelling cleaned up, and increasing the protection spells. He felt it was important they spend the night there after the festival, even if everyone would spend it in the clearing. As was the custom and tradition. As he was in charge, he could. What were Cormac's words? Oh yes, he could tweak a few things. That man spoke in the oddest ways sometimes.

He and Aidan, along with the help of other Ravens members, were selecting women who would help Harlow prepare for the ceremony. They handpicked women for Harlow's preparation for the ceremony. These women, who were loyal to the clan, knew which topics of discussion they could share with her throughout the day. Also, they ensured that each woman received every ounce of protection and blessing. Be it from spells, herbs, gems, and clothing. They went as far as providing extra protection to their families. They took nothing for granted. His people were important.

The side benefit was knowing the women hoped, if this went well, that Harlow would choose them as her permanent attendants. One he knew for sure would be. She was the latest member of Ravens Night and a talented magickal being.

Hayley bore the physical markings of an attack with other magicks. She, too, had no memory of her attack, much like Harlow. Kieran suspected her mind was protecting her until such a time she could deal with it. There were bits and pieces of her life before she could vividly remember. Whereas others have remained buried deep within and inaccessible.

Having found her close to their village borders, they had rushed to her aid. Welcoming her into their clan when she had nowhere else to turn. Quickly, she became a valued and active member. With her growth and development, they had sought her out for membership. Surprised when she cried as she accepted. She expressed her feelings of honor and shock that they would choose her. Kieran had just laughed and shook his head.

She was the one person he thought of as a little sister. One he also protected at all costs. Much to her annoyance. He had yet to even talk to Harlow about her. Hayley was already giving him trouble about it. But old habits die hard. It was normal practice, after all, to keep quiet about her. For her perfection. With her unable to recall her attack, they didn't know who or what to watch out for. So the villagers knew her well, but never talked about her. Well, not by name anyway. Only within the last couple of decades had people been referring to her as his little sister. Still, he was sticking with his plan to tell his Mate about her after the ceremony and festival.

He planned to introduce Harlow to the women in the morning. Since she would spend her next few days with them. They would decorate and preparing together. They would concentrate on getting everything ready they can do here within the great hall. Since it was the safest place for them. With the added spells and guards. Having Corrina among them also helped ease some of his worries. He had promised her he would be with her always. With adding the ceremony, there were things they each needed to do. Having already experimented with the arrangement of some ceremony rituals, he felt it best to keep others the same.

When he and Aidan returned, they found the table empty, which surprised them. They had hoped to share the evening meal. Odd, had they already eaten? They sat and ate, figuring they would be along, anyway. The plan was for them to all eat together while also discussing the day and any necessary changes to the plan. It was a time of day he looked forward to. He suspected so did Aidan. He had no blood relatives left, just like Kieran. This was a time of day that reminded him of past joys, albeit a little different. This meal was just to be the two of them.

When they finished, they were in a bit of a sour mood. They went in search of Corrina and Harlow. First checking their rooms, assuming they had finished early, and were just tired. Not finding them there, they went in search of the other side of the hall and found them deeply entrenched in a lesson. Both women looked frustrated, boarding on grumpy. Taking a chance to glance at his friend, he nudged his head in their direction while mouthing 'Should we', raising a brow in question. Aidan nodded in quick reply.

Offering their help, the three of them guided Harlow through her spell casting lesson. The poor thing was having quite the challenge. Between her pronunciation and timing, there seemed to be something missing for her. The harder she tried to focus, the worse she got.

Deciding to take a step back, he talked to her and ask her questions about her lesson. During the chat, he saw the spark of light brighten in her eyes. Something had triggered for her. So they started again, and this time things ran rather smoothly.

Seeing as both women looked like they were about to fall asleep where they sat. They encouraged them to call it quits for the night. There was always time after the festival to learn more, and to train.

CHAPTER 20

awning, Harlow raised her hand to cover it. She desperately tried to suppress the urge to be impolite to the women she was with today. After the last two days, well, to be honest, more like the last few weeks, she felt drained. Her body felt like it could use another week of rest. But no such luck for her. Today she had got up bright and early with Kieran to share a morning meal. Since she wouldn't be seeing him tomorrow at the festival. He surprised her this morning while they ate by telling her. Why hadn't he mentioned it before then? She had just chalked it up to his being a man and forgot to.

When they finished; they got ready for the day. Her heart overflowed with gratitude as she received not just one, but two handmade outfits from a kind woman in the village. They were both so beautiful. Similar to her usual clothes, she put on the outfit in layers. A woman in the village handcrafted the outfits for her, using a fabric that was soft and lightweight. As she put on each layer, it fit her perfectly. It resembled clothing she had seen others wear, but she fashioned it more similar to her clothing. Today's outfit was stylish and comfortable, at least. She only had a quick peek at tomorrow's outfit.

When she was ready to go, she turned around, only to see Kieran had been staring at her. His gaze traveled the length of her, making her blush nice and bright. Which only seemed to arouse him more. Before she could blink, he was on her. Holding close and consuming her mouth in the most devastating kiss. Moaning, she had kissed him back like a starving woman. He had more control than she did, pulling back to whisper in her ear.

"If only we had more time, little one."

Then he licked and nibbled her lobe. Sending shivers to her core. That man could light her up like a, oh what had they called it ...... oh yes, a firework display.

Taking her hand in his, he led her to the other side of the hall. There, he introduced her to a group of women. She would be with their group for the preparations today and tomorrow before the festival began. It all seemed a little confusing to her. As nice as these women were, she felt out of place. Which seemed strange to her after her experiences in the few days. Not once had any of the clan members made her feel out of place. She felt that this treatment resembled how people treated her at home.

The only ones to include her in conversations were Corrina, and a woman named Hayley. She liked her. A very spunky and witty young woman. Perhaps reserved, though. Harlow got the feeling that this woman had seen more in her life than all these others combined. Even reminding her a little of herself.

Could this be why she perhaps felt out of place, feeling on a level par with Corrina and Hayley? The rest of the women seemed to only want her opinion on things. Once she shared it, they got right back to the task. Taking over and leaving nothing for her to do. At first, she thought they were just taking pity on her cause she didn't know what to do. Now, though, she got the impression they believed they needed to do it all. So strange.

At least she could have a pleasant conversation with the other two women. They were happy to talk about her training and her troubles with casting spells. She also explained what it felt like in her head. How it was once like a maze chock full of knowledge, only for another section to be added on again and again. Confusing her even more. After last night, however, a light seemed to shine, and every-thing morphed into a massive spider web. All connected but each separate, too. Easy for her to navigate with confidence and speed.

Hayley said she had shared a similar experience herself. Frowning and becoming quiet.

"It's like giving birth to yourself. The one hiding deep within. I understand."

Corrina reached out, placing a hand on her shoulder, giving her a gentle squeeze. Then turning toward her to whisper.

"Hayley here has a situation similar to yours. She experienced an attack before she lived here. She lost her memory of the attack itself, and bits and pieces of her life before."

Before Corrina could finish, Harlow was up and out of her seat, taking Hayley into a deep, motherly hug. When she too whispered.

"Oh my dear, I'm so sorry. I am here for you anytime you need."

Before she could pull back, Hayley wrapped her arms around her, hugging her in return. If she had to guess, this woman didn't allow just anyone to be close to her. It likely had been eons since she let anyone hug her so. It brought back the sorrowful memory of her embrace with Rowan during his time of pain. Sometimes even scared. Pulling back, she tucked a few stray stands behind Hayley's ear. Looking her straight in the eye with her motherly glare.

"I mean it now. Anytime. Ok?"

Not looking away till she got her answer. A gentle nod accompanied a whisper..

"Ok"

Looking over at Cora, who was now standing too. She looked amazed, almost stunned at their encounter. Which just confirmed some of her inner suspicions. Taking Hayley's hand, she glanced over to the other ladies working away.

"What do you say we three go over to the kitchen and prepare a snack for everyone here?"

While both women looked confused, they agreed.

After they were in the kitchen a little while, she understood their confused looks. Neither woman could cook or prepare anything. She found it funny to ask how that was possible. Both had replied together.

"We just go to the kitchens like everyone else."

Well, that explained it, she guessed. Rolling up her sleeves. They were way too pretty to be getting dirty.

"Well, then I guess this lesson I will be the teacher. Let's each take inventory of what we have here, and we'll go from there, ok?"

Both nodding their heads, they scurried about the room taking stock. Seeing what they had, she presented a couple of options for what they could make. Once they decided, she guided them step by step through preparation, manufacturing, and cleaning up. Then they all took their delights out to share with everyone.

Once again, people looked at them with surprise. It seemed they hadn't even noticed they had left, and that they had prepared the food. Harlow was quick to defend her new friends and also encouraged the ladies to relax and enjoy. They had been working hard on other tasks, so they had taken this one. After all, that was what teamwork was for.

With that, everyone seemed to relax and have a good afternoon. Lots of talking, and sharing of family stories, and tales. All of which Harlow enjoyed very much. Who knew people could be so funny in their everyday lives? She found out she wasn't the only one to struggle with learning about magick and all its gifts and spells. The more they talked, the more she was feeling like she belonged. Her favorite stories were the ones shared about the ancient past. The ones no one knew if they were true or just fairy tales told to teach a lesson.

All too soon, the day ended. Everyone would spend the night here in the hall. They had set up cots in the area they had used during the day, to one side for the women. She and Corrina would be in the makeshift rooms they stayed in before. Hayley would take the one set up for Aidan. Seemed weird to her. Why couldn't the women just go home to their families and sleep? Forgetting her curiosities, she was ready for bed in no time. Crawling in, she wished Kieran was here beside her. She felt safer with him near. Hopeful she would sleep a dreamless sleep, snuggling deep, she closed her eyes and drifted off in no time.

Kieran and Aidan, along with several other Ravens members, were in the clearing managing the set up for the ceremony. He felt it had to be just so. Everything needs to be perfect for his Mate. Why, that was, he wasn't sure. It wasn't like she even knew what was going to be happening. Again, he made a decision. He just feared the outcome if he revealed the truth to her. Time was valuable in this. It would garner her more protection. Once fully connected, they would grow to know each other, and the connection would be that much stronger. With only fables left to describe the mating bond, they will be the first couple to rediscover all the ins and outs.

That was another thing he hadn't discussed with her either. She was his Mate, and he was hers. He knew she felt it, at least on some level. She trusted him from the moment they met. It was like an instant tether bonding between them. Their connection grew stronger every day. So too did her confidence. Something he suspected was lacking for her before.

Still, Hayley and Corrina had mentioned their displeasure this morning at him keeping Harlow in the dark. He had wanted to meet with them in private, but that hadn't happened. They only had a few moments while the other women introduced themselves to Harlow. He reminded them even though they were to be friendly, and a part of the preparations. They were guarding his woman. Their reply was to vent their opinions, and well, they knew their jobs. Especially Corrina, who was also a founding member. Both had stormed away in a huff.

His only thought was someday he hoped they would be in his position, and then they would understand. When that day came, he would snicker and laugh, and remind them of their responses. Not to mention their attitudes. As quickly as he could, he hugged Harlow, kissing her on the top of the head. Wishing her a pleasant time, he left. If he kissed her properly in front of all the women, he still would've likely tossed her over his shoulder, taking her bed. Where they could enjoy each other naked.

Shaking off his thoughts, he returned to the tasks at hand. They were constructing the platform for the ceremony. With the entire clan likely to be in attendance, he thought it best to have one. This way, they all could see. With the Priestess standing on the highest level in the center, it gave them room to build enough behind for her personal guard to stand there with her. Whereas Harlow and himself would stand in front of the Priestess, on a level higher than the guards behind. At each of the four corners, pillars stood tall, ready to be draped with a multitude of blooming flowers and vines.

This morning, they altered the plans to include a canopy over the platform. Some clansmen were already busy at work weaving together reeds. In which to create a base for blossoms to rest on top, while others could hang beneath. The effect of which would look like they were entering a floral built structure. He liked the idea the more he thought about it. Plus, the fresh blooms smelled amazing. With all the ideas flowing, it kept everyone involved, and being a part of their day. Making it even more special.

With so many people running about and executing all the plans. Even with all the extra add ons, they managed to finish things in no time at all. With an abundance of flowers, vines, and ribbons left, they erected several extra standing poles. With a criss-crossing of flowers, vines, and ribbons, they adorned each pole, then joined them together using ropes of vines dripping with blossoms from the tops. The effect was stunning. Every member of the clan went above and beyond. The ceremony and festival tomorrow would be the most beautiful one to date.

With a lightness in his step, he left the clearing and headed toward his dwelling. He completed all the basic repairs and added extra protection spells. They wouldn't need much for the next little while. It was just very important to him they spend their first night here. His heart swelled with appreciation as he beheld the stunning hand-carved bed in the room. The headboard displayed an amazing work of art, with a combination of triquetra and a crescent moon carved into it, beneath a raven with its wing splayed. It was so intricate he had to run his fingers along the carved wood.

Pulling himself away, he set about getting the place ready for them tomorrow night. With his day all planned out tomorrow, now was the only time. Even this morning, he wasn't sure if this place would be ready. Now he suspected he knew why. Whoever carved and made that bed must have worked tirelessly on it. Rushing to finish in just a few days, such talent.

This year, they truly received an abundance of blooms. There was more than enough for the clearing, and even some left over for his dwelling. Someone had even started by hanging them all around, then used them to create a pathway to the magnificent bed.

With not much else to do, he prepared for bed. Might as well get a good night's sleep. They wouldn't be sleeping tomorrow night. At least he planned on being busy, very busy. He and his Mate would devote all their attention to each other, and ignoring the outside world. Smiling to himself, he fell asleep thinking about all the things he wanted to show, and do to Harlow.

CHAPTER 21

*H*arlow woke the next morning groggy, and stiff. Even her vision was a little blurry. Rubbing her eyes, she had sat up, taking stock of how she felt. Blinking a few times, she noticed she was still in the position she went to sleep in. Not moving through the night would explain the stiffness. She must have been dead to the world, so deep in sleep. Yawning, she stretched her arms above her head. Before tilting her head side to side to work out the kinks. It had been ages since she had a night's sleep like that.

Well, enough with the self analysis, she got up and dressed. Today was the festival, and she needed to be ready. Apparently, they had something special planned for her since it was her first time celebrating. No one would tell her what it was, only that it would take all day. It was driving her crazy, trying to figure it out when not one person would reveal any clues. She didn't know whether or not to be worried.

Corrina had insisted it was nothing to be worried about, and that she would enjoy it. Whatever it was? At least she would enjoy right along with her, so that gave her some comfort. Yesterday she also found out Hayley would join them. Not sure why again, but that too made her happy. Liking her new friend, and discovering her old friend in a new way, filled something within her.

Her situation was complex, yes. Sometimes, though, it wasn't. Life was continuing on here with bumps and turns. It had been a challenge to figure out the whys, and hows of how she came to be here. The biggest challenge is that no one was around from the time of the arches' creation. With no folklore or tales verbal or written left, it was a guess at how it operated. With so many of the pieces missing in the puzzle she had been trying to solve, they might never know.

She secretly however hoped that Caden and Rowan would come through as well. She had left behind the book along with clues. Her son could likely read that book better than she did and could get them both here. Unless Caden had come through already. He was present when she had gone into the vortex of the arch. But there have been no sightings of others like her.

Plus, her brother wasn't alone when she went through either, so it was likely if Caden had come through, so would the others. Word would have spread like wildfire if that were the case. It had her wondering how many people had seen her before Kieran. Why leave there? I mean, word had spread about her fast enough.

Arg, she was doing it again. Shaking her head, she focused on the now. Morning meal, that's what she needed. Leaving her makeshift room, she went to the kitchenette in search of something to eat. Her tummy was rumbling on the way. Laughing to herself, she covered it with her hand, assuring herself she would eat. Rounding the corner, she stopped still in the doorway. The little room was full of women scurrying about, all talking at the same time. How they kept up with the conversation baffled her. It was quite the talent. Multiple languages were her thing, not this speedy talk. Her eyes darted from woman to woman to track the conversation.

When one of them noticed her standing there like a statue, she rushed over. Talking so fast, it was a challenge to answer her questions. Finally, she answered with.

"Anything prepared sounds wonderful, thank you."

They urged her to take a seat in a chair at the table in the room's corner. Someone placed a plate of food in front of her, along with a steaming brew. Without questioning, she murmured her thanks and dug in. This seemed to please all of them, her hungrily inhaling her food. Smiles spread across all of their faces while their postures relaxed. Who knew watching a woman eat could make them so happy? Before taking another bite, she mentioned it.

"This is good. Thank you."

Turning back to her plate, she finished eating. About to pick up her plate to clean it, it disappeared from in front of her. Looking up, she saw the woman who had snatched it.

"Thank you, but I don't mind cleaning up after myself. I mean, you are the ones who prepared it. The least I can do is clean up."

Getting up from her seat, she intended to do just that. However, the women wouldn't have it. It was time to head towards the first surprise. She raised her brows in question. There was more than one surprise. Her internal uh oh was giving her tummy butterflies. One surprise, maybe she could handle, but many. Nope, that was hard for her. In her history, others had made surprises at her expense for their amusement. So hesitantly, she followed the others. It was then she realized she had yet to see Corrina and Hayley. It was on the tip of her tongue to ask when she saw them, standing and talking together by the door. Corrina's grin spread across her face at seeing her.

As she laughed, she said.

"Well, good morning there, sleepy head. Or should we say good afternoon?"

Shocked, she had slept all morning and through the night. Really? With a hand to her chest.

"Wow, it's afternoon already? I've never done that before. I'm so sorry if I've made anyone late."

Everyone shushed her for her nonsense. She must have needed it. Trying once again, she asked.

"So where are we off to?"

This time it was Hayley who laughed.

"Nice try. You will see when we get there. So let's go."

As she maneuvered her arm to herd us all along.

"Let's go."

Leaving the hall, they stepped out into a beautiful sunny day. It had been a while since she had been out in the sun. Considering the world she had left, that was normal. No sun, only shades of gray, and dark gray. Where here, however, everyone had a lovely glow, one she wanted to. It felt so nice when the rays kissed her skin. Taking a minute, she stretched her arms out, tilting her face up to the sky. Closing her eyes, she spun in a slow circle, just taking it all in. Inhaling deep she opened her eyes, so beautiful. Smiling to herself, and relaxing her arms, she looked around. Everyone was staring at her. Confused by their stares, she stated. With a shrug of her shoulder.

"It's just so beautiful. It deserves to be appreciated."

She didn't want to give away too much information. Only Ravens Night members were aware she had come through the portal from the future. Even then, they weren't aware of what her world comprised. Or why she would feel so fascinated with the sun, and its warming hug each time she stepped out into it. It seemed necessary to her to guard such revealing information. It would be easier if she didn't continue to do strange things or blurt things out. Her behavior seemed a little foreign to her, while also natural at the same time. Like she could finally be herself.

At least her comment went over well, maybe a little too well, for the ladies all started buzzing. How more like Harlow they could be, the better everything else would be. She felt this was getting weird. Looking at her friends, she saw the same odd expressions displayed on their faces as she felt. What was going on here? It was like multiple agendas. Just what they might be, she hadn't a clue.

For the rest of the day, she would just go along with the show. Doing what needed to be done. The less crazy she could stir up, the better. All she wanted was to spend tonight with Kieran at her first ever festival. Just thinking about it made her excited. So whatever she had to do to get to that point, she would do it. When Corrina gave the nod, they all followed her on their way to the first of the day's surprises.

If she had known before what all her surprises would be, she would have adamantly refused. First was a bathing ritual, they performed all together. Some ladies had even wanted to wash her. Like she couldn't do that herself. They seemed hurt when she refused. Only accepting when she further stated only Kieran could touch her like that other than herself. How odd, she had thought. It sent an eerie shiver down her spine.

The next surprise happened before she could even form a complaint. Next to the river where they were bathing, they had set up cots running alongside it. When she was told to just go and lie down, she did. The breeze felt wonderful on her skin. But when four sets of oiled up hands began massaging her limbs, she screamed in surprise. Not wanting to offend again, she snapped her lips shut. Praying they hurry and finish. Noticing then that Hayley and Corrina were receiving the same treatment. Odd, why were the three of them being singled out?

When they finished, they gave her a beautiful white flowing robe to wear. It felt indecent to be walking around outside naked beneath a gauze robe. Then again, she had just been laying naked on a cot for a massage. So this was an improvement. She did like it, though. The fresh air and sun felt amazing. Now she was to sit in a chair that was almost laying flat. Its back only held a slight angle.

Sitting in the chair, she closed her eyes in comfort. This was nice, feeling so relaxed and calm. Who knew she would enjoy a massage? Even when given by four strange women. Feeling a gentle tugging on her hair. Opening her eyes, there were two women, one on each side of her, working through her hair. About to protest, they shushed her, telling her to relax. Well, if they insisted, she would. After the massage, her body felt like a rag doll, and the more they played with her hair, the sleepier she got. Deciding it couldn't hurt, she closed her eyes for a quick nap.

She woke a short time later, feeling refreshed and energized. It was amazing what pampering and relaxation could do for a person. Still, it felt a little odd to have people waiting on her. She just wished she knew why they were so insistent on doing so. At least she wasn't alone. Corrina and Hayley had had the same treatment from the women. It would seem they also took turns treating themselves after as well.

After everyone finished, they all headed back to the great hall. It was now time to dress for the festival. Feelings of excitement rushed through her on the way. Everyone seemed in high spirits and couldn't wait for the party to start. She understood the appeal and excitement that the village had displayed a week earlier. It was no wonder if this was what they had in store for them to look forward to.

They were making their way through the village when the women leading the charge began shouting in a tizzy and gathering around her. Curious about the behavior, she tried looking around to see what had caused it. Only she was much shorter than them, and even when she tried to jump up to see it was no use. She heard booming laughter.

"It's ok Red, it's just me. I have a message for Corrina, OK? You ladies carry on."

As one gigantic mass, they hustled her into the great hall. Feeling weirded out by their reaction, she could breathe a sigh of relief upon entering the grand space. As each woman then branched off in a different direction, Harlow just stood there. Only Hayley stayed by her side. Turning to her, she said.

"That was strange, right?"

Nervously, she pondered whether her question would come across as impolite. All she got in return was a head shake.

When they revealed the final touches to her outfit, Harlow was so stunned she needed to sit. It was beautiful, taking her breath away. Whoever had made did some exquisite work. The fabric was like the robe she had worn earlier in the day. Only this time displaying color hues green, trimmed in gold. Someone had created an outfit with many layers of flowing, triangular pieces of fabric.

She wore a very simple crafted two piece undergarment that somehow almost matched her skin tone. On top of that were the many triangular layers, forming a top with flowing sleeves. Her multi layered bottom could look like a skirt if she stood still. Or depending on her stride as she walked, and moved around, would reveal more or less leg.

Spinning in a circle with her arms outstretched, she smiled, feeling like a princess. Her actions caused everyone to giggle. She didn't care, though; she felt and looked amazing. Amid her happy display, they stopped her. It was time to work on her crazy mass of curly hair. It took three of them to wrangle it in, creating an intricate creation. Incorporating her crazy kinky curls with soft braids interwoven with ribbon and blossoms. They worked with what her hair wanted to do. Some curls framed her face as the rest formed the stunning creation down her back. She couldn't help but smile from ear to ear.

Before long, everyone was ready to go and looking stunning. Again, they left the hall en masse to the clearing where the festival was being held. As soon as they stepped outside, they could hear the music and singing, lifting all their spirits that much higher. Even Corrina and Hayley, who had been silent today, were smiling and laughing along with everyone.

You could feel the vibrations of the group's excitement as they traveled along the footpath. As they moved through the forest, most of the women joined in on the songs. Singing to their heart's content loud and proud. It was quite beautiful. Coming upon the clearing, Harlow thought this night was going to be special.

Kieran woke with the sun. Stretching his limbs, he rotated his head from side to side. Hoping today will go well for Harlow and the women in her company. With the need to hurry and get going if he wanted to complete his agenda today, he jumped up to dress. Why he packed so much into one day, he didn't know. Old habits of always trying to impress his dad, while also trying to do everything at once. Perhaps he should get some help today, though. Liking that idea, he began getting dressed. As he didn't have a functioning kitchenette yet, he was heading over to Aidan's for his morning meal.

When he arrived; he discovered that there were many Ravens Night members there. As soon as he entered, they rushed him to sit and began his meal. They were all sharing stories of old times or new ones they heard around the village. Asking questions about what it was like to discover his True Mate for the first time. Also, were the rumors true about the connection that formed and only grew stronger?

Most questions he could answer, others he couldn't or wouldn't. Some things were just meant to be between the two of them. He would not share Harlow with anyone, not even personal information. His animal like reaction to some of the more personal questions became answers themselves. Surprisingly, everyone gathered. Having enough, all he would say was.

"When your time comes. You will truly understand."

It was then they all realized they had wasted most of the day away talking and eating. Many people had kept arriving with food from the main kitchens for them to try. Confirming their approval for the festival, insisting it had to be perfect. Kieran only cared what one person thought, and that was Harlow. He knew he was brewing a kettle of fish without revealing everything to her. It was just timing that had not been on their side, nor the situation with Neera's followers. Her safety came first.

At least with her now knowing of Neera and her followers. There was a better chance of her understanding his position. It was his job, and right to protect his Mate, she would always come first. She was his just as much as he belonged to her. Even now he could feel inklings of happiness from her. He could only imagine what it would be like after tonight, and the ceremony, when their mating bond was complete. Smiling to himself, he also couldn't wait till he had her alone in their dwelling for the night.

As much as he'd like to follow all the traditions. He wasn't about to expose her to all the crowd gathered at the festival. Even if it meant they both could receive a much stronger connection or even greater power. He had enough as it was and didn't need anymore. That was another thing he needed to discuss with her after he figured it out for himself first. He hadn't even touched the edge of all the knowledge and experiences he now processed. Even his mate possessed a great power amount, herself. More so than he'd seen in anyone apart from himself and Cormac.

Standing to stretch his stiff limbs, he brought up all his tasks that needed doing today. Surprised at how quickly everyone jumped in, taking a task for themselves to complete. He found himself with the only task he could do himself, which was getting ready. As everyone left, he was thankful for his clan. They all worked together as a familiar unit. Striving for the best of everyone. As he went towards the river to bathe, Aidan went to tend to the only task he specified to a certain person. He was to gather all of Harlow's clothes and belongings from their makeshift room within the great hall, then take them back to their dwelling.

Her things belonged in their home. He wanted her to have all she wanted and needed. Even if they were going to spend their first few hours naked within their dwelling. She would require her clothes, to leave it, of course, eventually. The more he thought about the more he liked the idea of her just being naked all the time. She was stunning. Even with the signs of motherhood displayed proudly on her body. It made her even more beautiful. To create and carry life is the truest gift. He realized she knew he had seen the evidence. Until she was ready to talk, he would wait. The thought of how this must be for her was beyond his imagination. To be here without her son.

He only hoped that her son was as gifted and smart as his mother. Finding all the clues she had found to bring her here and acting on them. He felt a surge of joy, realizing that both of them would find satisfaction in that result. He knew what it was like to miss a mother. His having died, he had no hope of a reunion. Whereas Harlow might have one. He'd been praying to the mother goddess for such a thing. Deep down, he knew that the mother goddess would grant his wish. For she saw and knew all. She granted it when and how she saw fit.

At the river, he stripped, leaving his clothes on the riverbank. Wadding into the refreshing water, he hoped his woman was enjoying her day as much as he was. Even if he wished, he could have spent it with her. Dunking himself beneath the moving waters, he rose, shaking the excess water from his hair. It was a tradition to come to this river and bathe right before the festival. Laying back to float along, he strongly believed she deserved to be pampered. It being her first time, he had arranged for her group of women to access the river first. No need for his mate to worry about being in the river with the rest of the clan. Figuring a smaller audience the better. He just forgot to consider her curious nature and desire for answers.

She might not understand the women's natural behaviors and actions. Having still not told her he is the chieftain of the clan, and the village, and her True Mate. Therefore, they will treat her with the highest regard for her station. He just wished for her to be herself, with no worries or airs. Today was a special day for them and the clan.

That's how their world operated, and failing to give the women in her company the chance to pamper her would offend them.

Rising from the water, he pushed through the remaining lapping waters to the bank. Gabbing his clothes, he dressed. If he knew his woman like he thought he did, there was a very good chance of her figuring it out. It was just a matter of which part she would figure out, and when. He remembered her referencing his father as a leader, and their relation. But had that information sunk in he wondered? Perhaps not. She hadn't brought it up again, and neither had he. He was filling the kettle, and it was about to boil over.

Instead of worrying, he jogged his way back to Aidan's. The two of them were to finish getting ready there before the ceremony began. At least his part would start before Harlow would arrive. She was to walk amongst the people on her way to him. Corrina and Hayley were her guards and honor maidens. There for her in times of need, and a sign to the priestess she came with a wealth of her own. He was about to have Aidan and Cormac at his back. Only with him not returning after his most recent disappearance, he would have to choose another. Still, he was hoping he wouldn't have to, and he would show up at the last minute. A talent he had a very great knack for.

Inside Aidan's home, the two of them readied for the evening. Their clothing was refreshingly unpretentious. Not requiring many hands to help dress, they could take care of everything themselves. Were as Harlow's clothing for the evening, and like all the other women, would require help to get into. When they moved about, they appreciated all the work. Shimmering, and shining in the fading light of the sun or the flames of fire. Revealing bits and pieces of skin here or there. They all looked like the radiant goddesses they all were. For there was a piece of her in each, and every one of us.

All too soon, he was standing up on the platform. The ceremony began with the music of people singing with either their voices, feet, or drums. Many fires were already lit with offerings of herbs and spices for the celebration of the season. Hearing the o's, and ah's from within the crowd, he knew Harlow and her women had entered the clearing. Smiling, he knew they would soon form an eternal bond.

CHAPTER 22

The Master is pleased with me. Very pleased, I believe, for my plan has worked. Even if the first one failed. All because that demanding uppity woman had to be involved. Serves her right, being snatched, and sentenced along with her better than you are, mother. He wouldn't have to worry about their meddling anymore. Good riddance, he thought. They even fell for his acted persona. Stupid and thick, selfish women. Who needed them? They were a means to an end, and that was all. Even the Master had said so.

Slipping away had been so easy. The guards were so busy trying to deal with both women; they had never noticed he had gotten away. Even with the increased guards around the village afterward, he had been allowed to come and go as he pleased. Further proving his scrawny stuttering persona worked like a charm. Not a one of them knew he was the one who had cast each one spell needed to gain access. Or had killed the guard standing duty at the door. Not even when he infected the entire village into chaos and hysteria. That was funny to watch, smiling to himself as he remembered to panic. So easy, so easy.

He had tried to make his chieftain see. He didn't need her, he could just use her. Now he would let his Master use her. He listens, and he agrees. Soon all would be right, and the way it should be. He would see to that.

That is why he and Master were sneaking into the village while everyone was in the clearing for the festival. Not a one of them suspected him, nor should they. He had been good, real good. So good, in fact, Master said so. That had made him smile. He understood when Master had to punish him for not getting the girl. He would do better next time, and he had, he really, really had. For they were now standing right where they needed to be, to do what Master wanted to do.

Master again said he had done good. Real good. Smiling.

Master was pleased. Master would get what wanted.

Smiling, he hid them away within a cloak of magicks, until the time was right. Then, and only then, would he reveal them.

Good. So Good.

CHAPTER 23

She was stunning, so much so that she took his breath away. The clothing she wore shimmered and shone in the firelight surrounding them. She moved with a seductive grace only she could possess, revealing just enough skin to make his mouth water. Her skin was aglow, matching the radiant smile across her face that shone in her emerald eyes. A wide smile adorned her face, expressing her sheer happiness at his presence. He liked that, liked it very much. The women had outdone themselves today. For she looked like a Goddess.

That was saying something among their kind. Yes, they were Gods and descended from Gods. However, only a select few among them ever received worship and truly deserved it. They were the ones who cared about their people and would take care of them. His Mate was glowing as one in this moment. Imprinting this image of her was framing it in his mind, to remember her like this always.

Even the magic they had worked on hair was stunning. They had braided some of her curls and pinned others back, creating a stunning cascading effect down her back. With ribbons and blossoms inter-twined within. Her hair shone with a burning flame of a majestic red. Like a gem, his gem, his Mate, his partner, and his lover.

Offering her his hand when she finally stood before him. His blood sang the instant she placed hers in his. Grinning at her, he helped her up the steps of the platform. With their hands still joined, he presented them to the Priestess. Bowing slightly to her, Harlow quickly followed his lead and did the same. With that, the ceremony began in their mother tongue. Another thing he had not mentioned to Harlow. His list was growing at a rapid rate of things he needed to discuss with her. He knew in the end she would forgive and understand. It was just a matter of how much time that would be. He wasn't sure.

After blessing the cord; the Priestess wrapped around their joined hands. That was when Harlow took in a sharp breath and glanced at him. Her face displayed a mirror-mid of emotions. From shock to surprise, love, desire, and hurt. The last one surprised him the most. He had never intended to hurt her. He tried to convey reassurance through his eyes. Squeezing her hand, he moved his eyes back and forth between her and the Priestess, before raising a brow.

She hesitated but blinked slowly, turning again towards the Priestess. It was at this point they needed to repeat the verse. Again he squeezed his Mate's hand, repeating after the Priestess. Harlow did the same, only she tightened her grip on his hand with so much strength it was all he could do to not wince in pain. His woman was strong. As the ceremony prolonged, his woman softened. He could feel the connection they shared strengthening. It was fascinating.

Just then, he felt a warmth in his palm. Looking at their joined hands, he noticed in his peripheral Harlow do the same. Sparks of light started emerging from them as the heat increased. Looking up at the Priestess in question. Seeing her expression, he now understood, more of their childhood fairy tales were true. For he and Harlow were now receiving the universal mark of the blessed True Mates. This wasn't to appear until after the ceremony and mating. Was this why Cormac had suggested he rearrange the order of things? He wished he could look at the permanent marking. But tradition dictated they keep their hands joined till after they circled the crowd. Finally, he heard the Priestess shout.

"So mote it be,"

Together he and Harlow shouted.

"So mote it be,"

With the crowd shouting thereafter. Raising their still joined hands in the air, he maneuvered them so he could grab her around the waist. With their arms still raised, he kissed her, to the continued roar of the crowd. Smiling, he pulled back just enough to rest his forehead against hers.

"Let's enjoy the festival, little one."

Turning them to face the crowd, they stood still as some of them came forward, each carrying a wooden box. On the last step, each held their box high, when Corrina and Aidan appeared from behind them. Opening each box revealed massive gold torques. Taking them, they raised them above their heads for all to see, and then placed them around his and Harlow's necks. Next, they removed the delicate crowns of three interwoven ropes of metal, placing them on each of their heads. Finally, the three brought forward the tapestry and placed it across their shoulders. His honor, Harlow's honor, and the clan's honor. With that, Aidan and Corrina, along with the chosen representative, shouted in unison.

"We give to you."

With that, the clan erupted in hooted cheers and hollered praise.

For the next while they made their way around the clearing, talking, and celebrating with the clan members. Still, with her safety in mind, they were never far away from Aidan, Corrina, and Hayley. As the night wore on, and with food and drink long finished, the celebration flourished. He felt things were going well, all things considered. Still, he was concerned that Cormac never showed. It wasn't like him to miss an important celebration like this. It must be something of great importance to keep him away. He felt a deep sense of gratitude towards Cillian for being willing to stand by his side as his other.

As the energy shifted within the crowd, so did theirs. It was nearing the greatest time. He moved their swaying bodies into the center of the standing stones amongst all the other swaying bodies. Happy to hold his Mate close in his arms.

The shock was still very much present in her mind. Having just married Kieran, he never asked or demanded it. No, he just made it happen. Was the festival even real or just a ruse to achieve his desired plan? A plan he executed because he loved her, wanted her, or just to protect her. Once he had taken her hand, and the Priestess spoke, she knew. She didn't want to believe or hope. Secretly, she wanted to be tied to him. As the cord wrapped around their joined hands, she knew, knew this was real. When she felt the warmth grow in her palm, and the combining sparks, she was confused. Even more so by Kieran's reaction. Was this not to happen? At least the smile of the Priestess warmed through her, calming her.

Her emotions were all over the place. Joy filled her heart, but it quickly transformed into a fiery rage. Followed by hurt, then desire, and then confused again. She wasn't able to hang on to one for long enough to decipher its true meaning. Which confused her even more. After completing the rounds with the crowd, they could eat and drink a little. As if by magick, the tapestry disappeared from around their shoulders. Why did the weight of that bother her? She couldn't put her finger on it? She seemed fine with the torque around her neck and the crown on her head.

She remembered putting the connection together about Kieran's father being the leader. It just never registered that he was now the leader. Therefore, then she would be of importance as well. She knew that was how it had worked from reading all the books in the archive. Putting it into real life was a different matter. It still just didn't seem real. It was too much like all her dreams. Could it be that her dreams were preparing her for such an outcome? Like some kind of sight, similar to Cormac's gift. Someone had mentioned during her ramblings when she first met Corrina that it sounded like she had the sight.

Then there was the matter of the tattoo marking on their palms. She remembered both Corrina and Hayley had drilled it into her earlier in the day, that she was to take Kieran's offering left hand with her left hand. When she questioned why, the only answer she ever received was 'it was a valued important tradition among their people. Since she was also one of them, she needed to follow it.' So here they were now marked on their left palms.

A marking, a brand, a tattoo, not sure what to call it. Even Kieran seemed surprised by it, a little anyway. Why did they have it? What was it for? What did it mean? Again, way too many questions were swirling around in her head. It was becoming difficult to interact with anyone. She needed to shelve all her questions and curiosities for later. This was a celebration, after all, and she should enjoy everything she could. It was too dark anyway. She couldn't get a good look at the marking.

With her decision made, the energy shift within the crowd seeped into her bones. Following the internal sway she felt, she allowed Kieran to move them around the clearing once more. They settled in the middle of the stone circle. She had always felt a great energy surge within this place. This one, in particular, had the greatest pull. She enjoyed the warmth of his body as he drew her close. Sparks of desire were igniting deep within her.

Moaning when Kieran bent down, taking her mouth in a scorching kiss that turned her world upside down. Reaching her arms up, wrapping them around his neck, locking her fingers together. She wanted more, needed more of him. Pulling herself up to her toes, groaning when he pulled back, moving to whisper in her ear.

"Want to finish this? Making it official?"

Nodding her head in agreement, not knowing what it would require of her. She just felt her desire for him grow. The growl he released next to her ear when she swayed her hips with his had her dampening for him. Feeling him stiffen, she held herself up, wrapping her legs around him. Grinning, when she felt him grow harder still. In the blink of an eye, he had released himself and was sliding home in one quick thrust. Before she could throw her head back and gasp in painful pleasure, Kieran had his hand fisted in her hair at her nape. His lips sealed over hers, swallowing it with a searing kiss.

While he continued to consume her mouth with dueling tongs, she took advantage. Moving up and down as best she could. Moaning when he would squeeze her rear. She wanted more, squeezing him tighter with her thighs. He got the hint, and with a firm grip on her cheek, he started lifting her down. It felt so good she was grabbing fists full of his hair.

They were moving to their very own music, taking enjoyment and fulfillment from each other. Before too long, everyone seemed to just disappear, and they were the only ones left. Staring into each other's eyes, it was a rush to the finish. Faster and harder, with cries of plea-sure, moans, and groans. She wanted to make him cum. When his hand crept from the back of her head down to her core, she knew she would go over the minute he touched her. A sound erupted from within her, a plea for what she didn't know.

Kieran did, though. For a brief second, there was a smirk in his eye, as if to dare her. Tightening the grip she had on his hair, she hoisted herself up a little higher to take him deeper. He pinched her nub. They went over together, shouting their release for all to hear. Causing a chorus roar from the crowd.

Harlow could feel the blush coming. It started low, growing and settling in her cheeks, turning them a beautiful scarlet. Still gazing into Kieran's eyes, she saw them filled with absolute love and pride. With a grin stretching from ear to ear. Tilting her head, she asked.

"So, that was official?"

A burst of light swirled around them. This time, her entire body began to warm and turn into a fiery burning. With widening eyes, she tightened her grip on Kieran as the heat grew to a fever pitch. They were coming together once more, with a strong pulse of energy zinging inside and around them. It was over too quick, when in a whirling whoosh it was gone.

They were both shaking, staring into each other's eyes blinking, while trying to catch their breath. Kieran then helped her place her feet on the ground, and steady herself. Taking her head in his hands, he kissed her with the passion she had only ever read about. Wanting so much more, she leaned into him. When he pulled back, rubbing his thumbs on her cheeks. With a loving smile and a twinkle in his eye, Kieran asked.

"Want to disappear for a bit?"

Nodding in answer, he grabbed her hand in his, leading the way through the throngs of celebrating people. As they made their way back to Kieran's dwelling, her euphoria lessened. Once again, her questioning thoughts crept in to take focus. They left the magick that had been freely flowing in and around them behind, and with each step, she felt more of herself returning. Well, more like all of herself. What happened back there was only a portion of her inner self. Taking a glance up at Kieran, she knew he was not aware of her shifting mood or train of thought. She realized he was ready for more of the action they shared in the clearing amongst all the people. How she knew what he wanted so clearly was so strange.

She would need some time to process this all. Determination to get the answers she sought would not hold her back when she had some words with Kieran. Who apparently was now her husband. The further they got from the celebration, the madder she became. It also was getting harder to keep up with Kieran's pace. Out of breath and panting, she called out to him.

"Kieran ...... slow down."

When he turned and looked at her, he then reached for her, swinging her up into his arms. Cradling her to the chest, breaking into a run back home. He had them there in record time. She was still out of breath. With her still cradled in his arms, he murmured some of the ancient words before opening the door. Carrying her over the threshold, he let her down. Sliding down against his front, cradling her head in his large hands, taking possession of her mouth. Growling, he began walking her backwards when she tried murmuring a muffle.

"No"

Against his lips. She maneuvered her hands to his chest, pushing hard. She again said.

"No."

As he pulled back, his face displayed a look of utter confusion.

Dropping her shoulders.

"Kieran, we need to talk."

Reaching for her, she stepped around him, and out of his reach, saying.

"No Kieran. We need to talk now."

Feeling his arms wrap around her from behind. She loved the feel of him, and his scent did something to her. Shaking her head, she maneuvered out of his hold, turning to face him at a distance asking.

"Why lie to me about tonight?"

Kieran was still looking at her like he wanted to devour her. Looking like they did in the stone circle. Why had she snapped out of it, and not him? Staring him down with her hands on her hips, as she waited for an answer. When he didn't answer, she asked again with growing anger.

"You lied to me about tonight. Why?"

After a pause, she tossed some kindling onto the fire, so to speak, when she said.

"Do you not trust me? Or do you only want to control me to protect yourself and your people?"

With an angry snap.

"That's it isn't. Just like those Neera people. Is that it, huh?"

As she spoke, Kieran was shaking off his lust, and getting angry himself. He seemed to grow larger, when he firmly replied.

"No, of course not."

Softening his tone, he said.

"I did not lie to you, little one."

Huffing as she spoke through her teeth.

"Yes, you did, Kieran. That was more than a festival tonight."

Waving her arms towards the way they had come.

"Why couldn't you have just told me the truth?"

Raising a brow in question, she stared at him down. She could feel herself getting more worked up. Her feelings of hurt growing. Why wasn't she enough?

With a deadly grace, he moved to stand in front of her with his challenging stare. Speaking through his clenched teeth.

"I did not lie, Harlow. I just didn't give you all the facts. That's all."

Hissing her reply.

"That still counts as a lie, Kieran. It's lying by omission."

Turning in a huff, she gave him her back. She didn't want to look at him anymore. It hurt.

"You don't trust me. You are just like all the others in my life. Using me for what you want or need from me."

Defeated, her shoulders slumped with her changing mood.

She could hear his hands running fingers through his hair as he said.

"That's not true, Harlow, and you know it."

After a long exhale, he questioned.

"You are mad at me over this?"

Wrapping her arms tightly around herself.

"Just go, Kieran. It's clear you don't trust."

Moving toward the dwindling embers of the fire, she slumped down on the floor beside it.

"Just let me be. You've got me now. I'll do what needs to be done to save the people. But for now, I want my space."

Confused at how this evening had turned out, he shook his head as if trying to clear it. Pivoting on his heel, he left her sitting by the fire. Leaving her to have her space.

After he had left, she sat for a while just staring into flickering embers. Watching the hues change. She should add more logs to the fire. Standing, she grabbed a few, tossing them on as she walked past. Wanting to change, she made her way to the bedroom. Her outfit reminded her of all Kieran had done, and not told her. With the room bathed in darkness, she felt her way around, finding what she wanted. She made quick work of removing layer upon layer of the hand crafted garment. Then dressed in her clothing. Before returning to stoke the fire in the main room.

Placing a few more logs on the fire when she heard movement behind her.

"I said I wanted space."

She said as she turned around. Thinking it was Kieran who had returned. It wasn't him, however. The man standing there was taller than her, so full of hatred she could taste it. It was so bitter and fowl. She could tell he was a none magick. With each step he took towards her, scared her. Snarling at her.

"You are coming with me."

233

Taking a step back, and in as firm a voice as she could.

"I'm not going anywhere with you. Who the hell are you, anyway?"

Again in his snarling, snapping voice.

"Let's go."

As he reached out and gripped her arm. Her fear spread, and she tried in vain to wiggle herself free. She was far too scared to think. This stranger, and his hatred for her that consumed him, was suffocating her. Pulling her in closer to him, he simply stated.

"I don't think so."

Smiling down on her, before placing a foul smelling rag over her nose. In her panic, she was breathing too deeply and rapidly. Whatever was on the rag made her feel weak as her vision blurred. Now she was terrified as he lifted her over his shoulder like a sack, and strolled out of Kieran's dwelling like he owned it. She tried to call out but wasn't sure if she did or not. It was getting harder for her to stay awake. She possessed all these powers and the moves her brother had taught her. Not to mention all her recent training. She hadn't used one of them to protect herself, was her last thought before blackness took over. Apart from hearing a familiar voice whispered.

"Harlow."

CHAPTER 24

*K*ieran stormed from his dwelling in a frustrated huff. How had the night come to this? One minute all was well, hot and heavy between them. Then, in a blink, it was the complete opposite. What had he missed? She was right there with him, wasn't she? Running his fingers through his hair as he trudged his way through the village. He was feeling very edgy, and similar to how he did before entering battle. Why was that?

Was this how Harlow felt as they left the clearing? It would make sense if she did and explained her behavior. Even if what she accused him of was true. There had been circumstances beyond his control at play in all his decisions. Still, she was right, he should have told her. Looking at it from her point of view, it would seem he didn't trust her. That had not been his intention. He had only wanted to protect her. She was his True Mate.

Upset with himself he made his way to the cliff edge of the village. It was a great place to think. Many clansmen came here to ponder and plan. One could see for great distances in the daylight, sometimes in the moonlight too. The scenery was beautiful and inspired deep thought or sometimes relaxation. Tonight, he needed a little of both. He was feeling very emotional, and charged.

Reaching the cliff edge with careful steps, he sat near the ledge, taking a deep breath. Scanning in the vista surrounding him. The moonlight lit up the mountains, hills, forests, and glen with a sprinkling of fairy dust. Shining a unique view on life. Taking another deep inhale, he closed his eyes to just be. Needing to center himself before he could even consider thinking up a plan. Or even a well deserved apology.

Hearing the softest of footsteps, he knew his friend was coming up behind him. Opening his eyes, he turned to look at Aidan.

"Red called you out. Didn't she?"

Without saying a word, he just nodded his head with an uptick of his lip. He knew he deserved it. He had been hoping it would take her a while yet to get to it. No such luck there.

"You should have just been frank with her man. She deserves it."

With acknowledgment, he agreed.

"You were all right. I should have told her everything."

Running his hands through his hair again in frustration.

"It's just she's my Mate, and I need to protect her."

With a supporting hand on his shoulder.

"She'll forgive you eventually, you know. With the mating bond, she'll know and understand. You just need to give her some time."

Discontent with himself, he admitted.

"I know you're right. I'm more upset with myself than with her. It makes me proud that she stood up to me and expressed her desires. Needing time."

Shrugging.

"It just hurt my pride more than anything."

As Aidan opened his mouth to speak, fear suddenly overwhelmed him. Hands flying to his gut, he sucked in a sharp breath, trying to breathe. Through clenched teeth.

"Something is wrong. All I feel is her overwhelming fear."

Without another word, both men jumped up, racing back to Kieran's dwelling. On their way, he could feel her terror increase. He tried to push feelings of reassurance her way, and that help was coming. But he couldn't break through.

"I feel her growing fear, Aiden. I can't get through to calm."

Trying harder, he wasn't sure if he could get through or not. His connection to her gradually faded to silence. It seemed they had arrived too late. Bursting through the door, there was no trace of his Mate anywhere. Only the once dying fire that was now roaring with life. Why hadn't she used the flames to defend herself? She had been amazing during all her training classes.

He was still standing frozen beside the fire when Aidan found him after searching the place. Coming to stand beside him, he said.

"Red's not here. I know she changed into her old clothes, man."

Lifting a piece of the fabric she wore to the ceremony and festival tonight.

"She has all her gear. Hopefully, she'll use it."

Looking into his friends' concerned eyes, Kieran sank to the ground, sitting there staring into the flames. Feeling his Mate's terror was not an experience he wanted to repeat ever again. For his first ever actual connection to her, it was not a happy one as he had planned. Holding his head in his hands, he was at a loss.

Aidan, seeing his friend's trouble, and dismayed, sounded the alert, summoning Ravens Night to notify, and put people into action for a search. Hopefully, they could find her, though he seriously doubted that would be the case. They were dealing with someone skilled at the art of dark magicks. He knew Kieran had not sensed the telltale signs left behind when they entered his dwelling. The fear for his mate was too strong. He could hardly function, even now. He sat staring into the flames of the fire she had created. For him, and for her, he would find some answers.

His suppositions were growing about who the dark magick user might be. Also, who now was the possible kidnapper as well. He didn't like that possibility, because it would mean someone close to them had done this or aided in this abduction. Depending on who answered the call, he would have his answer to his question of who.

If it turned out to be who, he suspected, they would need to be very careful. Members arrived and their shock was evident when they looked at Kieran. And rightly so, his friend experienced over-whelming devastation. At least knowing Red was one of them, with a smart outlook. Assured him she would protect herself as best she could. More arrived, taking up action for a search. Others inspected the established magick boundary. Looking for any signatures of ill will.

Cillian completed his task and stormed into the dwelling, confirming his suspicions, with his face displaying a murderous look. A very prominent member, and a distant cousin of Kieran, and himself he took betrayal seriously. Especially when it involved his younger brother. Stopping right in front of him, he growled.

"You knew?"

Shaking his head, he whispered.

"No. I only suspected. I had no proof."

Placing his hand on his friend's shoulder, he continued.

"I am sorry Cillian. I didn't want to be right. I had hoped that I was mistaken."

Sagging in defeat, closing his eyes, he nodded in acceptance.

"It's ok Aidan, it's not your doing. All the blame belongs to him. I suspected he was up to something, but not this. He promised me eons ago he would stop with the dabbling. Clearly, he has lied to us all."

While feeling for his friend, his next statement surprised him.

Firming his posture, he looked up, making eye contact.

"He will surely pay with his life for his betrayal....."

With his mouth open, and no words, he paused. Closing his mouth, he thought for a moment before turning to look at Kieran and whispering his question.

"Does he know?"

Turning back to face him. Shaking his head, he said.

"No, I wanted to be sure before I told him."

Cillian tilted his head with a brow raised. In a silent question.

Understanding, he answered.

"No, I don't believe either of them is aware."

With a snort, Cillian said. As he nudged his head in Kieran's direction.

"Well, I understand her not knowing. But him."

Just then Kieran finally noticed his surroundings, and the multitude of conversations going on around him. The most intriguing was the one between Aidan and Cillian. Jumping up with speed, he moved their way to stand by them in an instant.

"What is it I should know, but don't?"

Looked between the two for any clues he may have missed. He was losing his touch if he was this out of it. Aidan just rolled his eyes as Cillian said, laughing.

Slapping him on the back, saying.

"So many things, man. So many things,"

Growling in frustration, he demanded.

"Spill."

With a long sigh, Aidan said.

"Have a look at your left arm Mate."

Aidan raised his brows, nudging his head, when Kieran gave him a confused look. He already knew he and Harlow now possessed the mating mark on their left palms. As directed, with a firm grip, he took hold of his sleeve and gave a good tug. Tearing the fabric to reveal the intricate markings traveling up his arm from his palm. The markings on his arm showcased interwoven vines of clovers, thistles, roses, and various animals. His arm also featured symbols they grew up hearing about, dotted across it. On his upper shoulder was a raven with splayed wings clutching an interwoven crescent moon and triquetra. They carved the same symbol on their bed.

It was beautiful. When the meaning flashed through his mind, he staggered back a step. Open his mouth to say something, anything he couldn't come up with a thing.

Aiden looked to Cillian, stating.

"Told you."

With his statement, the room fell eerily silent, all turning in their direction. Gasps of shock sounded, followed by echoing wows. Finally, everyone placed a right fist over their heart, took a knee, and bowed their head. Kieran looked around the room, still in utter shock. He was no longer the chieftain of his clan. No! He, and he suspected Harlow as well, were now the blessed God, and Goddess, destined to rule over all. This was not what he wanted.

Hearing a soft, simple whisper.

"And that is why."

Somehow, he also heard her smile.

"Blessed be."

Blinking rapidly, had he just heard that in his head? This time, he heard the softest laughter before it was gone. Shaking his head, he looked around him at all the kneeling men and women.

"Please get up. I need your help to find my Mate."

In unison all replied.

"Gladly blessed one."

He couldn't think of how this would change things for them. Let alone fathom the whys and hows. It just was. Hopefully, whoever had taken her didn't suspect or know of this change. She, in an instant, was now in even more danger. Scared for his Mate he looked to his long time friend Aidan, who was rising.

"We will find her….."

Before he could continue, Kieran cut him off.

"Don't even say it. Just don't. I don't want this any more than I received it. I am still just Kieran to you."

With a firm look, he stared at him down. Until Aidan nodded.

"Whatever you wish."

A smirk spreads across his face.

"Kieran."

With that out of the way, for now, they all gathered around their fire. Everyone listened as Aiden and Cillian filled them all in on their suspicions and findings. It was Cillian's younger brother who was responsible for the magick component of the abduction. Though they doubted he was the head of the snake controlling all the attempts and attacks. Unanimously, everyone agreed too.

The revelation of Ozel's connection to this has caused many emotions to surface. Angry he would betray his people and clan this way. Furious that he harmed his True Mate. With his last thought, he could feel the earth beneath them begin to rumble and move. That is until Aidan and Cillian each placed a hand on his shoulders. Their calming reassurance helped calm him to the point he could focus.

Acknowledging their caring with a simple nod. He assumed control of the discussion and motivated everyone to share their ideas and suggestions on where Harlow could have been taken and by whom. After a few rounds of talking back and forth, it was then he noticed his sister and Corrina were absent. He swore they had been here. Hadn't they?

Leaning towards Aidan, he asked him discreetly where they had gone. The whisper back surprised him. He had asked them, along with two others, to track Ozel and his movements. Since his gut was screaming to him, he was involved. Until he had proof, though he hadn't wanted to say for Cillian's sake. After confirming his concerns, he felt justified in sending them out without solid proof. He felt a deep sense of gratitude for his friend's foresight, which allowed him to relax.

Together they made plans for different scenarios. Hoping that the women came back with more information. This continued all during the night, and into the next morning. When the village found out about Harlow's abduction, and who was involved, all kinds of information and support came flooding in. Corrina and Hayley found the Ravens Night members in deep discussions when they returned, and joined as they made the final plans.

CHAPTER 25

*H*arlow came to slowly. Where was she? Why did she hurt so much? Try as she might, she couldn't recall anything that would cause her so much pain. As she tried to ease the throbbing pain by moving it was, then she realized she couldn't. Panicking, she opened her eyes and cried out when the bright light blinded her. It was like blades stabbing into her skull. Wow, that hurt, squeezing her eyes shut once more.

A discomforting familiar voice spoke.

"Ah, you're finally awake I see,"

Seemingly quite annoyed with her.

Carefully opening her eyes this time. Squinting to ease the pain, she tried to find the source origin of the voice. Recognizing the blurry figure as the creepy, scary man. The one so full of hatred that had taken her. Licking her parched lips, she could barely ask.

"What do you want?"

"Well, you of course."

He snarled at her.

"Why?"

She was so confused and scared. She was also having trouble thinking.

"What did you do to me?"

Trying to move again, she realized that someone had tied her wrists behind her back and secured them to the floor. The stone floor beneath her also carried up the walls and across the ceiling. They made sure her body was facing the only source of light, which came from a very narrow window. To the side of that wall was a wall of bars. Her captor was sitting in a chair on the other side. Great, she was in a prison cell.

"Feeling sore, are we? Well, you deserve it after all the trouble I went through to get you. You wouldn't stop mumbling and moaning. So we had to steal a cart to toss you in. That way, we could cover you and muffle your crazy murmurings."

Looking all put out, he continued to sneer at her.

"I don't even know you. So why take me?"

Moaning as she tried to sit up. Feeling very much like something had run her over, it took her several attempts. Sitting up, she felt a little woozy. Swallowing past the bile, she focused on a spot on the floor till it stopped moving.

"You still didn't answer my question. Why me?"

"Oh, I think you already know, my dear."

Rising from his chair in an attempt at a regal fashion, he failed miserably. His limbs shook uncontrollably, making it difficult for him to move. Despite his attempts to conceal it, the situation worsened with each effort he made.

"Now if you wish for your suffering to end, give me what I want."

Who did this man think he was, anyway? Squaring her shoulders, she looked him right in the eyes, as best she could anyway, with a firmly stated.

"No. I will never give you anything."

With the scariest laugh, he turned.

"Suit yourself. I will get what I want in the end."

Laughing as he walked away. Shouting

"I always do."

Laughing until he was too far away for her to hear.

Shaking off the chills of his laughter, she took in her surroundings once more. How would she get out of this one she wondered? Scared and alone, a crazy man held her in a prison cell. A man who did who knows what to her while she was out cold. She shook with her fear, allowing it to consume her.

Sometime later, she wasn't sure how much time had passed. Between her all-consuming fear and drifting off, she had no sense of time. Waking up, she wished her brother were here. He would know what to do, and how. Panic gripped her as she yearned for his presence. Having tasted the level of that man's hatred for her it made him very dangerous and unpredictable. Also, the separation from her twin for this long was taking its toll. Whispering her brother's name in a plea.

"Caden"

Suddenly, she felt as if Caden was there giving her a warm hug. She could smell the familiar scents of him. Cracking her eyes open, she scanned her cell in search of him. Finding nothing, it was her in the cell, with arms still bound to the floor. Still, that smell was everywhere. Whispering again.

"Caden?"

"Harlow"

Alert now. She scanned the room again, coming up empty. Curious, she whispered,

"How Caden?"

"In your head Harlow. Just think your questions. I can hear you."

Laying as still as she could to pretend to sleep. She continued this strange conversation with her brother.

"Wow, Caden. But how?"

"I have no idea, sis. What trouble have you gotten yourself into now?"

Grunting, she rolled her eyes mentally, saying.

"I didn't get myself into this."

Hearing her brother chuckle as she spoke.

"Some creepy guy took me. He's got me in some kind of prison cell. There is only a slit of a window nearer the ceiling and a wall of thick bars."

She tried to project the image cell to him as she described it to him. Her shoulders were aching. Trying to rotate, she couldn't tell if she was moving them. The numbness firing through her limbs was too great. She had long ago lost feeling in her fingers.

With brotherly concern, he asked.

"What's wrong, sis?"

Might as well be honest, she thought, to which he replied.

"Yes, you should. Now tell me."

"I have my arms tied behind my back and secured to the floor. My shoulders hurt, and I've lost all feeling in my fingers."

She could hear fierce growling echoing in her head.

"What else Harlow? No lies, remember only the truth."

"I have something he believes is his, and if I want my suffering to end, I have to give him what he wants."

Pausing, she had trouble thinking about the last part.

"I also deserve all I have coming to me for inconveniencing him."

Her head filled with growling.

"That's bullshit, Harlow. You don't deserve any of this."

In a blink, the connection was gone. She could feel it severed. Still, she thought.

"Caden?"

Trying whispering aloud this time.

"Caden?"

As strange as that had been, with the comfort gone. The pain of her aching body took hold. Closing her eyes, she allowed herself to drift off, again.

She could hear voices in the distance. Anger and frustration contorted their faces. She could tell by the tone each speaker was using. Confusion clouded her mind as she struggled to decipher if their anger was towards each other or someone else. They were too far away for her to understand what they were talking about. Maybe if she was still asleep on the floor, when they strolled by, they would continue their chat. Then perhaps she could get some more information.

As they approached, she realized she was the topic of discussion. They expressed their disapproval of how the Master treated her. They considered it wrong and cruel. Neera's crazy plans and weird ways were understood and agreed upon by them. They agreed upon and followed her instructions, not his. Regardless of what he thought. It didn't seem to matter to him in the slightest. Kidnapping a woman, just to force her to relinquish her power and gifts, to transfer them to him. He was crazy, cause for her to do that she had to die.

Well, now she knew what he wanted from her. These two had just confirmed what she had suspected. Wasn't it always about power? Why can't people simply appreciate the blessings they have and be content? Sadly, that was not the case. She agreed with them on one thing, however. He was crazy. Wondering if they or anyone else knew how crazy. She would never give him what he wanted. No matter what.

Loud echoing voices were thundering off the stone walls, interrupting the bothered voices. Fighting to stay as still as she could and cracking one eye open only a little. It was best to give the illusion of sleep. She confirmed they were bringing in another prisoner. A man from what she could see. The large men carrying the unconscious prisoner were talking about how they had found him laying out by old ruins. They knew he was up to no good, and perhaps he could be useful. He was wearing clothes that were just like the other prisoners.

They beamed with excitement, confident that the Master would be overjoyed by their performance. They assured the unhappy followers. Demanding they open another cell, tossing the man in like a sack of discarded trash. They continued to boast as they all left., in the opposite direction. Leaving Harlow to wonder who the unconscious man could be. Was he a member of the True Guard? Or was this someone she knew and came for her? She could only cross her fingers and hope for the best. He didn't look like Caden, so it couldn't be him.

She was missing Kieran as well. She hated their last words together were her getting so angry and yelling at him. Hopefully, Ravens Night was out looking for her. Unable to stay awake any longer, she went to sleep thinking of her intimate times with her man.

CHAPTER 26

*K*ieran was feeling sick with worry. All their plans of attack and searching had resulted in nothing. Not a thing. He knew dark magick was strong, but this, this was just outright worrying. As he paced the floor.

"This is crazy. Why can't we get a trace of her?"

He was hoping, when the women had come back the other morning, they had some good news to share. They had found nothing, absolutely nothing. How could a woman be here one second, and gone the next? Her trail started and ended at his dwelling.

Aidan sighed.

"She's obviously being cloaked in magicks. If only we knew who Ozel was working for. That slimy weasel."

Growling further in anger, he too paced the floor, faster this time.

Looking up from his seat, Cillian replied. Before twisting his fingers into a knot, turning them white with the tension. Anger and regret were clear.

"Hey guys, I'm sorry for my brother's actions. I just wish I knew more and hadn't been so blind to what was going on right under my nose."

Still pacing, Kieran said.

"Not your fault, man. It's your brother's fault. He shall wear the blame, not you. He lied to us all. Deceived us all."

After a while, he continued.

"Has anyone come close to revealing the identity of Neera's followers' new leader?"

Everyone shook their heads. They hadn't a clue. Only the knowledge that he was a man and that he had kept himself very well hidden, and secret.

If only their mating bond were stronger, he could just feel her out. But if Aidan was right, and she was being cloaked with magicks, there was no hope he could've used that avenue. Either that or she was unconscious. Which could explain him feeling nothing from her. If only he had told her everything, talked with her. Maybe things could have happened differently.

This type of thinking wasn't getting him anywhere. It only made him feel worse about himself. He needed to snap out of it. The what if solved nothing?

Everyone then retreated to the spot they had occupied since the festival. All of them were in his dwelling, fearing the worst if they left. It was easier, better, and safer to all stay together. If only to console Kieran. Plus, this way, they knew where everyone was at, making it easier to make and execute plans.

The hurried banging on the door had everyone freezing, sucking in a breath, and holding it as if frozen in time. Everyone that was to be here was here, well except for his Mate that is. This was their home. They should enjoy each other after their vows. Instead, everyone in Ravens Night gathered here hoping to rescue her. Shaking off his surprise, he went to answer the door. On the other side, he found one guard who usually stood at the entrance of the village. Confused, he squinted at the man asking.

"What is it?"

Out of breath but in a hurry, the man spoke.

"He said you are all to come. To be ready, for the Raven must fly tonight. Then all will be as it should be."

Confused for a moment, he asked the man to repeat the message, after which he asked.

"Who gave you this message?"

"Oh well, the man at the gate. I refused him entrance. Saying I will take the message to you. If it is then valid, you will understand, and be on your way."

Nodding his head at the man.

"You did well. I thank you for the job well done. Return, and tell this man we will be ready, and meet him shortly."

At once, the man took off towards the gate. Closing the door, he turned to see everyone in action. All getting ready for battle. His dwelling had quickly become a home base for them. With every standing member except for Ozel moving in. Able, and ready to fly at a moment's notice. They had gathered and organized all manner of gear, gems, crystals, and potions. They could be ready at a moment's notice. So this news of a message was what they had been waiting for. The raven must fly tonight, was one code they had established with Cormac.

It reasoned he had news and information needed to go into battle. He just prayed it involved the rescue of his True Mate Harlow. Being bonded, he couldn't fathom a life without her. She was his other half, the good half. The best of all of him. She brightened his world. He would kill anyone who harmed a hair on her lovely head.

In only a matter of minutes, every member of Ravens Night was ready for action. They would bring his woman home, and see justice served to her abductees. Or else.

Harlow could hear movement in the other cell. It sounded like the man was regaining consciousness. His timing seemed to be perfect for her. She was trying to summon up enough energy to at least burn off the ropes holding her wrists together. Succeeding just a few moments ago, when the man's moaning helped to cover her audible response to the very painful release of her arms. The amount of energy this took gave her thought. There was something in this prison dampening her ability to use or access her gifts.

With that thought, she could recover the feeling from her shoulders down to her fingers. Hoping there was no permanent damage done. She was thankful that whoever tied her hadn't been bright enough. In freeing her hands, she also freed herself from being secured to the floor as well. At least one good thing, she thought. Well, two perhaps. Her prison mates manning and groaning had helped her.

If only she had used her talents in Kieran's dwelling, perhaps she wouldn't be in this predicament. But maybe she was supposed to be here, for what she wasn't sure of yet. What could she learn or do by being held prisoner by a crazy man?

The man in the next cell was mumbling now, and she wondered how he would respond to waking up in a cell. If only his voice weren't so scratchy, she was hoping to figure out if he was from her time or not. Or if she knew him. When she heard him say,

"What the hell? Where am I?"

With a rustling of movement, she could tell he was moving around. Moving herself toward the bars of her cell, she peeked out, glancing in his direction. He was looking around, taking in what was all around them. When his eyes met hers, Harlow sucked in a breath. It couldn't be. Shaking her head adamantly when he opened his mouth to speak. With questions in his eyes, she again shook her head.

In vain, she tried to keep her silent tears at bay. They fell silently down her cheeks. They were now in trouble. Without knowing it, the crazy man now had the power to get whatever he wanted from her. She would do anything and everything to protect her son. The man found unconscious and placed in the cell next to hers was Rowan.

He had obviously found her clues, only it seemed a great deal of time had passed. The son she had last seen was fifteen years old. For her, she had only seen him off to training three or four weeks ago. Now she had to think on the fly and do what she could to protect him. He knew nothing of the world he had just woken up to. Hopefully, in protecting him, she could also protect herself too. He likely had gifts in this time. They would want him for his gifts, just like they wanted her. Before he could speak again, she asked him.

"What's your name?"

She wondered if other magics were blocking her access to her gifts. Those in power were likely listening or possibly watching. If the latter were true, they were in big trouble. Their body language and reactions to each other were a dead giveaway away too. Still, she would protect him regardless.

Again, with questioning eyes, he replied.

"Rowan. What's your name?"

"Harlow."

She squinted her eyes at the pain as she moved her arms to hang onto the bar's infant of her.

Mimicking her movements, he asked.

"What are you in here for, Harlow?"

Tilting his head in concern.

She could see his lips thinning, knowing she was in pain.

"They want something from me, and I won't give it to them. You?"

This time she mimicked him by tilting her head.

Rubbing a hand down and over his face as he said.

"I have no idea."

Cautioning him, she replied.

"Well, be aware, they will want something from you or use you."

Ending on a whisper to hide the hurt and pain. She watched as understanding crossed over his face before he nodded and retreated to the back of his cell. Feeling defeated, she too moved back to where she had been. Laying down on the cold hard stone, she pondered on how she could protect her son. If only she could use her gifts. They seemed to be a blessing and a curse to her. When she remembered to use them. With her eyes growing heavy, she drifted off to sleep.

CHAPTER 27

*L*istening in on the prisoners had been a fantastic idea. He was so glad he thought of it. Ozel was coming in handy on so many levels. Enchanting ordinary objects as listening devices was a genius if he said so. He felt a heavy weight of sadness settle in his heart, knowing he would never receive what he needed from him. Would have been much simpler that way. Alas, the man just didn't possess enough power for him. He needed more so much more.

He thought he had been lucky when he had found Neera. Believing she was a part of the prophecy, he couldn't believe the universe would hand her to him on a silver platter. She convinced herself, believing she was the star of the foretold vision. It had been easy then to pull just the right strings and manipulate her the way he wanted. What he hadn't seen coming was that she was just as power hungry as he. A wave of sorrow washed over him, as he had truly cherished her.

Now this Harlow, as she said her name, was. This woman, she had power, possessing so much of it that Ozel feared she could make a successful escape. To dampen her gifts, he had laced her cell with herbs and poisons to further weaken her. It was just a bonus that the cart they stole, and tossed her into knocking her around a bit as they traveled. Weakening her just that little bit more.

He would get from her exactly what he wanted. It was only a matter of time. She would give him everything, just like all the others had. He had eons of practice behind him. One never reached the age he had not having the skills required. Laughing to himself, he recalled the faces of all those who said he'd never amount to anything. Well, look at him now, and where are they? Dead and buried along with all of their descendants. Good riddance to them, he sure showed them.

It was just his good luck: his other lackeys had found that unconscious man when they did. From the clothing they described, it matched that of the woman. If they come from the same place, they have to know each other. He will just use the man for whatever info he can gain, and use it against Harlow. With his history, he found women were so easy to break, and this one would be no different.

With the universe finally favoring him, he knew he was on the right path. He always got what he wanted in the end. For the first time, however, it appeared he was being proven right. He would show them, show them all. Soon, they would all be bowing down to him.

Grinning at the image his last thought created. He rubbed his hands together, creating some much needed warmth. Something he had lacked ever since he started down this path. Life was incredible, unbelievably incredible. He'd see to that.

Harlow woke up to loud voices and the sound of metal on metal. Disoriented from lack of sleep and low nourishment, it took some time to ground herself. A stone cold floor was horrible for anyone to sleep on. Add in that she wasn't trusting enough to sleep for long periods of time in her current situation. She was fuzzy at best. Saving her strength for what mattered. In hopes an opportunity to escape would present itself to her.

Her heart raced with a mix of fear and helplessness, pushing her to conserve every ounce of energy. Leaving her with either sleeping or thinking to pass the time. As she slept, her dreams were vivid reminders of all the lessons she had learned since coming here. All the time, she practiced her many gifts. How she could channel and focus on a specific trigger. Each of them was unique. She had been so frustrated at first because it had felt like trying to find a needle in a haystack. Once she found one, the rest just seemed to fall into place.

Memories of events past and present tossed together, transforming the rest of her dreams into a chaotic themed show. Like they were trying to tell her something important. Only she could never figure it out. Just as she was about to, she would wake. She would then forget everything until the next time she slept.

When she was awake, her thoughts strayed all over the place. Stirring up all kinds of emotions. Thinking of Kieran made her wish she could be in his arms instead of this wretched place. Regretting the argument, she started. Had she not sent him away, he could have protected her from being taken. If that were so, she wouldn't be here now knowing that Rowan was here now too.

She needed to be at her best for her son. Knowing deep down in her gut he was going to need her. It was her job to protect him, and she would do that. Just not sure on the how yet. Saving her strength for such a likely event instead of healing herself. Amidst her wandering mind, something pulled her back to what had awoken her.

A group of enormous animal looking men who all seemed a little too cheery came into the dungeon, in the middle of the night she guessed. Since no sunlight peered through her tiny window. The mass stopped in front of Rowan's cell. Watching as the men entered and pulled him out of his cell. She couldn't believe her eyes. Her son had grown so much, almost the size of Kieran. He was most definitely now a man. How was that possible though, with their journeys through the arch vortex only weeks apart? Or did they just land weeks apart? Oh god, had she abandoned her baby for years? That had never been her intention. All she had wanted was justice for Cora's murder, and to complete the cause for which someone killed her.

Who knew it would land her here and now? Or that Rowen would find all her clues, yes, but so many years later. Arriving only weeks after her. This could give her a headache if she tried to figure it out. She realized the archway had a complicated and unpredictable nature. Right now, she has to help her son. Without endangering herself. She also feared what that man would do with all her gifts. It scared her the more she thought about what was going to happen with Rowan.

Watching as the two men dragged her son along the hall; she decided they must have drugged him. There was no way he was that uncoordinated. His movements were far too sluggish for a member of the True Guard. Or was it an act he was putting on for the posy of animal like men? She couldn't be sure. Instead of taking him up the stairs from where they came, they rounded the corner. Then she heard a large, heavy door open and shut moments later.

She kept her eyes fixed on the spot where she had last seen her son. Her heart pounded with a mother's fear and worry, terrified to avert her eyes in case she missed something. Suddenly, the heavy door opened again. This time there was no cheerful chatter, just the sound of shuffling feet. When she saw them round the corner, they were all but dragging Rowan down the hall. The closer they got, she noticed her son was only semi conscious. Arriving at his cell, they just tossed him in. Hearing him groan when landed on the stone floor.

As a group of men left in an exhausted hurry, she heard some rustling around from Rowan. Then in a garbled voice.

"Well, that was fun,"

With a half hearted chuckle before it turned into a cough.

Softly, she asked,

"What did they do? You were in there for hours."

"Just the usual questions and interrogation."

He said before groaning again in pain.

She doubted it was just questions and interrogation. There had to have been physical aspects that went on in that room. Her son was lying to her, trying to protect her. That was her job, not his.

"It's nothing I can't handle. So don't worry about me. I'll be fine."

This became a routine for the next three days. It also became how she could tell the passing of time. Everything happened the same way. She wasn't sure how she knew, but these men preferred the ritual. Only this night, a little while after they took Rowan, the two brutes came back for her. Now she was worried. The need for her twin to be at her side was overwhelmingly intense. In a desperate, fearful plea, she shouted in her mind.

"*CADEN. Caden, if you can hear me, please. They have Rowan. Caden. Please help us.*"

CHAPTER 28

*H*e couldn't believe the distance they needed to travel. They considered themselves blessed as they made preparations and traveled light. It meant they could also travel great distances fast. Which is what they had to do. This would explain why they had no word on Harlow. They had taken her to an area that was so many regions away from theirs. Deep into the area where the ungifted lived. Whoever had taken her must have had transport of some kind. Still, that was rare in his world, for they did not need such items. Only the non magicks used such things. Which seemed to fit with this current location.

They were dealing with nonmagicks who could influence both the gifted and the non. That was a dangerous person to be dealing with. With that knowledge, the stakes just rose a bit more. He hoped that somehow, someway, Harlow would rely on her gifts, and tap into her newly awarded power upgrade. If she could tap into them. He was suspecting she was being hindered somehow, and not able to access her inner gifts. He had yet to feel anything from her. Now with them being bonded Mates that was very unusual.

He had got moments of connection where he could feel her fear and her worry. Just as he would get an inkling it would fade just as fast as it came. Instead, he had sent her reassurance and strength when the inkling would start. Figuring she needed that more than he needed to feel her. Anything he could do to give her the upper hand, he would try.

Waiting at the destination dictated in the second portion of the message. They all became anxious when no one was there waiting for them. As patiently as they could, they waited. Either something had happened or they traveled faster than they had thought.

Just as the sun was setting in the distance, Cormac came flying over the hill. If the man was in a rush, that didn't bode well. With his concern growing, it was all he could do to wait. It was best they all heard the message, and that Cormac only had to say it once. The closer he got, he noticed he was in a dreadful state. What on earth had happened to him, and where had he been all this time? Before he could say a word, Cormac shouted.

"Come, we have to hurry. She doesn't have much time left."

Everyone was stunned into a moment of silence. Kieran thought, how did Cormac know this much? He never felt her that grave when they connected, however briefly. Was she able to connect with him? But how was that possible? Was it even possible? So he asked.

"How do you know?"

"If we hurry now, we may save more than one life."

With a come hither arm move, he continued to shout.

"Come quickly, follow me."

With that, the man took off at the speed of light.

They hurried to follow for fear of harm to Harlow and another life. All hoped they would get there in time.

They brought her into the interrogation room. It smelled of sweat, anger, and hatred. For the first time in days, she felt free of the bonds.

Someone had indeed enchanted her cell to restrict her use of magicks. She could now feel the energy flowing through her as she could breathe. It just wasn't enough in her current condition. Then there were her emotions, still being all over the place. In this situation, she wasn't sure how much control she would have. The possibility of hurting her son as well was high.

Looking around, she noticed this room was just like the other cells, well the only few she had seen, anyway. A massive heavy door resided instead of bars, like all the others. With a huge clanging lock that made her jump when it was engaged. Studying the room she noted, besides herself, and the two animal like galoots that retrieved her, her son Rowan sitting in a chair bloody and bruised. He looked horrible. One of his eyes had swollen shut. Behind him stood her abductor, and another animal like man. This one was larger and angrier than the others. He seemed to possess an air of authority. Out of the blue, she just asked.

"Why?"

The man, full of hatred towards her, only laughed, saying.

"Because I can."

Knowing full well he had her right where he wanted her. He saw the flash of concern in her eyes when they landed on Rowan. Proceeding to use the situation to gain information from them. He started peppering her with questions. With each question he asked, she studied the man more. Her abductor seemed familiar to her. There was just something out of her reach. She couldn't put her finger on it. Increasing her frustration the more she tried. Having enough, with her passive answers, it seemed Harlow was now given a choice. Snarling to the point of spitting as he spoke. Her captor demanded.

"Give me what I want, and your friend here won't die. Refuse, and we'll let you watch as he takes his last breath."

Nodding his head to the man beside him. The room filled with the sound of clothes ripping and the hollow sound of bones popping. Staring in fascination, and with wide eyes, she watched as the man standing behind her son sifted. Large amounts of fur appeared all over his body as he grew to become a giant wolf. With an upward tick of his lip, his beady yellow eyes zeroed in on her.

Eyes that triggered the memory of the insistent whinny and

demanding little man from in front of Cormac's cottage. The same man she realized, she had set alight with fire. Instinctually this time she tapped into her gift, to protect herself and the others. If she did it then with such accuracy, she could do it now too. Refocusing back to the moment, she couldn't help but smile, just a little. For once, she believed in herself and her abilities.

Rowan struggled and tugged, trying in vain to move and free himself. Looking at her with pleading eyes, he shouted.

"Harlow No. Don't do it."

She had heard of shapeshifters from Kieran, and Aidan, but never seen or met any she was aware of. Those that were in this room, though, were not as they seemed to be. She wasn't aware of how she knew that, she just did. With confidence building, she looked her kidnapper in the eyes, straightening, while she stated.

"Why the ultimatum? You'll do it, anyway."

"True."

Nodding his head.

"I thought I must try."

He stated as if he was doing them a favor. Such an eerie man. He gave her the creeps.

Glancing towards her son, she had an idea. Holding eye contact, she pushed the image of what she wanted towards him. As his eyes glossed over for a moment, she knew her attempt had worked. When his eyes cleared with understanding, he blinked his reply. Decision made, it was time to act. Even if she didn't like how it had to be done. In the end, Rowan's life was on the line. From what she had learned, only other magicks could survive a shifter bite. Still, they had only heard rumors and had found no proof thus far.

As traditionally, shifters were born, and not made. With what she was about to do, she hoped that a bite would be the worse outcome. If she was a magick, then so was her son. Best case, Rowan could move at a great speed, and free himself without another scratch. Worst case, she didn't want to ponder that.

At least they now had a tiny upper hand. Even if her son wasn't aware of it. He hadn't seen the shifter shift, only heard it. His focus had been solely on her. Taking a deep breath, she apologized to the universe for what she was about to do. Placing her palms onto the two men holding her in place, it was important to have direct contact. She drew all the energy she could from them. Draining their life in a matter of seconds. As she did so, she healed herself as much as possible. She needed to protect Rowan.

The ramifications of this choice could be severe. Life was to be protected and treasured. Even the evil ones. However, in this case, the treasured lives were hers, and her son's. If she acted as a Goddess passing judgment, and a sentence. Then, so be it.

Her actions caused chaos to erupt within the tiny room. As the men behind her slumped to the floor, dead, the remaining shifter growled as he clamped down onto Rowan. His glowing yellow eyes burrowed right into her, full of hatred. Guilt filled her. She wasn't fast enough to intervene in the gruesome bite. Pulling her eyes away, she watched as people were flooding into the room from a hidden door she hadn't noticed.

In a full rage, she stepped forward to take on the room single handedly. Throwing fire in every opponent's direction. Her strongest gift, as well as her favorite. Raising her hands, she danced around the room, sending intense flames this way and that. The room filled with smoke and the smell of burning flesh. When screams and cries ceased, and only the silence of death remained, she scanned the room. Finds only herself and Rowan alive. Using her gifts once more, with a flick of her wrist she uses the air within the room and snuffs out the smoke in an instant.

Surveying the carnage once more she realized her abductor and his shifter companion were not among the dead littered on the floor. Instinct told her to go after them and make them pay for their crimes. It was also telling her family first. She proudly showcased her unmatched maternal instincts. Stepping over the bodies, or whatever was left of them, she kneeled beside where Rowan lay. Carefully, she lifted him, cradling his upper body. Placing one hand over the still bleeding wound on his shoulder. Hopefully, applying just enough pressure.

Acknowledging too, from the placement of the bite, the intention had not been to kill but to turn. It looked like they wanted another lackey. How could they have known? Did yellow eyes sense the magick within? Well, they had another thing coming. They couldn't have him. With her other hand, she moved his hair off his brow. Smiling down at him, she whispered.

"You will be alright my boy. I promise."

Boy? No, her son was now very much a man. An adult, it seemed. Just how old was he? she wondered.

Rowan opens his eyes. His gaze was so unfocused, he smiled, whispering.

"I know, Mom."

His eyes rolled back into his head, and his body went limp.

CHAPTER 29

*W*ith Cormac in the lead, they charged into the extensive structure. It was a sight they had never seen before. It was an imposing massive thing, constructed entirely of stone. The roof appeared to touch the sky, disappearing into the blackness. The building had teeny tiny windows scattered around it. Their use is unknown. It would seem to be impregnable. Fortunately for them, they constructed the main door with wood. Easy to burn or ax down. In their case with magicks on their side, a door was an easy feat.

However, in the Cormac fashion, he had men inside already. They were waiting, and ready to aid in the fight. Granting them easy access into the colossal maze. For nonmagicks, these two packed a punch.

Like a snake slithering through the tall grass, they moved. Going through this place in, and out of the secret passages. Conquering each level of the massive structure, one floor at a time, flushing people out. On the upper levels, minimal fighting was required as most surrendered upon seeing them. It wasn't until they were about to enter the underground levels, revealed to them after, that the battle began.

Being greeted by some nasty looking shifters in a wolf form took some of them aback. It appeared that they had been compelled to remain in their animal form for an extended period of time. They went as far as chaining some of them to the wall. They now exhibited behavior resembling crazed animals due to the forced transformation. Guard dogs for entrance access behind them. With weapons raised the charged attack pushed forward. In a synchronized ballet, their group moved forward, thrusting blades up into their hearts. Or with a calculated forceful swipe to sever the head. These were the only ways to kill magick.

Lunging, Kieran thrust his weapon into the first shifter, for an instant kill. Grunting as he pulled his blade free to swipe at the next charging creature. Luck seemed to be on his side in this battle. Taking the next victim's head cleanly off, and pushing them back, and further into the room. Looking over his shoulder he saw Aidan slicing his weapon through the neck of a creature who had popped up behind him. Nodding, and grunting.

"Thanks."

Aidan rushed to say.

"You're welcome."

As he lunged for his next opponent.

Kieran weaved his way through the chaos. He had noticed a door at the end of the room, which was now unguarded. His people could easily handle themself. He needed to get to his Mate, she needed him more. Kicking the door open, it wasn't a room like he expected. The door revealed a downward staircase of stone steps. A glance behind him, making eye contact with Aidan. He jutted his head toward the steps. As his eyes lit up, he maneuvered to join him.

Together they managed the stairs. At the bottom, they were expecting more guard dogs to charge them. Only there was nothing, just a stone room with several doorways leading to stone lined hall-ways. Looking at each other in question, the stench of burned flesh reached their noses. Wrinkling their noses they both covered their face, before walking along the hall, toward the foul smell. When it vanished in an instant. Knowing it must be a magick, they rushed forward. Stopping in their tracks when they heard Harlow speak to someone.

"You will be alright my boy. I promise"

Followed by a husky reply.

"I know Mom."

Heads whipping to look at each other in shock, they quietly made their way into the room they had heard her speaking from. Freezing in their tracks when they saw it, it was littered with burned remains of bodies. Harlow must have been able to use or access her gifts. He felt for her having to kill. It wasn't a straightforward decision to make. Given who she was, it was something she would avoid at all costs. Unless it came to those who meant something to her. Like her son, being a protective mother through, and through, she did what she felt she had to. He wasn't sure of what went on here. Just that knowledge filled him, his Mate had protected herself all while defending her family. Stepping over, and around the remains he moved to Harlow's side. As she said.

"A shifter bit him."

While she stroked the man's cheek the way a mother would.

How could she be this man's mother, when she didn't look any older than he appeared? Looking between them he realized they looked more like siblings, rather than mother, and son. How could this be? They noticed that whenever they answered questions, more seemed to rise in their place. Would they ever really know, he was wondering.

When she looked up to him, and her face was full of silent tears his heart broke for her as she pleaded.

"We have to help him."

Blinking furiously she continued.

"I won't lose my son again."

Cormac was at their side, he and Aidan took over taking care of her son. He took his Mate into his arms hugging her close and whispering in her ear.

"I was so scared, little one."

Pulling back, he took her head in his hands, rubbing her tears away with his thumbs.

"I'm so sorry Harlow."

Pausing for just a moment. He seemed to have trouble speaking. With pleading eyes he continued.

"You were right. I just love you so much."

Before he could finish, she threw her arms around him kissing him, holding him tight. When they both needed air, they rested their foreheads together. She whispered.

"I love you, Kieran."

Had him standing with her, and lifting her, and into his arms.

His poor Mate looked way too thin, with dark circles under her eyes. She needed rest, and healing herself. When he was about to leave, he felt her icy fingers on his cheek. Her simple request.

"Rowan"

Was all he needed to know where her concern was at the moment. Turning he nodded his head towards her son who was now resting on a portable cot. They took great care in wrapping his bitten wound. Other members of Ravens Night were now entering the room to aid with his care and transport. Cormac came up to her smiling. With a familiar tenderness, he touched her shoulder. In a soft reassuring tone, he said.

"Your son will be alright my dear, just a little different. Now let your Mate care for you. You'll do no good to your son otherwise."

As if that was enough, he double tapped her shoulder. Turning his attention towards Kieran he said.

"I will alert Aramis, and the others in the triad on my way. I must leave."

With that, he spun leaving the room in a flash.

At Harlow's confused look, he explained that Aramis, an alpha wolf shifter King, Flanna, an alfa bear shifter Queen, and Hakan, an alfa dragon shifter King. Ruled over all the shifter kinds. Typically, they would stick to their shifter breed, however, they equally share the power, and responsibilities in their unique ruling trifecta. It's necessary to inform them about what has happened here tonight.

It was an offense to create a shifter from a bite. So the perpetrator could be dealt with. The triad will want to speak with her since she was a witness. Gaining any information she could share with them. Would make their ability to take action easier and go along with their decision. They were also the best people to treat Rowan's wounds and help him heal. Her son was in for a rough road ahead of him. He assured his Mate however that they would help him in any way they could.

It was best if they all left this place so they could care for him. Making the preparations for his transition as smooth as possible. Not to mention she would need rest, and healing herself if she expected to care for Rowan. As they followed the stretcher carrying her son, she insisted on checking everybody. Needing to verify that her abductor and Rowan's attacker had escaped. Unfortunately, it was confirmed that her suspicions were correct. She had recognized none of the deceased, only the two who had aided the clan members.

So now they were hunting for three traitors, Ozel being one of them. Leaving with the knowledge they were looking for a trio of evil left a heavy feeling in his gut. One of magick, one to shift, and one who leads. Hopefully, they would soon learn the names of the last two, from their sneaky inside helpers. They made a promise to offer protection in exchange for any information they had. For Harlow and her son only having seen these evil beings. They were never once revealed names.

He didn't think she would sleep long. With her mind so preoccupied with concern for her son or the fact she still needed healing herself, she needed sustenance. So he made them something to eat. One they could share in bed. He could only imagine how depleted she had been after taking the life essence of two shifters, and the firepower she had used, and extinguished. He also still needed to bring up the subject of their now new position, and everything else that came along with it.

Well, everything he knew anyway. It was buried deep within him somewhere. All thanks to the power transfer from his father when he died. He wasn't sure how to share that information as well, but he had to.

His father's parting gift was much more potent than he ever had realized. The knowledge was extensive. All he needed to do was go searching into the recesses of his mind. The more he did, the more he acknowledged the truth. A truth of what, and who his father had been. Of who, and what he, and his Mate now were. They had been bestowed with all the power.

It was dealing with the hurt, and sense of betrayal he felt, that he was having trouble dealing with. Also, the only person he wanted to discuss it with was Harlow, his True Mate. She was the only one who understood and knew what to do.

Hearing Harlow shift, and move around he knew she was waking up. Gathering all their snacks together he maneuvered his way towards her. She always took his breath away when she fluttered her eyes open upon waking. That unfocused dreaming look was his favorite. He smiled as her eyes lit up upon seeing him at the bedside with food. His woman was hungry. Her rushed klutzy movements caused him to laugh in her haste to sit up in bed, and she again tangled herself in the bedding coverings.

"There is no rush my little one."

Once she righted herself after many attempts, and her toppling over, he sat beside her. Offering to her a small plate with bite sized pieces of food on top of it. Which she dug into without a word, only releasing a sigh or moan here or there. With a gentle chuckle, he joined her in their snack all the while watching her in fascination. Eating always seemed to be a great pleasure of hers. Although you'd never know to look at her. She was so tiny.

When they finished, he took both their plates and set them on the floor beside the bed. He'd take care of them later. Now however it was time they talked. Since many things needed to be brought up. He wasn't sure where to start. When he turned and looked back at Harlow, her growing smile lit up her entire face. She muttered as she reached out to touch his arm, squeezing it.

"Thank you, Kieran. I needed that. Now spit it out what you want to say."

Tilting his head confused he asked.

"Spit it out?"

To which she smiled and laughed.

"Ya, spit it out. It means to say what you have to or need to say, and fast."

Understanding, he nodded.

"Well, I'm not too sure where to begin."

He said as he rubbed the back of his neck looking down into his lap. He was feeling nervous, though he wasn't too sure why. He acknowledged that there was no changing what had been done. There was no going back now. Feeling another squeeze on his arm, he looked up into his Mate's eyes. Seeing her love for him in them he smiled wrapping his arms around her and hugging her close. Murmuring a soft thanks he kissed the top of her head. As he pulled back Harlow whispered.

"Why not start at the beginning?"

"I could. Though l think it would make more sense if I start in the middle, or the now maybe."

While he spoke, he positioned them in a way that she was cradled against him as they sat in bed.

"I would very much like you in my arms as we talk. Ok?"

Her answer was a simple nod as she relaxed into his hold. Once again kissing the top of her head he said.

"Alright."

He began as if telling her a story. A story of them, and their beginning.

The day he had found her, he had not intended to go towards the protected ancient site. However, he felt an unbelievably powerful pull in that direction. He was almost there when he saw someone fall from the sky. As he rushed to them, he felt shocked to see her and how suddenly he felt rooted. Like a lightning strike, and an instant bond all at once. It took his breath away, with the internal knowing the unconscious woman was his True Mate. It was also comforting, and apparent that she felt the same way when he touched her.

Harlow had curled in towards him, seeking comfort. Also calming at his touch, and voiced reassurance. It was an amazing thing. Something they had been told were tales to inspire dreams. Only now were they finding this tale was true. As happy, and as good as that was, how many other tales were true then? Why did they lie to them? Some information was missing. That thought would have to be a tale for another time. Other things were far more pressing and required their attention first.

He then fast forwarded to the festival and the ceremony. She had been right about the binding ceremony. It was what she had suspected. Fear had ultimately kept him from telling her the truth. He could not take the risk of her saying no or let's wait. That wasn't an option for him or for her, as he saw it. Now though he realized he should have talked to her and explained his side of things. As well as the situation side of things.

Even though they are now bound, Mated for all time, there was more. As Harlow turned her head up towards him in question. He covered her open mouth with his finger.

"Shh little one. Let me finish the story before you ask questions. Alright."

Staring into her eyes he waited for her response. A gentle nod.

"Good. I will continue then."

Smiling at her, and grateful for her patience he proceeded.

There is a tale of fated Mates as he had told her before. There was just more to the tale. Ignoring her glare. If Mates go through the complete mating cycle, they receive a full mate bond. That cycle includes an official bonding ceremony, physical mating followed by physical marking, and blood exchange. To become one. Not only had they performed each of the cycles they also had the priestess perform the bonding ceremony.

While he was telling her these details Harlow glanced down to look at her left palm. As if only just remembering. She traced her finger along the delicate, intricate tattoo marking on her hand. In a gentle whisper.

"I remember now. Feeling the burning. If only for a second or two."

He too placed his left palm next to hers. Revealing the same tattoo marking. Her soft delicate finger traced the same lines. Knowing she still hadn't seen the rest and was still only accessing what he had just said.

"Look further, little one. There's more."

He watched as she hesitated and blinked a few times before gasping. Smiling when her awed face looked up to him, and her mouth a gape. Nudging his chin forward encouraging her to continue he watched in fascination as she explored both of their new tattooed markings. They each had intertwining symbols and picture imagery representing their newfound status covering their left arms. Any who looked upon them would know. The God and Goddess of all was standing before them.

He and Harlow were now the ones responsible for all things. In charge of all the magick, and nonmagick alike. An eternal father, and mother if you like. Why they were given, this gift was a mystery. Although if he had to guess Harlow came by it naturally. The woman was seriously talented, and gifted with the experience of an actual mother. He only processed the ancient knowledge. Working together as a team, they would be great.

When she again looked up to him saying.

"This is so beautiful, Kieran. What does it mean?"

He placed a finger under her chin to draw her closer for a small kiss. When she moaned for more, he pulled back smiling and kissing the tip of her nose.

"It means the powers have blessed us to be God and Goddess over all."

Watching Harlow's eyes change from desire to wonderment and surprise, he whispered. He emphasized that alongside their new status, there would be a sense of responsibility and a few adjustments. The chieftain of their village would no longer be him. That responsibility would have to be given to another. They would now have the freedom to roam, and travel, wherever they wished. He could further show her this world.

He understood her need to be nearer to Rowan. Especially now, given the circumstances he was in. Helping him to heal, and transition into a new way of life. Her son was their priority, all other worries would wait. They would deal with all the other issues later. Establishing, and cementing their newfound hierarchy would take time and patience. Time being something they possessed, having such a long life span, being immortal beings. They first needed to surround themselves with trusted individuals. With Ravens Night they were on the right track. Then there were the issues with Ozel, and the others to be dealt with.

They could plan for various options. In the end, however, time would tell what actions were necessary. He trusted himself when he looked inward on matters of worry. Knowing they just had to wait for things to reveal themselves. Then, and only then would everyone come together to extinguish the evil that plagued them.

Hopefully, with his help, Harlow will blossom more into her gifts. He suspected the real reason she hadn't noticed their markings was that she was still thinking, and looking at herself through other's eyes. When she just needed to look within, see her amazing wonders, and believe.

When she did that her eyes sparkled. The window that reveals the true identity within. Those moments were happening more, and more often. His heart overflowed with gratitude as she welcomed him into her life, and now they could embark on a journey of growth together. They had forever together. Yes, they were of the God race before. No one knew though how long they would live. Most just passed when they felt it was time. While others didn't have the same luck and someone killed them. Sickness or ill health never plagued them, only the nonmagicks suffered so. They now however would not have any such worries, they were infinite, never ending. Together for the rest of the time.

Harlow woke feeling warm surrounded by big muscular arms. Inhaling confirmed she was in Kieran's arms. Smiling, she snuggled closer, enjoying the heat. She had been so cold, right down to the bone after laying on that stone floor for so long. Not to mention all the aches, and pains that had accompanied the overall chill. Having the ability to heal yourself was amazing, yes, when you could. However, the price of it sometimes had a cost, and that was life. Even if they were bad people intent on harming her, and her son, she still struggled with taking their lives. In the end, she needed to protect Rowan. To do that, she needed to heal herself to the point she could fight, and use her gifts with ease. Feelings of melancholy, and guilt grew within her, and her train of thought was a danger of taking over. All too quickly they shifted to joy as the arms tightened around her with a whispered murmur.

"Good morning little one."

Burrowing her face deeper into his chest she too mumbled.

"Good morning Kieran."

This man could shift her moods from sour to sweet in the simplest ways. Kissing his sculpted chest, she then lifted her head. Looking into his sleep filled eyes. Asking the question that popped into her head.

"You think it's still ok for us to be here? What if Rowan needs me?"

She watched the concern fill his face as he raised a hand to cup her cheek, rubbing his thumb along it. Catching the single tear she allowed to fall. Her emotions were all over the place this morning.

"He will be alright, little one. If we are needed, we will be aware. Trust me."

He slid his hand to the back of her neck. She allowed him to guide her to his waiting mouth for a good morning kiss. Moaning at the instant contact. This man could send her flying in desire with the simplest touch. When he kissed her though she soared, craving more. He ignited her desire, and need for him. Raising her leg to straddle him, she positioned herself above him. Placing her hands on his chest giving him a seductive smile.

His responding growl, and the transferring of both hands to her hips, had her bending down for another kiss. While he held her in place allowing her to devour his mouth. The hungrier she was for him, the harder he became for her. So much so that he lifted her hips at the same time he pulled back from kissing her to demand.

"Harlow, take hold of me, and put me inside you."

Wanting to scoff at his demand, she instead moaned. Trailing her fingers down along his chest, smiling as he again growled his pleasure. Taking him in her hand she gripped him tightly. With varying firmness she gently moved her hand up, and down. Resulting in him jutting his hips upward on a lust filled moan. Lining him to her core she eased herself down onto him. When Kieran lightened his hold she angled her hips, swallowing him deep inside herself.

Kieran was quick to reprimand her in a breathy stern voice.

"Careful, little one. I am big, and you and my love are so tiny."

Her only reply was to squeeze her internal muscles. Resulting in both of them groaning in pleasure. He then tightened his hold on her hips, moving her up, and down. Before long they were moving in tandem with each other. Each vying for breath.

With her hands on his chest, she sank her fingers into him for stability. At the fire lighting behind his eyes, she increased her speed. Anything for more friction. He felt so warm, hard, and big inside her. She loved it. Wanting more of him.

As soon as that thought popped into her head he flipped them. In the blink of an eye, he changed positions. It was as if he could read her mind. He knew what she wanted or needed before she did. Gasping in surprise, she was all too happy when he dipped down for a melt your bones kiss. Sighing in pleasure she kissed him back with all the lust she could. Grabbing tight and threading her fingers into his hair on the back of his head. She devoured him right back, as he slowly moved within her.

When they finally, came up for air. She stared up smiling while trying to catch her breath. Watching him as his smile shifted to a look of pure lust. With one hand he grabbed her wrist, then the other, placing them above her head. As he did so, she felt herself grow wetter and squeezed him tighter.

With a devilish smile, he said.

"Oh, my little one likes that."

As she nodded her head vigorously, he continued.

"Good, leave them there."

He emphasized his demand by applying pressure to her hands.

"Now wrap your legs around me, locking your ankles at my back."

She complied. Continuing to get wetter with each demand. As he placed his hands beside her shoulders, he lowered himself. Rewarding her with a quick kiss. Followed by a whisper.

"Good girl."

As he rose above her, his movements were slow and erratic. He truly felt amazing, but she wanted more, harder. It was like he was trying to drive her crazy.

"Kieran please."

She whispered. He only shook his head in reply. Taking his time moving within her. Deciding then to take matters into her own hands, she lifted her hips to meet his. Taking him as much as he was taking her, he responded by grunting.

Lowering himself he tucked an arm beneath her, holding one of her cheeks in his hand, gripping it tight. With careful precision, he moved at an ever increasing pace. Before long he was pounding into her like a man possessed. He was, and so was she. They were equally possessed by each other. As the friction increased, and he was sliding against the best place inside her, she tossed her head back to groan. Rolling her eyes closed in delight.

Her resulting cries and sighs of pleasure earned her a

"Good girl Harlow. That's it. Yes."

While he tightened his grip around her. Bringing her even closer, intensifying the wonderful friction.

All bets were off, both of them were moving in a frantic race to the finish. Tangled in arms, and legs. Combined with kisses of dueling tongues, moans, and groans. Suddenly, she felt Kieran's finger pressing on her nub as he rammed into her. Eyes opening wide she held his gaze. She needed something more, just not sure what. She tried to get closer to him. Still, it wasn't enough, she needed what? Opening her mouth to say something, only for a moan to come out instead.

Out of breath, Kieran chuckled, while smiling.

"That's it, little one. Now COME."

Just as he demanded, he pinched her little nub.

That was all she needed. She came and came hard with an ear piercing scream. She came once more when she felt Kieran coming inside her while he shouted her name. Loved it when he collapsed on top of her. Even then he still kept his full weight from her. Always, always protecting her. As he rolled them to the side she smiled whispering,

"I love you, Kieran."

Unable to keep her eyes open she allowed the darkness to swallow her. As Kieran's arms enveloped her, a sense of safety washed over her, enabling her to surrender completely.

CHAPTER 30

They arranged a temporary bed for Rowan within their bedroom after arriving back at the village. It would be much easier to care for and monitor his condition if he remained close. It gave them the ability to take shifts caring for him. While still being close to each other.

Thankfully, the community here was proud and strong. Each helping in their way to provide care for Rowan, and anyone looking after him. The community provided food. Along with many taking shifts of their own to care for the tending of the dwelling. People were always buzzing around, willing and ready to help. Still, however, this was going to be a challenging road for everyone. For a multitude of reasons.

The change and healing her son was going through. He had lied about his condition after all those interrogations. Which she had expected, just not to the degree of which he did. He had so many broken bones, bruises, and lacerations. Still, she wondered if those interrogations caused all of his broken bones, bruises, and lacerations, or if they could have occurred before being apprehended. Sadly, they couldn't ask at the moment.

With him coming in and out of disoriented and intense fevered transition episodes, any answer given could be gibberish. There was a tiny chance of a truthful reply. Why make the effort when we couldn't confirm it until after, anyway? They might as well wait and allow the shifter venom to work its way through his system. Doing its job to change and alter the magick being. On some level, he seemed aware of what was happening internally, though. Begging for the change to stop, he couldn't take any more of the inner twisting, turning, burning fire.

Healing the various amounts of wounds he had sustained also took some time. The transition change, however, made that even more difficult. For it in itself caused wounds, too. His poor body was working overtime between the two. With constant healing, changing, and shifting on every level. His natural healing abilities, activated upon arrival here, were at work between the injuries and the transition. Forever, it seemed like a cycle in an endless loop.

Their challenge had been getting enough nutrition into him. When he slept, he was dead to the world. No one wished to wake him and attempt to feed him. In the few waking moments, his screams and moans were ever present, in tandem with his thrashing and bashing about. He ended up wearing more than he could receive. His strength seemed to thrive. For his safety, they were considering restraining him to the bed.

Not that it would do much. Perhaps giving a few moments more of time. Only Kieran and she seemed to possess the strength needed, so they fed him only twice daily. While one of them held him, someone fed him as best they could.

What concerned Harlow the most was why this was taking so long. In all the stories that she had heard, the transformation had taken only one or two nights at the most. Why Rowan's had been three nights, and counting, had her anxious. Her only reassurance was that Aramis would arrive tonight.

He, along with healers from his clan, were coming to assist her son in his transition. If he was stable enough for their liking, they would take him back with them for further healing. As well as to aid him in adjusting to his now new way of life. A world in which he was born a member of the god race. However, he now dwells, startled, within the shifter clan. He will need time to take in all that has happened to him and what his new world will entail.

There was also the thought amongst them that there would be a power struggle with Rowen. As the days passed, everyone who came within a specific range of him could sense the power within him. Each day shifting and growing stronger. Many had suggested that he was to emerge an alpha. If that were so, the question then became: what would happen to him? The shifter clan already had its leaders. The triad of wolf, bear, and dragon shifters.

Could there be room for another, or was that asking too much? No one could say for sure until Rowan awoke. Only then could they know the speculation. At least, though, they might establish provisions at the meeting tonight. Some thought that Aramis sensed this as an outcome as well. For he had sent word ahead of his arrival. Asking for such a meeting, as well as the assortment of people he intended to bring with him. Followed by his intentions and wishes.

Having never met this man, she liked him already. He seemed to care more about her son and his needs than about finding justice. At least for now, it looked that way. Insisting on a reply to his condition while also offering advice on his care until their arrival. A ruler who seemed to want all the facts first before he demanded justice. Needing to discuss all sides of the events leading up to her and Rowan's taking. As well as happenings during their time in captivity. They had to discuss how all this would affect both tribes and magicks at large before deciding on a punishment.

Ravens Night was having an official meeting, and for the first time except for her, was hosting outsiders. It would also, in a way, announce its existence to the world. Members were still keeping tight lipped about it itself, keeping themselves secret; instead saying they were now the newly formed guild to the God and Goddess. Anyone interested in becoming a member was to apply. They needed and wanted members of magick and nonmagick alike. A secret society within another.

They were making it known: Kieran and Harlow's new status. Although she suspected most knew anyway, at least they seemed to when they were in their vicinity. All bowing and paying verbal respect. Something she had trouble getting used to, while Kieran appeared honored by their regard. Always smiling with a small nod of his head. For her, she would always freeze up. It was strange having people be nice to her. Her Mate insists over time she will grow accustomed.

Still, she suspected that those magick beings who possessed great power themselves would have already sensed a change within their world. Knowing that a significant change had happened and was near. Would explain Aramis's actions and requests, plus the need now for further changes. Like, Aidan will take over the post of chieftain, therefore allowing Corrina to run Ravens Night, still in secret. While Cillian would be the head of the guild. Surprisingly, they received few arguments, since the guild would be answering to the God and Goddess. It was awe-inspiring how many wanted to join. Aramis just laughed, wishing them luck while congratulating them at the same time.

Never had so many different magicks worked together as a team, let alone with nonmagicks. It was history in the making. A step in the right direction, all working as one, she thought. It was such a successful meeting as well. Based on reports, they decided Rowan would leave tonight with Aramis and his fellow clans. A small contingent of newly formed guild members would also go, further protecting the group. After they had a quick, detailed briefing.

The healers had insisted that Rowan had passed the worst of his conversion and recommended moving him tonight. They were impressed with the level of care he had received thus far. They insisted on being allowed to teach guild members all they knew if this were to happen again in the future. Since they might not have the access he had had in the initial stages. They were, after all, magick beings and should know the ins and outs of each other.

Cillian agreed, saying they should prepare to leave while he selected the team members who would accompany them. He also agreed to the multiple suggestions made to keep Kieran and Harlow's new status secret as long as possible. Hoping his brother Ozel, along with those he is aiding, doesn't discover their true identity and change tactics. Everyone took part in the planning to set a trap by making it known where Rowan would be going. However, only after he is already safely there, of course. With Harlow to follow later, to see to his continued care.

Only Ravens Night members along with Aramis know of the

mother son connection between Harlow and Rowan. It was best kept secret for now, too. Still, they quickly made and put into motion plans. All were ready to perform their part and take action. Involving the god clans, and the shifter clans increased their numbers but also united them together in more ways than one. They now had plans to discuss involving other magick clans. Bringing them into the guild, or at least giving them the option at least. Kieran was adamant they decided for themselves.

With the meeting concluded, everyone went their separate ways. Some went to their homes, while others prepared for their newfound duties. Most had a lightness in their step never seen before. How wonderful to see when coming together to work as a unit can physically and emotionally change you. Harlow left with the contingent, intent on taking Rowan. She wanted to see her baby one last time. Knowing tomorrow was another day, and she would see many changes in him. She just knew deep down a change in more ways than one was coming. Other than her son's shift, she wasn't sure what that change would be.

He could tell his Mate was nervous, and a little distressed. Her continued pacing only further added to her emotions. Which he felt her broadcasting loud and clear. She needed time to process everything after the meeting. Then there were all the life events she still had yet to come to terms with. So he stepped back, allowing her mind to work, remaining close, just in case.

She impressed him with her strength and compassion. Her ability to fend off all those opponents while defending her son. Or when she had protected Aidan and himself at Cormac's cottage. The natural way the gifted powers came to her and flowed through her made him a little jealous. It had taken him years to come as far as she had in a matter of days. He also had years of learning and practice.

Sitting back in his chair, he watched as she continually bit her bottom lip while deep in thought, hands flying about as if deep in a conversation. Well, maybe she was with herself. His last thought made him laugh. Harlow froze, turning to look at him. Staring him down with her hands on her hips, he only smiled back. Throwing her hands in the air with a hmf, she marched his way. Plopping herself into his lap.

Wrapping her arms around his neck, she smiled up at him saying.

"Thank you. I needed that time to think it through."

Breathing in deep, she paused.

"So much had happened. I'm still adjusting and processing. As crazy as it is, though, I'm ok with it. I believe this is the way it was all supposed to be."

Tilting her head up to him, she asked.

"Is that weird that?"

Running a finger down her cheek, he smiled down at her saying.

"No little one. If that is what you know, then it is."

Bending, he kissed the tip of her nose.

"I feel as though I am missing something though, Kieran. The more I try to piece things together. The more pieces I seem to have. Plus all the whys. My head is hurting."

As she said the last, she rubbed her temple with a grimace.

With reassurance, he wrapped his arms around her, saying.

"Don't worry, little one, the answers will reveal themselves in time."

Smiling to himself when she relaxed, and snuggled into his embrace, murmuring a soft thank you.

"Close your eyes, and rest. It won't be long till you leave for the triad kingdom."

When he felt her body go limp with sleep, he too leaned his head back. Resting it against the wall. He hoped their plan worked. They swept Rowan away under guard as secretly as possible. They still weren't sure who they were all dealing with yet. Ozel, yes, was the one pulling all the magick strings. Briggs was the rogue shifter attempting to create an army to further his aspirations. Everyone was guessing and fearful about what those aspirations were. The unknown could be very dangerous.

Their unidentified leader was perhaps the most dangerous of all. Other than Harlow and Rowan, not a single soul has a recollection of seeing him. Which scared many, as it should. Was it he or Ozel casting spells of memory play or obscurity? What did he want, and how far would he go to get it? Why was he after Harlow? It just couldn't be for her power? All of this scared him.

Trusting his, and the shifter clans, as well as the newly formed guild, and Ravens Night alike, to come together. Along with close friends and his beloved Mate. To all work together, bringing their talents and gifts to see justice for Rowan. Along with all the others, who unwillingly turned and became savage. It looked as though that had been the intention. However, his gut told him that had not been the reason for his stepson. Just thinking of him in that way made him smile, while a warmth spread through him.

Briggs had his personal agenda and wasn't above using others to achieve it. Or so Aramis had informed him. This was not the first time he had performed such acts. It was, however, the first time the degree of which was so severe and savage. Still, no one was sure of his end goal. So he inspired more fear than our unknown foe.

Next in the plan was for Harlow to travel with a contingent of guild members. Some of whom were Ravens Night members as well. On the very visible path on route to the shifter kingdom. Making it well known she was going to see her fellow friends, each a victim of a kidnapping. They weren't telling anyone yet that he was her son, but they wouldn't hush rumors of that either. Hoping that the knowledge would protect them. While also allowing for more plausible reasons for her to travel. Everyone knew how fast information could travel.

The hope was anyone hearing it would side with mother and son. With a desire to keep them safe. If perhaps they had been favoring their yet unknown enemy, it would change their minds. If only to protect, but just maybe reveal more information too. He wasn't putting much stock into this stream of the plan.

He only went along with it for a few reasons. First, his Mate had insisted she go, it was her son after all. He needs her. No argument there. She seemed to tap into her gifts and believe in herself. In that dungeon, his woman achieved acceptance and pride in herself, while not letting it go to her head. Very few could say the same. For that reason, she was awarded the honor of the Goddess. It was the strength and power of her gifts, along with her ability to use them. That had him accepting she could handle herself if needed.

While he and the others would travel to the same kingdom through the night. Hoping to go unseen. This would also give them the advantage of being able to travel faster. Well, it would be a normal pace for a magick. To a nonmagick, it would look as though they were flying, and likely terrify them. Hence many rumors about them already. They had long since stopped paying attention. However, safety and the element of surprise were important. So night travel was best for him, and his team at least.

Harlow was traveling with the two survivors who had aided them in her rescue. They had shared any information they could. Offering to take her to their kingdom. As they were shifters, mouse shifters to be exact. They had been young and had believed Neera's lies in hopes of a better life. To only realize they became slaves. Now proud of their home, and actions for the many thanks they had received. Mostly from Harlow and from Aramis himself. The former had surprised and honored them the most. There wasn't anything they wouldn't now do for him. Especially now that he had promised them priority jobs within his large house.

So they would proudly walk alongside their Goddess. Taking her to their home so she could see her son. Even assuring her if anything went amiss, they would protect her. Only for her to reply the same. Further endearing her to them. She did so with every person she met, without being aware. Truly, a Goddess, his Mate. Closing his eyes, he sighed. A little snooze would be just what they needed before setting their plans into motion.

When their enemies would strike, they would all be ready. The trap they had planned was strong. All there was to do now was wait.

CHAPTER 31

This time he would make Master proud. After the catastrophe in the dungeon, he would be more prepared. The magick beings in question were more powerful than he had thought possible. It was no wonder they were so desired. How Master knew, however, was the mystery he still couldn't quite figure out. No matter though, failure was not in the cards for today. They would at the very least be walking away with one of them, and perhaps the possibility of both.

He had received information that the female was heading this way. Having left the God clan early this morning with a small guard. A group meant to protect what his chieftain coveted. He couldn't have her, though. She belonged to his Master, and he had staked his claim. What he wanted, he got. It was only a matter of time.

He was grateful to have the crazy Briggs with him though. He knew the ins and outs of the shifter kingdom. Even possessing knowledge of the palace in which their newly turned shifter was being kept. If the so called king wanted him, clearly he was powerful indeed. It was just that he belonged to another. They had come to take him back.

Sneaking into the kingdom had been child's play. The so called guards meant to protect the entrance had been so easily distracted by his hallucinating charm. Making them believe they were on the battle-field about to charge, he sent them scurrying off. They had taken off with so much gumption Briggs had chuckled, calling them mindless buffoons.

His shifter partner in this endeavor was an unpredictable beast of a magick being. He physically resembled his animal while in his everyday form. Having only seen him change once, the thought of which sent shivers down his spine. He would gladly take dealing with this everyday stinky and snarling man. Who had an agenda of his own?

No matter how many times he had tried to warn the Master away from him. As always, he would receive the same reply with a sneer of disgust.

"Never fear the dogs of the earth."

Before ultimately turning away. It was only a matter of time before this so called dog of the earth would turn on the Master. He just had a potent feeling it would be himself. However, who would take the fall-out? That was why he had snuck away from the dungeon. His instincts of self preservation had kicked in with a force, and so he took off.

How was he to know it was the power of the prisoners he was sensing? That their force was the battle he had avoided. Only to feel the wrath of his actions after from both Briggs and Master. So now he was fulfilling his promise with a guard dog. To retrieve their newest creation from the shifter kingdom. With hopes of possibly taking both magick beings. If their timing and luck held out.

They were able to make it mostly uninterrupted from the main gate. Why Briggs had insisted on using it, instead of the delivery side of the domain, was a mystery. He had his suspicions, though, very like a snub to the kingdom's rulers. Knowing full well his companion thought lowly of the royal families. Still, his knowledge and instincts had gotten them far, and quickly, too. It was almost too easy.

They had only encountered a few who were easily subdued with either a sleeping or paralyzing charm. From his hands, at least. If his grizzly partner got ahold of them. He had wrapped his massive hands around their head, twisting with such a speed to force a snapping of their necks. To which he would then toss the dead aside like trash after the eerie popping sound. This creature was one he never wanted to get on the wrong side of. So he continued to follow where he led. Attempting in vain to use his charms on anyone they happened upon before big mitts could do more damage.

He still wasn't sure how he felt about the loss of life. It was more the fact they were leaving a trail. One that could easily lead directly to them. His partner seemed not to care whenever he broached the topic. Nothing ever appeared to bother him. Well, that wasn't quite true, really. He had a severe dislike for the rulers of this kingdom. Perhaps that was why he took great pleasure, and disregard in the deaths of his kind. Or anyone really.

They made it to the palace, this time entering through the back. However, Briggs led them through the main sections, walking freely. They encountered no one. The strange phenomenon was setting the hairs on the back of his neck on end. It shouldn't have been this easy. Something had to be amiss. Still, they had a job to complete. He couldn't be worried about such things. Only getting it done.

Entering the wolf shifter's wing, it grew eerily quiet. As if time itself were standing still. Odd that. At the transitioning shifter's door, they encountered a protection charm. One that Briggs snarled at the scent of it, though it would not block himself. He was quite adept at spells and charms. This would only delay them a little. He got to work to remove the magickal lock.

No doubt in his mind of his abilities. They would be walking away from here with the Master's new pet. Of that, he was one hundred percent positive on the subject. With any luck, the magick being on the other side of the door would be through most of the conversions by now, and they could just waltz right out of here. Just like they had come in.

Their trek here had been mostly uneventful. Only encountered a few others on the road. Some had supplied a simple greeting while most just continued on their way, ignoring them. It surprised her mostly because she had such a strong gut feeling about today, and running into conflict. She had assumed that would happen on the road. It was the easiest place to get to her. Even with the contingent traveling with her.

It would be a straightforward plan, she thought. However, she didn't know her enemies that well. Even though she packed a powerful punch in the gifts department, her companions weren't without their gifts. To her, it made more sense to attack out in the open, where they wouldn't have the aid of the kingdom behind them.

Her instincts proved right when she caught sight of the main entrance to the kingdom. Its doors were wide open, and not a guard in sight. Strange, she had been given the assurance that the place was well protected both physically and magicaklly. Something had happened, and that was no longer the case. She had noticed this first and had swung an arm out to halt her two guides. They needed to act fast. While changing or rather tweaking their plan. Turning to her companions, she asked.

" Is there another way in?"

Looks of worry and concern followed by nodding heads. Acknowledging with a nod of her own, she turned to the rest of the group, who had stopped not far behind her.

"Alright, I will go with our guides to enter another way. The rest of you go through the main gates. Be aware and careful. Something has happened. Investigate, and help if needed. While we continue on the mission."

She held up her hand when someone was about to comment.

"I know it's not ideal or recommended. Okay, I am trusting my instincts here. Both them and you have my trust. Now let's go. We need to hurry."

With more nods of reluctant acceptance, they each took off in their separate ways. What they encountered when they entered the main palace shocked her. Bodies were lying about, slumped here and there. All snoring loudly, so deep in sleep. This had to be a spell of some kind, for no one would sleep so deep that they fell awkwardly.

Well, there was a good possibility Ozel was here if Magick was being used. He along with the shifter were her likely opponents this time. Never having battled another magick with gifts before, she hoped she was ready. Not counting her fight to free herself and her son from the interrogation room.

She was so deep in thought it took a few tugs on her sleeve, and the whispers of "miss" to get her attention on the here and now. Shaking her head back into focus, she blinked a few times, before looking towards the speaker.

"Miss. We know of another way. Follow us this way."

Showing a hidden door beneath the staircase.

"It is a more direct way and will give the element of surprise. Come."

She forcefully tugged her arm while saying the last words. To which she was quick to follow. Entering the tiny door, revealed an opening into a rather large space. Complete with a maze of hallways and more stairs. Spaces blessed with magick were rather wonderful and quite spacious. This world was forever growing on her.

"This way, this way. Hurry."

As fast as they could, they maneuvered their way to Rowan's room. Stopping at a tall, slender door. They could hear the muffled sounds of bodies shuffling and arguing. Pressing her ear to the door, she could hear who she assumed was Ozel talking.

"You promised me he'd be agreeable."

Hearing a few more huffs and puffs, followed by groaning.

"Can't you control him?"

Came a snarl and an accompanying growl.

"NO. The mutt is an alpha."

With her emotions rising, in a hurried haste, she stormed through the door, and into the room. Seeing her son struggle against two men, she shouted.

"STOP"

They all froze, letting go of Rowan, causing him to collapse onto the floor. Her attempt to rush to him was stopped by her two guides as they each grabbed her arms.

With lightning speed, the large galoot shifter grabbed her son. Holding his neck in his beefy hand and lifting him to his feet. His face lit up with an eerie smile of recognition. With a "tsk, tsk." He shook his head.

"This mutt is mineeee."

He emphasized in his slimy voice. His statement and claim caused Harlow to growl.

"Stay calm sister dear."

Relaxing, she focused instead on the other man in the room. She knew this man. He was the one who had tried to take her from Kierans' dwelling. The whiny one. This was Ozel. He looked nothing like his brother.

"Well, this has worked out better than I had hoped it would."

He turned to look at his companion and smiled while turning again to her. Proudly, stating,

"Two for the price of one."

Harlow felt filled with fear. Trembles spread through her.

"Stall Harlow. Help is on the way. Get him talking."

Feeling an overwhelming wave of assurance and comfort, she did as told. Relaxing her posture, she asked.

"What is this, better than you thought?"

Tilting her head for effect.

With his brows together in question.

"Do you not hear? Or are you addled in the head?"

Staring her down, waiting for a reply.

As if she would give him one. If she needed to play a part for her son's safety, she would do it. After reading so many books, she could play the part. What was it called? Oh yes, she remembered, the ditzy one. So she stared right back at him. A dare nonetheless. To which her guides still holding her arms each squeezed, either in support or as a warning. She wasn't sure and didn't care. All that mattered was Rowan.

"Isn't obvious. We already got the guard dog, and now we have you as well."

He said with an air of triumph. As he appeared to stand taller.

"Our task to get both of you. We had just planned on getting you each separately. You, my dear, just made it easier, is all."

With a huff, she pulled her arms free, placing her hands on her hips, demanding.

"Oh, really. Is that so?"

Again staring him down. This man seemed to like the sound of his voice. She was able to keep him talking, slapping him with one liners, and body posturing. This slimy runt had some serious issues. She almost felt sorry for him. Almost he was Cillian's brother, after all. That should count for something. He just however kept proving that wasn't to be. He had decided, and his allegiances known.

"That's it, Harlow, almost there."

He sounded out of breath. This time, it was her turn to furrow her brow. Confused about how her brother could be almost here? She thought this was just some manifestation of her mind while in the dungeon.

"It's not."

She'd done it again, mind wandering, and at a very important time too. The slimy man in front of her did not seem to like her zoning out. He was flailing his arms and jumping about. He looked like a toddler having a tantrum. Not being able to help herself, she smiled, letting a giggle escape. Trying to hide it, she covered her mouth with her hand. Too late.

Gasps behind her, and Rowan rolled his eyes in front of her. She knew she had gone too far. For now, Ozel was shouting.

"ENOUGH."

Reaching into his clothes, he pulled a knife free. Placing it too close to Rowan's side for her liking.

"Make your choice. What's it going to be?"

Anger grew inside her, filling her. Everything became brighter in her vision. The blade, she could tell, would do some serious damage. Someone had blessed it with charms. Making it almost impossible for a magick to self heal from the inflicted wound. Provided it possessed an anti healing curse. Sucking in a breath, she weighed her options.

Before she could respond, however, the door behind the men flew open. In a flash, faster than she could blink, the grizzly shifter moved, and Caden appeared. In a dance so smooth, he wrapped his hands around the shifter's neck, twisting to the side. An awful cracking sound filled the room, followed by the thuds of falling bodies. Ozel in vain tried to peddle himself backward, all the while screaming and demanding fair treatment.

Standing frozen in place, it was a shock to see her twin. It was like an instant wave of memories washed over her. Past and present ones all collided at once. Only for her to realize that everything happens for a reason. That reason was to bring all of them to the here and now. They were right where they needed to be and supposed to be. That this time it was right.

Again coming back into the now, she wasn't fast enough to dodge Ozel when he shifted behind her. With a careful precision, he placed the knife to her throat. Feeling the tip puncture her skin, she hissed at the sting. Caden froze in front of her. Through clenched teeth, he retorted.

"I wouldn't if I were you."

Just as her twin spoke, Kieran burst into the room. Scanning the room, he tensed at seeing her. Whispering, he reached for her.

"Harlow."

Caden raised his arm and demanded.

"NO"

Halting him.

Looking at Caden, he studied her twin for the first time. Through their connection, she could feel a wave of confusion before understanding washed over him. Making eye contact, she knew she had hurt him by not confiding in him about her sibling.

"His name is Kieran. He is my husband Caden. Please trust him. He only fears for me and Rowan."

With his eyes burrowing into hers.

"I know who Kieran is. But let's take care of this scum, ok?"

With a smirk, and a tilt of her brow.

"Ok, brother mine."

Caden's audible snort brought them both back into the moment. As Ozel tugged her backward, she grabbed his arm to steady herself while he shouted.

"Who is he? What does he want with you?"

This time it was her turn to snort.

"Well, I don't know what he wants with me. This gentleman is Caden, my twin brother."

Attempting to shrug, she felt the knife tip penetrate further. Causing both men to hiss in response.

"Plus, you already met my husband, Kieran."

"I've had enough."

Caden growled.

"Release my sister."

Caden's stare bore into her, until he winked. Using the skin to skin contact, she pulled Ozel's energy. Taking just enough to weaken him. When she felt the blade slip from his fingers, she acted in a well rehearsed move. Using both hands, she wrapped them around his wrist while bringing her heel up from behind. After contacting his jewels, and his very loud whine of pain, she flipped him around, twisting. In a combined move, Caden swiftly connected his rather enormous fist into Ozel's face. Rendering him unconscious.

Turning, she rushed to her son's side. Rowan was just coming back around. It seemed when he fell, Briggs landed on top of him, knocking him out. Kneeling at his side, she watched as he blinked a few times, trying to focus. Kieran took position behind her, whispering.

"It will take a little time adjusting to your new vision, son."

The fact Kieran saw her son as his own. Filled her with pride. She opened herself to her husband and pushed her feelings towards him. His gentle squeeze of her shoulder made her smile.

Rowan shifted his attention from Kieran with a simple.

"Got it."

Back towards her. With a smile that reached his eyes, he said.

"Hi, Mom."

While he moved to a sitting position, he froze while sniffing the air, and then relaxed. Turning his head, he said.

"Hi, Uncle Caden."

In a few more movements, he removed a leather wrist cuff he always wore. Revealing a marking.

Caden came to Rowan's other side to kneel. He, too, removed a leather cuff he always wore. Revealing the same marking. She had assumed the cuffs had had something to do with the True Guard. Not that it had everything to do with the Ravens Night. At her shocked gasp, both looked up to her.

Then she too revealed she too had the same marking on her inner wrist.

Caden's gaze shot straight to her face where he demanded.

"Really? When?"

"While I was here, Caden."

He appeared to relax as he exhaled.

"Wow,"

He shook his head in disbelief, chuckling.

"I knew we went far back. Just not this far."

Looking up at Kieran, he extended his hand.

"Caden. Harlow's older brother, and Rowan's uncle."

Kieran took the offered hand. The skin to skin contact shot aware-ness through both of them. Well, and her too. Her connection to both of them allowed her to know. Her husband, and now the two of them, knew the fabled prophecy included not just her, but Caden as well. Just like her, her twin now knew of Kieran's, and her higher God status.

As they pulled back, Kieran smiled while saying.

"Wow."

With gentle hands, he cupped her cheeks, drawing her in for a loving kiss. They only pulled back when Rowan started coughing to get their attention. She could so easily get carried away with this man. Smiling at him, she turned to look at her son, questioning. When he jutted his head towards Caden's odd expression. She asked.

"Yes, brother mine?"

As he shook his head, and his eyes regained focus, he asked.

"What does he mean, wow?"

It was too much to go into now, and here, so she shrugged her shoulders while pursing her lips before saying.

"Beats me, brother mine. I have no idea."

Which caused Kieran to burst out laughing.

Caden rolled his eyes, shaking his head at her.

"He's perfect for you, sister mine."

Looking then at Kieran, he said.

"Good luck, man. Hurt her though, and you're ours."

With a puffed out chest and a sunken voice, Kieran stated.

"Wouldn't dream of it. She's been through too much already."

With softening eyes, he bent his loving gaze to her.

Besides, I belong to her as much as she belongs to me. I love her,"

to which both Caden and Rowan responded.

"Ew, gross."

Which was chased by a rather enormous yawn from her son. His attempt to keep his eyes open was also becoming ever more present. At least now he seemed to be over the worst of the transition process. Now it would be him adjusting to a new way of life. With another yawn, he said.

"As much as I love this family reunion, do you guys mind leaving so I can get some shut eye? I'm exhausted."

"Of course, sweetheart."

She whispered. Before she could even attempt to help her son, Kieran lifted her into his arms. As Caden moved, he assisted Rowan back into his cot. With an unfocused gaze and slurred words, she whispered his "thanks" before he went limp. As quietly as they were able, they motioned for members outside the doors to come and take the dead shifter's body. They had served justice in a way there. She felt death had been too kind of a sentence for him. He had hurt far too many people, magick and nonmagick alike, for that to be fair.

It took three members to carry his body from the room. The sight of this sent shivers down her spine. Unaware as to the way she demanded.

"Be sure to burn him right away."

She was further surprised at the shocked, and fearful expressions on their faces, which then relaxed.

"As you wish."

With a quick nod, they left.

Turning her attention to Ozel. Who woke, and who also seemed to suffer from a broken nose. He looked even more like a slimeball to her. They swiftly took off his clothes and outfitted him like the women she had witnessed being sentenced before. Similarly, they quickly bound him, but for him, everything seemed magnified many times. It was a wonder he could not move at all.

Jutting her chin in his direction, she asked.

"What's to become of him?"

As Kieran lowered her to the ground, he spoke while helping her steady her balance.

"He will under go questioning, judgement, and then sentencing."

His voice sounded finite and angered simultaneously. Taking her hand in his.

"Come now, let's go. Rowan needs some rest."

Looking up at Caden, he said.

"Plus, we need to be more familiar with each other."

With his nodded agreement, Caden followed them to the door. They were almost there when Rowan sat up to say.

"He's coming."

Before once again falling back and snoring.

Harlow and Caden shared a look. It couldn't be possible. Could it?

* * *

Please leave a review. I would appreciate it. Thank you

GLOSSARY

Names, pronunciation, and their meanings:
    Aidan: little fire, born of fire
    Caden: Strength
    Cillian (Kill-e-an): bright-headed
    Cormac (Kor-Mac): son of the charioteer
    Corrina/Cora: maiden; spear/maiden; heart
    Harlow: Army Hill
    Rowan: little red-head
Creed translation:
    Thar ceann a oinigh: For the sake of his honor
    A lá gaile: His day of valor
    Tá sé de bheith orm: I am fated
    í gcónaí: Always

PLEASE JOIN!

Holly's Newsletter!

Stay up-to-date on what events are coming up and how my writing is going. This is a good way to keep in touch and get release day links! Oh, and let's not forget the free digital gifts I have for you.

MY BOOKS

Book 1 Goddess Kindled

Book 2 God Awakened

Book 3 God Bitten

ABOUT THE AUTHOR

I am Holly MacGregor is the author of the magickal, portal, spicy romance, and fantasy novels Ravens Night Saga. Which includes Goddess Kindled, God Awakened, and God Bitten, coming soon. I live in Canada with her husband, their son, and four furry friends.

Want to know more? Check out my website, hollymacgregor.com.

I am also on social media. Consider giving me a follow. I post frequently and enjoy interacting with my followers. I am Holly MacGregor, Author on Facebook and Instagram I am @authourholly-macgregor.

www.ingramcontent.com/pod-product-compliance
Lightning Source LLC
Chambersburg PA
CBHW020432030726
47495CB00006B/1759